The
Irish Devil

Donna Fletcher

JOVE BOOKS, NEW YORK

This is a work of fiction. Names, characters, places, and incidents are either the product of the author's imagination or are used fictitiously, and any resemblance to actual persons, living or dead, business establishments, events or locales is entirely coincidental.

THE IRISH DEVIL

A Jove Book / published by arrangement with
the author

PRINTING HISTORY
Jove edition / February 2000

The Penguin Putnam Inc. World Wide Web site address is
http://www.penguinputnam.com

ISBN: 0-515-12749-3

A JOVE BOOK®
Jove Books are published by The Berkley Publishing Group,
a division of Penguin Putnam Inc.,
375 Hudson Street, New York, New York 10014.
JOVE and the "J" design
are trademarks belonging to Penguin Putnam Inc.

PRINTED IN THE UNITED STATES OF AMERICA

10 9 8 7 6 5 4 3 2 1

*To my own Irish devil
with love
Until we meet again*

Prologue

Talk of the Devil and he'll appear.

—Erasmus

Cork, Ireland, 1171

"The Irish devil rides in with the storm, his army following directly behind. He takes the lead, fearless he is, knowing his evil lord will protect him. He carries but one weapon, a sword specially forged for him. No one but the devil possesses the strength to wield it, the blade heavy with the souls and cries of those lives felled by it.

"In his wake he leaves destruction. Whole villages burned, men slaughtered and women ravished. The devil tastes his fill taking a dozen women or more—"

"Enough nonsense, Nora, I will hear no more," Lady Terra scolded harshly, entering the small sewing room to the surprise of the three young women who sat huddled around the table.

The two silent women focused wide, frightened eyes on Nora, their hands trembling and their capped heads bobbing as she persisted in continuing her tale.

"But 'tis true, m'lady. The Irish devil is known for his cruelty. He plunders and massacres for pleasure and profit. He cares naught for human lives, only his evil pleasures."

"Mind your ignorant tongue, Nora," Lady Terra snapped. "The Irish devil is but a mere man, exceptional at what he does, but nonetheless a man, not a myth or a legend. A man, need I remind you, who will be here within a month's time to choose one of my daughters for a wife. I will not tolerate such willful lies and I will not have my daughters upset by idle servant gossip."

"Yes, m'lady," Nora said obediently, her head bowed respectfully and her fingers returning to her stitching.

The other two women immediately lowered their heads and focused on their own work.

"If one stitch is out of line, you will all go without the evening meal," Lady Terra said and slowly circled the table, her tall, slim body rigid, her thin hands resting on crossed arms and her dark eyes scrutinizing their work.

With breaths suspended and bodies tense, the young women waited. Lady Terra was not known for her understanding and charm. She was known for her shrewish tongue and sharp hand. Not one of the house staff had escaped her anger; some even bore permanent proof of her cruelty.

The sharp slap resonated through the confined quarters, startling all of them. The other two women jumped, their stitching needles accidentally pricking their fingers, yet they remained silent for fear Lady Terra would deliver the same to them.

"Bridget," Lady Terra shouted at the young woman whose cheek instantly welted with her hand print. "That line is crooked. You will rip out the entire seam and begin again."

She completed another full circle around the table, her eyes intent on their work, before walking to the door. She stopped and turned. A cruel smile spread across her thin face, emphasizing the many deep lines and wrinkles that marked her for a woman much older than her four and seven years. "You both may thank Bridget for missing supper this eve." She cast a look of disgust at Nora. "But then you, Nora, could lose a few pounds. Your abundant girth must certainly interfere with your duties. I will inform cook that you are rationed to one meal daily until I am satisfied with your weight loss. And make certain those dresses are finished on time for my daughters to have new gowns to properly welcome the Irish"—she stopped herself and sent a scathing look to Nora—"to welcome Lord Eric of Shanekill."

"Lord of hell is more like it," Nora murmured after Lady Terra disappeared out the door.

Tears trickled from Bridget's soft green eyes. "I am so sorry."

Ellie offered a consoling pat to the girl's thin shoulder. "Do not worry yourself. You are the best seamstress in all of Cork. You could not sew a crooked seam if you tried."

"The Irish devil will put the likes of that one in her place," Nora said, nodding toward the door.

Bridget lowered her voice to a mere whisper. "Are the tales true?"

Nora cast a cautious glance to the open door and leaned over the table, the two women moving closer to hear. "I heard the guards in the keep talking. Their voices trembled when they spoke of him almost as though they feared he would appear out of thin air and silence them with his mighty sword. They crossed themselves when they mentioned that he rode for any king who would fatten his purse the most, each king attempting to outbid the other and win the devil's favor and services. I heard them say he holds no allegiance to Ireland, being he is a barbarian."

"Barbarian?" Bridget repeated.

Nora gave another hasty glance around the room and at the door before she answered. "His Irish blood mixes with the blood of the barbaric Vikings and that is where they say his evil dwells. He cannot help but plunder and kill, it is part of him. He even considered betraying Ireland's kings."

"How?" Ellie asked, engrossed with the tale.

"He intended to supply, for a price, information to King Henry II regarding the Irish kings and their intentions. The kings offered to fatten his coffer substantially if he held his tongue. They offered him a lucrative marriage contract and vast land holdings, and bestowed on him a fancy title, lord, when he is nothing more than a barbarian. Lord William of Donnegan was ordered by the king of Cork, Dermot MacCathy, to offer one of his daughters to the devil while the king of Limerick, Donal Mor O'Brien, pledged a small castle and land in Limerick, him being no fool. The devil will protect what is his and Donal Mor O'Brien and his holdings along with it."

Bridget's skillful fingers finished off the last of the shoulder seam stitches of the soft moss-green wool gown she worked on. "I hope he chooses Lady Margaret to wed. She is as shrewish and mean as her mother and she resembles her as well, tall and thin with no shape to her, just that pointed nose and those thin lips that always frown, and she is the oldest at two score. The devil and her deserve each other."

Ellie smiled, her brown eyes dancing with mischief. "I think he deserves Lady Teresa."

Nora and Bridget giggled.

"I do not think the devil will choose a woman who smells like a horse for a wife," Nora said.

Bridget defended the woman, though she continued to giggle. "She may smell like the animals she enjoys tending but at least she is pleasant to the servants. And she does have good, wide birthing hips."

The two bobbed their heads in agreement.

"How about Lady Claire?" Bridget asked.

"Perhaps," Nora said. "She cares naught for anyone but herself, forever worried over her appearance, and she is the most attractive sister though she is only six and ten."

"Old enough to be taking a husband," Ellie said. "I wed John at five and ten."

"And will birth your first babe within the month," Bridget said with delight. "Are you fearful over the birth?"

Ellie spoke with confidence, "Not with Lady Faith to help birth me."

Complete silence filled the small room and a sudden draft drifted in from the open door, sending the shivers through the three women.

"You do not think Lord William will offer Lady Faith to the devil, do you?" Nora asked, her voice trembling.

"The devil would not want her," Ellie answered with conviction. "She is too sweet."

"The devil prays on the innocent," Bridget reminded.

"Lord have mercy on her," Ellie whispered, holding back her tears. "She is no longer innocent, and she is left with the scar to prove her sins."

Bridget snapped angrily at her friend. "No finer young woman lives. And it is the evil wagging tongues that claimed her innocence. She fought her attacker and won but no one will believe the truth."

"Truth or not, I would rather die than live with disgrace," Nora whispered.

"Aye, so would I," Ellie agreed.

"Courage and strength saw her through her ordeal," Bridget argued. "And you, Ellie, would not be here had Lady Faith not fought for her life that night."

Ellie wiped the tears from her cheeks. "True enough, Bridget. She has turned into a fine healer and her skill saved me from dying of the fever. But who will have her now? No man of her station will accept her in marriage and she is already twenty and five. She keeps herself locked away with her plants, potions and drawings. She wants no one to see her and the scar she carries as a reminder. What life is that for her?"

"She spends time in the forest collecting her plants and in her garden," Bridget defended.

Ellie frowned. "By herself, always by herself."

"Rook goes with her," Bridget argued.

"That monster dog of hers lets no one near her," Nora said. "Her father saw to that after the incident. He wanted her guarded and not by a man."

Ellie shook her head. "Speak the truth, Nora, her father blames her for the attack. He was ashamed of her the night it happened, as he is ashamed of her now."

"Good," Nora said defiantly. "Then he will not offer her to the devil since he thinks her spoiled goods."

"And with that awful scar to always remind her, bless her soul," Bridget said, crossing herself and murmuring a prayer.

Ellie and Nora joined in with prayers of their own.

"Does anyone know who attacked her?" Ellie asked, not having been in Lord William's service when the incident had occurred eight years previously.

"Her stepmother ordered her silence," Bridget said, and shivered. "I helped to tend her after the attack. She lay bleeding badly, the bedcovers soaked through with her blood. Lady Terra warned her to keep her lies to herself and not speak the name of the man she tempted or she would forever burn in hell. Lady Terra ordered a priest to her bedside for confession."

Nora interrupted. "I was the one she ordered to summon the priest." She shivered, rubbing her ample arms. "Calm and in control she was, not her usual self, she frightened me she did when she instructed me to hurry and bring the priest insisting that poor Lady Faith had met an evil end."

Bridget shook her head. "Lady Terra cares naught for Lady Faith. She wanted no shame of a mortal sin on her dying stepdaughter's soul. No one knows if she confessed the name, but I heard her plead as they rushed me from the room, 'God, save me from the devil.' Some believe she spoke about the devil in herself, but I, I think she fought the devil that night and God saved her life."

Silence reigned for several minutes and cheeks were patted dry.

A rumble of thunder sounded outside in the distance and three sets of eyes rounded in fear.

"The Irish devil rides in with the storm," Ellie whispered and the three young women crossed themselves.

One

Heavy rain pelted the castle grounds and a chill autumn wind blew across the land, swirling debris against the wooden edifice. Thunder rumbled the earth, sending shivers through the castle occupants. The thunder was not of nature but of man—horses hooves, a hundred or more baring down on the castle. In the front, leading the way, rode the Irish devil, himself.

Lord William and Lady Terra waited in the great hall, their daughters lingering in their rooms until summoned and the servants standing in readiness though their limbs trembled as the horses drew closer, quaking the castle walls.

Shouts and snorting horses announced the arrival of the unwanted guests. Lord William and Lady Terra hurried reluctantly to the front door to extend a proper welcome. Lord William ordered the metal bolts drawn back and the six-foot-high wooden doors thrown open. The force of the mighty wind blew wide the doors, sending the servants running for safety as the heavy doors broke free of their grasps and crashed wildly against the thick wooden walls, bidding the Irish devil entrance.

He strode in with the force of the hellish wind, his black wool cape swirling around him; his long, dark hair glistening with rain water; and his deep, blue eyes intent and clear as he surveyed the room in one sweeping glance. His hand rested on the hilt of his silver sword that hung from a leather strap at his waist. Twelve men followed him in, six each coming to a halt

on either side behind him. All were of great height but none
equaled the devil's own. He stood a good head over them, his
stance one of power and potency. His shoulder width was
broad, his chest full, his arms thick with muscles, his waist narrow, his thighs solid in strength and his voice deep and direct.
"My men require food and shelter."

He looked to Lady Terra and she gasped, his sinfully handsome features stealing her breath away. She could not speak or
take her eyes from him. His face mesmerized, with blue lusty
eyes, lips that promised endless pleasure and with an arrogant
expression that commanded attention from all.

Lord William stepped in front of his wife. "We are honored
to have you here, Lord Eric. The comfort of your men will be
seen to immediately." He waved at the servants, who reluctantly obeyed. They took a wide berth around the devil and
beckoned his men out the door.

The men did not follow.

Lord William roughly cleared his voice. "Your men may
take their leave."

"My personal guard will stay with me. They will be housed
close to my quarters." He made no request; it was an order that
was meant to be obeyed without delay.

Lord William complied like a dutiful servant. "As you wish,
Lord Eric."

"I require a hot bath and food, then we will talk." The devil
glanced over the short, stout man, his appraisal brief and dis-
missive.

Lord William found his blatant scrutiny offensive but with
his band of giants surrounding him, he had little alternative but
to suffer the insult. He issued angry orders in Gaelic to the remaining three servants, instructing them to show the devil to his
quarters and arrange for his barbaric men to be bedded down
nearby.

Lord Eric took a step forward, his massive shadow rushing
over Lord William like a demon rising from the fires of hell.

The stout little lord recoiled in fear as the devil spoke in
clear, defined Gaelic, then switched to Latin, followed it with
precise French, changed to the distinct tongue of the Scandina-
vian and finished with a warning in Gaelic. "The devil knows
and sees all, and his wrath is endless."

Lord Eric turned and followed the waiting servant up the

steps, further insulting Lord William by not even extending a word of courtesy for welcoming him into his home.

Lady Terra moved to her husband's side and whispered in his ear, "Loathsome barbarian."

His glance followed her own to the floor and he stared with distaste at the thick muddy path that trailed the men up the wooden stairs. "We need to talk," he whispered in return and hurried her out of the room to his private quarters.

A fire in the hearth warmed the small room and a thick tapestry covered the lone, small window keeping the chilled, stormy night at bay. A wooden table, four chairs and a chest were the only furnishings within. Numerous large candles added sufficient light and a servant poured the lord and lady wine before hurrying out and closing the door.

Lord William spoke with anger. "How dare he enter my home and make demands. Why, he did not even offer me a proper introduction. He walked in and acted as if this keep was his, issuing orders to *me*. Me!" He thumped his chest. "Lord of this castle and holdings."

"What are we to do?" Lady Terra asked in a harsh outrage.

Lord William shook his head, the wrinkles around his eyes and mouth deepening in worry. "The devil bastard carries great favor with the kings. I must comply with their wishes or suffer their reprisals."

Lady Terra frowned. "He has no manners and the land Donal Mor O'Brien, king of Limerick, granted him is too far removed from any place of political or social prominence. The woman he takes to wife will be little more than a slave to him and his brutish needs. I want more for our daughters and ourselves."

Lord William rubbed his chin. "As do I. More appropriate and profitable marriage contracts can be made for our daughters. The devil has not so much as offered me his protection in exchange for this union. I gain not one miserable thing from this forced arrangement."

"We must think on this, William. There must be a way for us to appease the kings and this barbarian and still gain from the union."

"Well think, woman, you know I admire your intellect and cunning in such matters and trust your intentions. You want exactly what I do, more wealth and power, but how do we manage to achieve it and still remain in the good graces of the kings?"

"A good question, William, and one I intend to find an answer to."

"Eric, you require a healer, your leg wound worsens," Colin said with concern as he watched his long-time friend rise from the wooden tub set in front of the flaming hearth.

Eric reached for the large towel the servant girl had hastily discarded on the small stool before she fled the room. He had snapped at her in anger, her trembling hands doing more harm than good to his tense muscles as she washed him. He ordered her to cease her senseless fumbling and rid herself of her annoying presence. He had quickly finished the job himself, the tub too inadequate in size to hold him comfortably. And besides, his leg hurt like hell.

He toweled himself dry, careful to avoid the red swollen wound on his upper right thigh. "Would it not be ironic to die from a splinter injury after having survived numerous battle wounds?"

Colin relaxed in one of the wooden chairs grouped around a small table not far from the fireplace, a tankard of ale in hand. "The devil cannot die."

Eric wrapped the towel around his hips and reached for another one to tend his long, wet hair. "No, he just forever pays for his sins."

Colin intended to protest but Eric interrupted with an order. "Send Borg with instructions to demand, not request, the local healer be sent to me and have Borg inform Lord William I will meet with him early on the morrow."

Colin stood to his full height—a mere two inches under Eric's six-foot-five-inch frame. He stretched the stiffness from his sore muscles. Where Eric was thick in muscles, Colin was slim and lean. Many a foe mistakenly thought him an easy opponent only to discover he possessed an uncommon and remarkable strength and skill that made them regret ever engaging fists or swords with him. His sculpted features, sincere brown eyes, winning smile and charming nature made him a favorite with the ladies. But Eric was the one person who understood that Colin presented a mask to the world and beneath lay a vastly different man.

"Why the smile, Colin?" Eric asked.

"The man almost embarrassed himself at the sight of *you*, wait until he sees Borg."

"Lord William is no man. He is an impotent fool and fools irritate and disgust me. Go fetch me the healer before I perish."

"The devil cannot die," Colin reminded him, walking out the door.

"The hell he can't," Eric said, dropping into the large chair closest to the fire and stretching his long legs out for the heat to warm his naked skin.

He was glad to be here at Donnegan Castle, glad this ordeal would soon be over and glad finally to be returning to his own land where he would keep the promise he had made to himself when he was but a lad of five.

Eric closed his eyes and allowed the peacefulness of the quiet room to soothe him. He listened to the snap and crackle of the fire, felt its heat creep over his bare skin and he slowly slipped into a much-needed slumber.

Faith stood staring at the giant of a man who waited just outside her door, the top of his head partially obstructed from her view since his height didn't allow him entrance unless he bent down. He had to stand at least six or seven inches over six feet. He had long, blond hair that fell over his shoulders and down along his chest and his eyes were a stunning blue and the width of him simply amazed her.

Her dog Rook, a monster of an animal with too many bloodlines in him to determine his origin, sat beside his master, tilting his head from side to side as though not certain what to make of the tall man.

"The servant Nora told me that you were the best healer around," he said, his voice much too gentle for a man of his immense size.

Faith nodded. "So it has been remarked."

"My lord needs your skills," he said. "Will you please accompany me?"

Surprised at his manners, comfortable in his overwhelming presence and of course with Rook to protect her from harm, she inquired as to his lord's needs. "What is his injury?"

He seemed almost to blush in embarrassment. "A splinter that has been sorely neglected."

She smiled and his blush deepened, his odd reaction making her realize he was not comfortable around women. A strange character trait for a man whose good looks and strength would obviously make him appealing to the ladies. "Allow me to gather the necessary items to attend your lord."

He nodded and stepped away from the door, Rook sniffing after him.

"Behave, Rook," she called out as she hurried to gather her things.

Faith's hands trembled as she worked with haste, realizing that the ailing lord could be none other than the Irish devil. She had heard the gossip that preceded his arrival. It was all anyone spoke of and all anyone thought about for the last few weeks. Most of the wagging tongues talked of him with fear and awe and none spoke of him without first blessing themselves. His reputation was infamous and she shivered at the prospect of meeting the mighty dark lord.

She finished gathering her supplies and before joining the giant outside she pushed her long, fiery red hair away from her face, holding back the springy curls that protested and fought to remain as they were. She gently ran her fingers over the thin, pale scar that ran just below her right eye, closer to her temple and down along her cheek nearer to her ear, along her neck, over her chest all the way down her full breast to the tip of her nipple.

It would forever be there, forever reminding her, forever keeping her a prisoner of her own fears. She released the thick mass of long, flaming curls to fall and conceal what her step-mother referred to as "her shame."

She made certain the scar was sufficiently concealed, grabbed her healing basket and hurried to join the large man, who was busy patting the contented mongrel sitting beside him. "Ready," she said, and slipped the hood of her dark cloak over her head as they walked toward the castle.

"I am Faith," she said as she struggled to keep up with the giant's long strides.

He stopped, looked down at her and said, "Borg."

"Pleased to meet you, Borg." She held her hand out to him and her delicate fingers were soon lost in his wide palm.

He nodded his response and she smiled, realizing this large man may be a fierce warrior, but he possessed a shy and gentle soul. She hurried alongside him, keeping her head down and making certain her long, red hair concealed the side of her face. If her path crossed with her stepmother, the woman would have a fit if she didn't hide her *shame*. But, then, she did not plan on confronting the woman this night. She would hurry to do her task and be gone before her stepmother discovered her presence in the keep.

The keep was unusually quiet and her and the giant's presence went on undetected as they climbed the stairs to the guest bedchambers.

Rook took a guarded stance outside the bedchamber door which they had stopped in front of and on trembling legs Faith entered with a confident Borg.

Two men occupied the small quarters. One was half-naked and appeared to be asleep by the fire and the other instantly rose to greet them.

Colin stood and greeted her with a smile that could charm the coldest of women, but before he could introduce himself, Eric spoke from his chair by the fire.

"Colin, leave the woman be, she is here to tend me."

Faith was surprised by the man's response since she thought him asleep, his eyes closed, his posture relaxed.

"Come, have done with this," he ordered none too gently.

She slipped her hood off her head. She did not notice the smiles Borg and Colin exchanged. After setting her cloak on a nearby chest, she snatched up her healing basket from where it sat beside her and approached the man quietly.

"Make haste, woman, I wish to seek my bed before the sun rises."

Faith remained silent. This man was not far from Borg's height, perhaps two or three inches shorter. His girth almost equaled the giant's, and where Borg was gentle in nature this man possessed an arrogant manner that would easily intimidate man or beast.

She quietly walked over to him. So this was the man that had gossipy tongues wagging for over a month. She glanced at his features, so sinfully handsome he could only be the devil's own. His long, dark hair remained damp, the wet strands resting over his broad shoulders and glistening from the fire's light. His heavy muscled chest could only have been formed by constant strenuous exertion and his powerful legs were defined with the same thick muscles. She could only imagine the potency of what lay beneath the towel and shockingly, she felt a faint stirring in the pit of her stomach.

Unnerved by her surprising reaction to this man, she set to work forcing all of her attention on her duty at hand. The wound in the middle of his right thigh lay exposed to her view. It was red and warm to the touch—infection would set in soon if it had not already started.

She arranged a clean white cloth on the small stool she pulled close to her side and proceeded to set out her ointments, bone needles and linen cloths for bandages. She scooped warm water into a bowl from the bucket that sat near the fire, dropping a mixture of leaves in it and adding a small white cloth to soak.

When all was in ready she cleansed her hands with another cloth and set to work. Her touch was gentle as she repeatedly soaked the wound with the cloth from the bowl and when satisfied the mixture had worked sufficiently, she picked up her slim bone needle.

"This may pain you," she said softly.

"I doubt that," he said, his eyes remaining closed and his head resting back against the chair.

The solution had worked well, forcing the piece of splinter she was sure had remained embedded in his thigh to peek out from the reddish wound. Gently she probed and within no time she removed the thin sliver that had caused so much damage.

Faith cleansed the wound again and then set to work administering a dab of cream around the infected area and wrapping white strips of cloth around his thigh. She did not notice that the man had opened his eyes.

Eric stared at the woman who knelt at his feet. He wondered over her features, with such a soothing voice he had assumed she would be at least passable, but the young woman who knelt before him was a beauty.

Her fiery red hair fell in a mass of ringlets past her shoulders. Her skin was pale and pure as freshly fallen snow and her lips narrow and tempting. She filled out her body generously, full breasts and hips and a narrow waist. And then there was her soft touch; it simply aroused him. That was why he kept his eyes closed. He wanted to enjoy the feel of her delicate fingers probing his heated skin and imagine. *Yes*. Imagine how her hand would feel if she slipped it slowly beneath the towel and gently cupped him.

As he indulged in that lusty thought, Faith looked up and met his sensuous blue eyes. Breaths were caught for several rushed heartbeats, passions soared and destiny was set into place.

"Are you finished?" he asked, his voice roughly gentle and much too enticing.

She nodded and attempted to collect herself. "Yes, I am finished. The cloth must remain in place for two days time, and this cream"—she picked up a wooden container from her basket and placed it on the arm of the chair in which he sat—"must be rubbed over the wound for at least a week's time."

He gave a brief nod.

Faith hurried to gather her things and be off. This man or devil was having a disturbing effect on her senses and sensibility, and she wanted nothing more than to be gone from his unnerving presence.

She was about to stand when he spoke.

"Will you share my bed this night?"

His lascivious invitation so shocked her that she fell to her backside, her mouth wide and her eyes rounded.

He reached his hand out to her, the hint of a lustful smile tempting his mouth. "I will be gentle."

She ignored his offered help and shook her head, giving him the wrong impression.

"Rough, if you prefer it that way."

He did not wait for her response. He stood, the towel falling off him, his passion more than evident by the potent size of him, and he reached down for her.

Faith scrambled to her feet, tripping on the hem of her gown as she fought to stand and take flight.

Eric tried to help her, but she brushed his hands away, trying desperately not to look at his naked body. He laughed when his hand finally grasped her arm and righted her in front of him.

"We have all night, there is no reason for impatience."

Faith gasped, finding the hard, intimate feel of him brushing against her shocking and his hold on her much too possessive. She yanked her arm free, grabbed her basket and cloak and rushed toward the door.

"If it is coins you wish, I can be generous," Eric said, annoyed and strangely enough disappointed.

"Rook," Faith shouted with a mixture of fear and anger.

The monster dog charged into the room, teeth bared and snarling, and took a protective stance in front of Faith.

Colin and Borg grinned at Eric.

"Sit!" Eric commanded in a thunderous voice that made Faith quake.

The dog immediately obeyed though he continued to emit a low snarl.

"Not for all the coins in the world would I lay with the devil," Faith said and fled the room, Rook close on her heels and snarling.

Colin and Borg burst into laughter.

Eric did not laugh.

"She was not at all impressed with you," Colin said and threw his friend a robe.

Eric slipped into the black silk. "It matters not."

"Her rejection did not bother you?" Colin teased, familiar with Eric's prowess with the women.

Eric walked to the table and poured himself a glass of wine. "As I said, it matters not. I will have her before we depart."

Colin continued his teasing. "I never knew you to take a woman by force."

"She will lay with the devil—and most willingly," he assured his friend and slowly sipped his wine.

TWO

Faith made it to the front door, her trembling hand reaching for the iron handle when her stepmother's shrewish voice halted her.

"What are you doing here?"

Faith took a deep, calming breath before turning to face the woman. She would display no signs of distress, give her no reason to berate or belittle her, though the woman never needed a reason. She found fault with everyone.

With her chin up and standing as tall as she could at barely four inches over five feet, Faith slowly turned around.

Rook, alert to his master's tense emotions, took a guarded stance in front of her.

Lady Terra approached with eyes spread wide and her voice raised to such a squealing pitch that Faith expected the keep to shatter around her.

"I have warned you not to bring that beast into this keep."

Rook did not at all care for her tone and the dark hair on the back of his neck went up as he bared his teeth, emitting a low rumbling snarl.

Lady Terra halted abruptly. "Put him outside or I will have him disposed of."

Faith loved Rook beyond reason. He was her true friend and her only companion and she could not bear to think of any harm coming to him. And she knew without a doubt that Lady Terra was capable of harm. Faith often wondered if she purposely inflicted harm on others out of sheer enjoyment of watching people suffer. She was cruel and heartless and that made her dangerous.

She would not risk losing Rook simply because she was not capable of enduring her stepmother's harsh mouth or a slap that would but sting and then be done with.

Faith opened the door and gently, though firmly, ordered Rook to wait outside. The big dog focused his dark eyes on Lady Terra, gave her a departing snarl for good measure and reluctantly and with slow strides did as his master instructed.

Lady Terra was on Faith before the door was completely closed, her fingers biting viciously into Faith's slender arm. She was so enraged that she did not see Rook sneak back in and blend with the shadows that hugged the wooden walls. She dragged Faith down a dimly lit corridor and shoved her into a room, slamming the door behind them.

Rook remained in the shadows waiting.

"Explain yourself," Lady Terra demanded of Faith as she pushed the young woman away from her.

Faith feared her stepmother, but she feared her own weakness much more. She would not allow herself to back down and be trampled on. She had endured enough humiliation and refused to endure anymore. In her strength she found courage and in courage she found pride. Pride in who she had struggled to become.

She tossed her fiery red hair back away from her face, the multitude of ringlets flying and bouncing off her pale skin and exposing her scar.

Lady Terra shook her head in disgust, but Faith continued to hold her head up high.

The physical scar was something she had learned to live with, but it was what the scar signified to others that caused her the most suffering. Everyone had assumed that her attacker had raped her. No one would listen when she told them how she had fought, fought for her life and won.

When they had found her that night in the stables, bruised and bleeding and brought her to the keep, her stepmother had shouted vile accusations and hateful words at her. And when she attempted to speak, the woman had warned her to keep her lies to herself. That no decent woman would want to remain alive after such a sinful incident.

But she was wrong. Faith wanted to live more than ever that night and she had struggled hard to do so. Even when the healers told her father she had lost too much blood to survive and the priests were called to give her the last rites, Faith still fought. She had struggled even harder when she had heard her stepmother and father agreeing it would be best for all, especially for Faith herself, if she were to just die.

Faith found a strength in herself that night she never knew she possessed and she prayed to God to help heal her and that she would in turn help heal others. He answered her prayer and she kept her word.

And now nothing, not her stepmother or the devil himself would strip her of her courage and pride.

"I hope you had enough common sense to hide that hideous reminder of your indiscretion," Lady Terra said with a sharp-eyed look that could cut almost as painfully as a knife itself.

"I shame no one," Faith said, her solid brown eyes potent in their own focus and enriched by the long, fiery lashes that framed them.

"You shame yourself," Lady Terra spat. "No decent woman would so blatantly brand herself a harlot."

Faith spoke softly, but with such conviction that her voice resonated in the small quarters. "I did nothing wrong."

"Enough, I will hear no more lies. Now tell me what you are doing here."

Faith saw no reason to hide the truth. She was a healer and often called upon to tend the ill, to the disgust and disapproval of her father and stepmother.

"Your guest requested my service."

A malicious snare preceded Lady Terra's comment. "Which service is that?"

Faith was quick to respond. "Perhaps you should ask the devil himself."

"You ungrateful whore," the woman screamed. "Though a whore is just what the devil would want."

"I thought it was innocence he looked to corrupt."

Her face red with rage, Lady Terra took several quick steps toward Faith.

Realizing she intended to strike out at her, Faith wisely answered her. "Lord Eric required attention to his leg."

That stopped the woman fast enough and the startling change in her expression frightened Faith.

"Did he treat you properly?"

Faith did not understand the smile that spread across the woman's face where only moments before fury raged. And she did not trust the sudden shift in emotions.

Lady Terra did not give her a chance to answer before plying her with other questions. "Was he respectful? Did he imply anything improper or make improper suggestions?"

Faith was not certain what the woman herself was implying but her barrage of questions made her feel uncomfortable and uncertain how to answer. She felt as though she were in the snares of a trap and her answers would either free or imprison her.

"Tell me this minute," Lady Terra snapped. "And I will have the truth from you. None of your lies."

Faith hesitated and for a moment thought of not mentioning the devil's sinful proposal, but then the devil needed no help from her. So as quickly and simply as she could she explained how Lord Eric had asked her to share his bed.

This time the smile that spread across the woman's face alarmed Faith. It was as though she had received wonderfully delightful news and was rejoicing in its delivery.

Eric sat at the high table in the great hall deep in conversation with Colin and Borg. His men had finished their morning meal. Some were presently seeing to the horses, while others were engaged in their daily physical practice or seeing to the care of their weapons. A few stood guard over the wagons.

Eric took pride in his men and their skilled accomplishments. They had rode many years with him and fought many a harsh battle. Now was the time to reap the rewards. He had acquired a vast fortune fighting for the lord or king who offered him the fattest purse. With that accumulated fortune and this marriage and the land holdings it brought him he would no longer need to hire out himself and his men as mercenaries.

A good portion of his men, along with hired laborers, had remained in Limerick to continue the work on the keep and the surrounding buildings so that all would have lodging for the winter. His men were looking forward to settling down, getting themselves wives and raising crops along with children.

He had noticed that some of his men had wasted no time in sniffing after some of the servant girls and he would not be surprised if he had several requests for the girls' services to be bought out so they would be free to go with his men.

After all, he was here for the same reason and the sooner he made his decision the better, though the fiery-haired healer continued to torment his thoughts and kept his blood running hot. He may choose a wife today but he also intended to search out the healer. His first thought had been to persuade her to surrender to him but as he gave the idea more consideration he realized that he favored looking upon her and one tumble with her would not do. He decided to offer her a position at his keep. One that would definitely benefit her and him.

"He is thinking of the healer again," Colin said, looking past Eric to Borg who was finishing the last of the potage.

Borg nodded. "Pretty little thing and pleasant, too."

Eric grinned, surprised by Borg's response. His shyness around women was well-known around camp. The men often teased him about it. For all his brawn and size, he was a gentle giant. A woman would be lucky to have him for a husband, but until the man could find his tongue around women he was destined to remain without female companionship.

"She caught your fancy did she, Borg?" he said in a serious yet teasing tone.

The tall man turned several shades of red and lowered his head, focusing on his empty trencher as if it would save him from humiliation.

Colin and Eric laughed and Eric slapped Borg on the back.

"I think, my friend, we will find you a woman before we leave here. I cannot have my strongest man blushing like a nervous female at the mere mention of a woman."

His cheeks flamed an even brighter red and he shook his head. "I do not need a woman."

Colin roared. "Like hell you don't. Every man wants and needs the feel of a woman beneath him."

"Or riding him," Eric added to Borg's further embarrassment.

"I for one love the feel of being buried deep inside of a woman who can ride me with wild abandonment," Colin said and was about to continue when Bridget entered the hall and nervously stepped toward the trio.

"Excuse me, sirs," Bridget said softly. "I do not mean to interrupt or be disrespectful, but cook wants to know if you wish more food."

"We have had our fill, lass, thank you," Eric said with a firm authority that always managed to make the servants nervous.

"It is those damn eyes of yours and that rumble in your voice that excites and frightens them," Colin commented as the young woman hurried off.

"What are you talking about?" Eric said, catching from the corner of his eye the way Borg watched as inconspicuously as possible the sway of Bridget's full wide hips as she finally disappeared from sight.

"Your eyes," Colin reiterated. "Blue as the deep sea and as lusty as a needy whore."

That brought a laugh from Borg.

Colin continued. "And your voice, it is a deep rumble like distant thunder warning the surrounding area what is yet to come. It excites women and frightens men."

"It did not excite Faith," Borg said casually.

Colin shook his head as Eric slowly turned to face the big man.

Borg looked his leader firm in the eyes. "She is a decent girl she is and caring, remember that."

"A warning," Eric asked in the demanding tone of one who commands.

Colin held his breath, for as big as Borg was, every man in Eric's service knew that Eric could take the giant down. His strength and courage was what legends were made of and he had won the respect and admiration of his men after demonstrating just how fearless a warrior he was.

Borg laid a gentle hand on Eric's shoulder. "From someone who cares."

Borg had grown up alongside Eric and his concern meant a great deal so he clearly understood that the man spoke from his heart. "Then I will remember."

Borg smiled and Colin released his breath.

"Good thing you two settled that amicably," Colin said with a wide grin. "For a minute there I was afraid I would have to break you two apart."

That brought a hardy laugh from both men.

"You are a lover not a fighter, Colin," Eric reminded, though he knew the man to be extremely skilled at both. He also knew Colin preferred to be noted for his reputation with the women. He often commented that his adversaries never took him seriously, thinking him more concerned with women than with battle, thereby misjudging his abilities.

"Which reminds me," Colin said, "my eye caught sight of a rather pretty morsel this morning. Brenda, I think she was called. I think I may just go find her and see if she would be interested in some entertainment."

"After you have finished seeing to the men," Eric said in a tone that left no doubt it was an order.

"As you wish," Colin said, giving Eric the respect he felt he fully deserved.

Eric saw that Lord William had entered the hall a few moments earlier. He purposely ignored the irritating man and finished his conversation with Colin, after which he turned to Borg to speak. His blatant disregard for his host's presence was a slight any proud man would not ignore and while Lord William might consider himself proud, Eric felt him a coward who used other men to fight his battles. He doubted he had ever raised a sword or even his fist for that matter, unless of course it was against a weaker man or more likely a woman.

Eric spoke with Borg, continuing to ignore Lord William who came to stand in front of the table directly across from him.

"See to the restocking of supplies for our journey home. And find that girl Bridget and see if she will ask the cook to bake a few extra fruit tarts for us to enjoy on our return journey. Be generous with compensation as usual."

Lord William waited in silence for the two men to take their leave. They made no move to depart and William grew impatient and nervous with the devil's hellish eyes moving to rest upon him.

Only after sweat began to drip in earnest from William's forehead did Lord Eric speak.

"My time is precious to me," Eric began. "I do not wish to waste it. Make certain your daughters are brought here to the hall at midmorning. I will inspect them and see which one fits my needs. I will make my choice then, wed her on the morrow and be gone by the next day. I expect my orders to be followed explicitly. Do not disappoint me."

With that Eric stood and marched out of the great hall, his men following.

Lord William stood with his mouth agape.

Lady Terra entered the hall and stopped beside her husband. Her eyes remained fixed on the devil's back, broad and powerful, and she smiled. "Arrogant and insulting. But what can one expect from a barbarian who knows nothing of manners and respect."

Lord William slipped his thick arm around his wife's thin waist. "Once again, my dear wife, you comfort me. And your astute mind has derived a perfect plan of ridding us of two unwanted nuisances while keeping our part of the kings' agreement."

Lady Terra licked her thin lips in anticipation. "Midmorning should prove entertaining."

Three

Eric sat behind the long table on the dais staring at the three women standing a few feet away from him. He had been busy all morning listening to his men's complaints and comments and he was not surprised to discover there were a few who had found women who were willing to leave with them. One woman was a weaver, another was an undercook in the kitchen and he himself had his eye on the servant girl Bridget who he had learned was an excellent stitcher. He had a feeling Borg was interested in the plump, fresh-faced young woman and given that he was shy he would never find himself a wife; so Eric intended to find one for him.

Love mattered not. It was but a fleeting emotion like passion and once passed served little purpose. He needed a wife who would be a solid, dependable companion. One who possessed strength and courage and the ability to bear him many sons and daughters so that together they would raise a fine family which would carry on his name and see that his land flourished.

He had hoped for a woman whom he would find pleasure in bedding and whom he could give pleasure to, but the three prospects standing in front of him not only lacked sexual appeal but physical appeal as well, making him all the more determined to find the healer and offer her a generous compensation to join his household staff.

The three young women who huddled around their mother

ranged from attractive to passable to unacceptable. He had already discounted one. She resembled her mother and looked to be equally shrewish. Her thin lips and narrow eyes that harshly probed all around her made her even less appealing. The attractive one was obviously taken with her beauty. Unfortunately there was a coldness about her that made Eric think she would not welcome a husband in her bed unless heavily compensated for it. The passable young woman seemed not at all interested in her surroundings and even less interested in her appearance. But she did have wide hips which would give her an advantage when birthing, though getting her with child might be a difficult process since he was not the least bit attracted to her.

Colin leaned over his shoulder. "Go with the beauty—at least she is easy to look upon."

Borg grunted and Eric turned toward him where he sat to his right. "What was that?"

Borg shook his head and Eric could almost sense his thoughts. None appealed to the giant though once again he caught Borg's eyes straying to the servant girl Bridget where she and two other servant girls stood whispering near the hearth.

"Of course the unkempt one would probably have no trouble dropping a babe or two with those generous hips," Colin said with a smirk.

"Did I ask for your help?" Eric said irritably, annoyed that none of the three women remotely appealed to him in any way.

"No, but I am offering it to you anyway. You must choose, your lands depend on this union and besides you will only have to bed her when you want to get her with child. This marriage is not a death sentence, just a minor inconvenience that can be ignored after the vows and planting of a fertile seed."

He was right, but Eric secretly had hoped for more. Along with his fertile land that would grow and produce by the sweat of his brow and strength of his hands, he wanted a woman who would give to him the same. He wanted a woman who would willingly take his seed and tend their child with love and caring. Not one who would do her duty to him, complain while the child grew within her and then ignore the babe when he was born. He wanted a woman who nurtured, loved and cared.

The healer.

She would nurture a child she carried. He could tell by the

way she had gently cared for him with her soothing touch and her calming voice. She would give freely of her love to her husband and child and nurture them with her gentle soul.

"Well?" Colin asked impatiently. "Which one shall it be?"

Eric grumbled beneath his breath while both men sitting alongside of him grinned with the knowledge that their lord was not at all pleased with the offerings.

"Take the one easy on the eyes, I tell you," Colin whispered.

Borg threw in his own choice. "The one with the wide hips."

Eric needed to be sensible in his choice but at the moment he felt anything but reasonable and reason quickly eluded him when he saw the healer walk through the front door with that monster dog of hers trailing close beside her.

He studied her with keen eyes. She wore a deep blue tunic over a pale blue linen shift and her slim waist was bound with a simple white braided belt that held a small leather pouch which probably contained her healing herbs. Her clothes were simple, unlike the harsh gold and orange hues the others wore. But simplicity suited her, serving to make her all the more appealing. And her hair—lord but it raged in flaming splendor around a pale face that was exquisite and her dark eyes . . .

They startled him for a moment, for he caught a hint of fear in them and he wondered if he was the cause of her distress.

He watched with interest as Lady Terra sent her a scathing look and with a rapid wave of her hand motioned Faith to her side. The three other women grinned.

Eric sent a guarded look to Colin and Borg and each man nodded. Something unexpected was about to happen and Eric intended to be prepared. He never faced battle without preparation and though this would probably only amount to a small skirmish he had all intentions of being the victor.

He sat back and waited in arrogant silence.

Faith approached her stepmother with apprehension. She had wondered as to the unusual summons to the hall. She rarely graced the keep with her presence aware she was not welcome.

Her stepmother shot a sharp warning look toward the dog and Faith immediately ordered Rook to sit and stay by the door. He did so but kept steadfast eyes on his master.

Faith stopped near her stepmother, the woman took quick steps to close the distance and spoke low but with a sternness that frightened Faith.

"Keep your shame hidden and speak not a word." She curled her upper lip in disgust. "Do not disgrace us." She then rejoined her daughters.

Faith's hands immediately went to her waist-length, fiery-colored hair and fussed with the ringlets, making certain her scar would remain concealed.

"Now there is a beauty," Colin whispered without moving from his alert stance.

Borg agreed with a simple nod of his head.

Eric said nothing. He simply stared at Faith. His boiling blood and his rock-hard response to her unexpected presence only served to make him more determined to take her with him. He wanted to feel the glory of that flaming hair against his naked skin and touch, taste and torment her into willing submission.

The urge to have her so overwhelmed him that he felt a shiver of lust shoot through him, causing him to throb unmercifully. He had never wanted a woman as badly as he wanted her at this very moment and the raging thought disturbed him.

He would do something and fast. That was how he wanted her—fast and furious, a tangle of naked limbs and piercing thrusts that sent them toppling out of control. And he would see that she lost control, completely, crying out her surrender to him.

His hand fisted at his side.

Colin saw the struggle in his smoldering eyes and white-fisted hand. "Make your choice and then take her and relieve this unrelenting ache."

Eric took a deep breath and was about to speak when Lord William strutted forward with an arrogant confidence that kept Eric on alert.

"A serious matter has been brought to my attention," he began.

Eric remained silent, keeping a steady, sure eye on the barrel-shaped man.

William smartly kept his distance from the mighty devil while he continued. "You, Lord Eric, overstepped my hospitality last night when you made an inappropriate proposition to my daughter Faith."

Colin and Borg's startled expressions betrayed their surprise but Eric remained as he was, calm and silent.

William haughtily proceeded to demean the devil himself. "I do not take kindly to such a blatant insult to my precious daughter. How dare you treat her like a whore when I graciously open my home to you! You shame yourself, but mostly you have shamed my daughter and I demand that you rectify this matter immediately. I will settle for nothing less than an offer of marriage to my daughter Faith."

"Father, no," Faith said with mounting alarm. She wanted nothing to do with the devil or Lord Eric or whoever he was. She favored her freedom and did not care to surrender it or herself to a man who clearly lacked any emotion. A trait the devil most surely possessed.

"Silence," her father shouted. "He will do right by you. I will not have my daughter's virtue stained."

Lord William was obviously enjoying what he assumed was his upper hand in the situation, and Eric quietly allowed the little man to continue with his useless tirade while he focused his attention on Faith.

She obviously knew nothing of her father's plan though he doubted the man possessed enough brains to contrive it. No, dubious tactics seemed more Lady Terra's style. The only thing about this whole strange incident was that he had never been informed that there were four daughters, not three. Why had her existence been kept from him? Why had he not been told that the healer was Lord William's daughter?

The puzzling thought irritated him though he would not allow it to stop him from possessing Faith. *Nothing* would stop him from possessing Faith.

Lord William ranted on, enjoying this moment of power over the lord devil.

Faith stood in shock, her slim body trembling beneath her garments. This could not be happening. Her father meant to give her in marriage to this dark lord? She would have no say in the matter. And once they were joined he would rule over her. Command her every move and demand she perform her wifely duties.

Her eyelids fluttered and her breath caught. What would happen when he discovered the truth and eyed *her shame*? She scolded herself for even thinking of her scar as shameful. But he would think of it as such and would feel betrayed, slighted, and then what? He had to be told the truth. If he knew the truth he would not want her.

She moved to step forward, but her stepmother blocked her path and whispered a harsh warning.

"Not a word will you speak."

The cold, hard glint in the woman's eyes sent a shiver through Faith and she did as warned. She remained silent.

Lord William, winded from his recourse, finally stood silent. Not a whisper, a sigh or a breath was heard. The silence hung thick and heavy, and not even the autumn wind sounded outside. Everyone waited, waited for the devil to speak.

Eric stood, his heavy wooden chair scraping along the planked floor as the back of his legs gave it a hefty shove. He walked slowly around the table, his blue eyes fixed on Faith and every eye in the room fixed on him.

Faith refused to show her fear. She forced her trembling under control; only a slight quake now racked her body and she boldly met his blue lust-filled eyes as he approached her.

He was magnificent, though that one word seemed inadequate in describing him. His dark red tunic was the color of rich aged wine, and the material looked to have been spun by the finest weaver using the finest threads. The wool garment complimented his finely toned body.

His face, though, was what brought a frantic tremble to her stomach. His features were a blend of Irish beauty and striking Viking strength. His long, dark hair was combed away from his face and lay in shiny splendor over his wide shoulders, adding to his potent appeal.

If this was the look of the devil, it was no wonder why people fell into sin.

He stopped a short distance from her, Lady Terra moving out of his way as if she offered Faith for inspection. It was no surprise to Faith that he did just that. He took his time circling her, his blatant stare stroking her body from head to toe.

She prevented herself from responding to the shiver that rushed over her from his lusty perusal. She had no doubt that if they were alone it would be his hands slowly traveling the route his eyes now followed. The sinful thought sent another flourish of frantic flutters to her stomach and instinctively her hand moved over her nervous abdomen.

Her movement stopped him and he grinned knowingly at

her. He was well aware of the discomfort he caused her and he appeared to take great pleasure in it. Without taking his eyes off her, he spoke to Lord William.

"I will wed your daughter Faith on the morrow."

Stunned and frightened by what this union meant, she moved to speak.

Her father's quick response cut her off. "I am pleased to hear this. A banquet celebration will be prepared."

Faith again attempted to speak, but her father's bloated pride kept him uttering nonsense.

"A wise decision for all and one you will not regret. Faith is a good healer, a dutiful daughter and will make you a dutiful wife—"

"Father," Faith attempted to interrupt.

He simply raised his hand to silence her. "You say you wish to leave the following day. I will make certain you are supplied with all you need and—"

"Father, please," she attempted again.

"You have no manners."

The harsh scolding came from her stepmother who had returned to her side. Faith saw the look of fury on her face and quickly gave a signal behind her back for Rook to remain seated. She sensed the woman's loss of control and knew it meant a sharp and sudden slap, for which she braced herself.

"You will obey your father and when you marry you will obey your husband, you ungrateful child," she screamed and raised her hand swinging toward Faith with such force that Faith feared she would not remain on her feet.

Faith closed her eyes and prepared for the blow.

She felt the soft brush of fine material against her cheek and opened her eyes to see the dark lord's hand squeezed so tightly around her stepmother's wrist that her fingers drained of all color.

His blue eyes that only moments before were filled with blatant lust now raged like a winter storm out of control and when he spoke, his deep, chilling tone froze all with fear.

"Faith belongs to me now. Touch her and you suffer the devil's wrath."

Lady Terra spoke not a word, though her thin body trembled as she bowed her head in submission.

Faith was stunned. No one . . . no one but Rook defended

her with such ferocity. It was almost as if he actually cared for her and she felt a twinge of guilt that he was not being told the truth of the matter.

Eric looked to Faith as he called out, "Borg."

The large man was at his side in seconds.

"You will stay with Faith until our departure. Whatever her needs, see to them and make certain that monster dog of hers"—he stopped when he saw her face darken with fear—"is ready for the journey," he finished.

She smiled up at him and the sensual heat that had been tempered by more obvious matters suddenly soared, causing him great discomfort.

"Thank you," she said softly and laid a gentle hand of appreciation on his arm.

If Eric possessed full Viking blood he would have swung her up in his arms, thrown her over his shoulder and taken her straight to his bed where he would have proceeded to ravish her. But his Irish blood, though temperamental, possessed the iron will of determination and he was determined to wed her and bed her in that order.

He turned to Lord William. "Make haste with the wedding plans."

William was only too happy to comply, wanting to be rid of them both. "Yes, yes."

Eric returned his attention to Faith. "We will talk later."

And with that command given, he signaled Colin to follow him out of the hall.

Faith watched the dark lord disappear out the front door and shivered. He must be told the truth, but the vicious looks her father and stepmother sent toward Rook warned her it would be he who suffered if she dared to disobey them.

Her only choice was to trust in the devil.

Four

The wedding was over and the banquet celebration near to
ending. Faith could not believe she was married to the man who
sat beside her at the long table. She knew nothing of him except
that he was called the Irish devil, and for what many believed
was a good reason. He was strong—which was obvious from
one sweeping glance—and when one lingered to look upon him
it became even more evident why he was considered the devil's
own. Strength, potency, arrogance, determination and no fear.
The man simply looked as though he feared no man or beast,
and she could easily believe it the way Rook had responded to
his strict command the other night. And, of course, there was
the way her father either avoided the man or stood several steps
away from him when he was around. And her stepmother?

Faith raised her hand to her mouth to conceal the brief smile
that surfaced when she thought of the way her stepmother
quaked when in the presence of the dark lord.

Her hand also served to hide the slight frown that suddenly
darkened her features. Concern as to what he expected of his
wife haunted her. Would he demand obedience? Did he wish
her to fear him? Was there any gentleness in the devil's soul?
But then, the devil did not have a soul, so what was *she* to expect?

She had hoped to speak with him alone. She had soundly
convinced herself that his request, when first they met, to take

her to his bed was simply a misunderstanding. He had thought her a servant of the keep. He knew not that she was the daughter of Lord William. And while he had frightened her, the thought that he had found her appealing excited her. Not a proper or ladylike thought, but one she pondered anyway.

But her hope was dashed when it became apparent that her father and stepmother purposely saw to it that she and Lord Eric were given no chance to speak yesterday eve even though the devil himself had decreed it.

When Faith returned to her small cottage she had no sooner entered it when she was inundated by ailing villagers. She learned that it was her stepmother's doing since barely any man, woman or child who sought her skills were actually ailing. It was late in the evening when Bridget came to see her that she discovered Lady Terra's involvement. The girl informed her that Lady Terra had ordered the whole village to be seen by Faith. By evening's end she was completely exhausted and still had to pack her belongings, especially her herbs. Then there were a few rare herb plants she had to dig up carefully and preserve properly so they could be transplanted to her new home.

Bridget had offered to help, as did Borg, and the three of them had worked together, enjoying each other's company. For all of Borg's size and strength, his large hands, that could easily squeeze the life from a man, gently handled the delicate plants with care and attention. He had also seen to it himself that Lord Eric was informed that she was much too busy to meet with him. Since she received no demanding summons from her future husband she had assumed that he accepted Borg's message without question.

She was also happy to learn that Bridget had accepted Lord Eric's request that she serve as Faith's personal servant. She could not help but notice that Borg had been pleased with the news as well. The tall, quiet man remained close by Bridget's side the entire time they had worked together and had listened to her endless chatter without comment or annoyance. The man, though shy in his demeanor, was obviously taken with her.

Having not had the opportunity to speak with the man who was now her husband made the night that lay ahead all the more frightening to Faith. He was a complete stranger to her. How did one share intimacy with a stranger?

He had barely spoken with her today, though she could not lay the blame on him. The ceremony and this celebration had brought much activity to the keep. Scores of people wished to extend their congratulations to them and there was little time for more than a brief exchange of conversation between them.

She yawned, placing her hand to her mouth.

"You are tired," Eric said, leaning over, his smooth cheek not far from her own.

She was drawn to his stunning blue eyes. They captivated, tempted and seduced.

She nodded, not taking her eyes from his, not wanting to and not able to. "Sleep was something I got very little of last night."

"And of which you will get even less tonight," he said in a soft whisper.

Faith knew not how to respond. She simply stared at him wide-eyed and her hand rushed to press against her tummy in an awkward attempt to still the strange flutters. Instead the flutters took flight, sending a tingling sensation down between her legs and an unexpected shiver to race through her.

Eric slipped his finger gently beneath her chin and spoke so close his lips almost brushed hers. "I will satisfy that tremble more than once this eve."

Faith was certain he intended to kiss her right there and then. She sensed it, her body ran warm with anticipation, she grew light-headed and to her surprise she eagerly awaited his lips.

Shouts and startled cries caused her to jump and Eric to rise hastily up out of his seat.

A frantic young man rushed forward toward the dais and fell to his knees before Lord Eric, his hands clamped tightly together as if he were prepared to beg for his cause.

But it was to Faith he directed his plea. "Please, Lady Faith, I beg you. You must come with me. Ellie's time has come and she is fearful. She says you promised you would be with her."

The young man looked pitiful, as though he shared his wife's labor pains and had spilled several empathetic tears for her suffering.

Faith stood prepared to rush off when she realized she now was answerable to a husband. And with what had just past between them she wondered if he would deny his own desires for that of a woman about to give birth. An ordeal that could possibly take all night.

With courage she had fought hard to sustain, she faced him. "Please, my lord, may I have your permission to attend Ellie?"

She was certain she had caught a flicker of admiration cross his face before she heard her stepmother's shrewish tongue.

"This night is for the consummation of your wedding vows. Do not embarrass your husband by making such a ridiculous request."

Eric turned his head slowly toward Lady Terra, his blue eyes ablaze with smoldering fury. The woman drew back fearfully in her seat.

"If your tongue lashes at my wife one more time, I will see to it that you never speak again."

The great hall grew so quiet that the crackling flames in the large stone hearth sounded like mighty thunder in the eerie silence.

The young man on bended knees was close to tears and Colin and Borg rose to stand behind their lord.

Eric extended his hand to his wife and she readily accepted it, the warmth of his flesh and the strength of this touch reassuring. "Come, I will go with you."

Relief visibly flooded her tense features and she sighed. "Thank you, my lord."

"Eric," he corrected as they walked around the table. Everyone who was not standing rose out of respect for the mighty lord and his lady.

"Lord Eric," she said, trying his name on her tongue.

"No, Faith," he once again corrected gently. "Eric, simply Eric."

"Eric," she whispered with a smile as his arm slipped around her slim waist and together they disappeared out the door, the young man frantically following.

A chilly autumn night kept the men huddled around a fire outside the small cottage. The young, expectant father sat shivering next to the dancing flames even though two cloaks had been placed over his shoulders.

Colin and Borg sat nearby discussing plans for an early morning departure and Eric, with Rook sitting obediently by his side, sat with his eyes fixed on the one-room cottage, tensing along with the young man every time a shrill scream ripped through the night air.

Eric flung back the black cloak away from his arms, the gold brooch that secured the woolen garment at his shoulder, preventing it from slipping off. He extended his hands out to the fire warming them.

It was his new wife he wished he was warming his hands on and introducing her to his intimate touch. When he had caught sight of her entering the chapel his breath had lodged in his throat and he had fought to maintain his composure. She appeared an angel outfitted all in white. Shift, tunic and belt. Pale, slim, petite in form, except for her generous breasts he ached to get his warm hands on. And then there was her hair. Its bold red color startled the eye and sat in sharp contrast to her pale skin and white clothing and made her all the more passionately appealing.

Now, however, she stood in that small cottage, her wedding clothes discarded for a more practical blue wool shift and tunic and she had draped a large white cloth around her hips. The last time he had peered inside, sweat beaded along her forehead and her springy red curls hung limply in her face. He had wanted to go over to her and tie back her hair, but she was so engrossed in tending to the fearful, crying girl that he had turned and walked away, sending her only a simple nod to let her know he was near.

He asked himself several times why he had granted her permission to forego their marriage bed to birth a babe. Surely the women in the village were skilled at delivering each other's babes. But he knew why. When she had turned to him with courage and pride and asked him permission in front of all, she was acknowledging and accepting her position as his wife and extending him the respect due a husband. For that tribute to a complete stranger he admired her and could not deny her request.

Another scream ripped through the air and the campfire flames crackled and shook in protest. He had forgotten how many shrills had pierced the night, had stopped counting hours ago. It was at least two hours past midnight and the babe had refused to make its appearance. He was sorely tempted to curse the unborn babe but held his tongue.

Instead Eric concentrated on the future and thought about his lands and the castle that was under construction in Limerick. The keep was near finished and the castle grounds work

moving along steadily. He would have a good home to take his
new wife to and fertile fields that had yielded a generous stock
for the winter. He hoped his wife would be as fertile as the Irish
soil.

His love for this land at times overwhelmed him. His mother
had often told him that a son born on Irish soil who journeys far
always returns to the land that saw his birth. She told him Ireland was forever in his blood and she was right.

Ireland's beauty held no equal. Rolling pastures, emerald
green hills, enchanted woods, sparkling blue lakes—no other
country possessed such riches. And soil that grew the finest
crops. He had sunk his hands in that dark, thick soil when he
had returned three years ago a grown man of twenty and five.
He had buried his fingers deep, feeling the precious gift of life
it held. And then and there he had promised himself that this
land of his roots would sow his seed once again.

He had fought hard and long, his hands covered with blood
so thick he thought that the hardy River Shannon would not
even be able to wash the stain away. But he kept his eyes and
mind focused on the true beauty of Ireland. He remembered
vividly the majestic mountains of Donegal where several nights
they camped in its shadow, the rocky coastline that made land-
ings difficult and the white, sandy beaches that finally welcomed them. His eyes drank their fill of the peaceful Ardbear
Bay in Connacht. He dreamed about the many windswept valleys in the northwest, their rocky terrain and thick vegetation
making them perfect places to hide in wait for the enemy. He
listened over and over again to the legend of how Ireland's
landscape was created by the battle of the bulls. And he listened
to the people that were Ireland's heart and soul.

And while the warring kings fought for more and more land
holdings, caring little for the land and what it could harvest
them and caring even less for the people whose sweat and
blood made the land thrive, Eric fought to gain land so he could
remain on his native soil and reestablish his heritage.

He intended to get himself a little piece of heaven, for this
land so pleasing to the heart and soul had to be the closet thing
to heaven. And he would work along with his people, his own
sweat and blood mixing with theirs so they would flourish
along with the land and together their futures would be secured.

The pain-filled scream caused all four men to jump to their

feet and the already exhausted, expectant father turned deathly pale. Rook simply released a mournful howl.

"Ellie, you are fighting too hard," Faith said softly, wiping the frightened girl's perspiring brow with a damp cloth. "The babe will come in its own good time."

"I am so tired," Ellie complained and grabbed for Faith's hand. "Nothing is wrong, is there? You would tell me if I were dying and you would see that the babe lived, would you not?"

Faith ignored the painful grasp the fearful girl held on her and spoke in a gentle, reassuring tone. "You are not dying and there is nothing wrong with the babe. Your labor is long and tedious and, yes, painful, but it will come to a joyful end."

Bridget stood on the opposite side of the bed and Faith caught the doubt and worry that shadowed her soft green eyes. She was secure that she could get Ellie through this delivery, though she was apprehensive. She had a feeling the babe was in the wrong position and would need to be turned for a safe delivery. Not an easy task for the deliverer and even less pleasant for the mother, but also not an impossible one. What Ellie needed most was to remain as calm as possible. Every time she tensed it caused her labor pain to worsen and to exhaust her, robbing her of the strength and courage she would need for the delivery itself.

"Relax," Faith ordered, and this time sternly. "You have time before the next pain."

She walked away from the bed over to the table in the one-room cottage and washed her hands once again in the water bowl she had instructed Bridget to change with each use.

"Is she all right?" Bridget whispered behind her.

Faith turned and spoke quietly. "She will be if she would relax. I think the babe needs turning—"

Bridget almost gasped loudly, but Faith's quick hand to her arm prevented the startled reaction from reaching her lips.

" 'Tis not a death sentence for mother or child. My hands are small and agile and will serve both of them well this eve."

Her confident response eased Bridget's worries. "True, I have seen you save many a villager whose family had given up hope. Will it be long now for her?"

"Before sunrise." Faith prevented herself from cringing at her own response. She hoped her new husband would understand the unpredictable delay and not be angered by it. She had seen him peek in once or twice and perhaps even more since she was so engrossed in tending Ellie, she took little notice of anything else. That was the reason she had purposely kept her now-damp hair hanging over her shoulders. She normally tied the mass of red curls back away from her face and out of her way, but with her husband so close by and his entrance to the cottage unpredictable she could take no chances. She had no choice but to conceal her scar.

Her hair hung around her face and over her shoulders in limp strands, though the curls persisted with less than their usual bounce. She wiped her damp forehead with a wet cloth and wondered what her husband's reaction would be when he first looked upon her scar. Would he feel cheated? Would his disgust be evident in his eyes? Would he refuse to honor their marriage vows and cause her even more disgrace?

Faith realized she faced an uncertain future with the dark lord and she wondered why the thought disturbed her. Their brief acquaintance served as a reminder that she knew little of him and yet she felt he was a man of integrity. He had come to her defense without hesitation or question. Of course, she was considered his property and he was a man who defended what was his, but still she sensed there was more to the man called the "Irish devil" than he allowed people to see. Perhaps if she could reach that part he kept so guarded, she would discover a man worth loving.

The key to solving this dilemma was to accomplish that before he discovered her secret.

Faith forcibly pushed the concerned thoughts from her mind. She had Ellie to tend to and the birth required all her attention.

She reached for a clean cloth to soak in the bowl filled with fresh water. After rinsing it she returned to Ellie and passed the cloth to Bridget for her to wipe gently the young girl's flushed face. She walked to the end of the bed, rolling up her sleeves.

"Here is what we are going to do, Ellie, to bring this little fellow into the world."

"Oh, do you think it a boy?" Ellie asked with more enthusiasm than Faith had seen from her in several hours. She wanted more of that eagerness, especially for the task that lay ahead.

"Of course, 'tis a boy," Faith said with a grin. "Only a man would give a woman so much trouble."

Ellie and Bridget laughed and as the next pain hit, Faith gently delivered the necessary instructions that would help bring the night's ordeal to a joyful end.

"Was that laughter I heard?" Colin asked, stretching his neck and turning his head for his ear to pick up the sound more clearly.

"Why would they be laughing?" the young man asked nervously.

Colin smiled. "What is your name, boy?"

"John, sir."

"Well, John, let me tell you something about women," Colin said, resting comfortably back against the stump behind him. "They make absolutely no sense. Never try to understand them, never argue with them and never, ever tell them they are wrong."

"Oh, Ellie, my wife, sir, she is never wrong."

He spoke with such complete honesty and love that all three men looked at him and shook their heads.

"Besotted," Borg said, almost as if he wished what John had was contagious.

"He is finished," Colin said and laughed.

"Perhaps," Eric said in that deep direct voice that commanded attention. "He is a very lucky young man."

John bobbed his head. "Oh yes, sir, that I am. I love my Ellie, she is the most wonderful, beautiful woman in all of Ireland and I cannot bear to know she is suffering so because of me."

"It is a woman's duty to birth babes," Colin informed him.

"Yes, sir, I know, but to suffer so while we sit here and do nothing but wait. It seems unfair."

"It is the way of things," Borg said and offered a comforting pat to the young boy's tense back.

Eric remained silent, his thoughts his own. He wondered how Faith would fair when birthing their babes. And he wondered if he would be able to sit idly by, waiting and listening to her screams.

Eric stood abruptly, startling the other three. Rook immediately rose along with him and remained by his side as he walked toward the cottage.

"Is he angry?" John asked fearfully.

Colin shook his head. "Impatient."

John swallowed the nervous lump in his throat before responding. "I upset his wedding night."

Colin laughed. "You planted the seed that decided to harvest and upset his wedding night."

John began to tremble again.

"Do not worry," Borg said. "He will wait as long as it takes and say not a word."

"Lady Faith will not suffer because of this will she?" It took courage for John to ask the question and his inquiry earned him the respect of both Colin and Borg. "She is a good, caring woman and I would feel responsible if she—"

Colin stopped him. "Worry not. Lady Faith wisely asked her husband's permission and he willingly gave it. She will suffer naught for her actions here this night, though she may find herself mighty tired on the morrow's journey."

"I heard you leave at dawn," John said.

Borg nodded. "If the babe has arrived we will. If not?" He shrugged. "We will wait."

John relaxed for a brief moment before a scream ripped through the night air once again.

Eric was near the cottage door when the scream rushed out. He hurried his steps, Rook keeping up with his long strides. He slowly opened the door and peered around it.

Faith stood at the bottom of the bed, her hands lost between the young girl's white thighs and her voice soft and gentle as she delivered instructions.

"It will not be long now, Ellie, I almost have him turned. Hold tight, don't do anything, just let me get him turned a bit more and it will be over."

He watched the muscles in her forearms tighten and her face scrunch up as she fought to turn the babe inside the frightened girl.

"A bit more, just a bit," she said, easing the girl's fears.

"I need to push. I need to push," Ellie demanded.

"One minute, just one, Ellie, hold on," Faith urged and with all her might worked the babe around. "Now, Ellie, now."

The young girl groaned along with her laborious task.

"I have his head, keep pushing," Faith urged and with gentle hands assisted the babe free from the womb. Her fingers worked frantically to clear the cord that had lodged around the babe's neck.

"A boy," Faith said with excitement while her fingers hastily cleared the babe's mouth.

"Why is he not crying? Why can I not hear him?" Ellie asked with fearful tears rushing to her eyes.

"Lazy he is," Faith said all the while doing her best to get the still babe to breathe. After making certain his mouth was clear, she gently massaged his throat and his chest, turned him over and gave him several pats on the back.

"What is wrong? What is wrong?" Ellie said crying in earnest now.

Eric shook his head. All this and the babe was stillborn. He could not understand why Faith fought so hard when the little fellow was obviously lifeless.

Faith turned the baby over and bent down to softly blow her life's breath into his mouth.

Eric knew then that he had chosen wisely. This tenacious woman would never give up, she would fight right alongside him. She would bring courage, strength and honor to his name. She would never disgrace him.

"No, no," Ellie cried, clinging to Bridget's hand.

A loud and unexpected wail ripped through the cottage and brought startled gasps from all present, even the mighty Irish devil.

Faith turned toward the door before she placed the babe on Ellie's stomach. Her husband simply nodded to her and soundlessly retreated, closing the door and leaving the women to finish the task.

"You have a son," Eric announced and offered his hand to the young lad.

John grasped his hand, grinned and repeated, "A boy."

Colin and Borg delivered hardy congratulatory slaps to the young fellow's back.

"Ellie?" John asked, suddenly remembering his wife.

"She is fine," Eric said. "I am certain my wife will let you see her soon."

"Thank you, sir, thank you so much for your kindness and understanding," John said, all the while shaking his hand.

The door to the cottage opened.

"Want to see your son, John?" Bridget called.

Releasing Eric's hand, John ran toward the cottage.

"The sun rises in an hour," Colin said.

"We leave on schedule," Eric announced.

Colin smiled. "We could delay it an hour or two."

Borg grumbled.

"He is entitled to the consummation of his vows," Colin insisted.

"The woman spent all night birthing a babe," Borg argued.

Colin snapped right back. "She has a duty to her husband."

"Enough," Eric commanded sharply. "I said we leave at dawn. Go make certain all is ready."

Both men nodded and hurried off, their bickering voices trailing them.

Rook briefly whined, then took off. Eric looked to see what had caught his attention. Faith had stepped out of the cottage, her hand rubbing the back of her neck.

She dropped down at Rook's approach and gladly took his sloppy kisses while ignoring her own discomfort to rub behind his ears.

Eric approached slowly, allowing her time with the monster of a dog she seemed extremely attached to.

Faith stood, filled a small bucket with water from the rain barrel beside the cottage and placed it on the ground for Rook. The dog greedily lapped away at it.

She simply amazed Eric. She had spent the whole night attending a difficult birth and still she saw to her dog's needs before her own.

"Forgive me, my lord," she said as he stepped near.

"Eric," he corrected. "Forgive you for what? You did what you had to do and with remarkable success. I had thought for a moment the babe would not breathe."

She visibly relaxed, her shoulders drooping and her hand once again returning to rub her neck. "I feared the same."

"But refused to accept it."

She smiled. "I can be stubborn, my . . . Eric."

He stepped next to her and gently pushed her hand aside. His long fingers slipped behind her neck and began to knead her tense muscles with a firm hardness.

She tensed, at first fearful he might brush too near her scar, but soon she forgot her worry and simply enjoyed the relief his skilled fingers brought to her stiff neck.

"We leave at dawn," he informed her.

"Oh, I thought—" She stopped and said no more. How could she ask this stranger why he wished to delay their coupling?

She thought him the devil able to read her mind when he spoke in a soft whisper near her ear. "You are tired. There will be time enough to consummate our vows."

"Come, sir, see my son," John said with joy as he stepped outside the cottage.

Eric moved to take Faith's hand.

"I would like to clean up and gather my remaining belongings for the journey."

Eric nodded. "Is Bridget finished with Ellie?"

"She will be shortly."

"Then I will send her to see to you," he said and before he disappeared inside the cottage, he added, "I admire your strength and integrity and I am pleased that you are my wife."

The next hour was a whirlwind of activity. Faith received a tongue lashing from her stepmother for not performing her wifely duties and was given orders to promptly see to the task. Bridget arrived after Faith had finished cleaning up and packing the last few items she wished to take and together they saw to the care of her delicate seedlings.

Faith barely had time to consider Eric's parting words.

Integrity.

What would the dark lord do when he discovered his wife was not as honorable as he thought? Her unpredictable plight troubled her though she had no time to give it full thought. It nagged at her now and then as she was hurried along, Bridget insisting they would leave precisely at dawn as Lord Eric had commanded.

Dawn came, and so did departure.

Brief good-byes were exchanged with her parents and another whispered warning in her ear was given from her stepmother to see to her duties.

Orders were issued in loud shouts and Faith stood waiting, several yawns attacking her. The long night had finally caught up with her and she was completely exhausted. She had hoped to ride in the wagon with the other women, but was told she would ride with her husband. She wondered just how long she was going to be able to stay mounted without falling asleep.

Eric mounted a gorgeous black stallion and to Faith's surprise, Borg grasped her around her waist and handed her up to Eric. He situated her comfortably across his lap, wrapping the black wool cape he wore snugly around the both of them.

She sat braced against his warmth and strength, his hard muscles a comforting pillow to her tired body. Without thought she rested her weary head on his strong shoulder, nestling herself against him and sighing with pure pleasure.

He smiled, though she did not notice or hear him order her to sleep. She drifted into a peaceful slumber as Eric directed the mighty stallion away from the keep.

Five

Eric watched the sun peek from behind the cloud that only moments before had dusted them all with a light rainfall. Faith continued to sleep contentedly in his arms, stirring occasionally and then settling herself with a comforting snuggle against him.

A brief smile tugged at the edges of his usual stern expression. He felt content for the first time in a very long time. He was finally settling, with permanence, in the land of his birth, a place he had felt he always belonged. It was as though the land called to him like now when the sun washed over the meadows highlighting them in rich shades of gold and glorious greens. And the hills in the distance echoed the shades of greens in the meadow though ranging in color from the darkest green to the brightest. And the bright sun streaming down made the raindrops that clung to the blades of grass sparkle like diamonds. It was truly a magnificent sight to behold.

Even now he could picture his fertile fields at Shanekill Keep being harvested by his men and the women his men had joined with along the way. They would all forge new lives. Instead of battle and death, there would be growth and birth.

He slipped his hand down inside the cloak and gently splayed his hand over Faith's flat stomach. He was anxious to get her with child and watch her body grow with his seed. He had thought the process would be a chore, one that was necessary but one that brought him no joy. It pleased him tremendously to know that he actually lusted after his own wife. And given that she was pure and innocent, he could teach her not only to enjoy, but to look forward to his touch. The thought excited and pleased him. Finally, after all the senseless battles and spilling of blood, he looked forward to his future.

She stirred against him and he moved his hand slowly up along her narrow waist and came to rest it beneath her breast. While his hand applied a gentle squeeze to her plump breast, his one finger faintly traced her nipple. He smiled when he felt her flesh peak to hardness and he softly squeezed the rigid nipple, wishing the wool material did not block his path.

A shudder ran through her and she moaned softly, stirring once again. He told himself to stop, to wait until later this evening when he could find a spot where they could be alone. Where he could slowly undress her and drink his full of her, but his own passion was fast taking control and he did not want to stop touching, feeling, wanting her.

Her eyes fluttered open and his fingers continued to tease intimately and play with her responsive nipple. He was prepared for her to protest and turn from him in embarrassment; he was not prepared for her dark brown eyes to widen in passion or for her to gasp in pleasure. His new wife seemed forever to surprise and please him.

"You are not adverse to my touch?" he asked boldly.

Her reply was just as bold and pleased him all the more. "Your touch feels good."

"Then I should not stop?"

"Not if you do not wish to," she said softly.

"I do not wish to, but I do wish to touch more of you."

"Oh," was her only response.

He caught Colin's approach from the corner of his eye. "You please me, Faith, and I will take your innocence with as little pain as possible. Ours will be a good match."

He felt her body stiffen and assumed she grew nervous over his words and the thought of the consummation of their vows. He would alleviate those fears and replace them with desire soon enough.

He removed his hand from inside the cloak but not before he gave her hard nipple one last brief, strong tug.

She gasped again and turned her head into his shoulder to

hide her flushed face as Colin directed his horse beside Eric's stallion.

"There is a small lake up ahead. A good place to water the horses and take sustenance, since Borg is incessantly complaining of hunger."

Eric nodded. "Ride ahead and make preparations."

Colin tugged at the reins to leave, but momentarily halted his horse and grinned. "The devil has all the luck."

He laughed and rode off and for once Eric silently agreed with him.

Faith was amazed at the efficiency and camaraderie of his men. They all worked well together, each going about their tasks with a friendly pleasantry that surprised her. She had always thought of soldiers or warriors as disgruntled men who lived to fight, but then perhaps these men had seen enough battles.

She sat on the red-and-black plaid wool blanket that Eric had deposited her on when they arrived at the campsite only a few moments ago. He ordered her to relax, though she doubted he realized he sounded as though he forever issued orders, a habit she equated to his battle days and one she clearly understood and, therefore, took no offense at. He had told her he would return shortly after seeing to his men.

And she did just that, enjoying the beauty of the day. The bright blue sky was thick with big white clouds and the sun seemed unusually bright, the probable reason for the warm breeze that blew across the field where they were camped. The small lake lay calm and serene, its silvery surface sparkling like a polished gem. Many of the wildflowers that flourished around the countryside had already dropped their seeds in preparation for winter, but Faith spotted heather growing in abundance in the near distance and hoped to gather some before they broke camp.

Bridget approached carrying a good-sized basket and Faith immediately rose to help the girl.

"Oh please, m'lady," Bridget protested when Faith reached out to help with the hefty basket. "You must rest. You had a long, tiring night."

"You stayed alongside me, Bridget, you must be just as tired."

Faith sat back down and Bridget eagerly joined her, placing

the basket beside her. "I but assisted you and very little I did. And besides, I slept the whole morning away in the wagon." She blushed as she reached in and began arranging bread and cheese on the blanket. "Lord Eric instructed the women that I was to rest and not be disturbed. He is a thoughtful lord, and I is pleased I am to be joining his keep. And pleased to be serving you, m'lady."

"Thank you, Bridget, and I must say that I am glad you do not mind digging in the dirt. I will need help planting my herb garden once we reach the keep."

"I love plants, m'lady. And besides, I have requested Borg's help with any task that may prove difficult," Bridget said with a smile.

"I think the gentle giant is smitten with you, though shy."

Bridget giggled. "He is very shy. The poor man turns bright red every time I approach him."

"He is coming this way now," Faith said, watching the large man slowly, almost hesitantly approach them.

Bridget was not as hesitant. She turned her head and waved at him.

Borg stopped near the edge of the blanket and held out a flask to Bridget. "Fresh water from the lake."

"Please join us, Borg," Faith offered and before he could respond Bridget reached out to him.

"Sit here beside me," she said, tugging at his hand and practically pulling him down beside her. "Let me slice some cheese and bread for you, and give you berries. You must have the berries that we picked before we left."

Faith watched Borg watch Bridget. He had a solid, square face with rich, defined features. Though not as handsome as Eric, he was a striking man, due more to his height, the mighty width of him and his long, blond hair that he wore tied back. While he looked a fierce and mighty warrior, he was the gentlest of men, with a soft voice and tender touch. He was a perfect match for Bridget.

The young servant girl possessed a pretty face, round and plump without a mark or blemish on her creamy complexion. Her long, brown hair was sprinkled liberally with blond streaks and she wore it in a braid that fell to her waist. She stood well over five feet and her large frame carried her extra weight well, dispersing it in all the right places. Faith had frequently caught

Borg's gaze wandering to Bridget's generous hips. And where Borg was shy and silent, Bridget was gregarious and loquacious. They would be good for each other.

Bridget was explaining to Borg how she required his help with the preparation of the herb garden. Borg nodded in agreement while he ate the food Bridget continually handed him.

Faith nibbled at a piece of cheese, enjoying the one-sided exchange.

When Bridget had finally ceased her chatter, Borg surprised them both by asking, "Do you have everything you need, my lady?"

"Oh, yes, thank you, Borg. I have been well taken care of."

"You need only ask," he said softly and once again turned silent.

"I best get back and leave you to eat," Bridget said, and before she could stand Borg was on his feet offering his large hand to her plump one.

She eagerly accepted his assistance and casually slipped her arm around his, forcing him to trail along with her since he was entirely too shy to refuse.

Faith watched the perfectly matched pair walk off, Bridget chattering away and Borg listening in silence.

She tore off a small piece of bread from the hefty loaf and took another piece of cheese. She wondered where her husband was, having expected him to return by now. She actually missed his presence. She had not known him long and yet within that time she had grown fond of him. He was considerate, a trait she had not expected him to possess. He was warm and comfortable to sleep against—another good quality about him and one she had not even considered. And then there was his touch.

She lowered her head to hide the blush that stained her cheeks, not that anyone was near. It seemed that the lord and lady's blanket had been placed at a discreet distance from the rest of the camp. At the moment she appreciated the distance and solitude that gave her time to contemplate her predicament.

She favored her new husband in more ways than one. She had not given much thought to the intimacy of the marriage vows. It was a chore she knew she was expected to perform and so she would. But waking to his large hand intimately touching her had evoked a strange pleasurable sensation in her and one she would not mind experiencing again.

The blush once again rushed to her cheeks, heating them to a soft red.

Whatever was she to do? She liked this man and respected him and he genuinely seemed to like her. But what would happen when he discovered her secret? What then would he think of her? How then would he feel about her?

She could not hide her scar forever and once discovered he would want answers. Would he accept her answers as truths? Or would he think of her as most did—a soiled and tarnished woman?

He would learn the truth when he bed her, but what if he discovered her scar first? Would he still want her as his wife? The distressing thought plagued her and the only solution she could find was to attempt to build a firm relationship with him on this journey in hopes that he would grow truly to understand her. Once he knew her character, he would know the truth about her.

She sighed, half content with her decision. Besides—what else was there for her to do? She was at the devil's mercy.

All of a sudden, the devil stood behind her. She felt his presence; it wrapped around her, consumed her with a sudden heat that tingled her flesh and caused her heart to race. He truly was a man of extraordinary power.

He eased down behind her, near to but not touching her, though she could feel his warm breath on her neck, causing gooseflesh to consume her arms quickly.

"Have you eaten?" he asked softly.

"Some," she said, though she had no appetite left. "Have you?"

"No."

She immediately reached for a piece of cheese and turned to hand it to him. His eyes assaulted her with such a burning passion that she instinctively knew he wanted a different type of sustenance. She dropped the cheese, startled by his obvious desire and surprised that she not only recognized it but felt the same way herself.

His large hand scooped up the cheese, reached behind her for a hunk of bread and then he stood, offering his free hand to her. "Come walk with me."

Her hesitation was brief. She fussed with her hair, making

certain it concealed the scar well and then she reached her hand out to him.

They walked in a leisurely gait like a newly acquainted couple on a stroll who were attempting to become better acquainted. He released her hand once she stood and proceeded to eat his fare as they walked side by side toward a small gathering of trees not far in the distance.

"Tell me of your keep," she said, the silence too heavy for her and wanting to learn more about her new home.

His eyes shone with pride when he spoke. "Shanekill Keep sits on the most beautiful spot in all of Ireland. It is surrounded by hundreds of fertile fields, pastures that generously provide feed for the cows and sheep and glorious meadows that are covered with wildflowers in the summer and into autumn. A soft stretch of hills spread out in the distance and early in the morning a gentle mist kisses the land and sprinkles it with shades of purple that are astounding to look upon. The keep itself will take time to finish, though the main section of it should be completed upon our return. My men are using stone instead of wood for the keep walls so it takes time, though the castle walls were the first to see completion, the many rocks and stones that burrow in the soil cleared from the fields and used for its construction. The cooking quarters were naturally seen to immediately and I made certain our private bedchamber was also finished."

Faith found it odd that he referred to the bedchamber as "our." Usually the lady of the keep had her own chamber and yet he made it sound as though they would share but one chamber. Perhaps the bedchamber consisted of two separate rooms. Though she wished to ask, she chose a different query.

"There is room for my herb garden?"

He dusted his now-empty hands of bread crumbs and spoke. "The land is plentiful and fertile. Your herbs should do well there."

"I look forward to seeing Shanekill Keep."

Eric reached out and took her hand as they neared the small gathering of trees bordered by a row of ragged rocks that bid entrance to the secluded area. "I do not wish you to fear me, Faith."

Her heart jumped. Did he plan on consummating their vows now in the confines of the spruces and foliage that bid them

welcome? Her stepmother had stressed how important it was
that they seal their union. Without the coupling, their vows
were just words on paper.

"I do not fear you," she said courageously and with only the
slightest of tremors to her soft voice.

Eric gently squeezed her hand as he helped her over the
rocks to enter the cloistered area. "Then why do you tremble?"

She had no chance to respond. He took her a few feet in
where the spruce saplings grew thick and the abundant foliage
surrounded them and he stopped and turned to face her. She
stared wide-eyed at him, chewing nervously at her bottom lip
and thinking what a lovely setting this was for their first time
together. The thick pine branches hung overhead like a beautifully draped canopy and the rich scent of pine mingled with the
sweet scent of lingering wildflowers perfuming the warm air.

His finger moved to her lower lip, preventing her from nibbling on it. "I have yet to kiss you, wife."

She looked at him with surprise. He was right. He had
touched her intimately only hours before but he had yet to give
her a simple kiss. The thought delighted her and she smiled.

"You are eager?" he asked, surprised and pleased.

"Yes, I have never been kissed."

So innocent, he thought and again felt pleased. She was all
his. No one had ever touched her, soiled her, spoiled her. She
was fresh and pure and his lips would be the first to touch,
tempt and teach her the ways of passion.

He brought his head slowly down toward hers and she
squeezed her eyes shut and pursed her lips. No, she certainly
had never been kissed before. And she certainly was in for a
surprise.

"Relax," he whispered, his lips near to hers but not touching
them.

She opened her eyes and was instantly mesmerized by his all-
consuming gaze. His eyes stormed with passion and raged with
an indescribable blue color. They made her body turn to liquid,
her knees tremble and if his arm had not slipped around her waist
she would have melted to the ground. She was his captor and she
was about to surrender willingly.

His tongue touched her first, stroking her lips, teasing them
and tempting her to respond. And she did. She fed on him innocently, tasting with hesitancy and then with an awkward ur-

gency. He understood her innocent ache, expected it and fed it. His lips covered hers and his tongue slyly invaded her mouth. The combination was simply lethal. Her legs crumbled and she moaned.

He tightened his grip on her as his tongue and lips worked their sinful magic, forcing her hands to crawl up along his hard chest and around his neck. And her tongue—Lord, but it mated most willingly with his, causing his hard loins to ache unbearably.

She shivered and Eric instantly deepened their kiss.

He liked the taste of her—warm, sweet and tart—and he could not get enough of her. His tongue probed, invaded and conquered, though she surrendered with an urgency that startled and excited him. Her thin arms even hugged him with a fierceness he had not expected, and his desire soared.

Would this woman never cease to surprise him? He hoped not.

He purposely made the kiss more gentle so she could probe and learn and drive him crazy. He also wanted to draw her closer to him, feel her body against his, let her feel the strength of him and learn not to be frightened by him.

He had half expected her to pull away from him he was so hard, but she continued to surprise him. She let out a small gasp when he moved his body and rested his protruding manhood between her legs. And then she simply and quite naturally moved slowly, a little awkwardly but definitely curiously, against him.

After only a few moments she pulled her mouth from his, moaned softly and rested her head on his shoulder, both having developed a steady intimate rhythm that obviously affected her and most certainly affected him.

Her moans turned to groans and her hands gripped at his neck.

"Eric?" she whispered with a soft harshness as if asking him to explain this foreign yet tormentingly pleasing sensation.

"I wanted to wait," he said, his own words sounding harsh from his heavy breathing. "Tonight—"

Her protesting groan echoed in his ear. "Eric."

Colin shouted out his name and he cursed the man, which caused Faith's eyes to widen as she looked up at him.

"Please," she whispered. "Please?"

He growled low and dangerously and listened as Colin shouted for him once more.

He did not waste another minute. Colin would be near soon enough and he would have to disappoint her and that he could not do to her. He yanked her up against him and silently cursed their interfering clothing and then he moved in a hard, strong rhythm that widened her eyes further and caused her groans to amplify and echo in the small woods.

She climaxed abruptly, surprising herself and him, and he stood holding her tightly to him as she repeatedly shuddered against him and with a will born of too many battles he tempered his own raging emotions.

Faith remained melded to Eric when Colin entered the woods. Colin immediately stopped when he saw the intimately embraced couple and turned quietly around, leaving them their privacy.

After a few minutes Eric eased Faith away from him, though he lifted her up into his arms.

"I have never—" She could not finish; her breathing was too labored.

"I am glad you never," he said with a simple, "though I promise you will many times from now on."

With those orders given he marched out of the secluded woods with his embarrassed wife hiding her blushing face against his shoulder.

Six

Faith rode her own horse for the remainder of the day, silently absorbed in her thoughts. Her willing, almost demanding response to her husband's intimate touch shocked and embarrassed her. She found it hard to accept the obvious—the obvious being that she was physically attracted to her husband. An absurd notion, since she barely knew the man; and yet . . .

She shook her head, willing her nagging thoughts away, though they returned instantly to torment her. Was she insane for feeling this way? Wanting, actually aching for him to touch her again the way he had in the woods. And if he made her feel so out of control fully clothed, what would his hands feel like upon her naked flesh. For that matter, what would his naked flesh feel like to her touch?

Now she not only worried about him discovering her secret; she worried about this relentless, tormentingly pleasurable ache she had for her husband.

He rode beside her in silence, almost as if the incident in the woods disturbed him as much as it had disturbed her. Occasionally he would order Borg or Colin to ride beside her while he rode up ahead and conversed with certain men who appeared to be in command of different groups. She knew his warriors consisted of those proficient with longbows, crossbows and swords. She had heard her father speak with envy of Lord Eric's skilled troops and how no one could defeat them. Watching her husband, she understood why. He kept himself conscious of his troops every movement. He was alert to all about him—his men, the animals and the land. He was an exceptionally skilled warrior and perhaps that was why he was called the Irish devil. Anyone who possessed such uncanny power surely had to be a cohort of the devil himself.

Colin approached them with more speed than usual, Borg not far behind him.

"Looks like foul weather ahead," he said. "It may be wise to camp early and be prepared."

Eric looked to the distance and studied the sky that was heavy with a variety of suspicious clouds. "I thought the same myself."

"We need an area with sufficient cover from the storm," Colin added.

"Agreed," Eric said. "Borg, stay with Faith while I go see to the camp with Colin."

He did not bid her one word before he departed or even send her a nod. He simply galloped off with Colin, while Borg maneuvered his large horse beside hers.

"Help me understand him, Borg?" she said, startling the shy man.

"My lady?" he questioned as if her query was strange to him.

Faith spoke frankly, feeling she could trust the man beside her. He may be a warrior, she thought, but he was a caring soul and she clearly understood that he respected, admired and, if she was not mistaken, cared for Eric as deeply as a brother would.

"Lord Eric is my husband and I know little of him. I wish to learn so that our marriage may be a good one."

Borg nodded, accepting her explanation, and spoke softly. "He is a man who deals in truths."

His statement startled her and she grasped hard on her reins. Truth was something their marriage was definitely not based on. Her identity had been kept secret from him and her attack had been kept from him as well.

"He is accustomed to the lies the kings and leaders feed their people and knows how to deal well with them, but with his men he expects honesty. I think that is why so many of them would gladly give their lives for him for they know, without a doubt, he would do the same for them."

Faith made no comment and Borg continued. "He explained to all who joined him that they fought for their freedom. That he would acquire land and they would all be free to join him and work the land not only for him to prosper but for their own lives to flourish. And to prove he was true to his word, he would always see to their care in every battle they fought. He made certain his men were generously provided for, from food to fill their bellies to wraps to keep them warm to fine-crafted weapons. His soldiers did not suffer like so many did. He saw to their well-being and even to their deaths, their bodies always being properly and respectfully disposed of."

Faith spoke the truth when she responded, "He is a good man."

Borg nodded. "A man of true honor. I watched him sit beside a young warrior all night as he lay dying. He was frightened and Eric spoke softly and reassuringly to him and was beside him when he took his last breath."

This was not a man to be called a devil and Faith asked the question she was not certain would receive an answer: "Why is he called the Irish devil?"

Borg smiled and the difference it made in his usual somber face caused Faith to grin in return. "You are not afraid of him, this is good. And you care for him, I can tell, this is also good. He needs someone to care for him."

She did not ask why that was better left for another time; right now she hoped for an answer to her question.

Borg remained silent for so long, she feared he disregarded her query; but he spoke finally with the usual nod of his head. "Lord Eric is a fearless warrior. He enters every battle with no thought of losing his life, and it shows on his face. His adversaries insist that he must be marked by the devil, for the devil fears nothing. And those that have looked into his eyes during battle and have lived insist that they have looked into the lifeless eyes of the devil himself and begged for mercy."

Faith shivered.

Borg instantly regretted his words. "I am sorry, my lady, I should never have told you thus."

"Nonsense. I asked. I want to know about Lord Eric."

"Not tales of battle; such stories are not fit for proper ears. I should instead tell you tales of his youth."

"You grew up with him?"

He smiled again and it pleased Faith to see his joy.

"Let me tell you of Lord Eric's first fishing venture."

In minutes Borg had her laughing at a tale of a very young boy who landed in the lake, but had managed to hold onto his fish even though he could not swim. Though Borg assured her that he was now an excellent swimmer.

Borg entertained her with many tales and she grew more fond of the gentle giant with each story, for she came to understand how much each man really cared for one another and how through the years that friendship was forged with pain, sorrow, laughter, tears, respect and admiration.

When a rider approached them and informed Borg that camp was being set up several miles ahead, he nodded. And when they were once again alone he turned and with his somber expression said to her, "I am glad Eric chose you as his wife. You are good for him."

She smiled. "Thank you, though he did not have a choice. I was forced on him."

His expression did not change; he simply said, "The devil does as he chooses."

Faith stared wide-eyed at Borg, though his eyes remained fixed on the clouds that darkened the skies overhead. He implied that Eric chose freely without force, but her father had given him no alternative. Would he have denied her father's demand if he so chose? Had he favored a union with her?

The odd thought brought a sense of pleasure to her. To think that he had actually chosen her, as if he favored her the most of all who had been offered to him. The pleasant thought lingered and strangely enough made the idea of marriage to the dark lord sound more appealing.

"The sky will open up soon. Have you another cloak?" Borg asked with concern.

Before she could answer, the sky did as Borg predicted and within seconds the two of them were drenched, every article of clothing being soaked steadily with rain as the heavy downpour continued.

Borg directed Faith toward a good-sized tent in the clearing they came upon after coming up over a small rise. It was almost impossible to see in front of them, past the driving rain and through the gray fog that rolled into camp along with them.

Her dark brown wool cloak was completely soaked through,

causing her tunic and shift to absorb the excess water. Her body began to feel the dampness and her feet did not fare any better after dismounting. One step into a deep puddle and her soft leather boots quickly soaked with water.

Borg hurried her into the tent, Rook on her heels, assuring her he would fetch Bridget to help her. He disappeared into the downpour before she could protest. Surely Bridget would have much to do herself, such as securing adequate lodging most importantly, rather than tending to her.

Rook was about to shake his large body when Faith shook her head and held the flap of the tent back. He stepped outside, gave a quick and sufficient shake and hurried back in to sniff around and find himself a spot to camp for the night.

Faith saw that one of her small trunks sat in the corner of the tent alongside a larger trunk and that the ground had been covered with a thick layer of straw. Rolled bedding lay to the side in waiting and a small table with two benches beneath held two flasks, a thick candle and a covered basket.

"M'lady," Bridget said on a sneeze as she entered the tent with an appropriate yet hasty bob of her head.

Faith shook her head. "You must go get out of those wet clothes at once."

"After I see to you, m'lady."

"No, Bridget," Faith said with authority. "I will not risk you catching a chill for my comfort. You will do as I order and that is that."

"But m'lady, Lord Eric instructed that I was to look after you."

"You will do me no good if you take ill. It will be me looking after you then and possibly more if everyone does not see to getting themselves dry. Now do as I say."

Bridget attempted to protest but Faith did not allow her to speak.

"You will do as I say. I will have myself dry in no time."

Bridget nodded. "Yes, m'lady."

"Bridget, have tents been erected for all?"

"No, m'lady. The women are to share the few available tents and the men have fashioned shelter amongst the trees. Are you certain there is nothing I can do for you?"

"I am fine, see to yourself," Faith said with a smile and chased Bridget out with a wave of her hand.

Faith slipped off her cloak, draping it over her arm as she hurried to her trunk. Whoever had chosen her trunk had chosen wisely. There was linen toweling and a change of clothes within. Faith wasted not a moment in drying off and changing clothes. It would do her no good to have her husband find her naked when he entered.

She paused in her task of slipping off her shift. Did he expect her to be naked for him? He had mentioned *later.* Was that why this tent was prepared? For them finally to consummate their vows?

A shiver ran over her chilled, damp body and her fingers fumbled with the wet garments as she hurried to undress. She could only hope that with the chilled rain the devil would prefer to remain partially clothed during bedding.

Faith slipped on a dark green shift, covering it with a pale yellow tunic trimmed with an even darker shade of green. She dried her hair as best she could, making certain her long hair once again concealed her scar.

She was arranging her wet garments over the trunk to dry when Eric entered the tent. His presence filled the confined space to capacity, causing Faith to gasp softly for a breath.

"My lord . . . ," she said once she was in control of her voice. She averted her eyes from him, the picture he painted too sinfully appealing to gaze upon.

He stood soaking wet. Wet garments. Wet hair. Wet skin. Wet lips. He was simply wet in all the right places and she flushed with her embarrassing and unseemly thoughts.

"The weather is most foul," he said, breaking the silent tension.

She was grateful he chose the weather to discuss and not her heated face. "Will this delay our journey?"

"Only if it persists till morning," he said, removing the belt that held his sword and placing it beside the table. He proceeded to remove his tunic and Faith immediately retrieved a dry linen towel from the trunk and moved like a dutiful wife to assist her husband in undressing.

He accepted her help as if he expected it; but then, it was her duty and he was expecting nothing less than what she was supposed to give. She took his wet tunic and handed him the towel as she saw to the care of his garments and tried with all her willpower to avert her eyes from his naked chest.

Unfortunately that was nearly impossible. Her eyes simply insisted on straying to the muscles and bulges that comprised his impressive chest. Full of strength and power and yet comfortable enough to rest her head upon. And with the thick muscles glistening with rainwater, Faith found herself hard-pressed to ignore him.

Eric watched her nervous movements. She did not know what to expect of him or herself. He understood her concern and hoped to alleviate it. The sooner she grew accustomed to his presence in her life the sooner she would grow accustomed to his intimate touch.

But he did not wish to rush like a heathen in lust. He wanted her to grow to trust him, rely on him, perhaps even care for him. This marriage had been forced on her and he did not wish their union to be forced. He wanted her willing and wanting. So he would take his time, though by night's end he intended that their vows be sealed once and for all.

He walked over to his trunk, keeping his back to her, and searched for dry clothes. Finding the desired clothes, he quickly stripped off his remaining garments, presenting a completely bare backside to his new wife who pretended not to look at him.

He smiled, catching, from the corner of his eye, the way her curious and cautious glance drifted over him and the way she chewed nervously at her bottom lip which was already swelling from her repeated nibbling.

He wondered what her reaction would be if he should turn around; and having the devil in him, he did just that. He was not surprised to see her turn away from him as he turned toward her. And he was not surprised to see her neck and cheeks flame brightly.

Eric stifled his laugh, pleased with his new wife who simply continued to delight him at every turn. He wondered how long her blushing would continue but then with what he had in mind she probably would be in a continuous state of blush for some time to come.

"Are you hungry, my . . . Eric?"

"Yes, famished," he answered and finished dressing.

Faith searched the basket and was delighted to see that a generous meal had been prepared for them. Meats, cheeses, breads, tarts, berries and nuts weighed heavy in the full basket and Faith saw to arranging the mouthwatering fare on the table.

She also saw to Rook, who had made himself cozy on a thick cushion of straw near the tent flap. She brought him a good portion of meats and cheeses and filled a wooden bowl with rainwater for him.

Eric and she sat opposite each other at the table while the rain continued to batter the tent. A few drops managed to penetrate the corners, leaking here and there but not where they sat comfortable in conversation and in sharing their meal.

"Your leg is well?" she asked, having noticed he continued to wear the bandage as she had instructed.

"Yes, it pains me no longer and the redness has almost disappeared."

"A few more days and you should be able to remove the bandage."

"You will see to it for me."

He did not ask or order, but simply instructed. And she simply agreed with a brief nod.

Eric prided himself in his patience. He clearly understood it was a necessary virtue and while battle helped define that virtue, lust helped to eradicate it. Therefore, before he lost complete patience he intended to discover a few answers to a few nagging questions.

He poured wine from the one flask into each of the tankards Faith had removed from the basket and casually asked, "Why was I not told of your existence?"

Faith was caught off guard. How had she failed to realize he was a brilliant strategist? She should have been more alert. She had always kept herself alert, particularly after the attack. But he had managed to penetrate her defenses and cause confusion. Or had the confusion been of her own making? Was it simply the truth he sought?

Faith answered as honestly as she could. "I can only assume that my father felt I was not of an adequate nature for you."

He looked at her oddly. "Whatever would make him assume that?"

The truth.

It hung suspended between them and Faith was uncertain what to do. If she told him everything now, would he understand? Did he know her well enough to know *the truth*? She doubted it. They barely knew each other. Clearly, he would not understand; therefore she required more time with him before he would come to know and accept the truth.

Still she fought hard to answer as honestly as possible. "My father did not favor me."

"Why?"

Faith shrugged. "I disappointed him."

"In what way?"

How should she answer him? Did she tell him someone had attacked her in the stables when she was summoned late one night to see to an ailing villager? Did she go on to explain how she fought for her life only to win and yet lose at the same time? Did she tell him her father felt she was fit for no man? But then her father thought him the devil, so perhaps he thought her an appropriate wife for the dark lord.

He waited patiently for her answer. What would she tell him?

She partially told the truth. "I was not an obedient daughter."

He wanted me to die and I refused.

Eric reached across the table and brushed a stray crumb off her bottom lip. "Will you be an obedient wife?"

"Will you be a fair husband?"

"I will be a good husband."

"Then I will be a good wife."

"Then you will be obedient."

She laughed softly. "Do you always have your way?"

"Always," he answered as if in gentle warning and his finger slowly stroked her bottom lip.

Faith hesitantly moved back, his hand falling away from her lip. "I do not know you well."

"It is not necessary that you do. Trust me, all will go well."

"You are a stranger."

"I am your husband."

"Still, a stranger."

"Who made you climax in the woods today?"

Her cheeks rushed to a soft red. "I have never known—"

"Pleasure?"

"A man," she finished softly, almost on a whisper.

"Do you fear me?" he asked.

Her answer was quick and honest, "No. When first we met I admit that you did frighten me. But now you make me tremble and it is not from fear."

He smiled and held his hand out to her. She slipped hers into his and his large, warm fingers locked around hers squeezing gently, reassuringly.

"We will do well together, dear wife, if you remember but one thing."

She waited, his large hand swallowing up her delicate fingers.

"Be honest with me and I will forever protect you. Be deceitful and I will show you no mercy."

At that moment Faith was tempted to tell him the truth and allow him a choice. They had yet to fulfill their marital duties so officially their vows were not complete. He could return her to her family and demand retribution. But what would be the consequences? What would her stepmother and father do to her? How would they make her suffer for betraying them? But then how would the Irish devil deal with her betrayal?"

"Lord Eric," Borg called out from outside the tent.

Eric responded with a curt, "Enter."

Borg stood just at the entrance, his head bent and his hand holding the tent flap back. He was soaked and looked exhausted. "I am sorry to disturb you, my lord, but two of the tents have collapsed and the women are growing chilled and wet. We are working hard to repair them but the ground is nothing but mud and is proving to be a mighty adversary."

"Is Bridget all right?" Faith asked, concerned for her servant since she had been sneezing.

"Chilled to the bone," Borg answered with a worried glance at Eric.

Faith held back her smile. It was obvious what the large man wanted from his lord. He wanted permission to shelter the women in this tent until the repairs were completed. She waited and wondered if her husband would once again relinquish bedding his wife to assist another in need.

His response was what she thought it would be and made him all the more appealing to her.

"Bring the women here," he ordered sharply and stood. "I will come help the men with the tents."

Borg nodded and immediately left to carry out his orders.

Eric walked over to where his wife sat, cupped her chin and leaned down to steal a much longed for kiss.

His lips were gentle, probing slowly, easy along hers, but his tenderness was brief, his hunger strong. His kiss demanded what his body ached for and his hands yanked her up off the chair, slamming her against him with an urgent passion that startled her.

He was hard against her and she yielded willingly to him.

"Soon," he whispered against her mouth. "Soon or I shall go mad."

He released her so swiftly that she stumbled and Rook lifted his head, his eyes alert.

"Go to sleep," Eric snapped at the startled dog as he yanked the flap aside and marched out of the tent.

After regaining her senses and her balance she walked over to where Rook lay and scratched behind his ear. She lifted the flap and stared out into the dark night, the torrential rain making visibility almost impossible. But nonetheless she saw her husband's shadowed figure, not huddled or frightened by the storm, but defiant. His head was held high, his strides filled with confidence, his voice boomed with orders causing men to scurry. Even the rain seemed to bow to his commanding presence and fell with less fervor.

She sighed, released the flap and sat down beside Rook, the big dog's head falling directly to rest on her lap. "What do I do?"

Rook moaned in empathy.

"Strangely enough, I admire my new husband. I believe I even like him, maybe care for him and if all goes well perhaps I could even love him. In time, that is. Given time anything is possible, right, Rook?"

The big dog moaned in response, though Faith had no doubt it was from being rubbed behind his ear, a favorite spot of his. But it did not matter. What did matter to her was that she had a chance at a good life, with a man who would care for her and protect her from harm. She wanted that chance. She wanted that man.

Now all she needed was a miracle.

Faith helped the four women, including Bridget, arrange their bedding and settle down for the night. Bridget was the only one not startled by the generous actions of Lord Eric. The other three women repeatedly thanked Faith for her thoughtfulness.

It was late in the night, Faith sleeping soundly and alone on the bedding meant for her and her husband when Eric finally returned. He quietly stepped over the sleeping women and after replacing his wet garments with dry ones he joined his wife beneath the wool blanket.

She shivered when his chilled body wrapped around her warm one.

"Eric?"

"Go back to sleep, it is near morning," he ordered in a whisper.

She turned toward him, slipping her arms around his chest, snuggling her warm body against his cold one. "I will keep you warm," she said and kissed the crook of his neck where her head nestled.

He groaned, her warm lips so soft and gentle, so sincere and so potent. He sprang instantly to life.

Her lips once again nibbled at his neck while her hand explored his chest. "Warm. Are you warm?"

Warm? He was hot and lusting like a young boy who had just discovered the joys of sex. He managed to assure her he was now warm to calm her wandering hands. And he swore a silent and not at all proper oath that by tomorrow night his wife would no longer possess her virginity.

Seven

The heavy rain turned to a light drizzle before sunrise. The camp was dismantled with quick efficiency and they were soon on the way, Eric issuing orders that they would continue through noon to make up for lost time.

It was apparent that he was anxious to get home and so were his men since none protested his command. The women seemed in agreement as well, busy cutting bread and cheese to disperse to the men along route.

Eric ordered Faith to ride with him. She did not protest and smiled at Borg as he lifted her up to Eric. Before she could nestle herself comfortably across him, he grasped her waist and positioned her as he wished, her backside resting against his thick thigh. He then wrapped a dark red cloak around them both, circled his arm around her back beneath the wrap and took hold of the reins in his hand. With his free hand he signaled his men to take leave.

"Are you warm enough?" he asked as he maneuvered the stallion along the muddy path.

"Yes, and most comfortable," she admitted with a snuggle against his chest.

He did not smile though his blue eyes were blatantly honest in their desire and her body trembled in nervous anticipation.

"I will not ravish you on my horse though I am sorely

tempted. I wish you to ride with me so that we may become better acquainted."

Faith immediately smiled and said, "Tell me about the first time you went fishing when a mere lad."

Eric could not prevent himself from smiling and Faith was amazed at how the soft crook of his mouth made him all the more handsome.

"Borg has filled your head with nonsense."

"He insisted you were so obstinate about holding onto your fish that you almost drowned."

His fingers tightened at her waist. "I keep what is mine."

"Perhaps the fish had a different idea," she teased.

He shook his head. "Once I lay claim, it is useless for anyone to oppose me."

"And you wanted that fish?"

He laughed. Faith felt the rumble deep in his chest and it felt good.

"I was hungry."

Faith pursued her interest in her husband. "You and Borg grew up together."

Eric quirked a brow. "Borg's tongue has loosened lately."

Faith hurried to assure him otherwise. "No, I ask many questions, he gives me few answers and I piece together the rest."

"What have you pieced together about me?"

"That you and Borg were childhood friends, almost like brothers."

"We are half brothers. We have the same father."

She was not surprised to learn this. While Borg gave Eric the respect entitled a lord, there remained between the two men a unique bond. And when Borg thought it necessary he spoke to Eric more as a kinsman than as a warrior. One would truly have to be blind to fail to notice. "And you are close."

"Yes, we are," Eric admitted with an emotional sincerity that Faith realized he rarely demonstrated. "But it is your turn to tell me something of yourself. Who do you care for?"

Again his question caught her off guard, though her answer came easily. "Rook."

"That ugly monster of a dog," he said, casting an eye at the animal who trotted beside the horse with ease.

"He is not ugly," Faith said in defense of her friend. "He is quite handsome and most intelligent. And he protects me."

"From whom does he protect you?"

Faith felt the panic rise within her, racing her heart and parching her throat, but she kept her fear well concealed. "From strangers, shadows and . . ."

She stopped, almost having added "shame."

Eric lifted her chin that had dropped slightly as her words trailed off. Sadness filled her voice, sorrow pooled in her eyes and her smile faded like a fresh bloom denied sunshine.

"Tell me," he ordered, angry that her joy had withered before his eyes and not understanding the cause, but knowing she had suffered a deep hurt.

Faith thought quickly, realizing that the devil would not be denied an answer. "I but envy you your closeness with Borg. I have three stepsisters and none, can I say, was ever a friend to me."

"Borg is your friend now and Colin as well, and you will grow to know all at the keep and have many friends. And besides," he said with annoyance, "your half sisters were too jealous of you ever to be true friends."

"Jealous?" Faith asked incredulously. "Why would they ever be jealous of me?"

"You are beautiful and they are not. You are caring and they are callous. You have me and they do not."

She laughed, thinking he but jested with her. "Perhaps they did not want you."

"Perhaps I did not want them."

He was serious, she could tell by the firm set of his mouth and the intensity of his glance upon her. Did he truly want her? Had his choice been of free will? She found the idea hard to grasp, to believe. Since the attack no one had spared her a thought, she simply was not worthy enough. If truth be told, would he still feel the same? Or having become acquainted with her, would he judge her differently? It mattered not at the moment for she suddenly felt compelled to reach out to him. To touch him. To be close with him. To know him and allow him to know her.

She slipped her hand from beneath the cloak and reached out to stroke his lips tentatively. "I want you"—her pause was brief as if she thought to change her mind, but then she hurried on—"to kiss me."

He looked at her for a mere moment, his intense gaze hinting at the devil within him. His scalding look instantly heated her flesh and shivered her to the soul. And left no doubt, even to a novice, that his passion for her bordered on the verge of igniting.

His whispered response caught on her lips. "My pleasure." He sampled her like a rare nectar that was meant to be enjoyed. "I love the taste of you," he murmured, his lips brushing over hers, claiming them with a gentle fervor that stole her breath.

He took and she surrendered, his mouth feasting, his hands roaming and his heart pounding in his chest. She felt the heavy rhythm against her breast, beating wildly, maddeningly, and knowing that she was the cause made her willingly submit all the more.

When his hand moved to cup her breast and pinch her nipple she moaned and completely lost herself to him.

He brought their kiss to an end, reluctantly denying her, placing brief quick pecks along her mouth and over her chin. His hand remained firm on her breast but his fingers ceased their tormenting, though her nipple remained hard and aching.

"You truly like the taste of me?" Faith asked when she could finally speak.

"I would not lie to you," he said firmly and softly kissed her lips. "Your sweet minty taste pleasures me. And does my taste please you?"

A smile ran over her face and she laughed lightly. "Bold and quite intoxicating."

He smiled himself. "I like your honesty."

That word again. Would it forever haunt her?

His hand moved to settle at her waist. "You are slim."

Her face shadowed with doubt.

He explained. "I but wonder if you will have difficulty birthing a babe."

A babe. She had so wanted children. She loved delivering the newborns, so wrinkled and crunched and yet when they took their first breath, their whole little bodies expanded with life. She wanted to see her own babe's body quake to life.

"I see no reason why I could not deliver you a babe," she

said, hoping to alleviate his concern that she would not be able to present him with a child.

He shook his head as if her answer did not satisfy him. "But would it be a difficult birth?"

She answered honestly. "Births and babes are unpredictable. There is no telling how a birth will go until delivery begins and even then it is best to be prepared for surprises."

"You do not fear the birthing process?"

"Why should I?"

"You see pain and suffering."

"I see miracles," she said with excitement. "Every time a newborn babe slips into my hands and breathes his first breath, it is a miracle."

His taut features softened and his eyes took on a gentle longing, but it was his words that most surprised her. "We will make a miracle together and I will not allow you to suffer the birth of our babe alone. I will suffer along with you."

She could easily love this man and that thought brought with it a rush of fear. Could he love her?

"A thoughtful and rare act for a husband," she said.

His eyes drifted ahead to where his men were grouped in discussion, but he returned his glance to her when he spoke. "I take care of what is mine. You are mine and I will see to your care and protection."

"Yes, my lord," she said on a sigh and a turn of her head. She realized she was but his property and nothing more. She was being foolish, as foolish as a young girl who thought herself in love. The dark lord simply did not love.

He hooked her chin with his finger and forced her to look at him. "You are *mine*, Faith. Do you understand? *Mine*."

Colin approached and Eric immediately turned his attention to him.

"A problem. One of the men was injured while helping to move a fallen tree. He took a severe gash to the leg."

"I will see to him," Faith said, sorry for the wounded man but relieved by the timely interruption.

Colin looked to Eric and Faith realized she had failed to request her husband's permission. Her freedom had been severely restricted by this marriage and it would take getting used to.

"I am sorry, my lord," she said, "with your permission I will see to the wounded man."

He nodded to her and to Colin he said, "We will be right along."

Colin rode off and Faith remained silent.

"Faith."

She raised cautious eyes to him.

His blue eyes, so hypnotic and seductive, remained fixed upon her and he slowly lowered his mouth to hers and kissed her persuasively, purposely and potently.

And as they rode off after Colin, Eric whispered harshly in her ear. "*Mine.*"

The delay in their journey annoyed Eric. He wanted to reach Shanekill Keep as quickly as possible. He had lived too long on the road, in tents, on the ground, rained upon and heated from battle. He wanted permanence in his life. And that began with his land and now included his wife.

He stood nearby, watching her as she worked with skilled fingers, stitching the open wound of the injured man. When he first saw it he thought she might faint from the sight of such a ghastly injury. But she set to work immediately, her hands tender and her manner calm and reassuring.

He was grateful the rain had finally stopped and the clouds had disappeared, making way for the sun. It would take at least another day or two for the land to dry sufficiently enough to make their journey less difficult. Which meant a possible further delay. And while this time provided him with an opportunity to become better acquainted with his wife, it also severely limited their time alone.

Time alone.

He had never given thought to spending much time alone with his wife; for them to share intimacy, yes, but for the sole purpose of just spending time together?

He found himself shaking his head. He slowly circled the area where his wife sat on the ground beside the injured man, finishing up the last of the many stitches. She paid no heed to her audience. Many of his men watched her as she worked and their faces betrayed their curiosity and amazement. The wound had been wide, the flesh badly torn, and yet Faith had seemed to work a miracle. Her stitching had drawn the torn flesh completely together, leaving no gaping holes. His men were impressed and he was proud of his new wife.

He had hoped for a good match, never expecting to find a woman he actually enjoyed talking with or looking upon and least of all admiring. She was truly a special woman—skilled, intelligent and beautiful.

And she was his. Almost his. Until they consummated their vows he felt their union incomplete. It was as though when they finally joined together they would be one and she would then be . . .

Mine.

He needed her to belong to him, not as property or as a wife or mother of his children, but to be part of him and he part of her. She had easily recognized the bond between him and Borg. A brotherly bond that was solid and strong, each knowing they could rely on the other no matter the problem or the circumstance.

He wanted to forge a similar bond with Faith, though it was not brotherly love he had in mind. He wanted, hoped, she would grow to care for him, not out of wifely duty, but out of something more solid, more lasting, more fervent.

Love.

He shook his head again as he continued to circle the area slowly where Faith now carefully applied a creamy substance to the man's stitched wound.

Was he foolish in thinking that the devil could love? And why suddenly did love matter to him when before he thought it unimportant? And did not one need a soul to love? He had been told so often he had no soul, he had begun to believe it. How else could he ride so many times into battle not caring about life or limb, his only intention being that of victory.

His purpose, though, was firm. He longed to lay claim to the heritage of his birth. He may be part Viking and part Irish, but his heart had always remained in Ireland. He would never forget the day he sailed off on his father's ship, watching the Irish coastline disappear from view and promising himself—no, swearing to himself—that he would one day return to the home of his birth, to his true heritage and plant his roots firmly in his native soil.

It had been a long, hard battle, too many useless battles with too many lives lost, but for him each one had been a victory. He had achieved his intention—more so than he had hoped—and now his toil would see fruition in his land and in his wife.

Faith possessed many qualities he respected and admired and his choice to take her as his wife had been made without regret, though suspicion remained. He supposed it was his warrior side that questioned her unexpected presence in the great hall that day. While part of him was pleased and satisfied that she would be his, it was the warrior in him that had cautioned his actions. He had realized soon enough that her family held little regard for her and that puzzled him all the more. It also made him want to protect her, wrap her in his arms and ward off any harm or hurt.

Her courage shielded her vulnerability, but not always, and it was at those rare moments when her guard was down and the shield dropped that he felt her deep sorrow. He wondered over its origin, and he wondered why she did not speak of it to him. That was one of the reasons he wished to spend time with her. Yes, he wanted to be intimate with her, but he also wanted to know her. Know her likes, her dislikes, her fears, her joys and her sorrows. Only then would their union truly be consummated.

George, the wounded man, was thanking her profusely and singing her praises, insisting to all who would listen that Lady Faith possessed magical hands and that he had barely felt the sting or pain of the needle.

George wore a huge smile as four men carried him to a wagon where two women waited in attendance for him.

Faith was smiling as she washed her hands in a clean bucket of water.

"You bewitched him," Eric accused teasingly and snatched a clean towel from the stack in the basket and handed it to her.

Faith took the offered towel and dried her hands. "I used an herb solution that dulls the senses to the needle's pinch. It is felt, but not nearly as badly as it would be if it were not used."

Colin joined them, followed close behind by Borg.

"Lady Faith is the talk of the camp," Colin said with a grin toward Eric.

Borg slapped Eric hard on the back and simply smiled.

She looked with puzzled eyes at both men.

"We have wasted enough time," Eric snapped irritably. "Order the men ready to leave. Borg, bring Faith's mare."

Faith moved to clean up the bloody towels and gather her healing tools and herbs.

Eric grabbed her wrist. "Leave that, Bridget will see to it."

Faith always saw to her own things, especially her healing basket. "I prefer to gather my personal items."

The air seemed to still around them. Where only a moment before a soft autumn breeze ruffled the nearby tree leaves and whispered across the land, it now lay still as if in fright. And when Faith looked into her husband's eyes she understood why the air stilled and why Colin and Borg cautiously stepped away.

Eric's blue eyes blazed with a heated fury that raced a feverish chill over Faith.

"I meant no disrespect," she said and shivered.

His nostrils ceased their flaring, his stern frown softened and the heated fury in his blue eyes faded to a tempered passion.

He drew her gently to his side. "I am not angry with you."

She ran a tender hand up his cheek and into his long hair to tuck a few strands behind his ear. She then pressed her fingers to his temple and with just enough pressure massaged the vein that throbbed there. "You will bring on a headache."

His eyes closed though he had ordered them to remain open. Useless orders. Her fingers simply felt too good to combat.

"Why are you angry?" she asked, working her other fingers on the opposite temple.

The pressure-filled massage eased his warring emotions and began to dull his senses. He felt nothing but her touch, sensed nothing but her nearness, heard nothing but her steady breathing.

Instantly his eyes sprang open and his hands clamped down on her wrists, pulling them away. He never lost control. Never. Not even when he took a woman did he allow his senses to rule completely. He was always in command of himself and those around him. He never surrendered to anyone and least of all to his emotions.

She looked at him questioningly.

He owed her no answer. He was her husband, she would do as he directed without question or thought, just as his men did.

"Borg, bring her mare," he called out, keeping his eyes on her.

She waited, saying not a word.

Borg appeared shortly and Eric swung her up in the saddle, his fingers biting into her waist.

"Ride with her," he ordered and marched off toward Colin

who sat mounted and waiting with Eric's stallion. Eric seated his horse and the two men rode off together.

Faith looked to Borg, confused.

"Bridget promises to be careful with your healing basket."

She was grateful for his reassurance but remained upset with her husband. "I do not understand what I did," she said, after riding for a few minutes in silence.

"It is nothing you did."

"But—"

Borg stopped her protest with, "Care for him—that is all you need to do."

"I thought I was caring for him," she said, still puzzled.

"Care for him," he repeated without explanation.

"How? When he will not let me," she said with annoyance.

Borg simply repeated, "Care for him."

That evening Faith intended to do just that. She spent part of the afternoon's journey talking with Borg about himself and his plans and the remainder of the time planning the evening.

Faith learned that Borg wished to marry and raise a family, but he wished his marriage to be founded on love rather than being an arranged one. He described the type of woman he searched for and oddly enough her description fit Bridget perfectly. The man definitely was smitten. She intended to see what she could do to bring the two together.

As for herself, she counted on the tent being already in place on her arrival in camp. She then had plans to spend a quiet evening *caring* for her husband.

Her plans did not at all proceed according to her design.

A line of men waited at her tent as she approached with Borg and before he assisted her off her horse, he grinned and whispered, "This is why Eric was angry."

It was very late into the evening when Faith finished tending the last ailing soldier. She was bone tired and needed sleep. She had not seen her husband but once after entering the camp. He had been in conversation with Colin just outside the tent. Moments later Bridget had appeared and had begun assisting her. Several times throughout the evening Bridget had insisted she stop and have something to eat, but she had adamantly refused and continued treating the men.

Most ailments were minor, though one or two were near to

infection and the men were lucky she had seen to their wounds. Bridget had seen to cleaning up and had brought her a simple fare since she protested that she was not hungry any longer.

Eric walked into the tent just as she lay down on the straw palette. He joined her, draping a wool wrap over their fully clothed bodies. He hooked his arm around her waist and pulled her to nestle against him and she did, her head resting comfortably on his chest.

"Sleep," he ordered in that rough yet tender tone she was growing accustomed to.

She snuggled against him, wrapping her arm around his waist.

"Tomorrow, Faith," he whispered, his arm hugging her fiercely to him. "Tomorrow there is nothing, absolutely nothing, that will stop me from making you completely mine."

Eight

Eric swore beneath his breath.

Colin laughed heartily.

Borg shook his head.

"Give up," Colin said seriously, though he could not prevent his laugh from punctuating his advice.

Eric ignored him and kept tight rein on his stallion, who appeared to be as temperamental as he.

Colin continued even though Borg sent him a silent warning to hold his tongue. "We will be at the keep in three days' time and then your wife will be all yours."

"One more word, Colin," Eric cautioned firmly, "and I will take my frustration out on you. Now go find a place for us to stop and rest."

Colin wisely remained silent and did as instructed.

"If you are thinking of offering me advice, do not," Eric said to Borg without glancing in his direction.

Borg kept his eyes fixed on the road in front of them. It was a clear road, the men traveling along it without difficulty or delay. The weather was clear as well, the sun bright overhead and the day warm with a touch of an autumn breeze. A good traveling day, though Borg grumbled beneath his breath.

"You have nothing to complain about," Eric snapped.

"Foolish and stubborn."

"I assume you are referring to yourself," Eric said, finally turning his head to look directly at Borg.

The large man met his stern look with a smile. "She is your wife."

"Not exactly."

Borg snorted in disgust. "Your own fault."

His accusation rose Eric's temperament several degrees, especially since he did not at all agree with him. "My fault? My fault when I allow her to birth a babe, my fault when I allow drenched women in our tent, my fault when I allow her to see to the men's care, my fault when—" He suddenly ceased his tirade and shook his head, swearing beneath his breath.

Nature had interfered with Eric's promise and after five days of waiting, his patience had vanished and his temper took rein. He glanced back at the cart where Faith sat with Bridget. They talked and laughed and looked to be having a delightful time, which irritated him all the more.

"You swear, grumble and snap at the men," Borg said. "Go talk with your wife."

"Why? Are you depleted of conversation?" Eric asked, fighting to keep a firm rein on his stallion, which had grown more irritable.

"He senses your displeasure, as do all of us. Go do what you do well—command." With his challenge thrown, Borg rode off to join Colin.

Eric stared after his back, a large target and one he could not miss, and was sorely tempted to take aim at, but sensibly discarded the idea. Borg spoke the truth. He always spoke the truth, even when no one else would and even when he knew his words would anger Eric.

In three days' time they would arrive at Shanekill Keep and this endless journey of delays and frustration would be over. He had seriously considered waiting until that time to consummate their vows, but unfortunately his body was demanding gratification. Not that he could not control his desires. He had on countless occasions; this occasion, however, was different. Faith was his wife and copulating with her was his duty.

He grumbled harshly and his horse snorted. "My sentiments exactly."

He could convince himself of all the nonsense he wished, but the truth of the matter was that he desired his wife. She was like a precious gift. The more wrappings he stripped away, the more desirous she became. The only thing left was to lay claim to her.

Eric directed his stallion to turn, halted him one moment, cast a glance at the cart and rode straight for it.

Bridget caught sight of his approach and blessed herself as she prayed. "Sweet Lord in heaven, help us."

Startled and thinking them under attack, Faith followed the direction of Bridget's wide, fearful eyes. Her breath caught and her own eyes widened fearfully.

Eric rode straight for them. The wind fanned his dark hair, his deep red cloak flapped like giant wings behind him, his black and dark red tunic hugged his muscular frame and his blue eyes blazed like the hot fires of hell.

He was the *Irish devil.*

Faith and Bridget instinctively moved closer to each other.

Eric directed his horse next to the rolling cart. "You will join me for the noon meal."

Faith nodded, her voice lost somewhere beneath the lump in her throat.

"You are well?" he asked, causing Bridget to blush a startling red.

Faith nodded once again.

His eyes coveted her as only the devil's could, intimately and sensually, and both women shivered.

He rode off without a word or a nod, his command issued, her obedience expected.

"A bold one he is," Bridget said, finding her breath, though it was raspy.

"He is my husband," Faith said in his defense, though shaken by his blatant demand.

"Forgive me, my lady," Bridget apologized with a quick bob of her head. "It is just that I have never heard a husband ask his wife if . . ." Her words trailed off and her face heated to a shiny red.

Faith ignored the flustered young woman and stared after her husband. He was bold, but the desire in his boldness spoke clearly. He wanted her and cared not that Bridget was there when he spoke.

Though in many ways he still remained a stranger to her, in other ways they had become familiar with each other and it was that familiarity that would make their first time together less frightening to her.

She had discovered his tender side, though many would refuse to believe the devil possessed any tenderness at all. But she had seen it with her own eyes and that quality had endeared him to her. He cared as well, though he rarely showed it and only if one was diligent and watched him carefully could one catch those rare moments. She had, and it was another quality of his she admired.

He possessed another quality that few people did and it was one she had always respected and held firm to, though of late it had proved difficult to maintain. He spoke the truth.

Over the last few days, while she rode in the cart, she had given great thought to telling him the truth. She realized the more time that passed the worse the situation would become. And if she consummated her vows without revealing her past she could very well destroy any chance of a future with him.

Truth also brought with it risk—the risk of losing him; and strangely enough, that thought disturbed her more than she cared to admit. He made his intentions perfectly clear. He wanted her and intended no further delay.

What was she to do?

The cart rolled into camp and Borg was suddenly there helping them. Faith took delight in watching the large man lose his tongue around the gregarious Bridget. He simply trailed after her like a lost puppy, his eyes full of love and admiration.

Faith brushed aside the straw, which had provided a cushion in the cart, from her dark blue tunic and shift. She left her cloak in the cart; ran her fingers through the massive curls of her long, red hair, making certain to conceal her scar; and smiled down at Rook who sat patiently waiting by her side, his large tail thumping the ground behind him.

"Come on, boy, let us see what plants we can find in the woods."

Faith left the camp preparation to the servants, having been warned numerous times by her husband that her care would be seen to by others, not by herself. She used the time to take walks with Rook, search for plants and spend time alone.

She missed her solitary time, having grown used to being on her own and depending on herself over the last few years. And when she could, she sought a few moments of that cherished solitude. The time refreshed her, clearing her head and filling her with a sense of peace.

Rook led the way and Faith gratefully followed. She had hoped this time would give her pause to consider her dilemma and finally reach a decision that would benefit all.

Eric caught sight of Faith, disappearing into the small crop of woods after Rook, as he dismounted his stallion. He carelessly threw the reins to Colin, who stood nearby and took off after her.

Colin turned to one of the men a few feet away from him and said, "Tell the men not to rush. We will be here longer than planned."

It took Eric mere moments to catch up with her, his long, powerful strides accustomed to chasing down men, therefore finding his wife easy prey. Even with the heavy growth of spruce saplings and dense bushes her trail was easy to follow. She stood in a narrow clearing. Her glance wandered over the ground around her and Rook sniffed and pawed at anything that caught his interest. The dog's head rose; he cast a quick identifying look toward Eric and returned to the clump of greens that had caught his fancy.

The two made a strange pair. The beautiful woman with the flaming red hair and the big, ugly dog who faithfully guarded her.

But from what?

Eric stepped forward and Rook barked, startling Faith who had bent down to examine a plant. She would have fallen on her backside if Eric had not quickly come to her rescue. He caught her beneath her arms and effortlessly lifted her to stand on her feet.

She immediately took a step away from him and he allowed her the distance. "I did not hear you."

"I did not mean to frighten you."

"Rook usually alerts me."

"He saw me and made no move until I did."

Faith patted Rook's head. The dog wandered off to investigate his surroundings, pleased with receiving his deserved praise.

Eric took several steps toward Faith and she in turn took several steps away. She was nervous and he did not blame her, though he had no intentions of allowing her apprehension to stop him.

"You search for plants?" he asked, having seen Bridget and her on more than one occasion with a basket full of rooted plants.

She nodded and glanced at the ground around her.

Disregarding the obvious was doing neither of them good. He chose to be direct. "You understood this moment would come."

Her head shot up and her eyes widened. "Yes, I am but nervous."

He took slow, cautious steps toward her as he spoke. "Would it ease your worry to know that I do not consummate our marriage out of duty, but out of desire?"

Faith smiled. "Truthfully, you do?"

He stepped closer until he was but a mere inch away from her. "Truthfully, I do."

She spoke softly and did not retreat from his close presence. "It does ease my worry."

"I am glad," he said and reached out to run his finger over her lips. "The taste of you lingers on me and reminds me how very much I enjoy your flavor."

She spoke the obvious. "You wish to taste me."

"Every part of you, Faith," he whispered and lowered his mouth to hers, his hand slipping behind her neck to draw her to his waiting lips.

His kiss was potent. There was no tenderness or teasing this time; he demanded and she simply surrendered. And she wanted to. Truth be told, she wanted him as much as he wanted her.

And the truth?

It was being acted upon at that very moment. Nothing else mattered. Nothing else existed but the two of them and their desire to unite as one. She would hold on to that feeling of unity, of oneness with each other, and hope and pray that he felt the same as she.

His mouth briefly left hers to speak. "I will not hurt you."

"I know," she said just before he claimed her mouth again.

His kisses turned urgent and his hands roamed her body, starting at her breasts and running down along her slim waist and over her round backside. He pulled her up against him with an intimate roughness that excited her and she moaned softly into his mouth.

His smile was wickedly satisfying when he drew his lips off hers. "I will make the woods echo with your moans."

She blushed, her cheeks flushing a gentle red. "All will hear."

"I do not care," he said with a laugh. "Your moans please me."

"And your moans?" she teased daringly.

"You think to make me moan?" he asked with surprise and delight.

"I can try," she challenged and moved her hand to explore his hard chest, his flat midriff and courageously and with a brief hesitation she ran her hand between his legs to squeeze his bulging manhood.

He gasped, she moaned.

She was about to withdraw her tentative touch when his hand covered hers and squeezed harder.

"Your touch is always welcome."

His reassuring words pleased her.

"But now it is my turn."

Her hand fell away with his and his hand moved to intimately stroke between her legs. Her body instantly grew limp and she dropped her head against his shoulder, her hands grasping his tunic, her moans muffled by his chest.

"I am going to take my time with you and introduce you to all the pleasures of passion."

He continued to massage her intimately with a gentle roughness that left her feeling senseless and sensual.

His suggestive whispers caused her to shiver, especially when he said, "This time when you climax I will be inside you."

"Yes, Eric," she barely murmured, "come inside me."

He shivered this time, her innocent invitation fueling his passion to near eruption.

Rook's whimpers startled them both and they drew apart.

Eric ordered the dog to leave, his voice gruff and impatient.

The big dog simply ignored him and looked with sorrowful eyes to his master.

"For his own good, tell him to leave, Faith," Eric said, his hands moving to untie the cloth belt at her waist.

Faith knew Rook well and she suddenly grew fearful. "Something is wrong."

Eric groaned and attempted to remain calm. "Nothing is wrong. He wants attention."

"No, he is trying to tell me something."

"He is jealous."

"Nonsense. Something disturbs him."

"Yes, my hands on you," he snapped with anger.

"Eric, please," she begged. "I tell you, something is wrong."

He took a deep breath and gathered his warring emotions. Part of him wanted to kill the dog and part warned him to pay attention.

Rook's whimpers grew louder.

"What is it, boy?" Eric asked, his own senses on alert.

Rook took off into the woods.

Eric cursed silently and followed him. Faith was close behind.

Eric had no trouble keeping up with the large dog and Faith, surprisingly, was not far behind. Several minutes passed and Eric was beginning to believe his first suspicion was correct—the dog was simply jealous. But as Rook broke through several bushes and rounded a tree, Eric's breath caught in his throat.

Faith came up breathless behind him, took one look past Eric's stiff form and shocked face and wasted no time in running past him.

Borg lay in a small clearing, covered with blood from the arrow that stuck out of his chest.

Nine

"Faith, help me," Borg gasped as she fell to her knees beside him.

Blood covered his entire chest and for a brief second she froze, her nightmares rushing over her and the fear of death thick in the air. Then just as abruptly she sprang into action, taking command.

"I need my healing basket, cloths, and I need him moved to where there is more light as soon as I stop the bleeding," Faith said to Eric as he dropped to his knees beside her.

"How?" Was all Eric could manage to say. He had seen many a man lose his life or limb in battle, but this was his brother and he felt helpless watching his life's blood spill on the ground.

"Accident, I think," Borg said with difficulty.

"You will be all right," Eric commanded sternly.

Borg gave him a painful yet confident smile. "Yes, Faith will save me."

Faith wished she shared his confidence in her and reminded her husband of her request. *"Now,* Eric, I need those things now."

Eric gave Borg's shoulder a reassuring squeeze. "You will save him," he said to his wife. Not an order or a command, but simply a statement of fact. Then he fled the woods, Rook remaining behind to stand guard over his master and the injured man.

Faith tore off the end of her tunic and with a delicate touch began sopping the blood around the wound. At closer inspection she saw that the arrow had lodged itself more in the shoulder area and with luck no vital body parts were damaged. But she could not be sure until she removed the arrow and probed the wound.

She worked carefully and diligently on her friend, and he had become her friend. He spoke often with her, offering bits of advice concerning Eric and answering her endless questions. He truly was a gentle and caring soul. She could not, would not, let anything happen to him.

"How bad?" Borg asked, his voice strained from the pain.

She answered honestly, her hands busy cleaning the blood from around the wound. "I am not certain."

"Tell me." Borg barely got the words out when he coughed, winced from the pain and turned a deathly shade of white.

"I speak the truth," she assured him, sorry for his discomfort but with her attention more fixed on his injury.

"You will . . . ," His words trailed off as his stamina lessened.

She finished for him, knowing it was important to him. "I will tell you everything, good or bad."

He closed his eyes and his breathing eased, if only a little.

Eric burst through the woods, Colin fast on his heals with several men running to keep up behind him. Bridget ran beside Colin, keeping up every step of the way, her expression one of desperate concern.

Eric placed Faith's healing basket down beside her, his immediate attention going to Borg.

Faith read the concern in his eyes. "He but rests." She gave a reassuring touch to his hand.

"You will make him well."

Again a statement of fact, but one Faith intended to clarify. "I will try."

Bridget knelt opposite of Faith on Borg's right side. "What can I do?"

Borg slowly opened his eyes and smiled at Bridget.

She smiled back. "Now, Borg, do not go worrying yourself. Lady Faith will see that you are up and about in no time. And I will personally see to the care of your recovery."

That brought a wider smile to the large man's face and Faith was glad to see it.

"I need to make certain the bleeding has stopped before we take a chance and move him," Faith explained to those around her.

"How about the arrow?" Colin asked.

"That cannot be removed until he is taken where there is sufficient light for me to see the damage more clearly. Now if you gentlemen would step back and let me work. You block what little light I have."

Eric and Colin immediately did as she asked, stepping far enough away to allow the sunlight that filtered through the magnitude of trees to shine down upon her.

"Someone shot that arrow," Eric said quietly to Colin, his eyes remaining on his wife and surveying the difficult task at hand. "Find out who."

Colin nodded, his concern and eyes focused on the scene before him.

"Bridget," Faith whispered softly.

The young woman instantly gave Faith her full attention.

"You must come around this side and help me."

Bridget rested Borg's hand on the ground and scurried around to Faith.

"My other side."

Bridget finally realized what Faith silently requested of her and moved in position to block the side of her face that bore the scar.

"Now pull my hair back away but just enough so that it does not fall in my way," Faith instructed.

Bridget did as she was told, catching sight of the thin scar that marked her and saying a silent prayer for her well-being.

Faith finished cleaning up the wound around the arrow, packed the surrounding area with clean cloths and prepared Borg to be moved.

"Eric," she called out and he was immediately at her side, though not before she shook her hair free, making certain the long curls once again concealed the scar.

Borg's eyes drifted open briefly and he gave Eric a weary smile.

"Break the end of the arrow off as carefully as possible," Faith directed.

She placed her delicate yet skilled hands around the base of the wound while Eric snapped the arrow like a dried twig.

Borg winced, though his eyes remained closed.

Faith examined the wound again and seeing that only minor bleeding had occurred, she ordered Borg moved. She realized the arrow had to be removed immediately and the wound cleansed and stitched if he was to recover properly, that is, if the arrow had not done any severe damage.

A large cropping of flat-topped stones near the campsite had been prepared with a thick layer of straw and covered with a blanket for the injured man. The height of the makeshift bed provided Faith with easy access to work on Borg. She wasted no time in issuing more orders for boiling water and for Bridget to prepare several herb mixtures.

Eric and Colin assisted her in cutting away Borg's tunic and only after she had forced warm liquid down Borg's throat did she order Eric to remove the arrow. Again Borg winced, but not to the degree he would have if Faith had not given him the soothing drink to dull his senses.

Her freshly washed hands were instantly at his chest, probing delicately.

"Tell me," Eric ordered, unable to stand silently by any longer.

"I do not think there is any severe or permanent damage. The arrow hit clear and clean, and with stitches and rest, I think he will do well as long as I can keep the wound from becoming red with fever. But presently, I must get this wound closed and the bleeding stopped."

He heard the urgency in her voice and stepped aside, joining Colin but a short distance away.

Bridget could not remain beside her the whole time Faith worked. She required her help in preparing the thread and bone needles and seeing to preparing several herb mixtures. Faith had no choice but to allow her hair to fall in her way and as she continued to work she grew more annoyed with the interfering and persistent strands. But Eric, Colin and the circle of men that had grown considerably stood too close around her for her to tie her hair back away from her face and risk exposing her secret.

Faith cleansed around the wound with a special mixture of herbs that were meant to help heal and ward off fever. She washed her bloody hands once more before taking the threaded needle in her hand. The arrow's mark left a hole that would take considerable skill and patience to mend, but it was the blood that continued to flow slowly from the wound that worried Faith. If she did not close it fast enough she feared for Borg's life. While bleeding an ailing person was often thought effective, Faith held a different opinion. She had seen too many injured people grow pale and weak from blood loss and die soon afterwards. Borg had already lost enough blood; she could not chance him losing more.

She explained the immediate situation to Bridget, instructing the young woman to have all the needles threaded and ready to hand to her so that she could continue her task without interruption. Bridget would not fail her—she was certain of that. She knew exactly what needed to be done. Bridget had performed a similar task before, only then it had been Bridget herself who had done the stitching.

Bridget prepared everything as per her instructions, even cleansing her hands frequently upon Faith's insistence. All was in readiness for them to begin.

Borg fought to open his eyes and look at Faith. "I trust you." Then he looked to Bridget and said, "I care for you."

His simple declaration brought tears to Bridget's eyes and she hastily wiped them away, her hands ready with the needles that would help save his life.

Faith took the slim bone needle from Bridget with confident hands and set to work. Only minutes into her task she realized the stitching would be an ordeal. The blood began to flow in earnest, her fingers turned slippery and her hair refused to stay out of her way. No matter how hard she tried, the task was taking longer than she had planned.

She had two choices. Keep her secret and risk losing Borg or tie her hair back and face the truth. Her choice was simple.

She quickly cleaned her hands in a freshly filled water bucket at her side and without hesitation grabbed her mass of red curls and tied them back away from her face, exposing her secret to all those around her.

She heard the gasps, caught how Bridget blessed herself and mumbled a prayer for her, but she ignored it all and set to work at saving Borg's life. Without the interfering strands hanging in her eyes she was better able to see to her task and her fingers moved with agile speed and efficiency even though the blood continued to ooze, though with much less frequency as the wound was stitched closed.

Faith was so engrossed with tending the ailing man that she had not noticed that he had opened his eyes. He stared at her, though not in shock, disgust or sympathy. He stared at her with understanding and she was forever grateful for his empathetic look.

The wound gave her trouble near the end, where the gap was wide, and she bent down close to work tight, neat stitches in his shoulder. She felt confident that he would recover, even with the heavy blood loss. She would see that he rested and ate properly and within no time she felt certain he would be on his feet. And while it would take him time and exercise to regain his full strength, he would at least be up and around.

She did not bother to glance in Eric's direction; she did not need to. She could almost feel his blazing eyes burning into her and when she turned she knew full well she would face the full wrath of the Irish devil.

After cleansing her hands again, she applied a salve around the stitches that she hoped would help prevent the feared swelling and reddening that preceded the onset of fever. Bridget assisted her in wrapping a wide cloth around Borg's chest and over his shoulder.

Borg did not protest when she held a wooden ladle of warm liquid to his lips. He simply drank and once again closed his eyes; but not before saying thank you.

Faith fussed over him until there was nothing left to do but turn and face her husband.

"Bless you, m'lady," Bridget whispered and took Borg's hand in hers.

Faith turned not only to face her husband, but also the whispering crowd that had gathered to watch her heal Borg.

All eyes focused on her, though it was her scar they looked upon, which did stand out for all to see. The pale, thin scar stood like a beacon against her flushed face.

She was well aware what was on each of their minds. How had she come by it? And how far beneath her tunic did the scar travel?

No one made a move. The whispers suddenly turned to soft murmurs and drifted off on the late afternoon breeze, and then there was silence. The sound was more horrible than any battle cry for she knew that beneath it lay rage.

One look at her husband, and she forced her chin up and took a firm and proud stance.

His blue eyes blazed and he fought to maintain his enraged emotions. His hands were fisted at his sides, his breathing was too controlled and his mouth too firm. She wondered just when he would explode.

He marched forward, many of the men nearby moving out of his way, though they were not close enough to interfere with his approach. His overbearing presence just seemed to command it.

He stopped in front of her, his eyes purposely avoiding the scar. "How is he?"

Faith fought courageously to keep her voice from trembling. "With proper rest and care he should do well, though there remains the chance of fever."

Eric looked to Bridget. "See to him, Colin will assist you."

He reached out, his fiery gaze now on her scar, and grabbed for her arm. She made no move to stop him as he pulled her alongside him toward a small clumping of spruce trees.

Curious eyes and wagging tongues followed their progress and Eric did not stop until the few trees and the abundance of bushes provided them with the privacy to speak. He then swung her around to stand in front of him.

He was curt and demanding. "Explain."

Would he believe the truth? Did he know her well enough to judge her wisely? She was about to find out.

With her head held high, she spoke. "One night I was summoned to tend an ailing villager. I thought nothing of the late-night request and took myself off to see to her. On my way past the stables, someone grabbed me and dragged me inside. I fought him with all the strength I possessed." She shivered, recalling the dreadful memory. She could feel the man's heavy body on her, see the flash of the blade and feel the first slice to her tender skin. "Unfortunately, I was unaware that he possessed a knife. I carry this scar"—her hand went to her face—"as a reminder."

"Where does the scar end?" he asked, his face a mask of controlled fury.

Faith reluctantly and hesitantly moved her hand to rest over her breast.

He released her arm and looked accusingly at her. "Are you a virgin?"

His question felt like a knife pierced straight in her heart. She thought, hoped, he had come to understand her well enough to know the answer. Obviously he had not and how very foolish of her to think that he, the Irish devil, would be any different form all the rest.

She had suffered the results of the attack far too long and she had done nothing to warrant the abuse. She had done what any man would have done. Only a man would have been praised and his scar admired for his bravery. But a woman? A woman suffered the sting of shame for her bravery.

"Answer me," he snapped and startled her.

"Why? You already believe the worst."

"I want an answer," he insisted.

She remained mute.

He walked up to her and grabbed her by the shoulders. "You will answer me."

She thought to keep silent, but instead spoke softly. "You already know the answer."

Her words stunned him and he released her, shoving her away from him.

His anger consumed him and he spoke without thought. "Your father thinks to trap me in this union, but since our vows have yet to be consummated I can return you to him and demand retribution."

Faith stood firm, though her legs trembled and her heart felt as though it broke into a thousand unmendable pieces. "I have survived far worse, but can your pride?"

"How dare you speak to me of pride when you are haunted by shame."

She did not know how many more verbal attacks she could suffer before she crumbled. This man, her husband, whom she had grown to admire, respect and even care for treated her as a contemptible stranger.

The disturbing thought propelled her to speak. "My only shame is that I did not kill the man who did this to me."

She thought she caught a flash of admiration in his blue

eyes, but then they blazed with fury and she imagined it was wishful thinking.

"Your father will pay for this," he said, though it sounded more like a promise. "And you?" He pushed her away from him. "You will remain out of my sight."

Faith did as he ordered, hurrying off away from him, out of his sight. She had to make haste for the tears that gathered rapidly in her eyes were about to burst free and she would not allow him to see her cry.

She ran straight past Colin and Rook, who walked by his side and who immediately turned and set off after his distraught master.

Colin walked up to Eric, who stood alone, his face expressionless and his eyes fixed on his retreating wife. He raised a hand of warning for Colin not to speak. He was furious, absolutely furious—but with whom?

He was not certain who to direct his anger toward, his wife who had kept this secret from him, or her father who obviously used it to his advantage. And somewhere between the both of them lay the truth.

His fury had almost erupted when Faith had spoken of being attacked. He could think of nothing but the intense fear she must have suffered as her strength waned and her attacker slashed out at her. But what then? What then did her attacker do? Was she too exhausted, too fearful to prevent him from further pillage?

Was it shame that kept her from telling him the truth? And what now was he to do?

He motioned for Colin to speak.

"The men are already talking," Colin warned him.

"No doubt they are—and what are they saying?"

"You do not want to know."

"It seems a day of questions without answers."

Colin followed Eric who walked toward an old large felled tree, and sat, joining him.

"She would not tell you the truth?" Colin asked.

"She assumes I know it."

"Do you?"

"I know her father lied."

"And Faith, does she lie?"

Eric answered honestly, "I do not know."

"Then you must find out."

"Which makes this dilemma all the more difficult, for if I do not like the findings, I am stuck with the results."

"And you do not wish this?" Colin asked.

Eric shook his head. "My mother was a whore who bedded a Viking. She managed to instill in me a deep pride and love for this place of my birth. This Ireland. I still remember when I was five running through the meadows and fields so alive with color and feeling the strength of the earth beneath my bare feet. My mother wanted more for me than poverty and despair. She wanted me to taste all the riches this land could give. She named me Eric of Shanekill, after a monastery, so that I would always remember my birthplace. When I was five she took ill and contacted my father, telling him of me."

Eric stood and paced briefly before stopping in front of Colin. "Her last words were to remind me that my roots were planted firmly in Ireland's soil and that I would forever be Ireland's son. I made a pledge to return as I watched the Irish coastline fade away from the deck of my father's ship. And though my father taught me much, making me the man I am today and instilling his Viking strength and pride in me, I never forgot my mother's words or my pledge."

Colin stood. "You have accomplished all you have set out to do."

"No, I have not. I promised that I would replant my roots firmly in Ireland's soil once again."

"And you will," Colin said.

"Yes, I will," Eric agreed, "but not with tarnished seeds."

Ten

Rejected by her husband and shunned by his men, Faith spent much time alone or in the company of Bridget or Borg. Borg had healed well over the previous two days. A slight temperature had given her cause to worry, but lasted merely half a day. He was already complaining about the confines of the open wagon he was forced to travel in, though he did not complain about the company. Bridget had seen to his every need and the two had become inseparable.

The incident had been determined to be an accident, the young warrior who had released the near-fatal arrow doing penance for his error and suffering tremendously for the unfortunate mistake, the men unmercifully ridiculing his inept hunting skills.

Faith would ride her mare or walk alongside the wagon, Rook at her heels. In the evening when camp had been set up and Borg had been tended to, she would seek solace by the fire. She had been instructed by Colin to make use of the tent, but she ignored his offer and chose instead to sleep on a blanket on the ground near the fire.

She had not seen her husband since their confrontation. Any instructions he issued were issued through Colin. The mumbles and whispers continued around her, though the women paid them no heed. It seemed that Bridget and the few woman from Donnegan Keep had spoken with the other women and they were more accepting of her unfortunate plight.

The men, like her husband, thought differently.

Faith walked a good distance behind the wagon today, leaving Borg and Bridget alone to talk. Rook walked beside her though he would take his leave every now and then to forage and snoop. And while she had always enjoyed her solitude, today she discovered herself lonely.

She missed Eric. She missed sharing his horse, talking with him, laughing with him, cuddling against him, but most of all she missed the closeness they shared. She should be angry with him and yet she was not. He should have been told the truth from the beginning with the choice left to him.

He was made to look the fool and that was unacceptable to any man, especially a warrior of Eric's infamous reputation.

And she? She was but a pawn in this game her father played. So what was she to do? Sit by and wait and yet again be used according to a man's dictate.

She shook her head. No, that was completely unacceptable. She would do what she did best. She would create a good, independent life for herself at the keep, serving the ills of the ailing villagers.

Eric would reach his own conclusions, if he had not already. And his decision on the matter would be final. She could do nothing to change his mind. If he had not realized her true character by now, then what else was there left for her to do to convince him of her innocence? The truth was for him to discover. She already knew it.

Colin rode up alongside her. "Why do you walk? To irritate him?"

Faith tilted her head up toward him, her hand following to shade her eyes from the morning sun. "Irritate who?"

Colin looked at her oddly. "Your husband."

Faith smiled with the knowledge that at least Eric cared enough to notice. "I walk because it pleases me."

"It does not please him."

She felt the devil poke at her and with her smile remaining wide, said, "Is he afraid of me?"

"What nonsense do you speak?" Colin asked, startled by her question.

Faith shrugged. "I but wonder why a man of his courage would send someone to speak for him. I assume if he had something to say to me he would have the mettle to do it himself."

"You know full well he does not wish, nor does he desire to speak with you."

"Then why does he worry if I walk or ride?"

Colin hesitated briefly before he answered. "He sees to the care of all his property."

Faith raised her chin. "I am not yet rightfully his property, therefore, I will do as I please. And it pleases me to walk."

Colin was taken back by her bold remark and he smiled. "You tempt the fires of hell, woman."

Faith grinned. "With the chill of autumn upon us, a bit of heat will serve me well."

Colin laughed. "I will tell him what say you."

"I expected you would."

Colin rode off and Faith continued walking, her smile smug and her confidence suddenly strong.

Her mood grew even brighter by midday. Two women who had recently joined with two of Eric's men fell into step beside her. They asked many questions about her birthing skills and she in turn asked if either of them were with child. They both smiled and each admitted that they soon hoped to be.

Bridget joined her shortly after the two women left her side. The young girl talked incessantly about Borg, though not once did she mention his health. It made Faith feel good to know that at least one relationship would prove to be fruitful.

"I worry, m'lady," Bridget said rather suddenly.

"Of what?" Faith asked with concern.

Bridget hesitated to speak and Faith reached a comforting hand out to her. "Tell me, Bridget. I am not like my stepmother. There is no need to fear speaking with me."

"You are nothing like Lady Terra. She is mean-spirited and cruel. You are caring and honest."

"Then what is it you fear?"

Bridget lowered her voice, though the distance from those around them was sufficient enough for none to hear her words. "There is talk that Lord Eric plans to return you to your father. If that be true then I go with you; but truth be known, I would prefer to stay in Lord Eric's service."

Gossip was the mainstay of all villagers and often proved to be more often hurtful than helpful. But then Faith had faced wagging tongues before and survived; she would not capitulate now.

She spoke from the heart. "What befalls me will be my fate alone. You may stay wherever you wish. On that I give you my word." She added with a smile, "Besides, I think Borg will have a say in that matter."

Bridget's full face brightened. "He is like no man I have ever known. He is caring, tender, and does not grow annoyed with my endless chatter."

Faith was about to respond when Bridget's face suddenly drained of color and with a quick, respectful nod she took herself off.

There was only one man who could cause such fright—her husband. She turned to see him baring down on her. His stallion was in no gentle gallop and his stern expression and stiff posture alerted her to the fact that Colin must have finally repeated their conversation to him.

With a firm and steady hand he brought his horse to a gentle walk beside her since she continued along as though his presence did not disturb her in the least.

He spoke not a word, though his eyes glared at her. She smiled and walked without interruption.

"You will ride," he ordered, and none to gently.

Faith answered without looking at him. "I prefer to walk."

She heard that distinct low grumble like a small roar he always made when he grew irritated, and the familiar sound pleased her. Before he could repeat his command as she was certain he would, she said, "I hear we are close to Shanekill Keep."

"We arrive before nightfall."

"I look forward to seeing your home."

"It is not finished."

"I know, you have told me, but I still look forward to our arrival there, and of course seeing to my herb garden. It is a good-sized patch of ground you promised me."

That growling rumble sounded again. "I did not come here to converse with you."

This time she looked up at him, her hand having difficulty in blocking out the bright sun and causing him to appear a massive shadow hovering over her. "Then why do you?"

"You will obey me." His voice was firm, his order clear.

"I do obey you," she retaliated. "I keep from your sight."

"And you provoke me so that I go against my own dictates,"

he all but shouted, causing heads to turn and snap back just as quickly.

"I wish to walk," she said and stomped ahead, Rook trotting alongside to keep up with her purposeful strides.

Eric was fast beside her. "You will ride."

Why she was so adamant in disobeying him, she could not say. She only knew she would have this her way. "I will walk."

"Damnable woman, at least I learned the truth of you before it was too late."

His words stopped her and she turned a furious glare on him. "Truth? You know not the truth, nor do you wish to accept the truth. Your manly pride rules and dims your wit."

"Enough," he roared, his temper near out of control. "Hold the wagon."

With her hands on her hips in open defiance she said, "I will not ride."

Eric was off his horse in seconds. He scooped her up in his arms, marched over to the wagon and dropped her in beside a prone Borg.

He addressed Borg. "She stays here or she will suffer my wrath."

Faith felt Borg's hand clamp down on her wrist as Eric turned, walked to his horse, mounted and rode off without a backward glance.

"You tempt the fates of hell," Borg said.

"So I have been told," she remarked, settling herself reluctantly in the wagon.

Borg released her wrist as soon as he was sure she meant to remain where she was. "Why provoke him?"

She shrugged as she reached out to check the newly applied bandage that Bridget had helped her with just this morning. "I do not know."

"He is a proud man," Borg said, as if in defense of his half brother.

She raised her chin, though it quivered. "I am a proud woman."

"And so you should be," he said in earnest. "Any woman who can survive such a vicious attack deserves respect and admiration."

Tears sparkled in her eyes. "Respect was lost to me that fateful night. Where a man would gain honor for defending himself, a woman gains shame, for none believe her strong enough to fight back."

"More fools are they."

She wiped at her eyes. "Why do you believe me and not him?"

"Learn who he truly is and you will have your answer."

She smiled. "I but wish it were that easy."

"It is," Borg said. "Eric admires the spirit of the Irish people and does not realize he possesses it himself. It is a pride born of stubbornness and love, an indomitable pride deeply rooted and passed on from generation to generation. He wishes that for himself. Understand that and you truly understand the man."

Faith grew silent and Borg's eyes grew heavy. She watched him drift off into a much-needed healing rest and her thoughts drifted to her husband.

Irish pride.

How should she deal with that?

"Patience," she whispered to herself. The best way to deal with pride was always with patience.

Eric barked orders at several of his men as he rode past them, causing most to jump and immediately do his bidding. He was in a foul mood and he knew it, though he cared not.

He was furious with himself for speaking with her and even more furious that he had enjoyed the short conversation. It had made him realize how much he missed her, not that he needed reminding. He could think of nothing but her. She was on his mind day and night. And he had cursed himself most frequently for ordering her from his sight.

Seeing her today made him all the more aware of his betraying emotions. He only need look on her gentle features, her flaming hair and those thin lips that insisted on moving in the most erotic manner to realize he wanted her and all else be damned.

His loins had remained hard from his unexpected confrontation with her. The more she argued, the more she demonstrated her spirit, the more he wanted her. His main thought had been to reach down, swing her up and over his shoulder and disappear amongst the bushes with her and be done with it.

But his pride prevailed and until he could sort this mess out and settle it to his acceptance, he would not touch her.

The unsatisfied ache in his loins told him otherwise. And he had no doubt he would have trouble obeying his own dictates, but he would try—Lord, would he try.

He thought about the scar she wore and recalled that she had kept it concealed when he spoke with her. Did she feel shame? Did she hide the truth along with its reminder? And why not simply answer him and be done with it?

He had assumed the worst, and why not? What woman could fight off a man who welded a knife?

Faith.

Her name came easily to mind. If anyone possessed the strength, courage and will to survive, Faith did. She possessed a spirit that defied the common. She stood strong, confident and proud. She had faced the fires of hell and emerged the victor.

So why question her integrity?

He shook his head and swore beneath his breath. Perhaps it was his own integrity he questioned, and perhaps the answer was not to his liking.

One thing was certain, though—he would have his answers. He would see to it. Nothing would stop him.

He urged his horse forward. He suddenly wanted to be home at Shanekill Keep. Tonight he would sleep in his own bed.

Alone.

Colin joined him, ignoring his brooding mood. "You settled the dispute?"

"There was no dispute. She obeyed."

"With help from you," Colin said with a laugh.

"My men's tongues wag as badly as women."

"They eagerly await the next match."

Eric shot him an angered glance.

"Do not blame me," he said, holding his hands up in a helpless gesture. "I but deliver the news."

"Gossip is more like it."

Colin grinned. "Gossip makes for good entertainment."

"Gossip serves no purpose but to hurt and shame."

"That it does," Colin said, seriously. "Perhaps it is a good thing to remember." He rode off, leaving Eric to ponder his words.

They arrived at the Keep just before nightfall. Eric rode ahead, his excitement at returning home too much for him to contain. He longed to lay his eyes on what was his. What he had fought so long and hard for and what he would continue to fight to keep.

He directed his horse up the small rise slowly, anticipating the first sight of his home, and his breath caught in his throat. It was more beautiful than he had remembered.

The setting sun blazed over his land and painted the area a vivid gold. The land glowed in splendor; some of the fields remained pregnant with rich crops ready for fall harvest. The outer walls to the castle were complete, as he had directed. The large trail of mounted stones wrapped protectively around the Keep and all its buildings, and while his home remained under construction, the sight of it filled him with immense pleasure and pride.

The gatehouse was well guarded by three of his men, even though the portcullis remained open. Men and women worked the fields, carts carried their burdens and men guarded the surrounding area with keen eyes, protecting what was his and theirs. They had fought just as hard for a home, and their pride was just as evident.

Colin joined him on the rise. "The men have done well."

"Not an easy task, since I insisted on stone inside of wood."

"But a more sensible one," Colin said.

"War and battle are adept teachers."

"Let us hope they request no more lessons."

Eric nodded. "Agreed."

"The men are anxious and push hard these last few miles."

"We will be settled inside the walls before nightfall. See that Borg is taken ahead and made comfortable."

"I have already instructed such. He does well," Colin acknowledged.

"Better than I expected."

"Faith is a—" Colin stopped suddenly.

Catching the look of disbelief in Colin's eyes, Eric followed his line of vision.

Faith was absent from the wagon and nowhere to be seen. Not trailing behind it, nor a few yards in front. She was simply nowhere in sight.

"I will go find—"

Eric never let Colin finish. "No, I will go find my wife."

"But—" Colin attempted to protest.

"Enough," Eric ordered sternly. "She disobeyed my command and was warned of the consequences. See to the men."

Eric rode off and Colin rode directly to the wagon. "Where is she?"

"I could not stop her," Borg said with a weary shake of his head. "She grew upset when she called for Rook and he did not respond. She feared him in trouble after several useless attempts and hurried off against my protests."

"Eric went after her," Colin said.

Borg smiled. "And who do you think will win this skirmish?"

Colin laughed. "My coin is on the devil."

"More you the fool," Borg said. "Mine is on the healer."

"I will grow rich before this ends," Colin said confidently.

"You will be a beggar, your coins squandered on foolish bets."

"The devil never loses," Colin reminded.

"On this I am counting." Borg smiled and closed his eyes contentedly.

Eleven

"*Rook! Rook!*" *Faith* called frantically for her dog.

She had seen him wander in amongst the dense bushes and bruce saplings that had bordered the road they traveled on only a short time ago. Something had to be wrong. Rook always answered her summons. Her concern grew as she made her way deeper amongst the dense foliage. She shoved branches out of her way and continued to call out to him, but she failed to receive a response.

Faith stopped a moment and listened, thinking she had heard a noise. Birds chirped, branches rustled in the cool autumn breeze, and then . . . the distinct snap of a branch. She turned just in time, certain the sound had come from behind her.

Her husband bore down on her with such speed and agility that she had not a second to breathe. He swept her up and over his shoulder in one graceful movement, and turned and headed back to the road.

"No, stop!" she cried and beat him on the back, for all the good it did. He was solid muscle and she had no doubt her hand would be more sore than his back. She stopped the useless pounding and pleaded for his help.

"Please, Eric, help me find Rook. He must be hurt or he would have answered my summons . . . please." Her words seemed to fall on deaf ears, but she continued, her voice anxious. "I know I disobeyed you and for that I am sorry, but Rook means the world to me. He was there for me when no one else was. When I was ignored and shunned, he walked proudly by my side. He made me laugh when I thought I never would again and he loves me, truly loves me as I do him. He would never desert me no matter the trouble and I would do the same for him."

His steps slowed considerably until he finally came to a halt and gently placed her on the ground.

"How did you come by Rook?" he asked.

There was no time to wonder over his curiosity. She simply answered his question. "After the attack, my father decided I needed protection so he brought Rook to me. He was but a puppy with big floppy ears and a wet sloppy tongue, but I loved him on sight and we have been inseparable since that day."

"Why did your father not assign one of his guards to you?"

She answered honestly with no thought to herself; her only concern was for Rook and his safety. "He felt a shamed woman could not be trusted with any man, so he chose a dog for my protector."

Fury shot into his blazing blue eyes, his jaw grew taut and the veins in his neck looked near to exploding. "He said this to you?"

"On many occasions."

He looked about to speak, but seemed suddenly to have a change of mind. Instead he grabbed for her hand. "Where did you last see Rook?"

She grasped onto him, grateful for his offer of help and grateful to feel the strength of his large hand wrapped protectively around her small one. "He wandered into this section of bushes and trees as we passed by it."

"Does he always come to you when you call him?"

Faith chewed at her bottom lip in nervous thought.

"Tell me," Eric ordered.

"There is one thing that might delay his response to my summons."

"And what might that be?"

Faith tried not to smile. "Berries."

"Berries?" Eric repeated incredulously.

"Rook has a penchant for berries. When he was a puppy I would take him with me to gather herbs and pick berries. He would eat most of the berries before we returned."

"And you did not chastise him for this poor behavior."

She shook her head. "I could not. He so enjoyed himself that I did not have the heart to scold him."

"Women," Eric said with a rough shake of his head. "So he could very well be sitting in a berry patch feasting to his heart's content."

"That is possible," she reluctantly admitted.

"And you risk life or limb for a berry-loving dog?"

"He would do no less for me," she said softly.

"That I will certainly see to, and I will see to rectifying his poor behavior."

"He is mine and I will punish or reward him," she said firmly.

His curt words warned. "You both belong to me."

She did not argue; it was pointless. He spoke the truth. She and Rook were his property and he could do with them as he chose. She only hoped he would not rescind his offer of help.

"Stay beside me," he ordered as he turned and moved amongst the foliage.

Faith had no choice but to remain by his side. He held firmly to her hand and she wondered if his grasp was more possessive than protective.

She found it strange that he did not call out to Rook, but discovered his reason soon enough. They came to a small clearing and he abruptly stopped.

"Rook!" Eric bellowed his name so loudly that Faith could have sworn the trees shivered.

Within seconds they heard him; he was on a run and barking.

Faith was so relieved, she did not stop to think of her actions, she simply threw her arms around her husband's neck and planted a thankful kiss on his open mouth. And that was the problem.

As soon as her lips connected with his, as soon as he felt her body collide with his, as soon as her tongue touched his, he surrendered. His arms slipped around her and crushed her to him. His mouth feasted as hungrily as hers and neither of them took note of Rook who stopped beside the embracing couple, sat, and finished the mouthful of berries he had been enjoying.

They stopped simultaneously, their lips parting reluctantly, their eyes heavy with desire and their bodies aching to surrender. Eric rested his forehead against hers, attempting to control his erratic breathing and not at all wanting to part from her.

Faith fought to calm her racing heart and ease the sensual quiver low in her belly that warned she wanted more from her husband, much more.

They snapped apart at Rook's loud bark.

Eric glared down at the large dog, whose berry-stained tongue hung from the side of his mouth. Faith instantly fell to her knees beside the huge beast and threw her arms around him.

"Bad dog," she said, "bad dog." All the while she hugged and kissed him.

Eric was about to give him the reprimand he deserved but instead found himself smiling. The two made an oddly delightful pair, Rook a breed so mixed no one could distinguish his true line and with colors ranging from a golden brown to dark paws and ears and a face . . .

Eric shook his head. Rook possessed the biggest, saddest eyes he had ever seen on an animal and that long tongue of his was a weapon he delighted in using on the most unsuspecting person. One lick and you were finished. He caught you in his special spell and you instantly cared for the dumb dog. Though Eric had learned he was not as dumb as he seemed and those large teeth of his could do damage if provoked.

"You must come when I call," Faith instructed and Rook answered with a wet tongue to her face, leaving her cheek stained with berry juice.

Eric suddenly grew annoyed with himself. He had commanded her to keep from his sight and here he was breaking his own decree.

"Enough," he said angrily, startling the pair.

They both looked wide-eyed at him.

"Come," he ordered snappishly and turned to walk away.

"Eric."

Her soft, hesitant call brought him to an abrupt halt and he silently swore he would not turn around. He heard her approach, heard her small feet crush the dry pine needles that carpeted the ground and heard her breathing, steady yet anxious. He had attuned himself to sounds so that when he was in battle he could hear an opponent approach, hear a nearby weapon slice through the air, or hear the fearful breathing of his enemy.

But he was not engaged in a battle and Faith was not his

enemy. How much easier this whole situation would be if that were so. This was but a skirmish . . . and Faith?

Faith was the prize.

"Thank you," she said with a gentle hand to his back.

Her innocent touch caused a sensuous shiver to run through him and he closed his eyes against the unexpected sensation.

"Teach him to behave or I will," he said and stormed off, more angry with himself than his wife.

Faith and Rook took their time catching up with everyone, though she noticed that Colin kept a close watch on her steady but slow progress. The incident with Rook haunted her thoughts; actually it was the kiss she and Eric had shared that haunted her senses more than her thoughts.

She could not make sense of her eager and urgent response to him. How could she desire a man who ordered her to keep from his sight? How could she crave his lips and his intimate touch? She must surely be mad, though so must Eric.

His kiss was filled with as much passion and urgency as her own, that he could not deny. Even though innocent, she was not ignorant and knew full well when a man hungered for a woman. Eric was hungry for her. And truth be told, she was hungry for him as well.

She was relieved when he had left her and Rook to walk back alone, though he had waited until they had made their way to the open path. He rode off then, though not far enough that he could not keep them in his sight and only when she was in the safety of others did he take himself off. Colin appeared shortly afterwards and had since not let her from his sight.

What chance had she with Eric? He was a proudful warrior who had been deceived. He would not take such an insult lightly. His pride would demand retribution, but what of his emotions? How would he quell or satisfy his desires for her?

And how would she prevent herself from falling in love with him? She knew herself too well to think this anything less than love. She cared for this man, this proudful warrior who had fought so hard to gain respect. She did not wish to be a hindrance or an embarrassment to him. If he could not accept her with pride of who she was, then she did not wish to remain his wife.

Faith released a heavy sigh and Rook barked.

"Feeling sorry for myself," she admitted to the dog who looked up at her with large, loving eyes.

Rook barked again.

"Allow me my time to sulk," she complained.

Rook would have none of her complaints; he barked again and rushed from her side, sniffing the ground for a stick. His teeth clamped down on one and he hurried to her side, tossing the thick stick up at her.

She caught it. "So you will not let me wallow in my own misery, will you? Fine, we will play as you wish."

She threw the stick, though not far and Rook fetched it with joy, returning it to her to start again. They continued on and soon Faith was running along with Rook laughing and chasing the stick.

Eric stood on the partially finished battlement and watched his wife and her faithful companion playing. He grew annoyed at their joyful antics and grumbled angrily beneath his breath. He raised a hand to signal Colin in the distance, and his friend nodded in acknowledgment.

He turned away and took himself off to see to other matters, but tonight—tonight he would have definite answers to his disturbing questions.

Faith was stunned at the quarters she was shown. The room was large, the bed sufficient for two, a table and two chairs sat against one wall, two rich tapestries graced the other walls and large chests stood open and empty, waiting for her use. Three tall, iron candle stands beautifully crafted in design occupied three areas of the room, the thick candles they held providing more than sufficient light. This was obviously the master chambers and she was uncertain if there had been a mistake in the servants directing her here. But Bridget, with a pleased smile on her full face, was already busily seeing to unpacking Faith's meager belongings.

"My lady, sit," Bridget said, clearing off garments from a chair near the tapestry that Faith realized concealed a narrow window. "I have directed the servants to bring refreshments and afterwards I will arrange for a bath."

Faith did as Bridget directed, physically and emotionally drained from the journey. She realized a bath sounded much too appealing to turn down.

Rook found a rush mat to his liking near the end of the bed and plopped down on it, immediately drifting off to sleep.

Bridget's tongue was soon chattering away. "I have been told that Lord Eric specifically had these quarters built for his bride. His chambers are beyond that door." She nodded toward a closed door on the opposite wall from where she worked. "The servants I have met thus far have told me he wished for his wife to have her privacy, but I think he also wished for his own."

"Why?" Faith asked innocently.

Bridget's round cheeks flushed and she scolded herself. "Me and my loose tongue."

Faith smiled. "I count on you and your tongue. Tell me."

Bridget was about to speak when a knock sounded. She admitted the servant who carried a silver tray laden with a variety of refreshments, meats, cheeses, fish, fruits, pies and pitchers filled with ale, wine and one with hot water.

Bridget dismissed the servant with a generous smile and an appreciative word and then saw to serving her mistress.

"I had hot water sent up, knowing you would want to brew your herbs."

Faith sighed. "You will spoil me."

"Gladly," Bridget said with a wide smile.

"But tell me of what you spoke," Faith urged, taking dried, crushed leaves from the pouch that hung from her belt and dropping three pinches into the hot water.

Bridget seemed uncomfortable with her request.

"Please, Bridget, I would like to know."

Bridget accommodated her, though with a bit of reluctance. "Not all keeps have separate chambers for the wife. Lord Eric saw to it that his wife would have her own quarters."

Faith laughed, realizing Eric's intentions. "And assuring his privacy from a woman toward whom he was uncertain how he would feel."

Bridget nodded and after making certain her mistress was settled comfortably at the table and her needs met, she returned to tending to Faith's garments.

Faith nibbled at the small chunk of dark bread she held in her hand. Eric had planned on a wife who would fit his needs; whether or not he desired her would not matter. How disappointing for him to find a wife he desired only to discover he had been deceived.

Another knock on the door caught the attention of both women and Bridget immediately responded to the summons.

Colin stood in the doorway. Bridget stepped aside, admitting him.

"Lord Eric requests your presence in his solar within the hour."

Faith was about to agree when instead she shook her head. "I cannot possibly accommodate his request. I have yet to eat and bathe. I will not be ready for at least three hours."

Bridget looked upon her mistress with as much surprise as Colin.

The man appeared stunned speechless and it was several minutes before he responded. "I will inform Lord Eric of your delay."

"Thank you, Colin," Faith said with a pleasant smile.

He turned to leave when Faith asked, "I have not had a chance to see to Borg's care. Has he been settled in his quarters?"

Bridget looked anxiously to Colin as he spoke.

"He is resting comfortably and has asked when you will come to see him."

"After I speak with Lord Eric, I think will be a good time. Then I will see to settling him comfortably for the night. Bridget will see to attending to him for the evening meal."

The young girl's face brightened considerably.

Colin nodded. "I will tell Borg. He will be pleased."

Bridget hesitantly spoke after closing the door on a departing Colin.

"You do not fear the devil, my lady?"

Faith shook her head slowly. "I would be a fool not to fear the devil."

With her stomach full and a soothing bath, Faith was prepared to face the devil head-on, or at least she assumed she was. She had not counted on the fact that the extra time she had given herself, she also had given the devil.

A servant directed her to Eric's solar, one floor down from the bedchambers. She gave a gentle knock and his deep voice bid her enter. She was beginning to realize that Eric had spared no cost in constructing and furnishing his home. The solar was large and suited to fit a man's needs. Several thick wooden chairs and two tables filled the generous space, and iron candle stands like those in her room brightened the quarters as did the fire in the hearth. The tapestries that graced the walls were rich in beauty and tales depicting victorious battle scenes.

Her eyes finally came to rest on her husband and her breath caught briefly in her throat. He resembled the handsome lord of darkness.

He was freshly bathed and freshly shaven. His long, dark hair shined in silky splendor and rested over his wide shoulders. His garments were of dark red coloring, to the point that they appeared almost black though the touch of deep red gave the material a hint of color. He stood near the hearth, burning with dancing flames that warded off an evening chill which had crept through the keep.

His stance was relaxed and confident and his expression stern until his eyes met with her. He apparently was surprised at her appearance, but then so was she. Bridget had insisted on fussing over her tonight. She had adamantly insisted that Faith look her best and saw to it that she did.

To Faith, Bridget had worked miracles. She wore a pale yellow shift with an equally pale yellow tunic and the plain garments highlighted her fiery red hair. And there is where Bridget had worked her best miracle. She had fashioned it in a way that most of the temperamental curls appeared drawn up and away from her face while several irate strands fell around her face and down her neck, framing her beautiful face and of course hiding her scar.

If Faith ever felt beautiful, she did tonight.

Eric moved away from the huge stone hearth toward the table that held several flasks and trays of food.

"May I offer you anything?"

"No, thank you," Faith said softly. "Your servants have more than adequately provided for me."

"You are not disappointed in my home?" He did not know why he asked her or why he even sought her acceptance, but he could not rescind his words, so he waited for her answer.

"It is more than I expected and I am more than pleased. I am honored to be here."

Her sincere words touched his heart and he could not take

his eyes from her. She was simply stunning, more beautiful than ever, if that were possible. The raging red of her hair was a perfect color against the soft paleness of her face. Her dark brown eyes startled, her rosy lips invited kisses and her body waited, waited for his personal touch.

"I hear that Borg does well," he said, knowing a change of subject was wise.

"Yes, I go to see him after we speak."

"I visited with him only moments ago and he looks forward to seeing you."

She smiled. "As I do him."

His expression turned serious. "First we have a matter to discuss."

She had wondered over his summons; now she would find out.

Eric had thought about this meeting with his wife since he had decided upon it when he had been on the battlements. He intended for her to answer his questions fully and honestly so that he could make a wise and reasonable judgment. He would settle for nothing less and this she would know.

He walked back to stand near the hearth, still not having offered her a seat and not intending to. "I have been lenient with you since discovering your deceit."

Faith was fast to defend herself. She had expected this confrontation, actually had hoped for it, and now that it was upon her she intended to defend her honor. "I did not deceive you."

"You kept the truth from me."

"What truth? That I suffered an attack and survived? Does the scar I carry bother you? I thought it would not, since being a warrior you yourself must carry many reminders of your battles and be proud."

"I am a man."

"And I a woman who defended herself. Was that wrong of me?"

He had not expected to be put on the defensive. He had expected her to quiver, shake and relent to his commands. She was not at all cooperating and yet he found her courage admirable and her defiance challenging.

"A woman has a right to defend herself," he agreed. "But she also has the duty of informing her husband of the truth."

Faith needed no time to respond—she was quick with her

words. "But should not the husband know his wife well enough to know the truth without asking?"

He thought over her remark. Her question suggested more than she spoke.

"Perhaps the husband needs to hear the words."

"Perhaps the wife feels it unnecessary."

"Enough," Eric shouted annoyed they were getting nowhere and wanting this settled and wanting his wife in his bed. "Enough word games. You will answer me. Are you a virgin?"

Faith stuck her chin up and clamped her inviting, rosy lips shut.

"You will suffer for your silence," he said and immediately regretted his rash words.

For a moment she looked stricken by his threat and then her eyes glowed defensively and her chin inched up even further.

"You are stubborn," he shouted.

Her chin inched up again.

"And foolish!"

Just as she was about to jut her chin out further, he growled like an angry animal, marched over to her, grabbed the back of her neck and yanked her toward him, his mouth clamping down on hers.

Twelve

Eric fed on her like a man too long denied. He simply could not get enough of her. She was like an intoxicant that once sampled was impossible to ignore. His mouth bruised hers with an urgency that frightened him and it wasn't until his rational side interrupted his passion that he released her and abruptly turned away.

He kept his back to her, attempting to control his lusty appetite, calm his ragged breathing and understand his unrelenting desire for her.

Faith took several steps back and rested her hand on the back of a chair. Several silent moments passed for which she was grateful, needing time to gather her wit about her. She had not been prepared for the intensity of his kiss or the shockingly demanding way he took it. And she had not been prepared for her own surprising response to him. Her body instantly sparked to life and whatever he would have demanded of her she would have willingly given him.

She supposed that was why she felt such an overwhelming sense of disappointment. He had initiated the startling kiss and yet he had failed to follow through. How perfectly rude of him. She planned on telling him just that if he continued such uncivil behavior.

She almost gasped at her own audacity and took a deep,

calming breath to still her tumultuous emotions. Whatever was she thinking? She actually wanted her husband to ravish her!

Faith smiled a shy, hesitant smile that vanished as quickly as it appeared. And with it went her girlish fantasies. Her husband was the infamous Irish devil; did she really think this man cared for her? He was a man who lusted for the wife he had assumed would perform her wifely duties without difficulty. He had not bargained for a wife with a tarnished past.

He delivered his words with a cold fury that sent endless shivers racing through her. "I will contact your father."

She expected nothing less, though she had hoped. No, she had prayed that perhaps he had grown to understand her nature and then he would not find it necessary to ask her if she was a virgin. He would know.

Foolish.

Perhaps she was foolish. Foolish for dreaming, wishing, hoping that someone would accept and love her for who she was. After all, she foolishly accepted him for who he was, the infamous devil, and she would find it no great chore to love the devil himself.

Foolish.

Yes, she certainly was that.

Faith turned and without speaking a word she walked out of the room, quietly closing the door behind her.

Eric slammed his fist on a nearby table, sending flasks and goblets tumbling. He was furious. Furious that he had insinuated that she may be returned to her family. He no more wanted her gone than he wanted to lose his own limb.

"Stubborn and foolish," he shouted to the empty room.

"It is always good to admit one's faults."

Eric swung around to send Colin a scathing look.

Colin grinned and raised his hands in mock defense as he entered the room. "I am not the enemy."

Eric reached for a fallen goblet, filled it with ale and handed it to Colin. "I but wish I knew who the enemy was; it would make this senseless skirmish more sensible."

"Does there need to be an enemy?" Colin asked and walked over to sit in a chair near the hearth.

Eric filled another goblet and joined his friend, taking a seat in the larger wooden chair covered with a thick, beautifully stitched tapestry. "Where there is deceit, there is an enemy."

"Who is being deceitful?"

Eric sighed and rested his head back. "That is what I am trying to determine, but my wife refuses to cooperate."

"Perhaps she was warned not to."

"I gave that option thought and while she was at Donnegan Keep I could understand her succumbing to threats. But once we left?" He shook his head. "What was there for her to fear?"

"Discovery."

Eric sat forward. "The question, my friend, is discovery of what? If she truly has nothing to hide, why not just speak the truth and be done with it?"

"Would you believe her?" Colin asked.

"The length and severity of the scar would put doubt in anyone's mind."

"Not in Bridget's or Borg's minds."

Eric sank back in the chair. "So I have heard. Borg talked endlessly of my wife's many virtues. Until finally I suggested that since he knew her so well he could answer my haunting question."

"Which is?"

"Is Faith a virgin?"

"How did Borg answer?" Colin asked.

"Without hesitation he told me that she certainly was a virgin and that I better see that I take her virginity with as little pain as possible, or I will answer to him."

Colin laughed. "He has a soft spot for your wife and a hard spot for Bridget."

Eric laughed along with him. "Have you ever seen a man blush as much as he does when that servant girl is around? It is damn embarrassing."

"I think it is funny. The man is simply besotted and I wonder how he is going to get the nerve up to kiss her."

"My coin is on Borg," Eric challenged.

Colin shook his head. "I will grow wealthy with all this foolishness. Mine is on the servant girl."

"You will grow poor, my friend," Eric argued with a smile and stood to walk over to the table and retrieve the pitcher of ale. He filled Colin's lifted goblet and then his own.

"Then if I am to be a poor man let us enjoy this night," Colin said and raised his goblet in a toast. "To a night of good drink and good women."

Eric's goblet did not move.

Colin looked questioningly at him. "I have two willing servant women waiting to pleasure us. What say you?"

Eric dropped in the chair and let out an exasperated sigh. "I say nay. Too much clouds my mind."

Colin tempered the smile that tempted his lips, downed his ale and stood. "Then I have no choice but to please the both of them. If you change your mind, we will be in my quarters."

Eric waved him off and stared at the ale in his goblet. He ached for his wife, not just any woman, but his wife. He wanted to taste those rosy lips, strip her bare and lose himself within her. He had never wanted a woman with as much passion as he wanted Faith, and it frightened him. He did not understand it, or perhaps he did and perhaps he did not like the knowledge he had discovered; or perhaps he was not yet ready to accept it.

He downed the ale and refilled his goblet yet again. He would drown his sorrows tonight . . . and tomorrow?

Tomorrow he would send a letter to her father.

Faith made her way slowly to Borg's quarters. They were two floors down and while she wanted to see him, she also needed time to regain her composure. Her meeting with Eric had upset her and she was attempting to deal with the knowledge that he might very well return her to her father.

An option she was not ready to accept.

She did not wish to return to Donnegan Keep. Her life there had been limited and lonely. Here there was a chance for happiness. Could she make it work?

She found herself at the door to Borg's quarters much sooner than she had anticipated and she entered, pushing her nagging thoughts aside, eager to see her patient.

Borg lay in a massive bed, his head and back resting against a mountain of pillows so that he looked to be sitting, though he was actually stretched out quite comfortably. A white linen sheet covered him to his waist and he looked freshly bathed and shaved.

"I have been wondering when you would come," Borg said with a generous smile as she approached him.

"I had matters to see to," she said and immediately moved to his side to check the bandage that covered his wound.

"Bridget saw to changing it. The wound heals remarkably

well. It has almost crusted closed and the redness has all but vanished. You are a good healer."

Faith drew a chair near the bed to sit and talk with him. "Thank you, but you helped by following to my instructions."

"I had no choice." He laughed. "I was threatened by Eric, Colin and Bridget that I was to do as you directed or else."

"Or else what?"

Borg shook his head. "I decided not to find out. They were all too intimidating."

Faith could not imagine a man the size of Borg being intimidated. "You feel well, no pain?"

"None I cannot bare, but tell me what you think of Shanekill Keep."

Faith glanced around the large room. "I am surprised at the size of the rooms in the keep. They are so large, and furnished to meet one's every need."

"Eric has spared no expense in its building. He wanted the best in all he brought to his home."

Faith glanced away, unable to meet his eyes.

Borg reached out to take her hand. "You outshine all he has brought here."

She raised a thankful glance to him. "You believe me. Why? No one else does."

"Why should I not believe you? I have never known you not to speak the truth or deny an ailing person help. You are an honest woman and, therefore, you give me no reason to doubt your character."

"I wish Eric felt as you do."

"How do you know he does not?"

Faith gave his hand a gentle pat. "He makes himself clear."

"But do you hear clearly?"

Faith looked at Borg oddly, though held her tongue.

"I am well enough to leave this bed," Borg said, taking his hand from hers and demonstrating his strength by pulling himself up to sit straight. He did fine until he leaned over ever so slightly, then he winced.

Faith immediately saw to easing him back against the pillows. Then she wiped perspiration from his brow that had been caused by his exertion, using the damp cloth that had been left in the wooden bowl full of water near the bed.

"I know you wish to be up and about, but if you rush your recovery you will only serve to prolong it."

"Wise words," he reluctantly admitted.

"And besides, I thought you enjoyed the care Bridget gave you."

Borg's pale face turned scarlet.

Faith instantly felt guilty about teasing the ailing man. "I am sorry, I did not mean to—"

He shook his head, interrupting her apology. "No, it is all right. It is my own fault. I am dreadfully inadequate when it comes to dealing with women."

Faith found that as difficult to believe as Borg being intimidated by anyone. "You are a handsome and fit man. Why would you feel that way?"

"I do not know. I only know I have always felt tongue-tied around females. Eric tried to teach me the ways of women. He has substantial knowledge when it comes to dealing socially with them, though I feel his good looks would warrant any woman's surrender."

Faith stiffened at the thought of her husband with another woman.

Borg continued. "No matter how many times Eric attempted to educate me to women, I simply failed to grasp the concept and found myself tongue-tied as usual." He smiled. "Of course, there was that one time when Eric decided I would remain mute and he told the women I could not speak. It worked wonderfully and we had a—"

Borg stopped suddenly, turning a scalding red. "I am sorry, my lady, I forgot my manners."

Faith laughed. "I am only sorry you forgot your manners before finishing the story."

Borg grinned and obliged her with, "I had a good time."

"And Eric?"

Borg purposely avoided her eyes. "He had a good time as well."

The large man attempted to move to make himself more comfortable and moaned softly in pain.

"I warned you about that," Bridget said, entering the room and marching over to the bed. "You are not to move yourself about."

"She is right, Borg," Faith agreed. "Though you may feel the stitches have set well, the inside needs time to heal also."

"Now I'll be settling you for the night. You need sleep," Bridget said firmly.

"I will say good night," Faith said, standing. "Since I see that you are in good hands."

Bridget smiled at the sincere compliment.

Borg simply smiled, not taking his eyes off Bridget.

Neither one paid her attention, though she noticed that Borg remained silent while Bridget chattered on and on. The man was obviously in love and the thought warmed Faith's heart.

She returned to her room, collected Rook and took him downstairs and outside the keep for a stroll before bedtime.

The keep and the castle grounds themselves more than impressed Faith—they amazed her. Skilled hands were evident wherever one looked, from the rich tapestries that graced many of the walls to the new furnishings that had been crafted with care and to the fields that were ripe for fall harvest. Eric had taken care to bring the finest to his home, along with the people who cared enough to see it remained that way.

She glanced up at the battlements armed with men who paid strict attention to their duties, protecting the castle from unexpected intruders. She watched women engaged in laughter and conversation outside their small one-room cottages and men gathered around an evening fire sharing a tankard or two.

A few women bowed their heads respectfully at her and the men avoided looking her way, and she felt safe to continue her stroll knowing no one would dare disturb the devil's lady.

The full dark of evening was almost upon them and Faith was anxious to locate an area of ground for her garden. She followed Rook around the side of the castle and found the kitchen entrance to the keep, and smiled at the large garden that ran alongside it. Squash grew plentiful on vines, some cabbage and wild onions still remained and she was sure her eye had caught sight of parsley.

She bent down and grabbed a handful of soil to sniff and squish between her fingers. It felt rich and smelled potent. The soil was fertile and she smiled.

She stood, brushing the dark dirt from her hands. "Where do you think our garden should be, Rook? I know it may seem silly to plan a garden if I may not stay, but I itch to get my fingers in the soil, and who knows? Miracles do happen."

The dog sniffed at the ground by her feet, looked up at her, sniffed the air and barked before he trotted off. She followed until he stopped at a plot of ground a bit of a distance from the kitchen, nearer the castle wall. A towering spruce tree with thick, heavy branches shared the space and probably cast a good deal of shade over part of the ground, making it perfect for her shade-loving plants.

Faith turned slowly in a full circle, taking in the whole area. "It looks to be perfect, Rook."

The dog barked his agreement.

"Tomorrow we shall see how much sun and shade this area receives, and then if it fits our needs we shall ask permission."

"As you asked permission to take this walk?"

Faith turned, startled by her husband's accusing and unexpected remark.

He loomed a towering shadow in a darkening night and for a moment his overpowering presence frightened her and she shivered.

He stepped forward, pulling his black cloak off and swinging it to wrap around her. "Have you no sense that you leave the keep alone and without a wrap for warmth?"

He secured his cloak around her, tucking the soft wool over her shoulder and fastening it with his gold brooch before he stepped away.

The familiar scent of him invaded her senses, drifting around her and over her like intimate fingers at play. And she could not escape him; she was imprisoned by her own passion for him and his familiar garment would see that she remembered. Remembered his touch, the taste of him and the feel of him.

Her hands grasped the soft wool and drew it close.

"What are you doing out here?"

"You promised me a garden," she said with a touch of defiance.

Eric crossed his arms over his chest and shook his head in disbelief. The woman was amazing. Only a short time ago his remark had warned that she might be returned to her father and still she persisted in planting roots. She was full of Irish stubbornness and courage, and he smiled.

"This could not wait until morning?" he asked, his voice stern.

"Rook required his nightly stroll."

"Will this be a nightly ritual?"

"Of course. Rook and I always take an evening stroll."

"You will not go unattended," he ordered.

"I do not. Rook is with me," she reminded.

He took a step toward her, his tone adamant and direct. "Here you will have more than just a dog to protect you."

Rook took umbrage to that and barked.

Eric shot him a warning look. He whined and moved to sit next to Faith.

Her hand went to pat Rook's head. "Rook and I can see to ourselves."

"Not anymore," Eric snapped. "You are my wife and will do as I say."

Her emotions bordered a fine edge and she snapped right back at him without giving thought to her words. "I am not officially your wife."

Her remark shocked both of them, but Eric was a true warrior and immediately retaliated. "That can be settled right now with a simple answer to my question."

With the intoxicating scent of him still heavy in her nostrils, she was tempted to accommodate him, but her own pride interfered. She had been forced to wed the devil, then discovered him a man of pride and convictions, a man she could love, and then she was forced to defend her own honor to him. That she would not do. If he did not believe her an honorable woman, then he had no business being her husband.

He moved closer, his fingers reaching out to trace the scar gently, coming to rest over her nipple. "I want to make love to you. I want to strip you bare and explore every intimate part of you. I want to plant my seed deep inside you and watch you grow heavy with my child. I want you as my wife. Now settle this and be done with it."

Her passion urged her to surrender; her pride refused. "Only you can settle this, Eric."

And with her challenge delivered she walked past him, Rook trailing on her heels.

Thirteen

Blood splattered across Eric's bare chest and covered his fists. He stood firm, barely panting, barely demonstrating any exertion though he had just engaged fists with three men and was presently looking for a fourth to take on.

The group of men who circled the exercise field, numbering near sixty, cheered with excitement, their loud voices echoing off the stone walls of the keep that loomed on a rise only a few yards in the distance. The imposing stone edifice stood as a symbol of their lord's strength and bravery.

"Enough," Colin shouted, pushing past the circle of men who had watched with an odd mixture of thrill and fear as their leader had repeatedly demonstrated the reason for his notorious reputation as a warrior.

"You now command?" Eric asked much too calmly, and Colin was wise enough to heed the warning behind his controlled words, though he did so with his usual humor.

"Nay, my lord," he said, smiling, "but I fear there will be no men left to guard the keep if you continue to ravage in such a brutal fashion."

Eric nodded, though his annoyance was evident.

Colin waved the group off and quietly ordered the three men that Eric had raised fists against—one looking more bloody than the other—to go see Lady Faith. They eagerly acknowledged his command and took themselves off.

Eric walked to the water bucket near a stack of stones, picked it up and spilled the entire contents over his head. He wiped the blood from his chest and hands and then shook his long, dark hair before running his fingers through the wet, heavy strands.

"With your own heat rising along with the temperatures these last two days, a dunk in the nearby lake might suit you better," Colin said, coming up behind him.

Eric turned on him. "Watch it, Colin, I am in no mood for your teasing remarks."

"I mean what I say."

"Then it is a fight you are looking for?"

"Peace, actually," he answered candidly. "You have been unbearable for the last few days. Bed your wife and be done with it."

"Not until she answers me. And besides, it is none of your business."

"You are wrong."

Eric stepped toward him, his hand fisted, and Colin wisely retreated several steps.

"See," Colin said almost in a shout. "Your first thought is to pound on me and that is not like you. You have never raised a fist to me, nor have I to you."

Eric shook his head.

"Bed a woman and be done with this rage that eats at you."

Eric spoke the words that had haunted his every waking thought for the last four days. "I want my wife."

"Then speak with her," Colin urged.

"I have," Eric insisted, and she refuses to answer me.

"I did not say ask her a question, I said speak with her. The way you did those first few days after the wedding. You grew to know her."

Eric paused in thought. He had enjoyed that time with her. They shared an emotional intimacy he favored. She had spoken freely, and thinking back, truthfully, he was certain. He had looked forward to their encounters. Perhaps bedding his wife was not the only thing he wanted from her.

The idea that he actually found pleasure in conversing with his wife was a surprise to him. He had not given thought to forming a relationship with the woman he wed. He had assumed that he would choose a woman who fit his needs, get her with child and see to the running of his castle. He had never considered he would actually enjoy his wife's company or even wish to bed her.

"I will speak with her," Eric said, his words more of a confirmation to himself than to Colin.

"Good," Colin said with a laugh. "Because she is headed this way."

Eric looked to where Colin's glance fell and he watched his wife march toward him with determined strides. She wore the familiar dark blue tunic and shift that seemed to comprise her wardrobe, only this time a white strip of cloth was draped along the front of her and it appeared to have blood stains on it. He reminded himself to order new garments made for her. Her riotous red curls were drawn up and away from her face—a face that bore not only beauty but the reminder of the reason for their ongoing skirmish—and at the moment he was prepared for battle. He actually looked forward to confronting her.

"Leave," he ordered Colin.

"Not fair," Colin muttered his complaint with a grin as he obeyed his lord's command.

Eric stood his ground firm and ready, but was ill prepared for her unexpected maneuver.

Her astute brown eyes widened in alarm and she gasped, instantly reaching out to grasp his bruised and bloody hands. "You are hurt."

He remained silent simply because he was speechless, and when she tugged him along and made him sit on a large rock, he obeyed like an obedient child.

"Now stay," she ordered with a gentle sternness and hurried a few feet away to retrieve a water bucket. She soaked the clean end of the white cloth in the fresh water, squeezed it out and then went to work tending his cut and bruised knuckles.

The moment she touched him he knew he was lost.

"Whatever were you thinking?" she admonished softly.

He could not very well tell her the truth—that he had wanted her so badly that he took his sexual frustration out in physical combat. Instead he asked, "Are my men all right?"

Faith spoke while her attention remained fixed on tending his hands. "A broken nose, a split lip, two black eyes, a swollen jaw and two lost teeth, but the three will survive. Bridget and two other women are seeing to their care."

"And you came to tend me?" he asked quietly.

She soaked the end of the cloth once again in the water and started on his other hand, but first she glanced up at him. "I came because I could not believe that one man could inflict such damage and still remain standing."

He leaned forward. "The devil can," he whispered with a quick grin and stole an even quicker kiss.

She looked at him with startled eyes.

"You doubt my strength?"

She shook her head, ignoring her tingling lips. "I doubt your senses."

She purposely dropped her glance to his hand, gently cleaning his bloody knuckles.

Eric would simply not be denied. He lifted her chin with the weight of one finger, forcing her to look at him. "I know what I want. Do you?"

Faith knew he wanted her and she fought the urge to tell him just how much she wanted him. Lusting for someone was easy, but love was not, and she would not settle and surrender herself and her honor to him for lust.

Foolish.

The word often invaded her thoughts and reminded her just who her husband was—the Irish devil. How could she expect more than lust from this man? But then she had been afforded the time to become familiar with him and she had liked the man she had discovered. It was that man she hungered for, that man she wanted to love and be loved by.

But how did she get the devil to release him?

"Do you, Faith?" he asked again.

She answered the only way she could, honestly, though not completely. "Yes, I do know what I want."

She waited for him to question her further, to counterattack, so she was caught off guard when he responded with a kiss.

Slowly and sensually he took charge of her mouth, teasing with the skill of a master lover. He invaded her senses until she was thoroughly limpid in his arms, not even realizing he had captured her in an intimate embrace.

Her body curved like a responsive bow fitting in the hollow of his embrace. His naked chest felt hard, warm and comforting; his arms were thick with muscles and they wrapped around her possessively and protectively.

She felt safe and secure and at home in his arms, and while her body quivered from the passion his kisses had easily ignited, she sensed a deeper bond spark between them. And it frightened her.

"I will not hurt you, Faith," he whispered in her ear, feeling the subtle change in her body.

With difficulty she pulled away from him and stood on trembling legs. "You already have."

Eric watched her rush away and he suddenly felt empty, as if he had been robbed of a part of himself. He growled in annoyance at the odd and disturbing sensation, and stood.

He wanted answers and he wanted his wife. He would get both.

With that decision made, he stormed off toward the castle.

Faith attacked the solid ground with the pickax, her frustration being released with every swing of the slender tool. Rook quietly crawled to hide behind the large tree, keeping a safe distance from his master's mighty swings.

She was not certain if it was herself she was angry with or her husband. He saw only what was in front of him; he never looked beyond. But then, he was a warrior and a warrior judged with his eyes and his instincts, not with his heart and his emotions.

The ax came down upon the broken clumps of earth several times before she stilled her actions. She wiped the perspiration from her brow with the back of her hand and looked up at the full sun, bright and warm in the morning sky. Summer was paying its respects to autumn one last time and when it left the cooling days of autumn would be full upon them.

This was the time when the land prepared itself for winter, dropping the pine needles to nourish the ground through the winter's cold, thickening the bushes with an extra coat of growth and laying the land dormant with a rich covering of greens and purples.

She looked down at her plot of land almost ready for the bulbs she would plant for spring growth. Near the castle wall was a pile of pine needles she had collected and would use to blanket and nourish the soil through winter. In the spring she would add the seeds and seedlings she dug up from the surrounding hills and meadows and her garden would flourish in abundance.

If she was still here.

The thought annoyed and disturbed her. Was she being obstinate, or was her husband? She could easily settle this matter, so why didn't she? Why did she cling so tenaciously to the truth when speaking it would set her free?

She let the ax drop to the ground and walked over to sit beneath the shade of the tree. Rook made his way from behind it and joined her, his large head resting comfortably in her lap.

A tear suddenly peeked from the corner of her eye and she wiped it away, stubbornly refusing to allow any more to follow. She had shed too many useless tears and she would shed no more. She had foolishly thought that her father had loved her. She had even called out to him when she was being attacked. She never imagined that after surviving the vicious attack, she would suffer a far worse one.

She momentarily shut her eyes against the painful memories. Her father had entered her room and as she lay bleeding and fearful of death, she had reached out to him. His vile verbal attack so startled her that her fear dissipated and in its place she erected a wall of strength and courage. She had done nothing wrong, and yet she was made to suffer unbearable consequences because of ignorance.

And though her virginity remained intact, she had been robbed of her innocence. She was not prepared to, nor would she surrender, her honor. She had paid dearly for it and had survived. She had learned to hold her head up high, had gained the respect of the villagers and had diligently restored her pride in herself.

And with great difficulty she had accepted her father for who he was, a man who spared no love for his daughter.

Marriage was not a consideration after the incident. Her father had repeatedly informed her that a marriage contract for her would cost him dearly and he was not willing to surrender any portion of his wealth for a marriage merger that would not greatly benefit him.

Thought it had taken time to accept her solitary fate, she had done so and she had not complained. Instead she had educated herself in the art of healing and had taken great comfort in the knowledge that she was able to help people. In accepting her fate, she had discovered herself and she was proud of the woman she had become.

She had grown strong and held her head high and she would not surrender her hard-earned honor to anyone, especially the devil.

"My lady." Bridget's anxious voice interrupted her thoughts.

Faith immediately got to her feet. "Is something wrong?"

"The husband of Mary the cook has been feeling poorly for a few days and she is worried. She asked if you would look in on him."

"Of course," Faith said, feeling she had spent enough time on self-pity. It was much better to live life than to wallow in it.

The one-room cottage was a short distance away from the kitchen. It was clean and well kept, with everything in its place and the room itself smelling sweet. Faith noticed upon entering that flowers and herbs filled pots, pitchers and whatever Mary could find to hold them. There was a table with two chairs, a worn wooden cabinet, a large bed and a chest at the foot of the bed. A stone hearth remained cold, a sensible choice with the recent warm weather.

Faith followed Bridget over to the bed on the far right of the cottage. "Stuart, this is Lady Faith. She has come to make you well."

The sizable man groaned and shook his head. "Too late."

"Nonsense," Bridget scolded. "You will get well. You probably have nothing more than an ailing stomach."

Faith stepped closer to the bed. The mattress was thick with straw, to which lavender had been added to give it a sweet scent. One look at the man and Faith grew alarmed. He was deathly pale; his thick lips were dry, near to cracking; and his large brown eyes had difficulty focusing. He was over six feet tall, had a massive chest and solid legs and a thatch of bright red hair.

"Bring his wife here quickly, Bridget," she ordered.

Bridget looked at her with alarm before hurrying from the room.

Faith sniffed the tankard that sat on the small stool beside the bed. It seemed harmless enough, mint to soothe the stomach, though it appeared to have little effect on the ailing man.

She located the rain barrel outside the front door, filled a wooden trencher with water and proceeded to bathe the man's brow with the cool water. He ran no fever, which alarmed more than puzzled her.

Mary filled the small doorway with her almost six-foot height and solid weight. She was far from heavy, her muscle tone firm and her weight evenly distributed on her large frame. She had a pretty face and expressive eyes that openly expressed a fearful concern.

Faith could not help but envision the little giants this couple would conceive.

"What is wrong?" Mary asked, rushing to her husband's side. She kneeled next to the bed, grabbing his limp hand in hers.

"I need to know what you have been giving him," Faith said gently.

"Mint," Mary hurried to explain. "I thought it nothing more than an ailing stomach, or a bad piece of meat or fish."

It was not uncommon for food to turn bad and stomachs to protest, but Stuart had been ill for a few days, which meant he suffered from more than a piece of food gone bad.

"What have been his complaints?" Faith asked.

Mary was quick to reply. "He stopped eating and complained of feeling light-headed.

"Has he eaten anything today?"

Mary shook her head. "Nothing in the last two days except the tea I have given him."

Faith looked puzzled and worried.

"Is there nothing you can do for him? Is it the fever?" Mary asked anxiously.

"He has no fever, though his complaints trouble me."

Bridget entered the cottage breathless. "The servants in the kitchen need Mary. The mutton stew needs flavoring and a young servant boy added too much parsley to the bread and turned it green and—"

"Enough," Faith said. "Mary, go see to your duties. I will tend your husband and if I need your help I will send Bridget to fetch you."

Mary looked torn between her duty and her husband, but Faith knew it would be best for her if she busied herself with work while Faith saw to the care of her ailing husband.

Faith reached out and placed her hand over Mary's, which

continued to keep a firm grip on her husband's limp hand. "I promise I will send for you if I need to."

Mary nodded and Faith walked over to where Bridget stood in the doorway, still panting. "Bring me my healing basket and have a fresh bucket of water drawn from the well for me."

Bridget nodded and left.

Mary joined Faith by the door. "Is there anything you need?"

"Nothing I cannot see to myself. Go and do not worry."

Mary smiled awkwardly and walked toward the kitchen, her steps reluctant.

Faith paced the one-room cottage, uncertain as to what steps to take to help the man. It was difficult to make a decision of how to treat an ailing individual when the reason for the ailment was unknown. She could do more harm than good if she was not sure of what troubled him.

Stuart slept on and off, mumbling incoherently. He seemed worried about leaves, forever insisting he must have them now.

Bridget announced that it was near time for the evening meal and that she should come bathe and dress. Faith dismissed her with a shooing wave of her hand. She had no appetite and was too concerned with Stuart to worry about the evening meal.

She had thought about purging him, but was not certain if it would do him any good in his already weakened condition. She continued to concentrate on all she had learned of herbs and their proponents over the years. She had made several unusual and surprising discoveries and she hoped one might apply to Stuart's condition.

Faith lit several candles as night began to fall and she called on the recorded knowledge she kept tucked in her mind.

Eric looked out from the dais on the occupants of the great hall. It was full of his men and their women laughing, eating and enjoying the evening meal. Colin sat with him and even Borg had grown well enough these last two days to join them. But his wife was conspicuously absent.

The meal was excellent, the mutton stew flavored perfectly, and he had to remember to compliment Mary on the green bread that held the stew; the coloring caught the eye and taste. Normally, he would have eaten the entire bread trencher, but his thoughts were elsewhere, taking his appetite with them.

He wondered over the whereabouts of his wife.

Was she purposely avoiding him? He intended to find out.

He looked about the room for Bridget. Not seeing her, he turned to Borg. "Where is your woman?"

Borg almost choked on a piece of mutton. "My woman?"

"Have you not made the servant girl your woman yet?" Eric asked irritably.

Borg blushed and shook his head.

Colin laughed. "I think you two are in dire need of instructions on how to bed a woman."

Eric silenced him with a lethal look.

"Where is Bridget?" Eric asked Borg.

To no one's surprise he knew exactly where she was. "Bridget is helping Lady Faith tend the cook's husband. He is ailing."

"My wife ignores her wifely duties to tend an ailing man?" he asked of no one in particular, and much too loudly.

The hall suddenly quieted to a few whispers and mumbles.

He had had enough. This was his castle, she was his wife and she would obey him.

"Tell the cook I wish to see her," Eric ordered a nearby servant girl.

The poor young girl trembled as she approached the dais. "The cook was summoned to her cottage by Lady Faith, my lord."

Eric stood, his towering height casting a menacing shadow over the fearful girl. She quickly stumbled out of his way as he rounded the dais and headed straight out the keep's front doors.

"My coins are on the devil," Colin said to Borg.

"You will grow poor." Borg laughed. "My coins are on the healer."

Bridget stood outside the closed cottage door and instantly took several steps away as Eric bore down on her. His long, dark hair glistened in the moonlight, his dark garments blended with the shadows of the night and his blue eyes blazed with a fiery brilliance that bordered on anger.

"Is she inside?" he asked.

"Yes, my lord," Bridget answered with a respectful bob of her head. "But she does not wish to be disturbed."

"You are dismissed, Bridget," Eric said with a firm calmness. "You will go attend Borg."

Bridget looked apprehensively toward the closed door and at that moment Eric clearly understood where the young girl's loyalties lay.

"I will not repeat myself," he said with a harshness that immediately sent her scurrying.

He reached for the wooden handle and instead of storming in, he slowly and quietly opened the door but an inch and listened.

Faith and Mary sat at the table while Stuart slept soundly.

"He keeps talking of potion, Mary. What does he refer to?" Faith asked the tearful woman.

"I do not know," Mary said with a regretful shake of her head. "It is important?"

"It could be. I need to know if he has been adding anything to his food or drink."

Mary thought a moment and then shook her head again. "I do not recall seeing him do so."

Faith sighed and proceeded as delicately as possible. "Then I must ask you a personal question that might help me to discover if he has been taking a potion."

Mary looked strangely at her. "Personal?"

"Aye, and if you do not wish to answer that is up to you but your answer may help your husband to make a successful recovery."

Mary nodded. "I will answer whatever you ask of me."

"Good," Faith said with a gentle pat to her hand and continued with reluctant necessity. "I need to know if your husband has sought his husbandly rights more than usual as of late."

Mary's eyes widened. "An illness can cause a husband to seek his wife more often?"

"Nay," Faith assured her. "But a certain herb called henbane is believed by some to be an aphrodisiac."

"That is why he has not been able to keep his hands off me?" Mary asked with a mixture of surprise and disappointment and answered Faith's question.

Faith shook her head. "No, the herb has no aphrodisiac qualities; it is actually poisonous."

Mary grew alarmed. "Stuart will die if he took this?"

"If he took too much," Faith confirmed.

Tears sprang from Mary's eyes, but she volunteered the information most willingly. "When Stuart returned from fighting, he had a problem."

Faith listened quietly, not commenting.

"He tried so hard night after night, but nothing happened. Then he left to accompany Lord Eric to Cork. He had not attempted to touch me for a week before he left. Then he returned, and his first night back . . ." She smiled with pleasure. "It was like when we first wed and has been ever since until he took ill."

"Did he bring anything back with him from his trip?"

"He has a pouch he keeps things in but it is private, I would never intrude."

"I would," Faith said. "Get it for me."

Mary hesitated.

"Do you wish your husband to get well?"

Mary did not think twice this time. She stood and fetched the pouch from the wooden chest at the end of the bed.

Faith probed the contents with care. The large leather pouch contained a number of items and she found herself opening leather boxes and unwrapping cloths only to be disappointed with each examination. She thought her search a failure when she came to a cloth pouch tucked in the bottom corner. She opened it slowly and spilled out a small amount of the contents into her cupped hand. She poked at the crushed leaves and then gave a sniff. She drew back her nose in distaste, the fetid order of henbane confirming her suspicions.

"This is the problem," Faith explained patiently. "And you can thank the lord that whoever gave it to him had added only a minute amount of henbane to the potion, or your husband would be dead.

Mary's eyes teared again. "Will he be all right?"

"He should be fine," Faith said. "He is very lucky. Make sure he rests, drinks the brew you make him and try to get at least some broth in him tomorrow. In a few days I think you will find him much improved."

Mary nodded and cast her eyes to the dirt floor as she asked, "Will his problem return now that he can no longer use the potion?"

Faith reached for her hands, forcing the woman to look up at her. "The potion almost caused him to die. It did not help his problem; he only believed it did."

"But now he will believe his problem has returned," Mary said sadly.

"Then he will need something to replace the potent potion."

"You have something," Mary asked anxiously.

Faith nodded and retrieved from her healing basket a small leather pouch. "These leaves are very potent. You must only brew a pinch in hot water."

"And he will have no problem?"

"No problem at all," Faith assured her. "Why, I would not be surprised to see you birthing a babe by the summer."

Mary threw her arms around Faith and hugged her tightly before realizing her actions were inappropriate. "Oh, my lady, forgive me." She stepped away, shaking her head and continuing to apologize.

"Nonsense, I am glad I could help. Now fix yourself an herbal brew and relax. You have had too much to worry about lately. You should rest yourself."

"You are truly a gracious woman," Mary said and bowed her head in respect.

"Thank you for your kind words," Faith said and gathered her things.

"I will see that a supper tray is brought to your room. You have not eaten since morning and must be starving."

Faith attempted to protest.

"Please, my lady, I would like to do this for you," Mary said.

Faith nodded. "As you wish."

Faith looked the sleeping man over one more time, assured Mary he would be fine and walked out the door, right into the arms of her waiting husband.

"One question, dear wife," Eric said quietly, making certain the door was closed behind her. "How do you know henbane is considered an aphrodisiac?"

Fourteen

Faith could not help but notice the look of him in the moonlight. A saint would fall to sin looking upon his handsome features, especially with the glow of the full moon bathing him in its silvery splendor.

"Stare at me with such wanton lust and I will have no choice but to satisfy you," he said in a rough whisper.

Her defiance rose with her chin. "Without first satisfying the question of my virtue?"

His intense blue eyes blazed with a wickedness that could not be ignored. "You forget our brief encounter in the woods."

Heat rushed to sting her cheeks as she recalled the pleasure he had given her.

He brushed his cool cheek against her warm one. "You tempt the devil."

"The devil lures the innocent."

"Are you innocent?" Eric asked in an anxious whisper.

Faith responded quickly. "Innocent of evil."

"You play with words," he said sharply.

"I speak the truth," she insisted.

"Of that I have yet to learn." He turned to walk away and ordered, "Come with me, you have yet to answer my question."

Faith followed him, though her strides were slow and measured. The day had been long and busy and she now regretted taking her anger out on the garden plot with the pickax. Her arms ached, her healing basket growing heavier by the minute and her stomach rumbled in hunger, putting her in no mood to answer any more demanding questions.

Eric slowed his pace, aware of her weary condition. He reached out as she drew near him and snatched the basket from her arm. Before she could protest he shot the question at her again. "How do you know henbane is considered an aphrodisiac?"

A question she did not mind answering. "I have made a study of several herbs and their properties. The plant has a fetid order and the noxious smell seemed more a warning than an attraction. I decided to study it further before making use of it. I was glad I did, since after being called to a nearby keep to see if I could aid the ailing lady I discovered she had been given a special potion by her husband, the one ingredient being henbane. Unfortunately, the lady succumbed to her ailments."

"How did you learn it was thought an aphrodisiac?"

"Gossip is the mainstay of any keep. The servants did not know I was Lady Faith; they thought me one of them and spoke freely. It seems that the lady of the keep was adverse to her husband's touch and he tired of her denying him. He sought the services of a nearby healer who prescribed a potion, supplying the cook with specific instructions on how to prepare it. The cook protested when the healer insisted she add henbane; the smell was so odorous she felt certain it would spoil the potion. The healer had explained that the foul scent actually worked as an aphrodisiac, causing the coldest of women to respond to their husbands and the most impotent of men to succeed."

Eric stopped at the door to the keep. "And what is this potion you gave to Mary to replace the one that made Stuart ill?"

"Chamomile and mint leaves."

"This works?" he asked skeptically.

Faith smiled and laughed. "I drink the potion all the time." She grabbed her basket from his hand and hurried into the hall, her husband's thunderous shouts trailing after her.

Eric failed to catch up with her upon entering the hall. Many of his men, deeply into their cups of wine, pounced at the chance to comment on his exceptional skills on the exercise field that day. It would have been rude of him to protest their praises, though he would have much preferred to follow his wife and demand an explanation. Which he still intended to do once he maneuvered his way through the gregarious crowd.

Colin and Borg lounged in their chairs on the dais, watching him with broad grins, and if he was not in such a hurry he would take the time to wipe the smug smiles from their faces.

He dealt in a good-natured manner with his men, all the while drifting closer and closer to the stairs. Until he was finally free to make his escape.

"Lord Eric, come share one last drink with us," Colin shouted, his glass raised as Eric turned a murderous look upon him.

He could not refuse to drink with them. His men respected and admired him and to them it was an honor to raise a toast with him.

A path miraculously opened among the crowd as he marched across the great hall straight for the dais and Colin.

"Easy with him," Borg cautioned Eric when he drew near. "He has sampled the new wine and found it too much to his liking."

Colin grinned foolishly at him. "My coins are on you."

Eric looked to Borg.

"A harmless bet." The large man shrugged.

"And who are your coins on?" Eric asked.

"The winner," Borg said with a confident smile and handed him a goblet of wine.

Eric nodded knowingly. "A wise answer, brother."

Anxious to be off, he turned, lifted his glass high and spoke for all to hear. "To the brave and mighty warriors who fight by my side." He downed the contents of the goblet.

A loud and lingering cheer echoed through the great hall, fists pounded at tables and voices soon raised in robust song.

Eric turned back to Borg. "Are you well enough to mount the stairs on your own?"

"I am well enough to mount most anything," Borg grumbled.

Colin snickered. "I wager the fair Bridget will be pleased to hear that bit of news."

Borg looked ready to pounce on him.

Eric intervened. "The wine speaks."

"The truth speaks," Colin mumbled in a drunken stupor.

"Both of you need mounting and neither one of you have the courage to do what is necessary."

"And I suppose you know what is necessary?" Borg asked.

Colin gave them a slow nod. "I do."

"And will you share this bit of wisdom with two fools?" Eric asked, placating his intoxicated friend.

Colin waved them closer as if he were about to impart with an invaluable piece of information. Eric and Borg obliged him, moving nearer.

It took three attempts before Colin got his finger to his lips in warning. "It is a secret."

Borg hid a laugh behind the hand he brought to his mouth and Eric played along. "We will not tell anyone."

Colin looked to Borg for the same confirmation.

"Promise," the large man said, his hand continuing to conceal his laugh.

Colin shook his head, evidently not believing them. "You are both too foolish."

"To do what is necessary?" Borg asked, his laugh having turned to a wide grin.

Colin still shook his head. "To know what is necessary."

"What is it we should know, my friend?" Eric asked.

Colin placed a hand on Eric's thick shoulder. "When you know what is necessary, you will do what is necessary."

"He talks in riddles," Borg insisted.

"I speak the truth," Colin argued.

Borg argued back. "You are drunk."

"I am a wise drunk."

That caused both Eric and Borg to smile.

"And I know the truth," Colin persisted, tugging at Eric's tunic. "You know the truth too, Eric, you know the truth."

His repetitive words disturbed Eric and he wanted to hear no more of them. He was about to signal one of his men to see Colin safely to his quarters when he caught the anxious eye of a young servant girl he knew Colin fancied.

He summoned her and she hurried right over to him. "Will you see that Colin finds his bed?"

"Aye, my lord," she said with a pleased smile and though she stumbled with the weight of him draped on her, she also smiled and laughed at the words Colin whispered in her ear.

"How does he do it?" Borg asked. "He is barely able to stand and the girl still falls under his damn charm."

"He has a special way with women, always has, and sometimes I envy the ease and wisdom with which he deals with them."

"You have never had difficulty finding a woman to bed."

"True, but there is a certain air of danger and intrigue in bedding the devil himself."

Without another word exchanged Eric marched out of the great hall, his own words troubling him as he mounted the stairs in search of his wife.

He did not care if he found Faith abed. She had taunted him with her answer and she would explain herself, though if he was honest with himself he would admit that he enjoyed talking with her. She was far more intelligent than he had expected.

His father had been generous in his education, insisting on its importance in dealing with foreign lands and their people. Most people assumed Vikings to be barbaric, and while the Viking heritage did contain a barbaric history, the Vikings also were excellent sailors, fine craftsmen and skilled merchants. To succeed in any of those trades, his father had made certain that mathematics and languages were an intricate part of Eric's studies. And while he chose none of these professions in life, his studies enabled him to succeed where many failed. He understood his adversaries' tongues, could calculate distances and troop movements for battles and could map a course in the blink of an eye.

Eric respected knowledge, which is why he so admired his wife's tenacity as a healer. She took pride in her skills and had obviously fought hard to gain them—qualities a husband did not often find in a wife and ones rarely sought.

He approached her bedchamber with a specific intent in mind—to clarify the answer she gave him and to learn more about the woman he had abruptly wed.

Her chambers sat directly beside his; his first thought when ordering them constructed had been that if he did not favor the wife he was forced to wed he could at least seek solace from her. Strangely enough, he now found himself seeking her chambers and he wondered if it would not grow to be a habit.

He gave no knock to announce his entrance. Why should

he? He was the lord of this keep and had the right to enter any room he chose.

Faith sat at the table, staring at the low flames in the hearth. A night chill had crept into the keep, causing several hearths to be lit.

"I saved you a brew of chamomile and mint," she said softly and turned a smile on him.

"Think you I need it?" he asked, closing the door and joining her.

She held the cup out to him. "If it is soothing you wish."

Eric accepted the offer and sat opposite her, tasting the hot brew. "A pleasant flavor. But why did you recommend it for Stuart if it but soothes?"

"He is anxious, he needs soothing."

"And this is his problem?"

"I will discover soon enough. If I hear no more from Mary, then I know I have treated him wisely."

Eric simply nodded, though he silently applauded his wife's perceptive intelligence.

"I am sorry if my absence from the evening meal caused you embarrassment."

"I know you have your faithful companion to protect you," Eric said, sending a brief glance to the dog sleeping soundly near the hearth. "And while I have no doubt as to your safety within the castle walls, I prefer to know at least why my wife will not be present for a meal."

"As you wish, my lord."

Eric understood that her formal response was issued with respect for his position, and took no offense. The blend of herbs did soothe and he found himself relaxing in the hard wooden chair.

"I am told you have single-handedly dug up a plot of earth for your garden."

Faith placed her cup on the table and pushed the heavy strands of curls away from her face as she spoke. "The location is perfect with the sun and shade being equal partners and it sits in a spot that will not be disturbed. That is, if you do not mind. You did tell me I could have a garden."

"I do not mind," he said, his glance settling on the pale, thin scar that ran down the side of her face, not far from her hairline. He did not find it unsightly, though it disturbed him to realize the horror she must have suffered. "Though I do mind that you labored alone. Ask and it will be done for you."

Faith looked at him as if insulted.

And for a moment he thought he had insulted her with the way he had stared at her scar.

"But it is my garden, my plants will rest and nourish there. Therefore, it is my concern to see that their home is sufficiently prepared. It would not do for someone else to labor over my patch of ground. 'Tis mine and I shall see to its care."

He was about to comment snappishly that if she carried his child she would not be laboring over anything but seeing to her own care. But he stopped himself, realizing there was no chance of her being with his child, and the thought left him feeling bitterly disappointed.

"I have also been told you have made your presence known around the castle grounds."

"I wish to explore and discover as much as I can about your home."

He noticed she did not refer to Shanekill Keep as her home, but then he had not given her reason to believe she would be staying. Yet still she wished to explore her surroundings.

"I see that besides your private chapel within the keep, a chapel has been erected in the courtyard for the castle residents, but I have yet to meet a cleric."

He smiled. "While I can coerce my men to follow me to hell and back, it is more difficult to get a priest to attend the devil permanently."

She laughed and strangely enough, seemed relieved.

He decided it was time to change the conversation in the direction he wanted it to go. "I am surprised you walk so freely, without fear, about the castle grounds."

"Why would I do otherwise? I fear no one here."

So she did not fear him. He was relieved to learn this, but interested in learning more. "I thought perhaps that the attack had left you with some fears."

She paused in her response as if uncertain, or perhaps memories haunted her. "I have faced my fears and they have made me strong."

Information was vital if he were to learn the truth, so he probed. "You mentioned the attack took place in the stables. You do not fear going to the stables here?"

She shook her head. "No, Rook always goes with me."

"Would you go alone?"

This time she shuddered, though she tried hard to hide her reaction.

Eric was persistent. "Your attacker was never caught?"

She looked hesitant to answer him and then seemed resigned, almost as if she was just too tired to object to his questions. "No, he was never found."

"Did you offer a description?"

Again the hesitancy. What was she hiding from him?

"It was late at night and dark, far too dark to identify the man."

"A face is not always needed—clothing will do. Was he dressed in peasant or a nobleman's garb?"

Her hand went to her neck and she rubbed at the thin scar that trailed down over her collarbone. She remained silent and he wondered if she gave thought to his words. She was obviously remembering something, but would she share the memory with him?

Faith shook her head. "I do not remember. I know he was strong, for I fought hard to keep the knife away, though he left his mark."

"At least he did not take your life."

She looked with sorrowful eyes at him. "But he did. He changed my life forever."

Eric could neither find words of comfort nor alter the truth of which she spoke. She had suffered greatly through no fault of her own and yet she had survived and had grown strong.

"You stare," she said bluntly. "Does my scar disturb you?"

Her candid question startled him as did the realization that he had allowed his gaze to linger much too long on her scar. And while he was the lord and could do as he pleased, it did not please him to embarrass her in such a rude manner.

He discarded his cup to the table before he rose, and walked over to her. He squatted down in front of her and her own eyes betrayed her, taking note of his firm thighs and the sizable bulge between his legs.

She forced her eyes up to meet his and was grateful that he had not taken note of her intimate scan of him. His one finger gently sought her chin and pushed her head to the side so that he could look fully upon her scar.

He ran his finger from the point to where it began beneath her eye, close to her hairline, down over her cheek, her jaw, along her neck and over her collarbone. He stopped when his finger touched her tunic.

"Take my finger on the path it travels," he said softly.

She did so without question, wrapping her fingers around his and slowly tracing along the scar where it traveled beneath her shift. The path ended at her nipple and she looked into those blazing blue eyes that could ignite the most celibate soul with one glance.

His finger ran in a tender circle around her nipple and the soft orb responded, instantly hardening to his intimate touch.

Faith dropped her hand away, feeling guilty, as if she had initiated his touch.

His hand fell away, along with hers. "You are a brave woman."

"Many thought me a coward." Her voice quivered.

"Why?"

His lips were much too close to her face and they were moist and full and so ripe for kissing . . . and the scent of him? If a man could smell virile, he did, and the assault of him on her nostrils was hard to ignore. But ignore the devil she did. Or did she? He seemed closer to her, but how could that be—he had not moved. Had he? Or had she?

"Why?" he repeated, his warm mint breath fanning her lips.

He was closer to her still, but who had moved?

She shook her head, softly attempting to clear her head. "Many felt I should have prayed to die, not live."

"More fools they."

She stared at him incredulously. "My scar does not shame you?"

He ran his finger over it once again. "You bear a sign of courage. Why would your courage shame me?"

She knew then that it was she who had moved for she slipped forward in her chair and tentatively touched her lips to his. He touched back gently. Her small tongue peeked from between her aching lips and reached out to stroke his lightly.

He moaned, but stayed as he was, allowing her to explore him.

His nonevasive response urged her pursuit of him and her tongue began to trace his lips over and over and over. The warm sweet taste of him made her feel giddy and she continued her innocent assault on him.

She slipped the tip of her tongue between his lips and he slowly parted his mouth, allowing her entrance. She darted in and playfully teased him, his own response just as teasing.

Her hands went to his shoulders, his hands went around her waist. She leaned forward, he leaned in and in a brief startling moment they were wrapped in each other's arms. The tamed kiss turned wild and their bodies melted against one another.

Eric's only thought was to carry her to the bed, strip her bare and lay claim to her. The consequences be damned. He wanted her. He hungered for her. He was hard, damn hard for her.

He stood, taking her along with him until he stood straight and then he scooped her into his powerful arms and carried her to the bed. He brought them down upon it together, their mouths and hands never leaving each other.

Rational thinking was impossible for Faith; her body simply had a mind of its own. She ached for him, wanted him and *loved* him. At that precise moment she realized that she had totally surrendered to the Irish devil. Fear of the consequences startled her and her body shivered.

"Shhh, easy," he whispered near her ear and placed warm, tender kisses along her neck. "I will not hurt you."

"Promise?" she asked softly.

He looked into her dark eyes, so pure and innocent.

Innocent.

Would the word forever haunt him?

He chose his words carefully. "Do you keep secrets from me, Faith?"

"I have no secrets."

His hand moved to press between her legs. "I will find none here?"

Softly and with strength, she said, "You will find the truth."

With suspended breath she waited. The choice was his. Did he truly know her? Did he truly care enough to accept whatever the consequences were? Did he truly desire her or was it simply lust?

An anxious knock sounded at the door before it swung open and Bridget rushed in.

Fifteen

Bridget gasped at the intimate sight of them together on the bed and immediately looked away. "My lord, my lady, forgive me."

"What is it?" Eric snapped.

Bridget refused to look directly at them. "It is Borg. He is in pain."

Faith instantly moved to leave the bed, but Eric stopped her with a strong hand to her stomach.

"Does he suffer?" Eric inquired.

"He requested to see Lady Faith," Bridget answered, her face flushed and her nervous glance focused on the floor.

"Please, Eric," Faith whispered. "He may be ill."

"He best be ill or I will ring his neck."

Faith suppressed the smile that wished to surface, knowing it would do her no good to demonstrate the pleasure his unexpected reaction caused her. He was angered by the interruption. Was the dark lord beginning to soften?

Eric gave quick instructions to the trembling woman. "Tell Borg she will attend him."

Bridget bobbed her head and fled the room.

Eric's muscled leg slipped over Faith when she made a move to leave. "We have matters to discuss, my lady."

The hardness of his knee resting so intimately between her

legs sent a flood of emotions soaring through her and she fought to remain in control. "I have told you—"

"Nothing," he finished for her. "But I expect you to tell me everything soon enough."

He swiftly removed himself from the bed.

She was startled by his words. Why should she admit anything to him? The decision was his to make, not hers. She told him what she would. She would say no more.

Faith hurried off the bed and grabbed her healing basket as she followed her husband out the door. He accompanied her to Borg's chamber, not a single word exchanged between them.

Closer inspection of Borg's condition did indeed confirm that he was in pain.

"See to him," Eric ordered Faith with a chilling command and with what Faith realized was a trace of fear.

Bridget stood beside the bed, nervously ringing her hands.

Faith calmly took control, sitting on a stool beside the bed. "Does the pain come from the wound?"

Borg nodded. "Lower portion of it."

Faith turned to Eric. "Do you carry a knife?"

He immediately reached down into his boot and produced a thin bladed one.

She took it and gently cut away the bandage.

Borg winced even though she carefully peeled the bandage off his wound.

Bridget gasped and Eric's jaw grew taut.

"That bad?" Borg asked, looking to Eric for an honest reply.

Faith answered. "Not as bad as it looks, though unnecessary. You had no business getting out of this bed before I ordered it."

Borg had the good sense to look contrite.

"Stubborn fool," Eric said.

"It runs in the family," was Borg's reply.

"You will stay abed until Faith directs otherwise."

"Is that an order, my lord?" Borg snapped.

"If necessary," Eric barked back.

"Enough," Faith ordered sharply, surprising the squabbling brothers. "I need to put a healing poultice on the inflamed area and then he needs to rest." She waited for no response but turned quickly to Bridget. "Fetch me hot water and clean bandage cloths."

Bridget nodded and took herself quickly off.

The time grew late yet Faith remained alert as she bathed the slightly reddish area clean, prepared and applied the poultice and bandaged the wound. She then made a soothing brew of Saint-John's-wort and chamomile to help Borg sleep. She did not feel the aches and pains of her long, laborious day until she had finally finished the task at hand.

A soft moan issued from her lips as she bent to retrieve her healing basket from the floor.

Eric brushed her hand aside and scooped her up into his arms. She did not protest; her head fell gratefully against his chest.

"Bridget, you will attend Borg until I order otherwise."

"But, my lord, who will care for my lady?" she asked anxiously.

Eric was about to scold her for even daring to ask when Borg spoke, low but firm.

"That is Lord Eric's concern, not yours."

Bridget looked with wide, surprised eyes at Borg, who motioned her toward him. She walked over to the side of the bed and he reached his hand out to her. She took it, sitting beside him on the bed.

Eric smiled and tucked his wife closer to him, her soft breathing a sure sign that she was close to a deep slumber. He returned her to her room and she did not stir when he placed her on the bed. He was tempted to undress her, but realized that would be unwise of him. Very unwise. He placed a light wool cover over her and brushed the wild riotous curls away from her face.

He leaned over her and faintly traced the thin scar with his finger. "What secrets do you keep from me, dear wife?"

His whispered words stirred her and she turned her cheek into his hand. He stroked her face, ran his thumb over her moist lips and groaned with the want of her.

He stood and stormed out of the room to his own. This had to stop, this obsession with her. He intended on getting answers and instead he found himself with more questions. Where once it was only her virtue in question, he now discovered he wanted to know about the attack. What had really happened that fateful night? Why wasn't the attacker caught? What was she hiding?

The haunting questions disturbed his thoughts and continued into his dreams as he finally took to his bed and slept.

• • •

Eric faced a busy morning, listening to the peasants' minor complaints, meeting with the stonemason, talking with the carpenter, drinking ale with a traveling merchant and seeing to the petty squabbles of the servants. He was beginning to think that it was easier to fight a battle than to manage a castle.

However, he amended that thought when he took his stallion out and rode to the rise to view his land. He still could not believe this all belonged to him. He had chosen wisely when given this spread of land.

The castle backed onto the River Deel and had access to two more rivers with connection to the River Shannon. Not all of the surrounding terrain was farming land, but that suited his purpose. He wanted a land that would protect and produce and his men had battled the elements and the land itself to dig the fields clear and clean for planting.

He had hired an army of men to build the castle and where it would have taken years to complete, he would see to its full completion in another two years. It was not the largest castle in Ireland but it would be strong and durable if under siege.

The woods to the west kept the larder stocked with its wealth of birds and beasts and the fields inside and outside the castle walls added to the abundant pantry. His people would not starve.

An autumn chill wrapped around him, racing through the black-and-red wool cloak he wore. Colors he often wore and he had ordered made into a plaid that would suit his taste. He looked to the gray skies that threatened rain, but even the dismal cloud covering could not dampen his spirits. His land lay before him in stark splendor. He had accomplished much and he would accomplish more. Next spring he would start building another keep, closer to the coastline, and he would give it to Colin to manage. He intended to firm his foundation and allow no intruders to take what was his.

This land, this bit of Ireland was his, and he would defend it with his life. He would nurture and nourish it and it would respond in kind. He would make certain his holdings and wealth grew and he would one day pass the legacy he had built on to his son.

A fine mist began to fall over Eric but he paid it no heed. His thoughts were busy with plans for the future and the seeds that needed planting now—the most important seed being the one he wanted to plant in his wife's belly.

With the mist turning to a fine rain, Eric made his way back to the castle with thoughts of finding his wife.

He found her in a small dilapidated cottage behind the kitchen, not far from her barren garden. She was looking it over with the delight of a young child who had just received an unexpected surprise. Rook sniffed around the one room, the space of which was barely sufficient for two people, and then darted past him out the door to answer nature's call.

The open door provided the only source of light and with the gray, watery skies that light was severely limited. A mound of ash lay in a cold hearth and a broken chair and broken bed were the only pieces of furniture to occupy the room. Yet Faith looked absolutely joyful.

The limited light quickly vanished when his large frame filled the doorway.

Faith turned with a start, though her smile remained constant.

"I frightened you?" he asked, stepping inside to allow the dim light entrance.

"No, not at all." Her answer was honest. "Rook would have warned me of an intruder."

"I do not intrude?"

Always. You intrude on my heart, my soul, my emotions.

The reply remained in her thoughts and she simply shook her head. "You are my husband. A husband never intrudes on his wife."

"Spoken like a dutiful wife."

She nodded and forced her eyes to remain on him, a difficult intent. He looked much too tempting. His damp, dark hair was drawn away from his face, heightening his handsome features and his devilishly sinful blue eyes. His deep red tunic appeared almost black in color and hugged his muscled body. And all she could think about was touching him.

Her sensual thoughts betrayed her and she blushed, thinking how it would feel to run her fingers over his naked chest. She turned her head away, hoping to avoid discovery.

"Did you seek cover from the rain in here?" he asked.

"No," she said, turning her back to him as if she were surveying the room. "Mary told me about this place. She mentioned how it was empty and I thought that perhaps if you had no good use for it, I could use it as my healing cottage."

She felt him walk up behind her and she continued talking, giving herself time for the heat to fade from her cheeks. "I require a place—"

"To hide from me?" he asked in a whisper near her ear.

His warm breath tingled the flesh on her neck, and she shivered. "Nay, I do not wish to hide from you."

His arm slipped around her waist and he slowly drew her back against him. "Then why do you hide that lovely telltale blush from me?"

She could not keep the quiver from her voice. "I do not—"

"Want me?"

His lips rested near her cheek and the strength of him pressing hard against her made his own desires obvious. Could she deny her want for him when he plainly displayed his?

"Would it matter if I want you?"

"A man prefers a willing woman."

"Even a husband?"

"Especially a husband."

She relaxed against him and he kissed her cheek. "Tell me what you want."

Would she be sorry if she spoke the truth to him? Would her admission of her desire for him help to solve their dilemma? No sound answer came to her. The choice would be hers alone, and she made it.

"I want to touch you."

He turned her around in his arms. "Touch wherever you like."

She dropped her head to rest against his chest and to avoid his eyes when she spoke. "I wish to feel flesh."

He raised her chin. "You want me naked?"

She shook her head, her cheeks once again heating. "Nay, your chest, I wish to touch your bare chest."

He obliged her, stripping bare to the waist.

She stood staring at him, unable to move, her eyes set on the wide expanse of his chest, bare of hair and so very hard of muscle.

"I am yours to explore, my lady," he said softly, extending his arms out.

She stepped forward, two small spots of heat still staining

her cheeks. He moved toward her, his hands remaining extended as if in supplication.

She advanced hesitantly, her hand reaching out, her fingers straining forward.

Eric made the next move, stepping into her reach.

Her hand lay flat upon his chest for a moment and then she faintly ran her fingers over him, skimming his soft nipple and running down along his ribs.

He had never experienced such exquisite torture, never had his own nipple harden in such pleasure; never had he hardened so painfully as he did without having laid a hand on a woman. And he cursed himself for surrendering to his own foolish desires, but he allowed her to continue, ached for her to continue, prayed for her to do so.

And she did.

Faith moved forward, her other hand running over his flat midriff, up along his muscled manly breasts and thick, hard nipples and then down along his narrow waist, only to start all over again.

She sighed with pleasure, but as she continued to roam, tease with a pinch here and a pinch there, her sighs turned to soft moans and her body swayed toward him, the sensuous motion defining her desires.

"You like the feel of me?" he asked, tempting her lips with a brief kiss.

"Aye, I do," she said, her lips pouting over the loss of his.

He gave her another fleeting kiss and she sighed in frustration.

Without thought to her actions or regard to the consequences, her hand roamed down his stomach, rushing to cup his bulging manhood intimately.

He tensed when she grasped him, though her touch was gentle and inquisitive, but if he allowed her to continue he was afraid he would not want her to stop. His hand covered hers, stilling it.

"Please, Eric," she said, her own pleas surprising her.

He realized then that he had allowed her to go too far, much too far.

A crack of thunder caused her to jump in fright and she slowly backed away from him, her eyes wide and her breathing labored.

" 'Tis a fool, I am."

"Nay, 'tis passionate you are." He advanced on her with determined strides.

She raised her hands in a futile defense. "You will have no answer from me."

"I seek none," he said and grabbed her around the waist. "You forget how I have pleasured you before."

She shook her head, attempting to deny him.

He laughed softly. "I will hear your moans of surrender."

The dust flew up and around them as he took her down upon the straw-filled bedding that lay in the corner of the room. His hand instantly moved beneath her shift, between her legs, and when his fingers found her rich moisture, she froze.

"You touched," he whispered gently. "Now I touch."

His finger entered her slowly and she cried out softly from the pleasure it brought her. She was so wet it was easy for him to insert a second finger and easier still to quicken and sharpen his strokes.

She moaned and moved to the rhythm he had set and he found his own body rubbing against her leg and his mouth reaching out to claim hers.

Their tongues tangled wildly and his own body protested most vehemently, forcing him to respond.

"Saints be damned," he mumbled, pulling his mouth away from hers, slipping his fingers out of her and spreading her legs so he could nest between them.

He cursed the heavens and all above for making him want his wife with such an aching tenacity. Then he cursed his own stubborn pride as he rubbed himself intimately over her. And he cursed the saints again when she threw her arms around him, moved against him with wanton desire and screamed his name as she exploded in climax.

He swallowed his own anguished cry of release. He had not spilled himself outside of a woman since he was a young boy. And he would not let it happen again.

He turned a scathing glare on his stunned wife. "Remember this moment well for the next time you touch me, I promise you will feel the full force of me inside you and the consequences will be yours to deal with."

He stood and stormed out of the cottage into the raging rain.

Sixteen

Faith lay motionless, her body shivering, though not from the damp chill in the room. It was his blatant promise that caused the uncontrollable shivers. She wrapped her arms around herself for much-needed warmth and comforting.

What was she to do? Swallow her pride, admit her virginity and submit to her husband's will? She would be a fool to deny that she wanted to copulate with him. And yet she wanted more from him than a lusty bedding. But why? What did she truly want from him?

The answer came easily. She wanted the dark lord to love her.

Faith got to her feet, smoothing down her garments and brushing dust from her hair. She walked over to where his discarded garments lay on the floor and picked them up, hugging the soft wool to her chest.

She had spent many years alone after the attack—barely tolerated by her family, not accepted by the villagers and loved by Rook alone. She had never dared to dream that one day she would marry and bear children of her own, so she rejoiced in every new babe she delivered.

Now, though, through a small miracle she faced the prospect of her dreams coming true, but at a cost that was dear to her.

Her honor.

How could she surrender the very thing that she had fought

so hard to maintain? Whenever she was called a shameful name, she held her head high. Whenever a man made an inappropriate suggestion to her, she held her head high. Whenever she thought she could bear no more insults, she held her head high. And when her family completely rejected her, she held her head high.

Throughout the whole sad ordeal she retained her own sense of honor, refusing to give in to the injustice of her situation. It had been a struggle in so many ways and there were times she often wished to give up and accept her sorrowful fate.

But her self-respect always won out, forcing her to fight, forcing her to retaliate, forcing her to succeed. Now she faced another battle. Would she turn tail and run, choose the easy path, or stand up for her beliefs?

She sensed in Eric a goodness that could not be denied and though he fought to conceal his own secrets she had caught a glimpse of his true nature. He was a man capable of loving deeply. She saw it in the attentive way he treated his men, in the way he cared for Borg and in his patience for his new wife who he unselfishly allowed to deliver a babe on their wedding night.

This man was no devil, and while lust filled his thoughts she truly believed love drove his emotions.

So what was she to do?

She smiled to herself and hugged his garments tighter to her chest. "I will teach the devil to love."

She called out for Rook, who had apparently fled the cottage without her knowledge. The large, wet dog stuck his head in the door, his wide sorrowful eyes searching the room.

"Lord Eric has gone, you may come in," she instructed with a laugh. Was there anyone who did not fear the dark lord?

She nodded as Rook shook the rain off him and answered her own question. "Me."

Feeling much relieved, she began telling Rook just how she planned to make the cottage her own.

Eric sat forward in his chair on the dais, his elbow on the table, his chin resting firmly against his hand and his intent glare focused on the double doors.

"Staring is not going to make her appear any sooner," Colin said, spearing a chunk of rabbit off his trencher with his knife.

"She disobeys me yet again," Eric said, a disgruntled growl rumbling deep in his chest.

Colin shrugged. "Return her to her father and demand one of her sisters in return."

Eric winced and sat back in his seat. "Even the devil does not deserve such punishment."

"Then what is it you plan to do?"

"Seek the truth."

Colin spoke low. "Will you be able to accept the truth?"

Eric did not answer. His glance caught his wife's hasty entrance and stayed steady upon her as she weaved her way around the trestle tables and benches to the dais. Rook, naturally, was right beside her.

Colin whispered near his ear. "The truth is wisdom in disguise."

Eric looked oddly at his friend.

"I am sorry, my lord," Faith said, breathless as she hurried around the dais and collapsed in the chair to the right of Eric.

Eric watched Rook make his nightly trip over to the servant girls who hovered nearby waiting to refill trenchers and tankards. They took pity on his ugly face and fed him enough for five men. He smiled, actually admiring the big dog's tactics.

Faith looked to his full trencher in disappointment. "You have already been served. Is there naught I can do for you?"

"Now there is an invitation I would not turn down," Colin whispered beside him.

"You would turn down no woman," Eric commented for his ears alone.

Colin turned an arrogant smile on him. "I would not dare deprive a woman of my exquisite charm and skillful touch."

"What of love?" Faith asked, startling both men.

Eric could have ordered her to mind her tongue—that the conversation was for Colin and him alone, and not a proper subject for a wife to discuss. But he wanted to hear her response to Colin's answer so he repeated her request. "Yes, Colin, what of love?"

"An elusive emotion, almost impossible to find."

Faith smiled and spoke as if instructing pupils. "You do not find love, love finds you."

Colin laughed. "Do you mean my chases have been for naught, and that love will strike me when I least expect it?"

"And from one you would never expect. 'Tis why the emotion is so elusive," Faith explained. "Many look in the wrong direction and lose their way when love is often right in front of them."

"How do you know of love?" Eric asked her.

Faith's smile turned serious. "I only know what I feel and love to me is not an emotion you can chase after or demand, it must be given freely, for only then can true love be known."

"I will remember your wise advice," Colin said. "And what about you, Lord Eric? What think you of love?"

Eric thought more of soundly thrashing his friend and the sharp look he sent him warned him to heed his taunting.

His wife waited patiently for his reply and would no doubt wait all evening until she received one. So he surrendered his opinion on a subject that sorely irritated him, more so lately than ever before. Another thought that irritated him all the more.

"Love is as fleeting as passion."

He had expected a stunned expression from her, but she simply nodded and gave his answer thought before expressing her opinion.

"I think love and passion sustain each other, blending together to form true love. Therefore, if passion is fleeting, then it lacks love."

Colin slapped Eric on the back. "You wed a wise woman."

Her words disturbed Eric more than he cared to admit and long after they left the great hall and he lay alone in his bed did her words haunt him.

Faith was summoned to Eric's solar early the next morning. She found him pacing the room, dressed in his usual red and black garb. She thought that he would not look so ominous if he dressed in brighter colors, but then, it was not her decision to make.

He gave her no salutation, but got straight to the matter. "The running of this keep is driving me insane. You are my wife and will assume your rightful duties."

It was on her lips to question him, ask if he meant for her to stay and remain his wife. But she wisely sought no answer. She would take what he gave with a grateful smile and continue to instruct the devil.

"As you wish, my lord."

He stopped pacing, his bold blue eyes upon her. "The cottage is yours to use as your healing place. But you will not spend all your time there. I wish for your presence to be known in the keep."

Her smile grew and she nodded. "Aye, my lord."

"And you will see that new garments are sewn for you." He grew tired of seeing her in the same few dresses. Her garments did not befit her new station.

"And you, my lord?"

"Me?"

"New garments. Would you not prefer a change of color on occasion?"

He glanced over himself. "These colors suit me."

Change was difficult for most, so she did not force the issue though she did suggest. "Perhaps more red in your garment for a change."

He shrugged. "Do as you wish, but the colors remain red and black. I will instruct the servants to pay you heed. And mind you, if there is any problem you are to come directly to me."

"Aye, my lord."

He stood staring at her for several moments before he continued. "I have decided that I no longer want you out of my sight."

His comment startled her.

"You have failed to obey my dictate and have caused me to fail to obey my dictate. Besides, it is better to keep one's adversary close."

"I am your adversary?" she asked softly.

"I have yet to decide," he replied firmly.

"I am not adept at battles."

He laughed. "This is not a battle, it is a mere skirmish."

She smiled with confidence. "Perhaps then I could win."

"A foolish thought."

"A possibility."

"The odds are against it."

"Because I am not a skilled warrior?"

He nodded. "Precisely."

"Then I will learn the way of the warrior."

"Courage, strength, tenacity," he recited.

"I possess them all," she said, elated.

"I have not finished."

She waited.

He spoke solemnly. "Bravery to do what *must* be done."

Would she be brave enough to walk away from him with her honor intact if she must, or would she surrender? And would he be brave enough to love her without his question being answered?

She ached to reach out and touch him, feel the warmth of his face, taste the fullness of his lips, but he had warned her and his warning had served well. She would not touch him.

She finally responded. "I do not know if I could do what must be done."

"Then you are not a warrior."

"No," she admitted. "I am a woman."

"That you are," he whispered with an ache that tore at her heart.

She definitely was no warrior, for at that moment the urge to surrender overwhelmed her and her only thought was to throw herself into his arms and demand he make love to her. However, her tenacity reared its persistent head and warned of the consequences. Her self-respect would suffer a loss and the skirmish had only begun.

It was time the devil met his match.

"Is that all, my lord?" she asked sweetly.

He looked at her strangely, his blue eyes more curious than lusty. "Aye, you may go."

Her hand was on the door latch when he asked, "Do you believe you would know love if you found it?"

Faith turned. "Yes, my lord, I would know without a doubt. Would you?"

She did not wait for his response. She turned and walked out of the solar, closing the door quietly behind her.

Why did he feel as though she had just scored a victory? He shook his head and his stern expression softened, his mouth spreading in a smile. At least now he was on familiar ground. He would approach all encounters with her as a skirmish. He would be prepared as he had been for all his battles. And he would be victorious, as he had been in all his battles.

He would have this matter between them settled before her father arrived and then when her father arrived he would settle it once and for all.

He suddenly felt elated and took himself off to the practice field.

Faith stopped by Borg's chambers after she had visited with the weavers and the women who tended to the sewing. She had given them specific instructions regarding the cloth that was to be made for Lord Eric's new garments, suggesting more red be added to his clothes and then detailed ones she wished made for herself, though she informed them that the embroidery would be done by Bridget.

She took time to speak with them and inquire as to their health and that of their families. The women relaxed and spoke freely with her. She promised to return with an herbal mixture for one woman who suffered from headaches and advised another that she would supply her with a paste that would remove the annoying wart on her hand. To their utter surprise she warned quite sternly that they were not to work themselves into exhaustion.

By the time she had bid them a pleasant day she had won their hearts and respect.

The door stood ajar and Faith listened, hearing Bridget's familiar though troubled tone.

"Do you care for me?" her voice demanded.

There was a momentary hesitation before Borg responded and Faith leaned in closer to hear. "I do. I told you I did."

"When you thought yourself dying you spoke, but now you say nothing?"

Faith could only imagine the giant's red face and she smiled, feeling sympathy for him, though credited Bridget with the tenacity to follow her heart.

"I-I-I am not good with words."

"I do not need a poet."

Another lapse of silence, and Faith strained harder to hear.

"I-I—" Borg stumbled over his words.

"I know what I want," Bridget said sharply and Faith pictured her standing near the bed, her hands firmly planted on her full hips, her rosy cheeks glowing and her green eyes steady on the shy giant.

Borg was able to speak but one word. "What?"

"I want you." Her voice softened. "I have since I first caught sight of you. My heart trembles when I am near you and aches when I am out of your sight."

Faith waited with bated breath for Borg's response, her own heart fluttering with excitement for the couple. That was why she was caught off guard when an arm slipped around her waist and a hand covered her mouth.

Fright raced through her.

Her husband's whispered voice comforted her. "Easy, it is me. You are safe."

He dropped his hand away from her mouth, though his arm remained firm around her waist. "You spy?" he asked, his voice low.

She tilted her head up to look at him and spoke in a whisper. "Bridget proclaims her feelings for Borg. I wait for his response."

Eric smiled and nodded and leaned toward the door with his wife.

"Come here, girl," Borg said in a tone that surprised Faith. It held no hesitation, but was confident and strong.

Eric whispered close to her ear. "He makes me proud."

She laughed softly and cautioned him to remain silent with a finger to her lips.

"I am not a man of many words."

"Honesty, a good way to start a relationship," Eric murmured and gave her waist a gentle yet possessive squeeze.

"Shhh," she scolded, her finger going to his lips this time.

His blue eyes blazed with such a sudden passion that Faith yanked her finger away as if it had been scorched. She returned her full attention to the couple, the flutters having rushed from her heart to rest low in her belly.

"It matters not, my mouth holds enough words for both of us," Bridget said and Borg laughed.

"I enjoy your endless chatter."

"Truly?"

"Truly," Borg said. "I could listen to you talk all day and never grow tired of a word you say."

"He may be sorry he said that," Eric whispered, and Faith jabbed her elbow in his ribs.

A nervous hesitancy filled Bridget's words. "You care for me?"

"I do."

"Do you not wish to know if I care for you?"

Faith grinned, the bold Bridget whom she was familiar with had returned, and along with her the shy giant.

"I-I-I—"

"Quiet, Viking," she ordered with a laugh. "You are to rest and get well and then I will show you how very much I care for you."

Faith wondered if this caring they spoke of was love. Neither had mentioned the word, and yet she felt certain the odd pair loved each other. But then Bridget was a servant and Borg a warrior. Could they ever truly unite?

She turned a frown on her husband.

"They will do well," he assured her quietly and tugged at her waist, silently instructing that she was to follow him—which she did.

They were descending the winding steps when he announced, "A traveling cleric has stopped at the castle. Do you wish to receive a blessing from him?"

Silence answered him and he turned curious eyes on her. She was deathly pale, to the point he thought she would pass out. He rushed up the few steps that separated them and wrapped protective arms around her.

"What is wrong?"

"I do not feel well," she said and buried her face against his chest.

He grew concerned and carefully scooped her up into his arms, feeling her body tremble. "I will take you to your chambers and summon Bridget to attend you."

"Do not disturb her. I need only to rest."

Her voice quivered and her body continued to tremble against his. He tightened his arms around her, his worry growing. His concern soared near out of control when he placed her on her bed and she grabbed at his hand.

"Please stay with me," she pleaded softly.

"I know not what to do," he admitted, feeling weak and inadequate for the first time in his life.

"A wet cloth on my forehead and your presence is all I need."

He nodded, finding cloth and water bowl on the small table in front of the hearth. He rinsed the linen square and before folding it to place on her forehead, he gently wiped her pale face. Once the cloth was in place he sat beside her on the bed and took her hand in his.

"Bridget would better serve you." He was fearful that she needed more attention than he could provide.

"Nay, my lord. It is you I need at the moment."

Her hand tightened around his.

He felt completely helpless. All he could do was lend the strength of his touch. "Are you in pain?"

She nodded and fought the tears that threatened her eyes. "My head pains me."

"Is there naught I can get you to diminish this pain?"

"Rest will see to its passing." She closed her eyes, her hand remaining firmly entrenched in his.

He kept his hand clamped tightly around hers. The protective pressure seemed to soothe her, for each time he loosened his hold, she grasped tighter to him. Her strange actions perplexed him. He was well aware of fear and what it could do to a person. He had seen it grab hold of many a soldier on the battlefield and he himself remembered his first confrontation with it. But he had learned to combat it and use it to his advantage.

Yet he never forgot the sickening feeling that had him retching and turning his face a deathly pale. He now saw that fear in Faith and could not understand the cause of it, but meant to find out.

Seventeen

Eric emitted a low rumbling growl as he walked through the great hall. If one more person sang his wife's praises he would strangle them. Her presence was now certainly known in the keep. The servants spoke of her as if she were a saint. To them she performed miraculous healings, always passed a pleasant word and forever wore a generous smile.

The last he had to agree with. Whenever his eyes lighted on her she was smiling. Whether she was busy cleaning and arranging her healing cottage, tending the soil in her garden or directing those in the keep, she always appeared cheerful and good-natured. And damned if it was not contagious. He had found the servants more civil and content since she took over the duties of running the keep. His own men even changed their attitude toward her, especially after Stuart had shared the secret of his renewed prowess with them.

Faith had teasingly informed him that she would need a large plot of soil just to grow mint and chamomile. He had found her tale amusing and had shared it with Colin. The next day he was stunned to find a large plot of land completely cleared and prepared for planting not far from her herb garden. His men had taken her remark seriously and saw to it that she got what she requested without delay.

The one incident that disturbed him the most, though, had happened just that very morning. He had grown annoyed waiting for his wife to join him for the morning fare. She was late as was her usual way, but for some reason her delay irritated him. If he had thought on it he would have realized that it was because he was anxious to see her. He had planned a tactical maneuver he thought would work well. He would ask her to join him on a ride to the lake. Once alone he intended to talk with her, hoping to discover more about her life at Donnegan Keep.

Unfortunately he had not known she had been attending an ailing peasant most of the night and when she rushed into the great hall appearing exhausted, he lost his temper. He had not meant to shout at her. He was annoyed she had worked herself to near exhaustion, but he had lost control of his emotions—a rare occurrence. He raised his voice at her demanding she obey him and she acquiesced with a respectful nod of her head. He had not been aware that the hall had grown silent and all eyes remained fixed upon them.

It took only minutes for him to realize that he had erred. All eyes looked with sympathy to the lady of the keep. Oddly enough, he had also realized at that moment that he had made a wise decision in taking her as a wife. That realization made the path to victory in their skirmish all the more clear and although the hall was filled with frowns, he smiled. Which annoyed the occupants all the more.

Now he intended to hunt down his wife and take her on that ride to the lake. He had ordered Mary to pack a basket with food. She appeared reluctant at first and while he did not have to share his intentions with her, he felt compelled to do so.

When she learned of his plans she spared no effort in producing a basket fit for a king and with a wide grin and a respectful bob of her head she handed the hefty basket to him.

The horses were set and all he needed now was to locate his wife. She was not in the keep. Bridget had no idea as to her whereabouts. The young woman barely left Borg's chambers and he made a mental note to secure Faith a new servant to see to her needs.

He marched out of the castle, those in his path moving out of his way as he stumped round the keep toward the healing cottage where Faith could usually be found.

He came upon an unlikely scene and if he had not seen it with his own eyes he would never have believed it. Two of his fiercest soldiers were busy helping his wife. One carried a chest into the cottage and another split wood, piling the pieces beside the front door for the coming winter. Rook lounged near the door, chewing on a big fat bone the size of his paw.

Chattering women's voices could be heard from within and Eric grew all the more annoyed that all seemed to be having a delightful time. That came to an abrupt halt as soon as his presence became known.

The men gave a respectful nod and Rook barked once and thumped his tail to announce his arrival and to welcome him. When he entered the cottage all chatter came to a sudden pause and the three women helping Faith to tie bunches of herbs together for drying immediately took their leave.

He was pleased to see that his wife wore newly sewn garments, a deep green shift of the softest wool and a tunic of a lighter shade. The pale yellow trim was embroidered by a skilled hand that could only have been accomplished by Bridget, and her belt matched the trim and was tied tightly enough to show off the slimness of her waist.

She looked beguiling and he wondered about the wisdom of his plans.

"My lord," she said, and waited for him to make the reason for his unexpected presence known.

That added to his irritation. He did not need a reason to approach his wife. And yet she made it seem that he only sought her out for a particular reason.

"You will come with me," he ordered.

She appeared startled by his curt command. "As you wish."

Tongues wagged as she followed him along the castle grounds. Eyes watched their approach with trepidation and whispers trailed them as the lady of the keep fought to keep in step with her husband's determined gait. And as the couple drew more and more attention, the devil's temper grew.

He stopped at the stables and signaled the guard to bring his stallion.

Eric mounted the mighty horse with ease and then he leaned down, grasped her under the arm and lifted her to sit across his lap. He loosened the gold brooch on his red-and-black wool cloak and wrapped the warm cloth around the both of them. He then turned the horse and galloped toward the open doors and portcullis of the gatehouse.

Murmuring gossip filled the castle grounds and did not settle down until long after the lord and his lady had disappeared from sight.

"You have kidnapped me, my lord," she teased with a smile and a snuggle against his hard chest.

"What other way would I be able to speak with you?"

Faith ignored his irritated tone and the fact that he only wished to talk. His sensual blue eyes told another story, but she would ignore his passion as best she could. She had determined that the next intimate touch they shared would be of his choice and the consequences of his doing.

"The weather has chilled considerably," she said, making minor conversation and enjoying the flowing warmth that his large body extended to hers.

"Winter fast approaches."

She felt the tenseness ease a bit from his taut muscles and continued on. "I see the fields have harvested a hardy supply and are ready for the winter rest."

"We will not starve."

"All celebrate the full harvest and look forward to a time of rest."

"There is still work to do."

She agreed with excitement. "Yes, many speak of the new weapons that will be forged and the cloth that will be weaved and the hunting that will be enjoyed and"—she paused in reluctance before proceeding cautiously—"and the children that will be sired."

Eric spoke not a word. News of expected summer births were frequent as of late and each time he heard of another babe to be born his thoughts turned to his wife. With his passion running near out of control, he doubted it would take him long to get her with child. And that surely pleased him.

He wondered often why he stopped himself from intimately knowing his wife and the answer was always the same. Could he live with the consequences of his lusty actions? He hoped to uncover the answer soon. It was one of the reasons why he sought this time with her. He felt that if he could get her to talk of the attack he might better understand the results. And in so doing have his answer.

"Where are you taking me?" she asked, peering out from the cloak that partially covered her face. "'Tis beautiful land."

"Aye, that it is," Eric agreed and slowed his horse to a steady gait.

"When I was a little girl the woman who tended me told me that Ireland was created by magical fairies and that was why the land was so beautiful. To this day I believe her for when I look upon meadows flowing with a preponderance of wildflowers and land covering so green that it startles the eye, I think that only fairies could produce such magical beauty."

Eric smiled with such sincerity that it stilled her heart. "The Irish are the best storytellers. My own mother kept me spellbound on winter nights with tales of the celtic gods."

"Druid tales," she whispered, as if fearful.

"You should hear the tales of the Viking gods," he said with a laugh.

"Fierce and mighty warriors, from what I hear told."

"The fiercest," he said, looking down on her sternly.

She giggled.

"You dare to laugh at a Viking?" he said, his own voice filled with laughter.

Her expression turned serious. "You are Ireland's son."

"Why say you that?"

Her answer came easily. "You were born on Irish soil. One born here is always Ireland's son or daughter. You possess the blood of hundreds of generations who have fought for the soil of this great land. You can no more deny your heritage than your right to breath. You are Ireland, as am I."

Eric was speechless. If he had any doubts that Ireland was his home, his wife had just dispelled them. He had never felt so much a part of this land as she had just made him feel. His chest swelled with pride for his long-lost heritage and for the woman he had chosen to wed.

"Do you know why Irish lakes sparkle?"

"No," he said, and waited anxiously to hear her tale.

"The fairies sprinkle their dust over them every hundred years or so."

"The woman who cared for you told you this?"

"Aye, she did and she told me if I wanted to see a fairy I should sit very still and watch and I just might catch a glimpse of one. I tried very hard to do as she directed; I did so want to see one."

Eric's smile broadened. "I cannot see you sitting still for long."

She poked him in the chest. "Neither could my caretaker."

They both laughed as Eric brought his horse to a halt near a lake that sparkled and shimmered with such beauty that for a moment he believed in fairies.

He wrapped a secure arm around her and lowered her carefully to the ground and then he dismounted. He tethered the horse to a nearby tree and reached for the basket and dark wool blanket that had been strapped to the side.

Her brown expressive eyes widened in delight. "You planned this."

He hastily amended her comment. "I took measures that would ensure that my wife was on time for a meal."

Faith snatched the blanket from beneath his arm and walked nearer to the lake. "We should sit close to the lake so we can look for fairies."

"Think you can sit still long enough?"

She smiled at his teasing, noticing that the tension had eased from his body and his manner. "I can try."

He left the basket on the ground and returned to his horse while she spread the blanket. He returned with her brown wool cloak, which had seen better days.

"Bridget tells me this is all you have for warmth."

She took it from him, draping it around her shoulders, the sun bright but the air crisp. "It serves well enough."

"Have the weavers make you a cloth of my colors and direct the women to fashion a cloak and a shawl," he ordered firmly, assuring she would obey his command.

She nodded, though she appeared more concerned with the full basket. She soon had the generous fare spread and quickly went to work slicing two thick pieces of the warm black bread and spreading each piece with a soft cheese liberally laced with parsley.

There were slices of cold mutton, sweet bread, berries and two flasks of wine. The fare was more than two people could eat, but having barely touched her morning meal, Faith found herself ravenous and ate with relief and pleasure.

"This is a beautiful spot. Do you come here often?" she asked.

"My time at my home has been sorely limited and when here

I am busy seeing to the building and fortification of the castle.
I did, however, have the opportunity to swim in the lake a few
times this past summer."

"You swim?"

"A necessity for a Viking."

"I have heard Viking ships are a sight to behold."

He popped a berry in his mouth. "Who tells you this?"

"As I told you once before many thought me a mere servant,
especially visitors to Donnegan Keep. All knew Lady Terra
held no interest in healing and those who required my skill
thought me a healer secured by the lord to tend his peasants."

"So they spoke freely in front of you."

"More often than not. A sizable merchant required my aid in
soothing an ailing stomach and spoke incessantly about his
travels as I tended him. He is the one who talked of the beauty
and craftsmanship of the Viking sailing vessels. He bragged
about trading with Viking merchants."

"We are a skillful lot," he boasted proudly, but turned the
talk to her wondering over her freedom at Donnegan Keep.
"Did not your father restrict your duties?"

Her smile was painfully sad. "My father cared not where I
went as long as I stayed from his sight. He did not wish for my
presence to embarrass him."

"So he simply gave you free rein?" he asked, incredulously.

She bowed her head and toyed with the red berries in her
hand.

What sorrowful memories so haunted her that they gave her
pause to speak? He wanted desperately for her to share her hurt
with him so he could understand her pain, and he wanted just
as badly to help rid her of it.

She looked at him, her wild red hair a perfect frame for her
beauty and his blood began to heat.

"At first, right after the attack, my father insisted I stay
within the confines of the keep itself. But my presence unnerved my stepmother and I soon found myself given a small
cottage within the castle grounds far removed from the keep. If
it were not for my interest in healing I think I would have gone
mad from the loneliness. But I busied myself with studies and
planting a garden of my own."

At least he understood why her body was in such good physical shape. Physical labor kept it toned, and he advised himself to allow her to continue to cultivate her own garden.

"When my skill as a healer grew, so did my acquaintances. I had no true friends. The peasants could not befriend me; after all, I was Lady Faith to them and I was ordered not to participate in any keep gathering. Bridget spoke with me the most, but then I think a special bond was formed between us the night of my attack. She helped to tend me afterwards and up until the time I could finally tend myself."

Important information he would not forget. "She was good to you."

"She was good and she was comforting, her voice being the only soft and reassuring one I heard."

Thoughts of how she must have suffered plagued Eric and made him even more anxious to get his hands on her father. It amazed him that with all she had been through, she had not only survived her ordeal, but had grown stronger and more courageous.

"Did your father have the castle grounds searched immediately following the attack?"

Faith shook her head. "I do not remember much of what followed except for my stepmother warning me to keep my lies to myself."

The passion in his blue eyes turned to anger and he controlled the fury he felt rising within him. "Lies?"

Faith hesitated and he could sense her discomfort. He reached his hand out, taking hers firmly in his. "We do not need to speak of this."

She looked at him with eyes that begged for understanding. "I spoke no lies that night. The truth is what I told, but perhaps it was not what they wished to hear."

He moved beside her and took her in his arms. "I believe you."

She laughed softly and tugged on a strand of his long, dark hair. "The devil believes me."

He pushed her hair away from her face, purposely exposing her scar. "Nay, Faith, *your husband* believes you."

The stormy anger in his blue eyes had subsided and where usually she saw passion she now saw a depth of caring that touched her heart and made her care all the more for the dark lord.

A cloud covering drifted overhead and with it a sudden chill wind whipped around them. She shivered and his arms tightened around her, hugging her to his warmth. She felt safe and protected in his arms. He would allow no harm to befall her. He would forever protect her, care for her. But could he love her?

With time, perhaps that was possible. But was her time with the Irish devil limited? Suddenly she wanted to know.

"I wish to ask you a question, my lord?"

He pressed a finger to her lips and his words sounded more like a warning. "But do you wish to hear the answer?"

Did she really want to know? Did she want to hear that her time with him was limited, that she would not see her garden flourish in the spring or birth her own babe in the summer?

He ran his finger over her thin lips. "What say you?"

She wanted this time with him. A time to know him, a time to understand him and a time to make memories.

Her answer came with a smile. "Teach me how to fish."

He laughed, a full hearty laugh, and with a glint of mischief in his eyes, said, "If you will look for fairies with me."

She completely lost her heart to him at that very moment. God help her, but she loved the *devil*.

Eighteen

Borg was finally up and about, feeling his usual self and enjoying his renewed freedom. However, his physical exercise was sorely restricted and though it irritated him that he could not practice with his sword or bow, he took enjoyment in watching the men go through their daily practice routine.

Eric, Colin and Borg sat on a blanket on a patch of ground near the exercise field, watching the men combat each other. Flasks of ale and wine sat beside them, as did food, though the three men had eaten their fill and were now basking in the contentment of full stomachs and satisfied palettes.

"Do you love her?" Colin asked, turning to look at Borg. "And do not try and deny it, since we already know the answer."

Red heat crept up his neck and rushed to sting his cheeks.

"I knew it," Colin said with a grin and a slap to his knee.

"Leave the besotted man to his suffering," Eric said, joining in the good-natured teasing.

"Huh, he is not the only one besotted," Colin said with a poke of his elbow to Borg's arm.

Borg joined in the fun. "He is right about that."

Eric refused to be intimidated. "You think me in love?"

"You think not?" Colin laughed. "You sniff after your wife like a stallion ready to mount."

"That is not love," Eric corrected him.

Colin draped his arm over Eric's shoulder. "No, my friend, it is not. If it is a lusty bedding you but wish for, you could have quenched that fleeting passion with any willing wench. I think you look for more. I think your pride stands in the way of love."

Borg grunted in agreement.

"Pride?" Eric repeated.

"Pride," Colin and Borg said in unison.

Colin reached for the flask of ale and handed it to Eric. "Your wife has won the hearts of many. They speak of her with love and respect and condemn you when you raise your temper against her. And have you yourself not come to better understand her?"

"The whole castle speaks of the lord and lady and how they sleep in separate chambers. They fear that Lady Faith will be sent away, that the Irish devil does not desire her," Borg said.

"Who speaks such nonsense?" Eric demanded.

"Gossip." Borg shrugged.

"Utter nonsense. Faith is going nowhere. Her home is here," Eric said. "Tell that to the gossips."

Colin shook his head slowly. "They have heard the news that Lord Donnegan is on his way to Shanekill Keep and they think he comes to take his daughter home."

"His journey has been delayed, his wife is ill," Eric confirmed. "Though I trust him not. It is but a ruse to delay meeting with me. But it gives me time."

"Time for what?" Colin asked.

Eric grinned. It was the grin of the devil. "To win my skirmish."

Colin raised his hands to the heavens. "A rich man I will be."

"Another wager?" Eric asked.

"A certain win," Colin grinned.

Borg grunted. "A fool he is and a poor one at that he will be."

A serious fight broke out on the practice field, catching their attentions.

"See to it," Eric ordered Colin. "And make certain both are punished. I will not have my soldiers fighting each other."

Colin advanced on the squabbling pair with a roar.

Eric kept his attention on Colin, while he spoke with Borg. "Bridget talks with you often?"

Borg laughed and this time he did not need to hold his side. "She forever chatters, but I enjoy the sound of her lilting voice."

"Does she speak of the attack on Faith?" Eric asked and turned to face his half brother.

Borg shook his head. "Nay, of that she had never spoken."

"Faith tells me that Bridget tended her right after the attack."

"That I would believe. She worries about Faith and sometimes I catch a glimpse of sadness in her eyes when she speaks of her even though she is singing her praises."

"I think Faith hides something about the attack, something that she does not wish to admit."

"That is understandable," Borg said. "The scar she carries proves the viciousness of the attack and perhaps the insanity of the attacker."

"Do you think Bridget would speak of it to me?" Eric asked.

"I am not certain. While she may fear the devil, she loves Lady Faith and would want to do her no harm. You could command her to."

Eric shook his head. "No, I do not want her to think she speaks with the Irish devil; I want her to know it is a concerned husband who requests the information."

"A wise choice," Borg said and pointed his finger toward the keep. "You have your chance; ask wisely."

Bridget was walking toward them.

"You will stay," Eric all but ordered. "She will feel safe with you around."

"I will be relieved when she finally feels safe around the devil," Borg said with a grunt and smiled as Bridget drew near.

"My lord," Bridget said and lowered her head. "My lady requested that I see if there was anything else you required."

Eric realized that Bridget did indeed fear him. She rarely looked him directly in the eyes, her glance always being slightly averted. He edged the sternness from his deep voice and while his timbre sounded far from gentle, it did not sound threatening. "I require a few moments of your time."

Borg extended a hand to her. "Sit beside me."

She gladly obliged him since Borg provided protection from the devil.

Eric purposely kept his eyes from hers and spoke as he watched Colin in the distance deal with the two angry men. "I

speak as a concerned husband and not as the lord of this keep."
He did not wait for a response or expect one. "Faith has told me
that you tended her the night of her attack. While I do not wish
you to betray her trust, I do ask you to tell me something of that
night."

He kept his focus on the practice field and waited.

Borg encouraged and assured her with a gentle squeeze of
her hand.

Bridget spoke softly, her voice more of a whisper, and both
men listened with interest. "I was summoned by Lady Terra to
see to Lady Faith. She lay deathly pale in her bed, the bedcov-
ering soaked through with her blood. Lady Terra ordered me to
do what I could since none expected her to survive the night. I
was to clean her up and sit with her and . . ."

Her voice faltered and Eric knew she fought back tears. He
said nothing and waited patiently.

Her voice was more stable when she continued, "Wait for
death to claim her."

Eric's chest tightened, as did his fist at his side. To think that
Faith had lain helpless, bleeding while her family waited for her
to die filled him with such rage that he wanted to lash out at
someone, that someone being her father.

"If it were not for Lady Faith herself, she surely would have
died."

That brought a turn of his head. "Why?"

She looked at him then and though her voice quivered she
held her head up with pride. "It was she who instructed me as
to what to do for her care. She lay in pain and near to death and
told me what must be done and how I possessed the skill to do
the task."

Eric remained silent and listened, his fist tight and his heart
aching.

Bridget took a deep breath before proceeding. "It was late
and all had left the room, Lady Terra instructing me to wait with
Lady Faith until death took her. Finally, when only I remained
did Lady Faith speak of what must be done. She lay so very
quiet while I cleansed her wounds as she directed and then she
instructed me how to prepare the needles for stitching."

Eric interrupted. "Did she not direct you to give her what
she gave to Borg so she would not feel the needle's pain so
greatly?"

Bridget held back her tears. "She could not. She had to remain alert so she could instruct me as I worked."

Eric raised his face to the heavens, shutting his eyes and emitting a low, ominous growl that brought the shivers to Bridget and even to Borg. He then turned to Bridget and waited.

She continued without delay. "The wound was long and I worried that I would not work fast enough. Lady Faith told me not to concern myself with the time it took me, that the bleeding had subsided and the wound now needed stitches to keep it closed and to help it heal. She instructed me to make my stitches small and tight." Bridget paused and wiped at a traitorous tear. "It took me an hour and over a hundred stitches to close the wound."

She stopped then, unable to continue.

"You did well," Borg said and slipped his arm around her shoulders to draw her near.

"Nay," she cried through her falling tears. "'Tis Lady Faith who did well. She did not scream, did not shed a tear, she simply continued to tell me what a gentle hand I possessed and how grateful she was to me for my help."

Eric stood, knowing Bridget was best left to the care of Borg and he himself needed time alone. "Thank you, Bridget, for sharing that with me." He turned to leave.

"My lord," Bridget called and he turned. "There is one thing that has troubled me about that night."

"Tell me," he encouraged.

"Lady Terra ordered the priest to bless Lady Faith, vanquishing her sins. I was ordered from the room but not before I saw the priest approach the bed and heard Lady Faith scream out for God to help save her from the devil."

"Why did that trouble you?"

She appeared almost reluctant to speak and with an encouraging nudge from Borg she continued. "Lady Terra told everyone that Lady Faith's own words condemned her. That she spoke of the devil within her and finally begged for God's mercy."

"You did not see it that way?" Eric asked.

Bridget shook her head. "Nay, I saw the fear in Lady Faith's eyes and knew she spoke of actually seeing the devil. She believed he was in her room."

Eric reached out and patted the girl's hand that Borg held. "Again, thank you. You have been most helpful."

Eric left the couple then, sending Borg a knowing nod that told him they would speak of this later. He walked past the practice field toward the keep, but veered off toward the cottage where he thought to find Faith. He felt the need to hold her, simply hold her safely in his arms.

She was not there, though he paused to give the place a glance. She had fashioned a warm and welcoming home for herself and he felt an empty ache inside. Her intentions were suddenly obvious. A large wooden chest sat against one wall with a row of pegs above it for hanging garments. A table and two chairs were centered in the room and a single chair with a soft tapestry cushion sat cornered by the hearth. A single bed was dressed with fresh linens and a blue wool blanket lay folded at the foot. A sweet scented wreath made of colorful flowers and herbs lay on the pillow and another scented wreath hung over the door. A rack with drying herbs stood between hearth and bed and the table was neatly arranged with the tools of her trade. There was even a thick rush mat near the bed for Rook.

This was to be her home if he refused to commit to their marriage vows. She did not wish to return to her family. Why should she? They cared naught for her, but here the people loved her and she them.

He growled again, a low agitated snarl, and stormed out of the cottage.

The dark lord was a sight to behold. He stormed into the great hall, his scowling face, blazing blue eyes, long dark hair and black garments that possessed but a trace of red making it appear as if the devil himself had just risen from the recesses of hell. Servants scurried for cover; workmen hurried out of his way, keeping their eyes from him; and the flames in the hearth even cowered as he rushed past them toward the kitchen.

Chatter ceased and faces paled when he entered.

"My wife?" he asked of a trembling Mary.

"I have not seen her, my lord."

He turned and left, heading back through the hall toward the steps when Faith called out to him.

"You have frightened the servants."

He turned and descended the two steps he had taken up the

stairway and ignored her remark to say, "Where were you?" He took one look at Rook who was licking his mouth most joyously and said, "Wait, do not tell me. You were berry picking."

Faith patted the dog's head and smiled. "Rook was picking berries. I was foraging for herbs."

He approached her slowly, sending scathing looks to any servant who remained in the hall. They all fled in haste. "You left the castle without my permission?"

"Nay, my lord, you were busy on the exercise field and I did not wish to disturb you so I told Colin I wished to forage in the nearby woods."

Colin had not spoken a word of this to him and knowing Colin would never permit her to leave the castle grounds unattended, he asked, "Who did Colin instruct to go with you?"

"Stuart volunteered to accompany me."

Stuart was one of his largest and fiercest warriors. He had charged into the worst melees and had always managed to emerge with nothing more than a scratch. The men thought him indomitable and since Faith had healed him and returned his prowess to him there was naught he would not do for her, even if it meant foraging in the woods for herbs.

Knowing her plan to remain here as healer, he suddenly resented the time she spent away from the keep and from him. She was putting a distance between them and he did not like it.

"Do you neglect your duties in the keep while you tarry in the woods?"

She was not at all affronted by his remark; she simply smiled. "Nay, my lord, I see to all my duties before I tarry in the woods."

She teased him and he grew annoyed, stopping before he drew too close to her. "There is a duty you have failed to see to."

"And what duty is that, my lord?"

She addressed him formally in order to irritate, and she was succeeding, though he was about to outmaneuver her.

"You have not seen to my wound."

"You are wounded?" she asked with concern.

His grin was purely carnal. "I speak of the one you tended to at Donnegan Keep."

She realized his game now and pursued her own course of attack. He would be the one who surrendered, not her. She would not touch him out of want. He must be the one to want, touch, submit.

"It is not healed?" she asked.

"I am not certain. You told me you would see to its care and failed to do so."

"You ordered me from your sight," she reminded.

His heated blue eyes remained steady on her. "Now I order you to finish what you started."

Faith hesitated. Her healing basket was in her cottage, to which she was reluctant to return, remembering what had occurred there between them. He, however, had a different idea.

"Let us go to your healing cottage, where you can *properly* attend me."

She could not deny his request; he was her husband—yet she wondered how safe it was for her to be alone with him. Not only because of what he might do, but because of her own reckless desire for him. Who would finally win this skirmish?

"As you wish, my lord," she said and turned and walked toward the door. He did not directly follow her. He waited several heart-pounding moments, and then he caught up with her.

She remained silent on the short walk to the cottage, his presence looming so largely over her that she felt a chill from the shadow he cast. She was not surprised when he ordered Rook to remain outside the cottage. The big dog obeyed dutifully, finding a comfortable spot nearby to rest.

Faith lit several candles, many along the mantel and two on the table as soon as she entered the lone room. She was glad she did, for the room darkened considerably when Eric shut the door after himself.

"Sit," she ordered, pulling out a chair from the table and fighting to calm her trembling hands.

"Do you not *want* me to remove my clothes?"

His deep voice was pure seduction, from the emphasis on "want" to the softness of "clothes." He was tempting her in ways she found hard to ignore. She realized then that he had no intention of laying a hand on her. His words would do the suggesting . . . and she? She would do the damage.

"I only need the wound area exposed," she said as calmly as her racing heart would allow.

She fussed with the items on the table, attempting to keep herself busy and her eyes off him while he removed part of his clothing. She did not expect to find his wound in need of care and it would take but a second to examine the area and be done with it.

She heard him sit in the chair and without hesitation she turned, wanting this to be over and done as quickly as possible. His legs were bare and the bottom of his tunic kept him from being fully exposed to her.

She breathed a sigh of relief and knelt before him, her fingers grazing the area that was so nicely healed one could barely determine the origin of the wound. She did not trust herself to press or probe his warm skin. Her fingers were already heated from the faint touch of him. And knowing what the tunic concealed only made the task more difficult. She had discovered she liked her husband's body and while she was not completely familiar with it, what she had seen and touched impressed and enticed her and she wished to explore him further.

"This reminds me of the first time I laid eyes on you."

His words startled her and she wanted this finished before she regretted her actions. "I tended you well then; the wound has healed nicely."

His curious remark kept her kneeling between his legs. "I wondered how your touch would be."

"I was gentle—"

He did not allow her to finish. "Not your healing touch; your intimate touch."

She could avoid his eyes no longer. She raised her dark eyes to his.

His words suggested and his sensual blue eyes promised. "While your hands tended my wound, I wondered how those same delicate hands would feel if they stole up beneath the towel and cupped me intimately."

Words escaped her and her senses betrayed her, stirring her passion to a fever pitch. His remark was purposeful, placing a vivid and suggestive thought in her mind—a thought that was hard to ignore and control. Her hands simply itched to do his bidding.

"What were your thoughts of me when first we met?"

Her reply came easily. "I thought you arrogant."

"You thought me handsome."

"I thought you foolish."

He grinned wickedly. "You wanted me."

"Nay."

"Liar," he accused with a laugh.

"I did not wa—"

"Do not deny the truth," he said. "I am familiar enough with the ways of women to know when a woman wants me. You wanted me then as you want me now."

She hastily looked down, away from his accusing eyes.

A mistake. A big mistake.

His arousal was obvious from the rise of his tunic.

"Did you grow wet then . . ." He paused abruptly as if allowing her time to recall, and she did.

Memories of that night flooded her mind and she remembered the odd reaction she had at the first sight of him. She had thought him handsome, his body in fine shape and she had—good lord, she had grown moist thinking about him.

She raised wide, incredulous eyes to him.

"As you do now?" he finally finished on a soft groan.

Only then did she realize that her hand had been faintly stroking his leg and had slowly inched closer and closer to the edge of his tunic. Shocked by her actions, she yanked her hand away and fell to her backside.

"A repeat performance," he laughed and leaned forward. "Only this time the outcome will not find you rushing out of the room."

She glared at him and spoke with a defiance that was hard to ignore. "What do you want from me, Eric?"

"Touch me," he all but ordered.

She shook her head most reluctantly while keeping her hands firmly clasped together, fearing they would betray her and do as he directed. "You warned me of the consequences."

"Consequences be damned. Touch me," he said, finishing on an angry whisper.

She was about to deny him with another shake of her head when he asked, "Do you not want to touch me, Faith?"

Did she deny the obvious? Could she tell him nay when all she wished, all she ached for, all she wanted to do was reach out and do as he had suggested—slip her hand beneath his tunic and touch him.

"Come on my little adversary—surrender," he urged. "Touch me."

She smiled then, a wicked little smile, and while he thought it capitulation on her part, she thought it a grand maneuver on hers. She would most certainly touch him, but the *dark lord* would be the one to surrender.

She got off her backside, up on her knees and ran her hands ever so slowly along his thighs, and whispered softly, "As you wish, my lord."

Nineteen

Eric closed his eyes and took a deep breath, steeling himself against the exquisite torment of her delicate touch. He was not a young boy incapable of control. And though he had lost control once with Faith, he would not do so again. He would maintain command of this situation. He would demand, he would instruct and she would surrender.

"Look at me, Eric, please?" she pleaded with a pout. "I love your blue eyes. Their vivid color reminds me of the sky just before a storm."

He did as she asked—it was such a simple request, after all.

She sighed with pleasure when his glance fell upon her and she continued in a lazy crawl up his thighs to the edge of his tunic and stopped.

He questioned her actions with a stern look.

Her fingers toyed with the deep red trim on the ends of his dark tunic and she released a long sigh. "I fear I am not certain how to proceed. Should my touch be light, or do you prefer it rough?"

If he were in command of his senses he would have realized she had thrown his own words back at him—the ones he spoke when first had they met. But being consumed with the anticipation of her fingers upon his already heated flesh, his thoughts were not of one in command, but one near to surrender.

"Whichever you favor," he said confidently.

Her dark, determined eyes remained steady on his blue ones as her fingers slowly stole beneath his tunic. "Gentle, I think." And her fingers tenderly cupped him until he rested full in her hand.

He shut his eyes against the pure, maddening pleasure of her intimate touch. Her fingers were cool and she softly squeezed, eagerly stroked and faintly rubbed his loins until they hardened in her hand.

"My lord, your eyes," she pleaded like a spoiled child. "I want to see your eyes."

He could not deny her, especially since her hand was moving to capture his aroused manhood.

The potency of his desire blazed in the blue of his eyes and she smiled as she roughly grabbed full hold of him. "Rough now," she whispered harshly and his eyes widened in surprise as her hand took full and complete control of him.

She massaged, stroked and aroused him to such a maddening hardness that he thought he would go insane.

He almost flew out of the chair. He had not expected this from her. He had thought she would remain shy and meek, then suddenly like a bolt of lightning from hell he realized her intentions, and at that moment she realized the warring Irish devil had returned full force.

He leaned forward and her hand stilled upon his throbbing flesh. "You think to play with the devil?"

She paled, the look in his eyes one she had never seen before and hoped never to see again. If this was the look he took into battle then she understood why no one ever defeated him.

His eyes held no mercy.

He was out of the chair in a flash. He grasped her beneath the arms, dangling her in thin air in front of him before she had a chance to take a breath.

"Now it is my turn to play," he said with a smile that promised retribution and sent shivers racing through her. He walked, holding her out in front of him as if she were nothing more than a sack of grain.

He tossed her on the bed and as she heard the crunch of the thick straw beneath her she also heard his query. "Gentle or rough?"

He did not wait for an answer and she thought he cared not whether she gave one. He hastily shoved her shift and tunic up and out of the way and as he descended down upon her she heard him say, "Gentle, for now."

Faith cried out when his tongue stroked her. She had not given thought to a husband demanding such intimacy from his wife and if given time to think on it she might have feared such a strange union, but with his skilled and determined tongue taking complete command and giving her such pure pleasure she could think of nothing else.

His tongue flicked across her in short, rapid darts, sending shivers straight through her; and then his strokes turned lazy, crawling intimately over her until she thought she would go mad. Her hands gripped the bed linen and she bit at her bottom lip to stop herself from screaming. Until she could stand it no more, and his name rushed pleadingly from her lips. "Eric."

He raised his head, looked at her and warned with a smile. "Rough now."

"Nay," she screamed just before his tongue dove into her.

Madness engulfed her; she lost complete rational thought. Her only concern was of surrendering to her husband fully and unconditionally.

"Eric, please," she cried, a single tear slipping down her cheek.

His response was to drive her further to madness.

Her cries turned to sobs of anguish mixed with pleasure.

Eric raised himself to look at her and spoke with the roughness of a warrior bent on victory. "Tell me you want me."

She thought to deny him, briefly, hesitantly, and he laughed.

"Damn you." She cursed him in a raspy breath.

He flicked his tongue over her swollen nub, causing her to shiver and she cursed him again, and then he grinned. "The devil is already damned. Now surrender and tell me you want me and I will give you the climax your body craves."

She bit on her lower lip to control the trembling. He was to surrender, not her. How had she allowed this to happen?

"Tell me," he demanded and teased her with another flick of his wickedly skillful tongue.

She shivered yet again but remained silent. She wanted him—there was no doubt of that—but surrender? Did she really wish to surrender to the devil? Did she not want that from him? Was it not important for him to admit he wanted her and not just out of lust, but because he truly cared for her?

Or was she simply being a fool? If that be true, then surrender was not possible.

"Nay," she said with difficulty.

"Tell me," he ordered and stroked her intimately with his finger. "Tell me."

He repeated the words over and over, her head ringing with his incessant command as his fingers took the place of his tongue. She bit at her lip and fought to control her raging passion, fought the urge to scream out her surrender, fought the panic as she realized just how much she loved the dark lord.

"Nay! Nay!"

"Damn you," he said and with his tongue proceeded to bring her to an exploding climax that had her screaming out his name.

By the time she regained her senses he was standing over the bed fully clothed. He leaned over her, bracing his hands on either side of her head and said with a determined anger, "Next time, wife, we end this madness."

The great hall was in its usual state of chaotic pleasure that evening. Everyone was enjoying the food, drink and merriment, bringing the day to a pleasant close. Colin and Eric were deep in conversation with a group of men standing not far from the large hearth. The nights had turned colder and the flames chased the chill that seeped and drifted through the keep.

Faith toyed with her trencher of food, feeling isolated amongst all the gaiety. Her mind was much too cluttered with serious thoughts to give concern to those around her. Those ponderous thoughts had haunted her since her husband had fled her cottage in angry haste.

Ever since her arrival at the keep several weeks ago she had studied her husband with interest. He was not one to waste words, emotions or actions. Everything he did was based on careful consideration and deliberate action and yet he had constantly lost complete control around her, rushing his words, his emotions and his actions—beginning with their first encounter.

Love, true love, often caused people to act out of character. Could he truly love her? Or was she being a foolish woman who ached to be loved?

Bridget had informed her that Eric could have availed himself of any number of willing wenches since his return home and yet he had sought out none. Could his fondness for his wife have prevented him looking elsewhere?

Or was she but daydreaming?

"Your thoughts are heavy?" Borg asked, sitting in the empty seat beside her.

"You are not overtaxing yourself, are you?" she asked with concern.

He laughed heartily and it was good to see that he did not wince or hold his wound in pain. "Bridget watches me like a hawk and swoops down on me if she thinks I am doing the slightest thing to harm myself."

"She cares for you."

"That she does, and I care for her. We know that, the whole keep knows it . . . but you have yet to respond to my question."

Faith attempted a smile, but failed. Her heart was just as heavy as her thoughts. "Much troubles me of late."

"Have you spoken of this worry to your husband?"

"He is my worry," she admitted freely, feeling comfortable in discussing Eric with Borg.

"Tell me," he said seriously. "I will attempt to help you."

She placed the knife she held in the trencher and then pushed it aside, not hungry for food, but starving for a sense of understanding concerning her dilemma. "Do you think Eric capable of truly loving a woman?"

Borg answered honestly. "I think Eric does not give much thought to love and therefore has trouble comprehending its meaning."

"He does not recognize love?"

Borg shook his head. "He is a warrior educated in conquering. He approaches everything he does as if in a battle or skirmish, the end results always being the same."

"Victory," Faith finished with a smile.

"Now you begin to understand him."

She sighed, exasperated. "But I am not skilled in battle techniques. How do I conquer a adept warrior when I am so inept?"

Borg laughed softly. "Surrender."

She was startled and disappointed by his advice. "I cannot."

"Cannot or will not?"

She laid a gentle hand on Borg's arm. "My husband must understand how difficult surrender is for me. I fought so hard to live and then to survive and finally to live again. I did not crawl away and pity myself; instead I fought back and refused to submit to defeat. I discovered a strength and courage I never thought possible and I cannot or will not surrender."

Borg placed his large hand over her small one. "When a warrior enters a battle he knows it will either end in victory or defeat. But there are a few rare warriors who understand that on uncommon occasions victory can only be won through surrender. And those brave warriors never actually taste defeat."

She stared at him strangely.

"What you refuse to surrender is what will make you victorious."

Faith's eyes widened and her smile was generous as understanding dawned. "You believe me a virgin."

"I have no doubt, and if my brother were not so stubborn and foolish he would know the truth for himself. But his Irish pride gets in the way."

She laughed. "Vikings are not stubborn?"

Borg grinned. "A Viking stubborn? We do not need to be. We know everything."

Faith's laughter trickled away and her expression turned solemn. "Do you think then that the Irish devil could love me?"

Borg leaned closer and spoke softly for their ears alone. "Eric fought for what he wanted most in his life. If he did not fight, then he did not find it important enough to him to matter. He fights now for you."

"For me?" she asked with surprise. "But who does he fight?"

"He fights the most dangerous opponent he has ever faced. One he may not be able to conquer."

Faith shivered and rubbed her arms. "Who? There is no one to stand in his way. No one would fight for me."

Borg whispered as if he should not speak the name. "The Irish devil."

"Himself?" she asked incredulously.

Borg nodded. "And he refuses to admit why he fights so fiercely."

"Are you telling me he fights his own love for me?" she asked with a shake of her head, not believing her own query and not giving Borg a chance to respond. "He thinks of me as nothing more than his property, a vassal who will serve him well. He is lusty, arrogant, stubborn, demanding and—"

"You love him," Borg finished with a smug grin.

Faith sighed, her answer coming directly from her heart. "Aye, I love him, the fool that I am."

"You are no fool. It takes courage to love the devil, and even more courage to surrender to that love."

"You favor the word 'surrender,'" she said, her dark eyes shining. "Have you ever surrendered?"

"Nay," he said with a wide grin, "but I intend to very soon."

"How soon?"

"How soon will I be fully healed?"

Faith smiled. "I think you can surrender this night if you wish."

Borg looked joyous, nervous and anxious and cast a quick glance around the hall until his eyes settled on Bridget. He sent her a smile that actually caused her to blush and then he turned his attention back to Faith.

"Will you surrender this night, my lady?"

She cast a hesitant glance around the hall, looking for her husband. Her cheeks heated when their eyes met and he immediately headed her way.

She looked with pleading eyes to Borg.

"Remember, he fights for what he most wants," Borg whispered near her ear as he moved to stand and walk away.

She felt deserted, alone, vulnerable and suddenly frightened. It did not help that her husband descended on her with fierce determined strides or that his handsome face was stern or that his blue eyes blazed with a lustiness that sent a shiver racing straight through her or that her body ached for his skilled touch.

Surrender.

The word repeatedly echoed in her mind and made her doubt her own sanity.

"You wish something from me, wife?" he asked, standing in front of the dais and staring directly at her with eyes that cautioned and promised.

The choice was hers.

She reached her hand out. "Eric . . ."

The door to the great hall flew open and a man rushed in, interrupting the gaiety and Faith's surrender.

Eric immediately turned his full attention on him. He looked to have ridden hard and long and he was near to collapsing from exhaustion. Colin and Borg followed behind the thin, tired man as he approached Eric.

"My lord," the man said with a respectful bow of his head. "Donal Mor O'Brien, king of Limerick, has sent me. He requests your help in quelling a skirmish at Finnmorgan Keep near the coast. He asks for your immediate presence in the area."

"How much of a presence does he request?" Eric asked.

"Enough to quell two disputing clans," he explained.

"Food, drink and a place to rest will be provided for you and we will leave at first light with two hundred of my men."

The man grinned. "That should end it right fast."

The servants took charge of the weary man while the hall waited for their lord's instructions.

Colin and Borg stood beside Eric, ready to do his bidding.

Eric spoke with the confidence and command of an aged warrior. "Colin, see to the preparations and send me Stuart—he is familiar with that area. I wish to form a battle plan before dawn. Borg, you will remain here and see to the safety of the keep. We have limited time before dawn and I want all ready for departure on time."

Colin and Borg agreed with a nod and took themselves off to follow his dictates.

Eric turned a quick glance and even quicker words on his wife. "I will speak with you before I leave."

He was out the door before the realization of the situation set in for Faith. He was going off to engage in battle, which meant there was a possibility that he would not return. Her heart plummeted and she felt near to fainting. She had not considered this moment, this time when she would bid her husband good-bye with uncertainty and so much left unsaid between them.

Suddenly surrender, victory, defeat seemed like senseless words and all she wanted to tell Eric was how very much she loved him and always would. She sat helpless, not knowing what to do, what action to take, what help to offer.

Then with a determination borne of pride and courage she took the matter in hand. If she could not speak with him now she would at least see to it that he and his men would not starve. She took herself off to the kitchen to talk with Mary.

The night grew late but the castle did not rest. Only when Faith was certain her husband and his men had all they needed

to fill their bellies and quench their thirsts did she rest, and it
was not until Bridget insisted that there was no more to be done
that she reluctantly took herself upstairs to her chambers. She
had hoped to catch a peek of her husband, but she learned he
had retired to his solar with Stuart to map and plan their journey.

Her chamber was warm from the hardy fire that blazed in
the hearth and after removing her clothes and slipping into her
nightdress she gratefully sought the comfort of her bed. She lay
still, her eyes heavy with sleep, thinking on her husband's
words. Would he seek her out before he left or would those
words be the last she heard from him before his departure?

The busy night had kept her from thinking of his leaving,
but now that she had time and her emotions were weary, she
found herself upset. She asked herself why his leaving so disturbed her. She realized that she would miss him, miss him ter-
ribly. She had grown accustomed to him—whether he scowled,
ignored or teased her it mattered not. He was always there,
making some ridiculous demand of her. And then there were
those times they had spent simply talking and then there were
the other times when intimacy and passion ruled.

She sighed, her eyes drifting closed. "I will miss you, my
dark lord."

Eric stood ready, his men assembled, dawn on the horizon, but
there was one last detail he had yet to see to. He gave Colin orders to prepare for departure shortly and left the great hall, taking himself to his wife's chambers.

He entered quietly, the heat of the flaming hearth reaching
out to him as he passed by it. He stopped a few away from the
bed and stared at his sleeping wife. She was beautiful—even
the long thin scar could not damage to her beauty. He sometimes wondered if she was real or nothing more than a dream.

He would often find himself hunting her down during the
course of the day just to make certain she was there—that she
was flesh and blood and belonged to him. His desire for her was
outrageous and yet his desire simply to talk with her, hold her,
spend time with her raged out of control as well. He simply
wanted to be with her as often as possible.

He supposed that was why he was presently having difficulty departing. He did not want to bid her farewell.

Anxious steps took him to the bed and he ran a gentle finger over her thin lips. He wondered what words she had intended to speak before she was interrupted this evening. He could have sworn he felt her need, her desire to surrender, and he had waited with stilled breath to hear her words.

He wanted so much to know what had been on her lips, but there was no time for discovery—only good-bye.

He leaned over her and brushed a faint kiss over her lips before whispering, "Faith."

She stirred, but barely.

He kissed her again, his lips more persistent though gentle and she sighed, her body stretching slowly beneath the covers. He slipped his one arm behind her back and moved his other hand to cup the back of her head and then he brought her up to meet his hungry mouth.

His kiss was not gentle and she woke immediately, wrapping her arms around him and pressing her body against his.

"I have come to bid you good-bye," he whispered in haste, his mouth finding her warm neck much too enticing to ignore.

"I shall miss you," she murmured in his ear.

"So you say," he said, his lips moving over her chin toward her mouth.

"So I mean." She barely finished before his lips anxiously and demandingly laid claim to hers.

After satisfying himself with the taste of her for several minutes he laid her back down on the bed. "You mind Borg," he commanded like a warrior.

"Aye, my lord," she acquiesced softly.

"And take care to behave."

She nodded, her eyes welling with tears.

The pool of unshed tears in her eyes tore at his heart. "I must go."

She nodded again, not trusting her voice and feeling much too close to shedding her tears.

The first tear fell when he moved to leave, the second as his back turned to her and the third when he turned around and descended on her like a man too long denied. He lifted her clear off the bed. She instantly wrapped her legs around his waist, her arms around his neck, and she locked her lips to his hungry ones.

Their kiss was urgent and filled with unfulfilled passion. They feasted like two starving souls needing nourishment.

He attempted to tear his mouth away from hers but she clung to him and only by grabbing the back of her fiery hair and pulling her head back could he disengage her lips from his.

He saw the ache, the need, the surrender in her dark eyes and cursed the two warring clans that would deprive him of his wife's capitulation.

His spoke harshly. "We settle this when I return."

She nodded as best she could given that his hand was gripping her hair.

He brought her mouth once again to his and then reluctantly grabbed her around the waist, yanked her off him and settled her back on the bed. Without a word or glance he turned and marched to the door.

"Eric," she called out to him.

He stopped but did not turn.

"I love you," she said without hesitancy or regret.

He made no response—he simply walked out of the room.

Twenty

A *heavy mist* swallowed up the large troop of warriors that made its way slowly out of Shanekill Castle. The eerie omen did not bother the seasoned warriors. Why should it? The devil rode at the lead, shielding them from harm.

Tales were shared of the dark lord's exploits into the mouth of hell and back again. More tales were told of the fierce enemies he courageously faced and how he always emerged victorious. The men spoke of the many wounds he suffered in battles and how most would have killed a mere mortal man. But most of all they whispered about how no one would dare look the devil in the eye during battle—if they did they would lose their souls.

Whispered chatter rippled through the ranks of warriors as they trudged along the hard earth, entertaining themselves with tales of their mighty leader. The stories fueled their own confidences and courage preparing them for what was to come.

And of course as they made their way away from the castle grounds, the mist finally began to dissipate. It was the dark lord's scowling look and intense blue eyes that were given credit for that—all the men agreed that the mist rolled away in reverence to the Irish devil's presence.

Colin, on the other hand, knew better. "Your thoughts are not on the battle."

"A skirmish I almost won," Eric said, his glance steady on

the land spread out before him. A mix of rocky terrain and flat earth awaited them and the gray skies overhead promised a wet journey—not an appealing prospect.

Colin remained silent, aware his friend was not in a pleasant mood and ready to listen if he wished to talk.

"Have you ever been in love, Colin?"

Anyone other than Colin would have been shocked at hearing the dark lord ask that question, but Colin knew his friend too well and understood. "I have made love to many women in my two score and seven years and I cared for each one of them in my own special way. But love?" He shook his head slowly. "I cannot honestly say I have experienced a love so strong for a woman that I would want to spend the rest of my life with her." He paused briefly and then continued. "Though I cannot say I would not want to. To know a love so potent that it tears at the heart and soul is an emotion I might one day wish to experience."

"I never thought to love," Eric said with a sadness that disturbed Colin.

"Why?"

"I thought nothing of love. It was a fleeting feeling that came and went at will, like lust."

"You think differently now?" Colin asked, adding, "Now that you have Faith?"

"She is a most unusual woman. She makes no demands of me, obeys me when it pleases her and makes it seem that she obeys me when I wish. She is gentle, yet strong. She challenges life and manages not only to survive but to thrive. And she is firm in her convictions. She is a remarkable woman."

"You tell me what you most admire about her. Tell me what troubles you about her?"

Eric answered, his words edged with frustration. "I find myself wanting to be with her all the time. Not only for intimacy but just to be with, to talk to, to hold, even to argue with. I find I ache to touch her, taste her, tempt her." He laughed. "How I love to tempt her."

Eric turned to face Colin. "I miss her when she is not near me. I want her in my bed, there in the evening when I retire, in the middle of the night if I wake I want to reach out and pull her into my arms, and I want to wake in the morning with my body wrapped protectively around hers. I want to plant my seed deep inside her and watch her belly grow with my child, not just one child, but many. And I want to grow old with her."

Colin laughed and gave Eric a hardy slap on the back. "My friend, you have lost your heart and if the devil had a soul I would say you surrendered that as well."

Eric was not amused. "You think me in love?"

"You think not?" Colin asked with a glint of humor in his dark eyes.

"I never surrender," Eric said fiercely, as only a true warrior would.

"You think to love is to surrender?"

Eric shook his head. "I do not know what to think any longer. Where once I made plans, implemented them and succeeded in my intentions, now I find myself changing my plans from day to day and not even knowing what my intentions are."

"Then this time away from your wife is good for you," Colin suggested.

"Why?" Eric snapped. "I foolishly miss her already and we are but a few hour's ride from the castle."

"This time away will help you better understand your feelings toward her. If you continue to miss her, think of her, want her, then what else can you be suffering from but love. This forced distance between you and she will give you answers."

"And what of her virginity?" Eric asked, annoyed.

Colin spoke seriously. "If you love her, will it matter? It is not as if she gave her virginity away. She was robbed of it, if at all."

"You believe her a virgin?"

"What I believe, my friend, matters not. It is what you believe, or rather how you truly feel about your wife that makes the difference."

Rain began to fall lightly at first but soon the drops would grow heavy and frequent and their journey would be delayed by the weather and the drudgery of the wet earth. Eric wrapped his dark cloak more tightly around himself and became lost in his own thoughts.

Faith's declaration of love had haunted his mind since he left her chambers. He would hear her voice soft yet firm and confident as she declared, "I love you."

Her unexpected remark had startled him and he did not know how to respond, so he had fled her chambers like a coward. That did not sit well with him. But giving the situation further thought, he realized that it was not her declaration he was fleeing from; it was his own sudden emotions that had reared up and frightened him. The words had rushed to his lips without thought or consideration of the consequences. His only desire was to respond in kind and tell her how very much he loved her.

But instead of surrendering, an unacceptable choice to him, he had fled with the words slipping softly from his lips, so his ears were the only ones to hear his whispers of love.

Now he sat in the pouring rain contemplating his cowardly actions. If he thought as a warrior he would not think them cowardly. He would view them as brave and righteous, a wise decision. A warrior never ruled with emotion; such an act would surely bring defeat.

But was this a warrior's decision or that of a man in love?

Love was not an emotion he had given credence to and now he found himself thinking of nothing else, if this gnawing feeling be love. It would not leave him. It haunted his waking thoughts as well as his dreams. His wife was forever on his mind and he did not mind, he liked her there. And at the moment he missed her.

He felt empty sitting on his stallion alone. He had enjoyed Faith's company on their journey from Cork to Limerick. She had fit him and his stallion perfectly and he had found pleasure in their discussions. And he could not deny how much he favored her body being so close to his. She had felt warm, soft and so good to the touch.

If he was truthful with himself then Colin's words would ring true. If he loved her, her virginity would make no difference, though if he truly loved her it would, for it mattered to Faith whether he believed her or not.

He turned again to Colin. "I think Faith keeps something from me about the attack."

"Do you know what it is?" Colin asked with sincere interest.

"I think she knows more about her attacker than she admits."

"Perhaps it is someone she knows but fears mentioning."

"Possibly," Eric agreed with a nod. "Or a person no one would believe possible of committing such a vicious act."

"You wish to find him."

"I wish to see him receive a just punishment for his crime."

"And you will be the one to deliver his punishment?" Colin asked, though unnecessarily.

"No other," Eric said with such certainty that for a brief moment Colin felt sorry for the poor unfortunate soul.

"How do you plan on finding him?"

"Faith."

Colin nodded in understanding. "She will give you what you need without even realizing it."

"That she will," Eric said confidently and smiled. "My wife will give me all that I request, upon my return home."

"This dispute between the clans may take time," Colin said with an earnest teasing.

Eric raised a brow. "Nay, it will not."

Colin unwisely argued, though with a smile. "The messenger commented how stubborn both clans are."

"I will convince them otherwise."

"They may—"

Eric shot him a deadly look that immediately quelled his response. "They will do as I command."

Colin wisely agreed with a nod. "Then we return home?"

"As soon as possible."

Colin's teasing nature could not be suppressed. "No time for me to dally with the wenches?"

Eric smiled then and gave Colin a potent slap on the back. "I think it is a wife you need. I will see if I can locate one for you."

"Do me no favors, I need no wife," Colin insisted with a laugh. "And besides, it would not be fair."

"Fair to whom?"

"To the women I have yet to bed?"

Eric laughed along with his friend. "It is time to lay your reputation to rest and find one woman to please."

"I please all women, my friend. There is none impervious to my charm and skill as a lover."

"Then I shall have no difficulty in finding you a wife," Eric said and galloped ahead.

"Eric, I warn you," Colin called out, riding to catch up with him and convince him otherwise.

●   ●   ●

Faith needed to speak with someone. She felt alone, lost and completely confused since Eric's morning departure. She did not know what had made her declare her love for him and now she wondered if her decision had been a wise one. She needed to talk with a friend, someone she could trust. That someone was Borg.

She knocked on his chamber door and opened it, accustomed to entering without a response from him.

A mistake, since he was no longer ill.

Borg and Bridget lay naked, wrapped in each other's arms.

Faith blushed, apologized and quickly fled the room.

Bridget was the one to find Faith in her chambers several minutes later. "My lady, forgive me for not being present when you rose this morning." Bridget bowed in respect and hurried to tend the room, though there was naught for her to do. Faith, accustomed to seeing to herself, tended to her own needs and care of her chambers.

"Nonsense," Faith said, attempting to calm Bridget's unease. "You had more important matters on your mind and I am more than capable of tending myself." She reached out a hand to Bridget. "I am happy for you and Borg and wish you well."

Bridget squeezed her offered hand. "Oh, thank you so much, my lady. Borg said you would be happy, that I was not to worry."

Faith moved to reach for her new dark red wool cloak that lay draped over the chair. Bridget immediately retrieved it and held it up for Faith to slip on. "He is right. There is no need for you to worry and it is I who should apologize."

"You, my lady?"

Faith nodded, draping the end of the cloak over her shoulder. "It was foolish of me to enter Borg's chambers before being properly admitted."

"You surprised me," Bridget said with a generous smile.

"And myself."

"Me as well," Borg said, standing in the open doorway fully clothed.

"Please forgive my untimely entrance," Faith said sincerely.

"Your apology is appreciated though not necessary, my lady," Borg said, walking into the room. "My concern is more for the troubled expression you wear."

"Now I know why you remain silent—you listen and ob-

serve and see much more than anyone realizes." Faith looked at
him with curious eyes. "I even wonder if you are as shy as people think you are."

"Oh, my lady, he is not shy at all," Bridget said before realizing of what she spoke. She immediately blushed profusely,
causing Borg to erupt in a robust laughter and Faith to giggle.

Faith was not only surprised when Borg walked over to
Bridget, grasped her around the waist, brought her flat against
him and kissed her soundly, but also surprised when she realized she was envious of the happy couple.

As silently as possible she moved toward the door, intending to give the loving couple time alone. Rook crept alongside
her. Borg's booming voice soon stopped her.

"Stay where you are, my lady—we need to talk."

Woman and dog both froze.

"I will see to food for you both," Bridget said, still wrapped
in Borg's powerful arms.

"And yourself," he ordered, then asked of Faith, "Where
were you off to, my lady?"

"To take Rook for a walk and then to my healing cottage."

Borg released Bridget after a tender kiss to her cheek. "I will
accompany you, and Bridget, bring the food to the cottage—we
will all share the morning meal together there."

Bridget stared at him in disbelief.

Borg looked to Faith. "Is there any reason Bridget would not
be welcome at your table?"

"None at all," Faith said honestly. "I would enjoy sharing a
meal with you both."

"Then it is settled," Borg commanded and gave a startled
Bridget a gentle shove toward the door. He then joined Faith,
holding his arm out to her. "My lady?"

She slipped her arm in his and they walked out of the room,
Rook following fast on their heels and Faith insisting they retrieve Borg's cloak from his chambers so he would not catch a
chill.

They strolled the castle grounds, Rook running off here and
there, visiting his favorite spots and cottages where many a
peasant would give him a treat. The rain had not begun though
the dark clouds overhead promised its arrival soon and a chill
wind swept down and around swirling leaves, dirt and twigs
throughout the courtyard.

"You love Bridget." It was not a question but a statement of fact Faith presented to Borg.

Borg did not hesitate to confirm it. "I love her very much— enough to spend the rest of my life with her."

"When did you know yourself in love with her?"

"When first I saw her."

Faith was amazed at his response. "Truly? You knew when you first laid eyes on her that you loved her?"

Borg briefly paused in thought before offering an explanation. "When I first saw Bridget her full face captured my attention and her smile held me spellbound. Her endless chatter fascinated me and her body—" He stopped abruptly and blushed, his cheeks heating to a faint red.

Faith pursued the subject with interest, ignoring the big man's discomfort. "You speak of the way she looked and her chatter—it was not her body, then, that first drew you to her?"

Borg's cheeks deepened in color but answered her query. "I cannot honestly say that I did not look at her body at first glance—all men look at a woman's body."

Faith spoke with honesty, causing Borg further embarrassment. "I must admit I thought Eric possessed a handsome body."

"What other qualities did attract you to the dark lord?"

Faith cast him a hesitant glance.

"Come, tell me. I would like to hear of my brother's attributes."

She acquiesced. "It was when he defended me that I found myself more interested in him."

"In the great hall, when your stepmother raised her hand to you?"

Faith nodded. "He captured my full attention and, if I were honest with myself, a part of my heart that day. I felt safe and cared for, for the first time in many years."

"Even from the devil?"

"He intimidated me, that I will admit . . . but fear?" She shook her head. "After that moment my fear was minimal, if existent at all."

"And when did you fall in love with him?"

Startled dark eyes met his knowing ones. "Is my love for my husband that obvious?"

Borg grinned. "To one who is in love himself, it is."

Rook ran past them with a fat biscuit clamped in his mouth and they turned to follow him as he headed for the cottage.

Faith answered his question. "His handsome features stole my breath on first sight, but he won my heart gradually with his thoughtful ways."

"The devil, thoughtful?" Borg enjoyed a good laugh.

"Eric *is* thoughtful," Faith insisted. "He allowed me to birth a babe on our wedding night, and he shared our tent in the rain, and he was patient when his soldiers sought my aid, and even when he thought himself angry with me he still helped me find Rook."

Borg continued to laugh softly as he nodded his agreement. "Thoughtful deeds."

"He cannot help his stubborn and foolish nature."

"Making excuses for the devil?"

Faith stopped walking, her dark eyes as intent as her voice as she solemnly said, "I want the devil's love."

"Then surrender," Borg advised seriously.

Bridget called out to them from the open door of the cottage and they hurried along, the rain beginning to fall and the skies darkening, promising a heavy and continuous downpour.

Surrender.

Her only choice.

And what of he? What would he surrender to her?

His pride? His foolishness? His love?

She would find out when he returned. She would be waiting for him.

In his bed.

Twenty-one

"You should not be riding," Colin said to Eric for at least the tenth time that morning. "You should be in the wagon with—"

Eric quelled any further comments would a curt, "Enough."

Colin shook his head and rubbed at the rough stubble of near two day's growth of beard on his chin. "You suffered a serious wound to your thigh, not to mention your arm. You continue to lose blood—"

"It but oozes," Eric corrected.

"You still keep losing it and that is no good. And you're stubborn enough to sit on your horse instead of riding in the wagon—"

Eric interrupted. "I will not have my men see me incapable of leading."

"You lead, the skirmish is over, and it was a fast one at that. The men are all bragging about the way you fought that stubborn leader from the Dermot clan and they are still laughing at how the leader of the Anise clan immediately fell at your knees in surrender afterwards."

"Fools, the both of them."

Colin could not have agreed more. "Aye, and not trustworthy. The combat was to be with fists and Dermot went and hid a dagger—and even injured and bleeding you fought him. Another tale to add to the Irish devil's legend. If his foolhardy stubbornness does not kill him."

"We will be home in a few hours' time."

That pleased Colin to hear, and he smiled. "Aye, and it is your wife you will be facing then."

"A prospect I look forward to," Eric said and grinned, though it was followed by a low groan.

"I do not think you will be enjoying the homecoming you planned."

Eric scowled. "Nothing will interfere with me spending this night with my wife in my bed."

"Faith might object," Colin argued.

"She will surrender. I command it."

Colin shook his head and smiled with confidence. "Not when she gets a look at your wounds."

"I will have Bridget tend them and—"

Colin's hearty laughter prevented him from finishing. "Faith will let no one tend you but her."

"She will not know," Eric insisted, intending for nothing to get in the way of his making love to his wife this night.

Colin grinned like a pleased man. "She already knows. I sent a man ahead to inform her of your injuries so that all would be in preparation for your arrival."

"I am going to kill you," Eric said quite seriously, then shook his head. "Nay, better yet, I intend to find you a *special* wife."

Colin laughed even harder. "Lady Faith will protect me from an unwanted marriage."

Eric reared up off his horse and pain tore through his leg, causing him to pale instantly and grow light-headed.

Colin reached out to him, steadying him until the blood rushed back into Eric's face. "You should be in the wagon."

"Nay, I will not lie down in front of my men—it is but a small wound."

"It is not—look at your leg," Colin insisted, concerned for his friend. "It bleeds."

Eric glanced down at his right thigh and watched blood ooze out from the thick cloth that had been wrapped around it several days ago. He had suffered far worse wounds and survived, but this wound was a persistent bleeder, and that was not good. He had wished Faith was with him. She would have seen to his care directly and had the wound almost healing by now. But she had not been at his side, a situation he found disturbed him. He missed her and he was relieved that within a few short hours he would lay eyes on her again.

He also wanted to lay hands on her and he did not give a damn how bad his wound was. He wanted his wife and he intended on having her this night.

"Faith will have you in bed for days," Colin warned.

"Then she will have me exactly where I wish to be and she will be right there along with me."

Colin laughed. "This I want to see."

"A wager?" Eric asked, ignoring his throbbing leg and casting a challenging glance at Colin.

"I am going to be such a rich man from all my winnings that I will be able to purchase myself a good wife," Colin said, holding out his hand.

They shook.

"Nay," Eric said. "I will have the honor and joy of finding you the perfect female."

They continued bickering as Shanekill Keep came into view, each man anxious to be home, but each for a different reason.

"My lady, they come over the rise," Bridget said anxiously, peering out the lord's chamber window.

"Do we have everything, Bridget?" Faith asked, her glance hastily perusing the table she had set up beside the bed for her medicinal tools and herbs.

Bridget joined her, carefully checking the table. "I think we have everything. Water boils in the hearth, clean cloths wait in the basket and fresh buckets of water wait in the hall."

"The messenger spoke of two wounds," Faith said, checking that the thin bone needles were threaded and prepared for immediate use.

"I would say he spoke more of Lord Eric's fighting skills than of the wounds."

Faith nodded absentmindedly and moved to the large bed to fuss with the clean towels that had been spread over the white bed linens. "True, but Colin is the one who sent the word, which means he must think Lord Eric's wounds serious enough for us to be alerted before their arrival."

"Lord Eric rides, my lady," Bridget said, having returned to peer out the window once again.

Faith hurried to join her.

"If my lord still sits on his horse then the wounds cannot be that bad."

Faith disagreed. "Lord Eric is stubborn and foolish. Even after suffering a serious wound I would wager that he would not allow his men to see him other than on his horse and in command."

Both women watched as the men approached. It was an awesome sight to behold. They walked in unison, a steady drumbeat announcing their arrival; and in the lead rode the Irish devil.

Faith's breath caught at the sight of him. The autumn wind caught his long, dark hair and whipped it back, away from his handsome features. He wore his dark cloak, a gold Viking brooch keeping it secured at his shoulder. And he sat on his horse like a true warrior, straight and proud and in total command.

Perhaps his wound was not as serious as she suspected—at least, she hoped it was not. But when she watched his slow dismount and caught a hint of pain rush across his pale features she changed her opinion and grasped Bridget's wrist.

"He should not climb the steps."

With that said she rushed from the room and down the stairway, meeting her husband as he entered the great hall, Borg and Colin flanking his sides.

"Carry him," she ordered in a shout, surprising everyone present.

Eric laughed. "A most odd welcome home."

Faith ignored his comment and hurried over to his side, her eyes immediately focusing on the blood-soaked bandage. "How long has this been bleeding?"

"Since the fool would not get off the horse," Colin said.

"Take him to his chambers," she ordered once again, not daring to touch the cloth until she had him where she could properly tend him.

Colin and Borg looked to Eric.

Eric looked to his wife and was about to chastise her when she spoke.

"Please, my lord," she pleaded softly, her hand going to rest on his arm near where the other bandage was also soaked with blood, though it was dry. "I am worried about you. Please do as I ask."

He paused briefly, taking time to study her face which was so filled with concern for him. How he had missed looking upon her and how grateful he was to be home. He was especially glad to know how much his welfare concerned her and therefore he did as she requested, though he did it his way.

"I will walk upstairs to my chambers."

She was ready to argue but thought better of it. It was important he get off his feet and the sooner the better. She nodded her agreement. "All right, but I will help you."

The three huge men laughed.

Her lethal glance quickly extinguished all laughter.

"Come," she ordered, taking her husband's injured arm and carefully placing it around her small but sturdy shoulders.

Eric did not argue—he liked the feel of her and he wanted to be as close as possible to her. He took several steps toward the stairway when the pain hit and almost sent him to his knees. If it were not for Faith's strength he would have hit the ground.

Colin and Borg were immediately by his side, their arms reaching under his to lift him off Faith.

"Please," she begged the two men. "The walk up the stairs will do the wound no good."

That was all she needed to tell them. They nodded to each other and as Eric moved to protest, Borg hefted his brother over his massive shoulder and carried him up the staircase. Colin followed behind in case Eric protested further and Faith trailed happily behind them.

"You will pay for this, the both of you," Eric insisted after being carefully deposited on the bed, though he sounded much too tired to carry out the threat.

When he made to move, Borg pinned him to the bed with one hand.

"Let me undress," Eric ordered.

"I will see to that," Faith said, directing Bridget to pour hot water into the wooden basin on the table.

Eric stayed as he was and remarked, "Do you plan on stripping me naked?"

All eyes turned on him.

"I want no company if this is her plan," he explained.

"I may need some assistance," Faith said.

"Do you need any now?"

Faith shook her head. "Nay, maybe later, if you require stitching."

"Borg, see to the men. Make sure it is a good feast they have," Eric ordered. "Colin, though exhausted, will no doubt enjoy himself and make certain the men are made aware that my condition is not serious."

"Do you not want one of us to remain nearby in case my lady needs our help?" Colin asked with a playful grin.

"Bridget can stay," Faith said, her attention on her husband's bloody wound.

"She can get me food. I am hungry," Eric directed, though food was the furthermost thought from his mind.

That seemed to please Faith. "You wish to eat?"

"Something light."

With all dictates issued the room was fast deserted, leaving the lord and the lady of the keep to themselves.

"Now what?" he asked.

"First, I unwrap these bandages and take a quick peek and then I rid you of these soiled garments. I think you will also need to be hand bathed. I want no dirt or dust from your journey disturbing the wounds."

"Can I help in any way?" he asked, reaching out and gently running a hand over her cheek, slowly down her neck, lingering over her breast and coming to rest at her narrow waist.

She shivered from his intimate exploration. "You can behave."

"Must I?" he asked and moved his hand to rest over her backside.

Faith backed away from him. "Please, Eric, let me tend your wounds without distraction."

"And then?" His blue eyes were intent and filled with such potent passion that she grew moist.

"First your wounds," she insisted, attempting, to ignore his desirous intentions and how they were making her feel, though having a devil of a time. She felt hot, ready and willing.

Eric obliged her by grasping his tunic to strip off.

Faith stopped him by placing her hand on his. "Let me remove the bandage first."

"Colin did what he could," Eric said in defense of his friend's ministrations.

"You mean he did what he could since you probably refused to sit still long enough for him to do anything more."

"You know me well," Eric hissed softly when at last she carefully removed the cloth from around his arm, exposing the wound.

Faith examined the abrasion carefully, touching and probing the blood-dried area. "This does not look bad. With a good cleaning, a healing salve and a clean cloth to keep it bound for a few days, I think it should be fine."

His upper garments were easily removed and Faith adjusted several pillows behind his back and head, covering them with towels to keep the linens clean. Eric made immediate use of them, sinking back against their welcoming softness.

She next set to work on his leg, taking extra time and patience in removing the blood-soaked cloth. She worried over swelling and fever and was glad when no stench but that of days-old blood rose from the wound.

It was difficult to determine the severity of the abrasion with so much dry and wet blood surrounding it, though the area was slightly red and warm to the touch. She wasted no time in ridding him of the remainder of his garments.

She casually draped a towel over his lower belly and impressive manhood, more for her own sanity than for modesty. She received a distinct chuckle from her husband for her ladylike actions. She ignored him.

His arm could wait; his leg could not. She went to work cleaning it with the water that had boiled over the fire and now was but warm to the touch. Eric made not a sound as she worked on him. She kept her touch as gentle as she could, but knew that at times she must be hurting him. Still, he made no sound of discomfort.

On closer examination she found the slashing wound to be deeper at one end than the other and that was why it had continued to bleed, especially since her stubborn husband had refused to stay off it. It would require stitches and bed rest.

When she was finished cleansing the leg, she removed the soiled towels beneath and replaced them with fresh clean ones.

"I am sorry if I hurt you," she said, handing him a tankard for him to drink.

He did not take it from her. "You are more gentle than you know. What is this you give me?"

"A potion that will soothe and relax so the stitches will not overly pain you."

"Nay," he said firmly. "I wish my wits about me."

"Why?" she demanded. "You require rest to heal properly."

"I will rest later."

"You can rest now, while I work on you."

"Nay," he repeated more firmly.

"You are being stubborn and foolish."

"Think what you will, wife, but I will not drink that sleeping brew."

"It will but rest you."

"Nay," he said once again and in a harsh tone that warned she was not to ask again.

"As you wish, my lord," she said with a shake of her head and placed the tankard on the table.

"Empty it," he ordered.

"What?"

"Empty it. I will not have you slipping it in my drink later this evening."

She did not argue. She spilled the contents into the dirty water bucket. "Satisfied?"

He was about to smile when the pain struck him again and he winced, cursing quietly beneath his mumbled breath.

She tossed the empty tankard on the table and hurried to his side, grabbing his hand. Eric gratefully took hers in his and squeezed gently.

"Part of the wound is deep and must first heal from within. I will stitch it to hold it fast so that it might heal, but you must promise me that you will stay in this bed and rest until I instruct otherwise."

He pulled her down toward him and she was amazed by the strength in his hand. She had thought that his injury would have weakened him and yet the potency in his grip proved her assumption wrong.

Her face rested not far from his. "I will stay in this bed if you will give me your word that you will keep me company."

His blue eyes ran hot with passion and Faith was certain he wanted more than friendly company, but she knew if she failed to agree she would have a problem of keeping him well rested, so she gave her word.

"You have my word."

He released her. "Then stitch me and be done with it so that you will be able to join me."

Bridget returned, knocking on the door and waiting for permission before entering. Faith was busy stitching the wound and Bridget hastily placed the silver tray on a small table near the hearth. After making certain neither Lady Faith nor Lord Eric required anything further form her, she hurried from the room.

Faith had the stitching done in minutes, the wound only taking ten and his arm required none. She applied salve after making certain his leg and arm were thoroughly cleansed and dried and then followed it with clean bandages.

"Do you prefer to eat first or shall I bathe you?"

While Eric wanted nothing more than her delicate hands washing his warm body, his leg throbbed unmercifully from the stitching and he required a period of rest before proceeding to seduce his wife.

"Food, I think."

"Good," she said with a smile and he could not help but stare at her stunning face. Her pale cheeks were tinted red, high along her prominent cheekbones, and her dark eyes were framed by the most exquisite long lashes that curled slightly at the very tips. Her flaming hair was tied back, the white braided stripe of cloth having difficulty keeping the mass of springy curls together. Several strands fell free along her temples, tempting his fingers to reach out and touch. But it was her lips that tormented him the most, thin and yet plump from her nervous chewing as she concentrated on her stitching.

They looked as if they ached to be kissed and he did want to kiss her.

He also wanted to rid her of that white, soiled strip of cloth, tied tightly around her waist, then her green tunic and . . . every piece of clothing she had on. He wanted her naked before him, stark naked so that he could see, touch and taste his fill of her.

Faith handed him a thick slice of dark bread and cheese and she sat a goblet of wine on the small table beside the bed.

"Join me," he said.

He asked so kindly that Faith found herself unable to refuse, though she said, "First let me clean up some and then I will gladly share the meal with you."

He nodded and enjoyed the bread and cheese, talking with her as she cleaned her worktable.

"Will I suffer with the fever from this wound?" he asked, wanting to make certain he would remain in good physical shape for the sensually strenuous nights and days he had in mind.

"Your arm worries me not. The leg is a different matter, though I see no signs for alarm. The skin is warm and only slightly red. I cleansed it well and the salve I applied should help heal it, but you must stay off it. You can participate in no strenuous activity until I am certain the leg has healed properly."

Eric swallowed the food in his mouth, washing it down with a swig of wine. "No strenuous activity?"

Faith removed her soiled tunic, discarding it to the bucket filled with the soiled towels. "None," she confirmed and helped herself to the dried fruit and a piece of cheese. "That is, if you want to be up and around soon. The more stubborn you are about allowing the wound to heal, the longer you will be unable to do as you wish."

I wish to make love to you.

Eric wondered how she would react if he spoke his thoughts out loud.

"More food?" she asked, but Eric shook his head and dusted his hands of any crumbs.

"Nay, I grow tired." And disappointed. How would he handle this dilemma? He wanted his wife tonight. He intended on having his wife tonight, the question being how did he seduce his wife if he could not move his leg?

"I will bathe you quickly so that you may rest," she said, his sudden frown disturbing her.

"Do not rush," he ordered, the thought of her hands rubbing him clean too enticing to have it over and done with before he could enjoy and respond to her touch.

"I will get your robe," she said, moving toward his chest at the end of the bed. "I do not want you getting chilled."

"Nay," he snapped, startling her. "I am hot."

She hurried to his side, pressing the back of her hand to his cheek. "You feel warm, though not feverish."

"I am comfortable," he insisted more calmly.

Faith looked at him oddly for a brief moment and then

turned away to gather the items she required to bathe him. She took her time, well aware that his blazing blue eyes watched her every move.

How she would manage to bathe him and not lose control of her senses was a question she had been attempting to avoid since she realized her husband wanted her. The realization startled her, for she had not expected an injured man to concern himself with passion. And at first she thought perhaps she saw what she had wanted to see, that her husband had sorely missed her and returned, wanting her with a desperate passion.

Now, however, she understood that she was not mistaken, he did want her and she wanted him just as desperately. He had warned her on his departure that they would settle this upon his return. But he was injured and she could not allow him to cause further damage to his leg. What was she to do?

Bathing him was certainly not going to help the situation.

She grabbed the rope handle of the bucket that sat by the hearth. The heat of the roaring fire kept the water warm but not hot and she carried the half-filled bucket to the side of the bed and placed it on the floor. She then gathered a clean cloth and a bar of soap that she had scented with a mixture of sweet wildflowers.

Towels were next, actually anything she could do to delay the inevitable, she did. She carefully arranged the basket of towels a distance away from the bucket of water. She slowly rolled up the sleeves of her shift. She retied her hair, fussing to make sure all the strands were tucked back away from her face. And finally, when she could think of no further acts to delay her, she dropped the scented bar and cloth into the bucket.

She reached into the bucket, grasped the cloth and twisted it so tightly that not a drop of water remained and then with a trembling hand she reached out to start on his face.

He grasped her wrist with a light firmness. "We settle this tonight, wife."

Twenty-two

Faith kept the tremor out of her voice though her hands continued to tremble after he released her wrist. She brought the cloth gently to his face and wiped his brow and cheeks, running over his chin and down along his neck. "What do you wish to settle, Eric?"

He was quick to answer. "This madness between us."

She returned the cloth to the bucket, rinsing it and lathering it with soap before she twisted the excess water from it and brought it to cleanse his chest. She ran the cloth over his thick muscles in slow circular motions. "You have suffered a serious injury. Your leg needs to rest."

"I have suffered far worse injuries," he insisted with a knowing smile, "and still returned to battle to fight again."

She rinsed the cloth yet again and motioned him to sit up, which he did slowly. "See . . . you have not as much strength as you think."

Her words disturbed him, for he had felt the weariness in his body. The wounds had taken their toll on him and she was probably correct in advising him to rest, but he did not wish to rest. He wanted his wife and it was becoming more evident by the minute, his loins growing hard as she moved the wet cloth down over his back.

"I have all the strength I need," he protested once he rested back against the pillows.

Faith said not a word. She continued to cleanse his body, moving the rinsed cloth along over his arm. She found it difficult not to admire the cut of his defined muscles and the smooth hardness of his skin. She found it even more difficult to ignore her own body's response to her intimate touch of him.

Her heart beat a fast, erratic rhythm; her nipples hardened most obviously beneath her shift and she grew so moist with the want of him that she thought she would climax without his hands ever touching her.

He sensed her thoughts. "You want this settled as much as I do."

She threw the cloth down into the bucket. "Aye, my lord, I do, but—"

He would not permit her to speak another word. "Finish bathing me."

"We need to—"

"Do as I order," he demanded.

She acquiesced with a silent nod, snatching the soapy cloth from the bucket, and proceeded to wash his one leg, the injured leg having already been cleansed before she had stitched the wound.

She gave thought to speaking her mind several times as her hand slowly ran the wet cloth over his leg and then reached for a towel to dry his sturdy limb. But Borg's advice kept echoing in her mind.

Surrender.

If that was her wisest move, then how did she surrender under the present circumstances? She did not wish to see him cause his injury any undo harm. His arm did not concern her— it was a minor abrasion. So what, then, were her options?

"Finish," he ordered again.

She reluctantly admitted to herself that his curt command actually seemed appropriate. This matter needed finishing once and for all. And though she chose to surrender, she would do it her way. She would be in charge. She would take command. She would surrender her virginity willingly.

"Aye, my lord," she responded softly. "I will finish this."

She brazenly yanked the towel off him and if there had been a hint of doubt as to his intentions, it vanished at the sight of his prominent arousal.

Determined to succeed in her own intentions, Faith made

certain a fresh cloth was rinsed in a bucket of clean, warm water before she brought the moist cloth to lay low on his belly. She placed her hand flat on top the cloth and lazily stroked it back and forth just above his nest of dark hair. She then ran the cloth on either side of his loins, venturing near but never intimately touching him.

Her intentional avoidance drove him mad with the want of her touch, but he forced himself to remain still and silently watch her.

She toyed with him, running the damp cloth near and around his sprouting manhood, coming dangerously close but never brushing his manly flesh.

What annoyed him even more was that her playful little game aroused him to a fever pitch. He grew harder with each deliberate swipe of the tormenting cloth, so that when she finally discarded it and grasped him full and hard with her own hand he groaned with much relief and much pleasure.

Her eyes held a bewildered yet intent look, a strange and dangerous combination. What would it produce? Where would her unplanned actions take her? Did she wish to indulge him or harm him? He waited anxiously and suspiciously.

His discovery was so startling that his merciful groans echoed off the stone walls as she stroked him with a tormenting rhythm that soon had him sitting up fast and eagerly reaching out for her.

A firm yet delicate hand to his chest pushed him back against the pillows.

"Nay," she all but whispered, "I will not risk you suffering further harm."

She stepped back a short distance away from the bed and as if fearing she would change her own mind she hastily shed her clothes. She finished quickly and stood perfectly still, baring not only her nakedness, but her vulnerability.

Eric's eyes feasted on her without restraint, roaming her exquisite body, savoring this long-awaited and intimate perusal of his naked wife. She was stunning—pale skin, full breasts, a narrow waist his hands itched to grasp and a thick nest of red curls that brought a wicked smile to his lips.

"Come here," he said in his usual demanding tone and held his hand out to her.

She made to move and then hesitated. "You must promise me you will not move your injured leg."

"With what I have in mind to do to you, that will prove difficult," he admitted, his smile replaced by a look of sheer determination.

She slowly shook her head. "Then I have no choice—"

He interrupted sharply. "I will not be denied—"

She finished just as sharply. "Nay, you will not. I will straddle you."

He had always successfully concealed his emotions. He had learned long ago that it did no good to allow anyone to see the effect their words or actions had upon him. But her candid remark shocked him speechless and his eyes widened with genuine surprise.

She approached the bed with a hasty apprehension as if wanting this over and done, but when she came to stand beside the bed she appeared to have a change of heart and she slowly, like a lazy cat, crawled over him until her naked body was completely sprawled over his. She carefully brought her legs up to flank the sides of his waist so as not to disturb his wounded leg. And there she rested, her head upon his chest.

His hands drifted up over her back. Relishing the smoothness of her silky skin, he moved down along her slim waist that gave way to rounded hips and a firm backside that he cupped solidly in his anxious hands.

She in turn tasted his chest with a tentative kiss, liking the cool, clean flavor of him on her warm tongue. She proceeded to lick, nip and kiss her way up his neck to his lips.

He took command from there, his hand grasping the back of her head and forcing a kiss from her that raced their emotions to a fever pitch. His hands moved to her waist, yanking her up to give his mouth easy access to her full breasts.

Rational thought completely escaped her. Passion hot and bold remained and took absolute command.

She managed to place her hands flat on his broad shoulders, steadying herself as he proceeded to suckle her hard nipple. There was no gentleness to his taste and yet his harsh feasting shot ripples of pure passion straight through her and she shuddered with a soft moan.

Her pleadful moan brought him back to her lips and there

was a whispered roughness to his query, "Do you want me, Faith?"

Her simple, "Aye," disappeared into his mouth as he claimed her surrender with a conquering kiss.

"Are you sure you want me?" he asked again, nipping at her sensuously swollen lips with determined bites.

Before she could respond or even think a coherent thought he yanked her up and slipped a finger fast inside her.

"Aye, you do want me," he confirmed with a sinful smile.

She gasped as another finger followed in pursuit and she heard his brief laugh mingle with a low growl.

"You feel so good," he murmured near her ear. "So warm, so wet, so ready for me."

His fingers were working their usual magic, making her lose her senses and thinking of only one thing.

Him.

She found herself willingly moving to the steady rhythm he had set and along with that incessant rhythm his kisses became more urgent, his mouth rushing all over her, wherever his lips could reach.

When they had both reached an unbearable heat that could only be quelled by the finality of coupling, Eric moved to push her beneath him.

"Nay," she protested, shoving his hands away and moving to mount him eagerly.

She settled herself near his bulging manhood and grasped him firm in her hand to guide him into her.

"Stop, Faith," he shouted and leaned forward, his hands grabbing her beneath her arms and pulling her to him. "You cannot do this."

His powerful hold was steady on her and their faces nearly touched.

"Why?" she asked, confused.

"It is too painful a way for you to lose your virginity."

The shock of his remark was evident in the drop of her mouth and the widening of her stunned brown eyes. "You believe me a virgin?"

"Aye, I do," he answered without a moment of hesitation and with a brief, tender kiss. "And I will not see you suffer pain."

Her shocked expression immediately turned to one of disappointment. "But I want you."

It took all his willpower to say, "When my leg heals, we shall finish this."

Tears of love pooled in her eyes and she shook her head. "Nay, my lord, I cannot wait."

With that Faith broke free of his grasp and moved once again to mount him.

Eric attempted to protest but she was quick and successful in her attempt to slip his swelled manhood inside her.

Her startled grasp jolted his emotions in opposite directions. He grew harder from the tightness of his partial entrance within her wet nest and he grew upset thinking of her suffering further discomfort and pain.

"Enough," he ordered, but before he could grab her arm she moved further down upon him.

"Eric," she cried out when his manhood attempted to penetrate her maidenhead and she felt the first painful sting.

"Enough, Faith," he insisted, though he throbbed unmercifully with desire.

"Nay, nay," she said, shaking her head back and forth.

He silently cursed his own raging desires and her stubbornness and as she slowly attempted to take the full hard length of him inside her, he reached out and took command.

"Forgive me, my love," he said and with his hands around her waist he brought her down hard upon him, sending him full length into her.

She let out a gasp and he gave her no pause to think. His large hands sat firm on her waist and he took command of her ride. Her hands settled on his arms and after the initial shock of his solid entrance faded, what remained was sheer, exquisite pleasure and she wanted nothing more than to stay astride and ride him forever.

Her head fell back and then forward, her fiery mane spilling down around her and her moans of passion filled the room, echoing eerily off the thick stone walls.

A barrage of emotions attacked Eric full force. His concern for her pain, comfort and satisfaction far outweighed his own desires. Actually, the concern he felt for her managed to rage his passion past the limits of sanity. He had never experienced the overwhelming sensation of feeling complete, as if two halves had been joined to form one solid, overpowering desire that fueled and fed them both. One could not now exist without the other. They were whole, no longer separate beings but one forever, and he liked the strange, empowering sensation.

His name spilled from her lips along with her pleading moans. She begged him to end her torture and then she begged him not to stop. She was lost in a void of pure pleasure, sweeping her up and out of reality.

"Come on, my sweet Faith, come on," he urged, his rhythm turning demanding.

Her ride turned fast and furious and with it his words repeatedly urged her to join him.

"Aye, my lord," she agreed with an urgency she barely understood.

Their naked bodies shined with a fine sweat and they rode together, each lost within the other, emotionally and physically.

Eric was near to exploding from the warm, wet, welcoming feel of her tight sheath and Faith felt the scream of final surrender deep in her throat as he repeatedly thrust the full thick hardness of him deep inside her.

Their cries of surrender rang out simultaneously and as one they erupted in a climax that united their souls and joined their hearts.

Faith collapsed on Eric, her head coming to rest on his moist chest, his arms wrapping protectively around her damp body. Several minutes passed before either could calm their breathing enough to speak, and then neither could find the words.

Silence hung heavily in the room as they continued lying joined together until finally Faith shifted to move off her husband. His powerful embrace prevented her from detaching herself.

"I like being inside you."

His blatant remark heated her already flushed cheeks and made her all the more aware of his potent size. Even with the climax she could still feel the strength of him snug within her.

"Do you hurt?"

She felt completely exhausted and utterly pleasured and could feel only the barest hint of soreness, and his thoughtfulness pleased her so her reply came easily. "Only a little."

Her ear flat against his chest picked up his low growl that erupted into words. "I should not have allowed—"

"Nay." She stopped him, raising her head to look at him directly. His stark blue eyes blazed back at her. "I wanted you."

His hands moved to push back her mane of raging curls away from her face. "And I wanted you." His kiss was gentle though probing and it was a rising heat they both tempered as they reluctantly pulled apart.

"Why now did you believe me a virgin?" she asked curiously, resting her chin on his chest.

His hands moved to stroke leisurely down her back. "In all honesty I must admit that I never suspected otherwise. It was my own foolish pride that interfered. I wanted to hear you admit the truth."

She smiled. "And my stubborn pride ruled my better senses. I wanted to believe you knew me well enough to know the truth without asking."

"Aye, sweet Faith, I know you well." His voice was low, his tone certain. His hand moved down over her backside. "And I will know you even better before this night is done."

She shifted once again in an attempt to move off him and again he prevented her leaving with a firm hand, though this time she winced.

"You hurt," he said, not asked, and with a gentle slowness lifted her off him and brought her to rest alongside him. "You should not have mounted me. Now you suffer."

She rested her head comfortably on his shoulder and draped her arm over his broad chest. "I am fine."

"If you speak the truth then you chance me wanting you again," he said candidly.

"Promise?" she asked with a wicked laugh.

"You tempt fate, wife," he said, enjoying her playful nature.

"Nay, I tempt you." She shivered, her damp body catching a draft from the tapestry-draped window.

"You are chilled," he said with concern.

Before he could move, she sat up. "I will fetch us a blanket." She was almost off the bed when she caught sight of his bandaged leg. The white cloth was soaked with blood. She did not hesitate to set to work tending the bleeding wound.

He was about to protest, but thought better of it. They would waste time arguing and she would win in the end. And besides, he favored watching his naked wife fuss over him.

A clean new cloth was applied to the wound in no time and

she covered him to the waist with a soft, wool blanket. She then took a few minutes to cleanse herself with a cloth by the fire and Eric looked upon the intimate scene with pleasure.

Her body was firm and trim from digging in her garden, her stomach flat, though he would change that soon enough. He would take her often, not only to get her with child but because he desired her. How lucky he was to have a wife he favored bedding and favored to look upon and favored to be with . . . and who he loved.

Was he mad to think himself in love with Faith? Why else would these strange emotions attack him so incessantly? Could he actually be in love? Could it not be merely respect and admiration for a unique woman that he felt?

He grew hard again as he stared at the way she intimately ran the cloth between her legs, stroking and cleansing the thatch of red fiery curls.

"Come to bed," he ordered much too harshly.

She smiled at his demand and obediently slipped naked beneath the covers to lie against him. "You must not move your leg or it will continue to bleed."

"Then we have a problem," he said and took her hand, placing it over his swollen manhood.

He felt warm, hard and sticky. "You need cleaning."

"That is not what I need."

She whispered in his ear before she moved off the bed. "I know what you need." She hurried over to the hearth and retrieved a warm, wet cloth from the bucket. She returned and folded the blanket down behind his feet.

He watched her, wondering what she planned. Was it a repeat performance? He could not allow her to mount him again. He was concerned for her comfort. He thought to mount her this time, though she would probably protest, given her concern for his leg.

She gently washed his potent erection. "Tell me," she said, reaching for a clean towel to dry him. "Is it permissible for me to intimately taste you as you did me?"

She managed to shock him a second time that night and seeing his stunned expression she laughed before stretching out between his legs and slowly introducing herself to the taste of him.

Twenty-three

Faith woke before her husband the next day just as morning
dawned on the horizon. So as not to disturb his much-needed
healing slumber she gently slipped out of his embrace, tucking
a pillow under his arm when in his sleep he reached out for her.
He seemed content with the substitute at least momentarily, af-
fording her time to see to her own care.

She found Bridget waiting in her chambers. A light early-
morning fare sat ready on the table, a pot of her favorite
chamomile leaves brewing, and a steaming tub of water scented
with rose oil sat before the warm hearth.

Faith squealed with joy. "Bridget, you are wonderful."

The young woman smiled at the compliment and immediately reached out to assist the lady of the keep. "Let me help
you undress, my lady."

Faith did not protest. Her limbs were sore from their unusual
exercises and she could think of nothing more soothing than
steaming water. She sank into the huge tub with a grateful sigh,
the almost-hot water a perfect temperature as it engulfed her
body all the way up to her shoulders.

Bridget placed a folded towel on the rim and Faith rested her
head back on it.

"You are too good to me," Faith said in appreciation.

"You deserve to be treated well, my lady," Bridget said,
gathering the mass of red ringlets in her hands and twisting the

strands to secure them with two combs at the top of Faith's head. "After you rest and before the water chills, I will see to washing your hair."

Faith closed her eyes. "Thank you, Bridget. I do appreciate your attention."

She listened to the crackles and pops of the large logs that flamed in the hearth and relished the toasting warmth that drifted over her. She had not felt this satisfied in a very long time. And it was all due to last night and her surrender.

She smiled like a contented cat who had just finished a fine meal, for that was the way she felt—full and content. She had not thought surrender could prove so worthwhile, but then surrendering did not necessarily mean defeat.

A soft sigh ran from her lips and a gentle blush stained her cheeks. She had acted like a wanton woman last night and had thoroughly enjoyed her wicked actions. She had never felt so in command, so powerful as she did sitting astride him. The pain had been sharp, but only for an instant and then . . . she sighed again, remembering.

She wished for more opportunities to couple with her husband and she wished to be more inventive in their coupling. The taste of him had been pleasurable and she had feasted like a starved cat. She giggled, recalling his demands and how those same demands had turned to pleas of surrender, with him screaming out her name.

She did so enjoy that moment, though he did promise retaliation. But then she looked forward to his promise.

Bridget got down on bended knees to wash Faith's hair. Her thick, strong fingers roughly scrubbed the heavy strands right down to her scalp and Faith remained with eyes closed as Bridget rinsed, twisted and patted the wetness from her hair.

Faith saw to her own bathing and drying and Bridget saw to combing her hair by the fire, after she had dressed in a deep red shift and tunic, and taken a few bites of warm crusty bread and a mouthful of potage.

"Are you all right, my lady?" Bridget asked with reluctance and concern.

Castle gossip traveled fast and Faith had no doubt that the daily topic of conversation was the bedding of Lady Faith and the Irish devil.

Faith turned to face Bridget with a generous smile. "I have never felt so grand."

Bridget giggled. "I know the feeling."

"It must be their Viking blood," Faith said with a laugh.

"Aye, it gives them stamina."

The two women giggled like young girls in love.

A knock at the door made them both turn their heads.

"You may enter," Bridget called out.

The door opened and Borg filled the doorway. Actually, part of his head was above the doorframe. He bent his neck and entered the room, coming to stand full height.

"Your husband demands your presence in his chambers, my lady," he informed her with a grin.

Without thinking, she said, "I thought he would sleep the morn away after such a strenuous night." As soon as the words escaped her lips, her hand flew to cover her mouth as if attempting to retrieve her remark.

Borg laughed and Bridget giggled.

"Lord Eric has frightened the servants who have brought him his morning meal, he yells at Colin who fights to keep him abed and curses the warring clans who caused his injury," Borg informed her when his laughter died.

Faith stood quickly, causing Bridget hastily to withdraw the comb from her damp hair. "The wound does not still bleed, does it?"

Borg shook his head. "Nay, his bandage is dry and he insists he is well."

"Another day abed and then limited use of the leg for a few days thereafter and he should be fine. He is not feverish?"

Borg found her question amusing. "That I cannot say. No one dares go near him."

"Tell my lord I will be with him momentarily. I have one thing I must see to," she said and rushed over to her wooden chest to grab her dark red cloak.

"Colin has seen to Rook this morning and Mary the Cook feeds him well at this moment," Borg said.

Faith nodded. "I had no doubt Rook would be well looked after. He has a way of winning people's hearts and when he knows I am in good care he does not worry."

Borg gave her a quizzical look. "Where is it you go, then?"

"To offer a prayer," she said.

Borg moved alongside her as she approached the door. "I go with you. Eric ordered me not to return without you or I would suffer his wrath."

Faith cast him a skeptical look. "He would not harm you."

Borg shook his head and smiled. "No, but his wrath is something I do not wish to experience. It chills the soul."

Faith stopped at the door and turned suddenly. "Bridget, you have been most kind. Thank you."

Bridget shook her head as Borg hurried to her side, kissed her cheek and whispered, "Lady Faith does not understand her position . . . be patient."

Bridget swatted him on the arm—not that it did much good. "She will always be a kind soul and I will always do what I can to protect her."

Borg winked at her. "So will I."

Faith hurried up the stairs, knowing exactly where she wished to go.

Borg caught up with her, finding her hasty flight curious. She had passed the chapel and yet she wished to pray. Where was her destination?

She made her way to the barican that viewed the River Deel. The river could only be seen from this height, though the morning sun was now cloud covered and a fine mist lay low over the land, preventing a view of the green fields and rolling hills that spread out for miles.

Borg hesitated, remaining a few feet away, giving her privacy for what obviously was the place she wished to pray.

Faith looked up, blue sky peeked through gray clouds with the promise of a lovely day. But for now the land lay shrouded in a eerie mist that frightened most—but not Faith. She often thought that God covered the fields, valleys and meadows with the all too familiar mist to protect the animals and give them time to forage and nourish without interference from humans. And to her it was the perfect time to get His attention.

She cast a smile to the heavens and spoke a simple prayer of thanks and appreciation for all He had given her. And she specifically requested that He look after her stubborn husband and help heal him. She finished with another prayer of thanksgiving, then turned to join Borg.

"Why do you not pray in the chapel, my lady?" Borg asked as she hooked her arm in his.

Faith paused briefly before she offered an answer. "'Tis the heavens I wish to look upon when I cast my prayer."

Borg accepted her explanation with a slow nod and together they made their way to Lord Eric's chambers, jumping aside to avoid the frightened young servant girl who ran crying from his room.

Faith called out to her, bringing her to a sudden halt, and she offered an apology for her husband's rude behavior. The young girl was stunned speechless. Faith then asked if she would take her cloak to her chambers. The girl bobbed her head and though tears still shined in her eyes, she smiled and hurried off.

"Do not dare attempt to stop me, Colin," Eric warned with a snarl that was meant to intimidate. "I am getting out of this bed now."

"Nay, you are not," Faith said, entering the room and going straight to her husband's side.

Colin had a firm hand to Eric's chest and quickly and gratefully vacated his position beside the bed at her approach.

"Where have you been and why did you leave me to wake alone?" he asked, irritated. Before she could respond, he shouted, "Borg, Colin, get out."

"It is not necessary for them to leave," Faith said.

"Out," he shouted at the two men and they both laughed loudly as they walked out and shut the door behind them.

"You lack proper manners," Faith insisted.

"Manners be damned. Why did you leave my bed?"

Faith noticed he had seen to his morning wash and his freshly combed dark hair lay over his shoulders and brushed his naked chest. The wool blanket covered him to his waist and she assumed he remained naked beneath. The thought thrilled her and she smiled.

"My query amuses you?" he asked caustically.

"Nay, my lord," she said, repentant, though her smile remained. "My thoughts were elsewhere."

"Why did you leave?" he asked again and reached out, taking her hand in his and gently tugging her down to sit beside him on the bed.

"I required a bath and fresh clothes."

"You could have bathed here."

"I would have disturbed your sleep."

"Your absence disturbed my sleep even more," he said, and

ran his hand up along her arm, over her shoulder and to the back of her neck where his fingers firmly stroked her sensitive skin.

"You need time to heal," she insisted, her words a warning not only to him but to her own traitorous body.

"I need time with my wife."

"We have all day."

"You robbed me of this morning with you."

"I apologize," she said, his fingers running up into her hair and stroking her scalp and sending shivers of sensuous delight racing through her.

"What thoughts were on your mind?"

She looked at him with odd confusion. Feeling as shameless as she did last night, mostly from those magically tormenting fingers of his, she spoke honestly: "Thoughts of you naked beneath that blanket."

He smiled, pleased. "When you were not beside me this morning when I woke, I thought perhaps last night was nothing more than an erotic dream, but your woman's scent clung to me and I drank it in, remembering."

His hand cupped the back of her head and drew her to him. "And I grew hard with the want of you." He brought his mouth down softly on hers. "Very hard," he whispered harshly, and his mouth turned rough and demanding.

She responded in kind, her own lips brutal in their need of him and her body growing just as needy.

He moved his mouth off hers long enough to demand that she rid herself of her clothes. She stood to do just that as a knock sounded on the door.

He cursed viciously and shouted for the intruder to be gone or face execution.

Borg laughed as he entered the room. "A message from Lord Donnegan."

Faith immediately dropped down on the bed beside her husband and Eric instantly reached out and took her hand. She grasped onto his reassuring hold, squeezing firmly.

"What does he say?"

"That his journey has yet again been delayed and he will send you a message when he is able to travel."

Bridget entered the open doorway with a worried expression. "Excuse me, my lord and my lady, but Mary the Cook is ill and requires attention."

"You cannot see to it?" Eric snapped and received a sharp warning look from Borg.

Faith stood, releasing Eric's hand. "It will take but a moment. And you should eat," she suggested, pointing to the tray filled with food on the table.

"I am not hungry for food," he insisted.

She leaned over and placed a gentle kiss on his lips, then whispered. "Satisfy your belly and then I will satisfy your passion."

He smiled and returned her kiss, nipping playfully at her lips. "Nay, wife, 'tis time for me to retaliate."

Faith blushed a bright red as she hurried out of the room, Bridget fast on her heels.

Borg dragged the table, abundant with food on it, near to the bed and pulled up a chair.

"Do you intend to eat it all?" Eric said, sitting forward and piling pillows behind his back.

"You said you were not hungry," Borg said, helping himself to the trencher of sweet potted herring spiced with wild onions and handing Eric a chunk of hard cheese.

Eric eyed the pitiful chunk of cheese with disgust. "You never were one for sharing food equally."

Borg popped a slim onion in his mouth and mumbled, "Food fuels the body, gives one stamina."

Eric reached out for the wooden bowl near the end of the table and smiled, pleased to find fresh salmon with leeks inside. "Hand over the bread."

Borg broke off a hunk of the black bread and handed it to Eric, then broke off another, even bigger piece for himself. "All went well last night?"

"More than well—perfect," Eric confirmed with a smug smile.

"Good. Now that you are finished acting like a fool we can concentrate on the problem."

"I was not acting like a fool, and what problem?"

"The problem of who attempted to murder your wife?"

Eric did not seem the least surprised. "You have reached that conclusion also?"

"How could I not? He attacked with a knife, meaning to kill, not damage."

Eric nodded. "I agree. I have been giving it thought as well and Faith suffered her wound because she fought him. If she had not her wounds would have been fatal."

"Which leaves the question of who wanted her dead?"

"You have your choice of Donnegans."

Borg scooped up a chunk of herring with the bread. "A stupid and greedy lot."

"Stupidity and greed make for a dangerous enemy."

Borg shook his head after emptying his tankard of ale with one swig. "Why would any of them want her dead?"

"That is the mystery that once solved will give us the attacker's identity."

Borg refilled his tankard and added more ale to Eric's near-empty one. "Have you ever seen Faith enter the keep's chapel?"

Eric was about to answer but paused momentarily in thought. "I cannot say I have ever seen her there. Why do you ask?"

"When I found her in her chambers she requested a few moments to offer a prayer. I followed her under fear of your wrath," Borg said, grinning widely, "and she took herself to the west barican."

"To pray?"

"Aye, to pray," Borg confirmed. "And when I asked her why she did not go to the chapel she remarked something about wanting to look upon the heavens when she prayed."

Eric thought this news over and added his own concerns. "You know Faith rarely grows ill."

Borg nodded. "Aye, she is a fine, healthy woman."

"The day that cleric stopped in his travels to offer blessings for those in the keep, I asked her if she wished to receive any blessing from him. She grew ill and spent the entire day in her bed."

"You think her illness feigned and that one of the clergy could be responsible?"

"I think Faith knows more than she admits and I think I want my wife to trust me enough to speak to me of her fears and concerns."

Borg threw his large hands up. "Not another skirmish."

"Nay," Eric said with a laugh. "The only skirmishes will be beneath the covers and I will always win."

"My coins are still on the healer. She will be victorious and have you calling out her name in surrender."

Eric laughed harder. "Brother, you win the wager. I thought the whole keep heard my pleading surrender last eve."

"Faith is good for you," Borg said seriously.

"Aye, that she is," Eric agreed. "And I would surrender my life not only to her but for her."

"Besotted," Borg grinned, raising his tankard in a toast.

Love.

The word echoed in his mind but his lips repeated the toast. "Besotted."

Mary lay on the single bed in the healing cottage, a damp cloth on her head, groaning. "'Tis dying I am."

A smile twitched at Faith's mouth. "There will be no dying today."

Rook sat beside the bed crying along in sympathy with the woman who gave him daily treats.

"Stop that, Rook," Faith scolded, her mouth again threatening to smile outrageously. "Mary will be fine and you will continue to receive those treats you think I know nothing about."

Rook immediately turned silent and cautiously made his way over to the hearth to stretch out. Mary continued the groaning on her own.

"How often have you had trouble keeping the food in your belly?"

"The last few days have been the worst and sometimes I do not even need food in me to have my belly protest," Mary said, rubbing her wide yet firm stomach.

Faith nodded knowingly.

"Tell me the truth, my lady, please. I need to know if my stomach rots."

She spoke so seriously that Faith grew alarmed. "You think your stomach rots?"

"Aye, I have seen it in other women," Mary insisted, sitting up, color having returned to her pale full face.

"And you think this is what ails you?" Faith asked.

"What else could it be?"

Faith smiled. "Think, Mary, you have been busy and not

paying attention to your body. The signs are there for you to see."

Mary frowned. "I am not a healer and do not know such signs."

"Every woman knows these signs and if you but think you will know what grows in your stomach."

Mary looked ready to shout at Faith when she suddenly jumped up and cried out. "I am with child!"

"Aye, you are," Faith said as excited as the tearing woman in front of her.

"Thank you, my lady," Mary said and scooped Faith up, hugging her to her ample bosom.

When Faith was finally placed on her feet again, she laughed. "I think it is your husband you should be thanking."

Mary's laugh was joyous. "I will do that tonight."

Faith found the servant and peasant women easy to talk with. They were candid and honest in their speech and took pleasure in simple duties and daily life. Their lot was not easy and yet they loved and lived with an honest and joyful intensity she often found lacking in nobles. They accepted hardships with courage and strength and continued to survive and flourish in their own unique ways. They were the true sons and daughters of Ireland, fighting the land, the elements and the nobles who warred continuously to fatten their holdings.

She felt a kinship more with these people than with her own kind. Her stepmother had often remarked how she belonged with the peasants and Faith had to agree. She had found their kind more to her liking.

Mary finally calmed down enough for Faith to sit with her and talk. Faith recommended a mint brew to help keep her stomach calm. She also told her that she would speak to Lord Eric about providing Mary with more help in the kitchen.

Mary shook her head. "Nay, my lady, 'tis my job and babe or not I must see to my chores."

Faith surprised herself when she said, "I am lady of this keep and if I wish you to have extra help in the kitchen you will have extra help."

"Aye, my lady, as you wish," Mary said respectfully.

"Good," Faith said, confirming her dictate more to herself than Mary.

After a few more instructions to Mary, Faith stood and with

a smile ordered her to go talk with her husband. Mary's expression turned sheer radiant and after many words of appreciation for all Faith had done for her and her husband, the joyful woman practically ran out of the cottage.

Faith was about to return to Eric when a castle worker showed up at her door, his hand bleeding. And so the next few hours passed by with one person or another needing attention. It was not until an hour or two past noon that Faith finished and with a rumble of thunder in the distance and heavy raindrops chasing her, she hastily returned to the castle.

Rook deserted her side upon entering the great hall, his nose having scented the makings of the evening meal. He seemed to have sensed she was safe once inside the keep and took himself off daily for regular visits to the kitchen before finding her once again. But if she stepped outside the keep he was always by her side.

She was pleased to see that Eric was sleeping when she entered his room. Pillows were scattered over the bed and he was turned slightly to his side. His long, dark hair fell back away from his handsome face and his arms hugged a pillow tightly to his chest. If she had been beside him she was certain it would be she he was embracing.

His hands had constantly reached out for her last night, not groping but to touch, to pull close, to stroke, to hold. He made her feel that he could not get enough of her.

"Come here," he ordered softly, waking from his sleep to see her standing beside the bed.

She took a step toward him and his words stopped her.

"Nay, wife, I want you naked."

She should have blushed, she should have protested, she should of reminded him of his manners, but instead she removed her clothes.

Twenty-four

Eric stretched his limbs, all the while keeping his eyes on his wife's every move. He had grown annoyed and then tired waiting for her return and had slipped into an unexpected slumber. Now he was glad he had. He felt refreshed, rejuvenated and ready.

Ready to make love with his wife.

Faith stopped when she reached the bed and looked down at him. She shivered at the intensity of his blue eyes and the firm set of his jaw. He was determined and resembled more a warrior about to engage in battle than a husband about to make love to his wife.

He sensed her apprehension and with a smile that belied his sensuous intentions he held his hand out to her.

She took it and joined him, slipping beneath the blanket, the soft wool coming to rest at her waist. "Your leg does not pain you?"

"Always the healer," he said and gently brushed his lips over hers. "My leg has caused me no pain and the bandage stays dry."

"Rest does you well," she said, tucking a strand of his long hair behind his ear and running her finger down along his firm jaw.

He nipped playfully at her finger as she passed it over his lips. "Rest bores me. I need activity."

"You will rest," she ordered sternly. "I will see you healed before you leave this bed."

His smile was followed by a soft laugh. "And I will see you pleasured many times before I leave this bed."

His intentions reminded her of Mary's condition and she happily relayed the news to him. "Mary is with child and I told her she would receive extra hands in the kitchen."

"As you wish." He pushed the blanket down so he could splay his hand over her flat stomach. "When you grow large with our child you will take care."

Faith placed her hand over his. "You have my word that I will take care of our child."

His lips drifted to hers. "I will give you many children."

"Promise?" she whispered, her lips reaching out to meet his.

"Promise," he assured her and sealed his word with a kiss.

A sharp crack of thunder brought them apart and made Faith snuggle closer to her husband's side. Eric felt her tremble against him and slipped his strong arms around her.

"Tell me of your fears, Faith," he said, holding her close. While intimacy was foremost on his mind, questions nagged incessantly at him; besides, he wanted her to realize and accept the fact that she could trust the devil.

Her trembles subsided and she relaxed within his protective embrace. "I fear not having strength."

"You have much strength for a woman and now you have me and I will always protect you."

Her voice grew low. "Nothing is forever."

Her truthful remark caused a ripple of fear to race through him. He had this moment here and now with his wife, but what of tomorrow? A day, an hour, a moment could change a person's life forever, just as it had for her.

He took a chance with his next comment. "When you release me from the confines of this bed we will go to the chapel and pray that forever lasts for us."

Her response did not surprise him. She stiffened.

He continued his pursuit of her secrets. "Borg mentioned that you prefer saying your prayers outside. Do you not like the chapel?"

"It is a lonely place," she admitted softly.

"Not when the priest is in residence."

This time she shivered.

He pulled the soft wool blanket up over her.

She changed the subject, choosing one he would eagerly respond to. She slipped her hand down between his legs and gently cupped him. "I like the feel of you, dear husband."

His hand followed suit over her body. "And I you."

The next crack of thunder did not disturb them, nor the sound of the torrential rain that drenched the land. The couple was lost in a world of passion, hearing only the sounds of their own surrenders.

Laughter and whispers followed all the servants of the keep. There was not one who did not comment on the incessant coupling of Lady Faith and the Irish devil. Wagers were being made on when the lady of the keep would be with child; others wagered on how many times Lord Eric would seek his wife out and they would disappear for a few hours or for the rest of the day. But the mainstay of the gossip was that the pretty healer had managed to tame the devil himself, and that topic would keep tongues wagging for some time.

Eric had been out of bed for near to two weeks. Faith had removed the stitches and pronounced him fit, though he could have told her that over a week ago. He had to admit that he did enjoy his convalescence in bed, especially since his wife spent most of the time there with him. He had learned more about pleasuring a woman's body in that time than in all his combined years. He'd had the time to explore and discover and the discoveries he had made simply astounded him. He now knew every point and place on his wife's body and how each would react to his touch or taste. He had even learned what words enticed and excited her and he often used them to his advantage.

On the other hand Faith had done her own exploring and he was surprised to learn just how crazy she could make him. She was well aware of how and where to touch him to get an immediate response, and a few of the places surprised him. They had grown to know each other well, though they still explored and made discoveries. Which was why he was presently searching her out. He felt the urge to discover.

It was a couple of hours before supper. Borg had sought out Bridget, Colin was presently entertaining one of the servant girls and Eric was still in search of his wife. She had not been in the keep, her healing cottage was deserted and those he met around the castle grounds did not seem to know where she was. There was one place he had not looked, though he doubted she was there, but he headed in that direction anyway.

The stables soon came into his view and he hurried his steps. He was probably wasting his time and yet if someone was in need she would go, even to a place she feared.

The scent of fresh hay mixed with the pungent odor of animals assaulted his nostrils as he entered the stable. He had a large stable erected to house his horses and as he walked along the stalls that held the mighty beasts that had rode into battle with him he was reminded of how many times a few of them had saved his life. He stopped along the way to offer a comforting pat and an appreciative word to the fine animals.

He spotted Rook; the large dog had stuck his head out from the last stall to offer a bark at his presence. Faith appeared next, exiting the stall, and was followed by a young stable hand whose arm was wrapped in a bandage up past his elbow.

Eric heard her edict upon his approach. "You will be fine and your courage deserves a reward." Rook barked at that announcement. She scolded the animal much too softly before continuing. "Go to Mary in the kitchen and tell her you are to have a special treat."

Another bark from Rook was quelled by a warning look from Eric.

Faith smiled and shook her head and asked of the young lad, "Will you take Rook along and get him a treat as well?"

Rook was about to bark again, but turned a wide eye on Eric and wisely chose silence.

The young lad and Rook was soon bounding out of the stable toward the kitchen.

"You spoil that animal," Eric said, stopping in front of her and reaching out to pull her into his arms.

She went willingly. "Aye, but I spoil you as well."

"How so?" he asked, playfully nipping at her neck and sending gooseflesh running along her skin.

"I always let you have your way with me."

He laughed. "Let me? Poor choice of words, wife. You want me and then you always surrender."

She gave him a playful punch in the arm.

He in turn hoisted her in the air and moved toward one of

the stalls that held a mound of hay, teasingly saying, "I will teach you to be a good wife."

He was about to toss her down on the hay when she buried her face in his neck, locked her arms around him as best she could and cried softly for him to stop.

Reality dawned on him and he could have kicked himself for being so stupid. He tightened his hold on her and eased her down onto the mound of hay along with him.

He whispered reassurances in her ear. "It's all right. No one is going to hurt you. You are all right."

She cried and sighed next to his ear and would not let go of him and he did not force her to. He held her, reassured her and comforted her, all the while berating himself for his stupidity. As soon as she calmed down he would get her out of here and into the keep. Maybe there he would be able to repair some of the damage he had done.

"I am sorry," she said on a hiccup.

She had finally released the tight hold she had on him and he looked with relief into her dark, teary eyes. "Nonsense, I am the one who needs to apologize."

She looked surprised. "Why, you did nothing wrong. You simply wanted me."

"Aye, that I did," he admitted freely. "But I should have been more cautious with my words and actions."

"Nay, Eric," she said softly, placing her cool hand against his warm cheek. "I cannot carry my fear around with me forever."

He gently pushed her hair away from her face and slowly traced the thin scar with his finger. "Let me rid you of that fear once and for all."

She shivered. Could she submit to his will here and now, and in a place that was familiar of her attack? Instinctively she knew she had nothing to fear from her husband and yet old memories haunted her. What if she agreed and then could not submit?

"Let me love you, Faith," he urged with a gentle kiss to her lips. "Let me show you there is nothing to fear."

But she did fear. She feared reliving the memories and the nightmares. She feared seeing her attacker's face, feeling the knife slice her skin, hearing her own screams. She shook her head slowly.

"Don't lock it away, Faith, let me help you," he said and kissed her again and again, not giving her a chance to respond verbally or deny him.

His gentle aggression worked; she responded in kind, kissing him most willingly, almost hungrily like a woman too long denied.

The sudden need for him startled her and yet she refused to fight it. She wanted her husband, ached for him, and there was no reason she could not have him here in the stable. She shivered at her own thought.

He took command, continuing to kiss her in between shedding his clothes. He would not toss up her shift and have his way with her. He wanted them both naked and he wanted her totally responsive.

It took some coaxing, kissing, and suggestive words to get her to let him undress her. And when they were both finally naked he began a slow, sweet seduction of her body that started at her mouth with lazy nips and kisses and worked its way down over plump breasts, nipples that rolled off his tongue taut and ready and a fiery red nest that welcomed his tongue with eager squeals.

Faith lost all sense of herself and her surroundings. She could think only of her husband and his wickedly delightful tongue, but then her eyes were closed. She shut them when he began and had refused to open them. She would think of Eric and only Eric and where they were did not matter—only what they shared.

Eric moved over her, ready to enter her but not with her eyes squeezed tightly shut. He wanted her looking directly at him. He wanted her fully aware of where she was and what he was doing and how she was responding.

"Look at me," he ordered firmly and she shook her head.

He shook his own head at her stubbornness, but could understand her reluctance, though it was her strength and courage he wished to see surface. He tried again, this time with a stern firmness. "Look at me, Faith."

"Nay," she said, and her ardor began to cool.

He would not allow her to retreat. He did what he did well and took complete command. He claimed her mouth with a demand she could not deny and she moaned when he released her lips with a biting kiss.

He parted her legs. "Look at me, Faith, watch me enter you. Watch me take you. Watch my passion for you."

He tempted her beyond reason. She wanted to watch him do it all. She wanted to see the full hard length of him slip into her. She wanted to watch as he set a pace she had become familiar with and she wanted to watch the passion fire in his blue eyes. But if she opened her eyes she would see the stable, and what then?

"Look," he urged, "Look how much I want you, Faith."

She could feel him. He purposely rubbed his thick shaft against her mound to tempt and torment and remind her of what she was missing. And her body demanded she respond, and quick. She felt the heat engulf her, felt the moistness ready to welcome him and felt the urgency to feel his entrance.

"Come on," he urged again and moved over her in a deliciously sinful way that had her battling herself. He watched her eyes drift slowly open and he kept talking to her, urging her, reassuring her and inviting her.

She finally surrendered her fear to him with full open eyes and a soft cry of his name from her lips. "Eric."

"Look at me, Faith, I am your husband, feel how much I want you," he said and slowly slipped inside her.

She watched his every move and gasped at his easy entrance and smoother penetration until he was completely sheathed deep within her and then he again convinced her to keep her eyes on him as he began to slide in and out of her with a steady, lazy rhythm that stole what little senses she had left.

The hay crunched beneath them, she smelled its freshness and heard the animals, only this time they were quiet, not screeching along with her screams of fright and the man that she saw was not a dark figure intent on murder but her husband intent on pleasuring her. And this was not the stable at Donnegan Keep but her home at Shanekill.

Her home.

She was home here with her husband and all was right and good and she could trust the devil. She smiled.

"I please you," he said with a confident smile.

"Aye, you do," she admitted and began to move along with him.

"Tell me you want me, wife," he said teasingly and rose high enough over her for her to watch him move in and out of her and make her feel his every controlled thrust.

She did just that. "I want you, husband."

"Then take all of me," he said on a whisper as his lips rushed down to claim hers and his body rushed to satisfy them both.

They were soon lost in a world of unbridled passion. Nothing mattered, not where they were, who they were, why they were—only that they were one at this moment.

Complete and whole.

They exploded together in a climax that left them stunned and breathless.

Eric collapsed on top of her and though he realized his weight was too much for her, he found it too difficult to move. He was panting and attempting to gain control of his strength. He felt drained—a pleasant drain, but nonetheless a drain of every last ounce of strength he possessed.

Faith felt pleasured beyond reason and safe, safe with her husband's strong body covering hers. She also felt warm, the heat of his damp flesh toasting her nicely against the chill that raced through the stable.

"Are you all right?" he asked in a whisper near her ear before he pressed loving kisses along her scarred cheek.

"I am," she admitted softly, rubbing her cheek to his.

He looked at her, his blue eyes gentle in their appeal. "I want you to know you are safe here at your home, no matter where it is you choose to go."

"That means much to me, Eric." She smiled and poked him in the shoulder. "But I truly wonder if the stable is a safe place after all."

His grin was wicked. "If it is a safe place you are looking to be from your husband, you will find none. I will have you wherever and whenever I or you please."

"There is a time and place for such things," she scolded, tugging teasingly at the long strands of dark hair that brushed her chest.

"The time and place is of my choice or yours."

"Promise," she said, wrapping the silky strand around her finger and drawing his mouth closer to hers. "Promise me that no matter when or where I ask you will not deny me."

He assaulted her lips gently and said, "I promise."

"Good," she said on a laugh and whispered in his ear.

"I will see to that most hastily," he assured her and slipped off her.

"Now?" She looked at him with startled eyes.

"We both need a good soak in the tub after this pleasurable episode in the hay, so why not together?"

"Truly?"

"Truly," he agreed with a nod and began dressing. She followed suit.

"The servants will gossip."

"They are already gossiping."

"They will think us strange," she said.

"They will know us happy," he corrected.

"You are happy?" she asked, standing after pulling on her boots.

Eric picked broken bits of hay from her hair. "Aye, I am very happy, and you?"

"I am most content."

"With me?"

She stood on her toes to reach his mouth as she said, "With you and all you have so generously given me."

His arm circled her waist and he hoisted her up so their lips could easily meet. Her kiss was ardent and it surprised him. By the time they broke apart he was fully aroused, another surprise, though a pleasant one.

"I could take you again, here and now," he said roughly, her lips plump with passion and her eyes flooded with desire, two sure signs that fueled his own heated cravings.

"Nay, 'tis your chambers where I wish to be with you for the rest of the day."

"Be sure of what you ask, Faith," he warned. "For once I take you there it is there we will remain, you and I, in the bath, in the bed and wherever else it is I wish to take you."

She gave him a quick peck to the cheek and a wide smile before she asked of him, "Can it be done in a chair?"

He laughed and swung her up into his arms. "Remember it was you who asked."

"But you did not answer?"

"Nay, I will show you instead," he said and carried her out of the stable, past many startled and whispering peasants and straight through the great hall, shouting orders that a bath be brought to his chambers.

Faith buried her blushing cheeks against his chest and he laughed even harder, promising her that he intended to make her whole body blush tonight.

And he did.

Twenty-five

Faith watched her husband deal fairly with the people who brought him their problems and though he was known as a good lord and well respected there were still many who feared being in his presence.

Looking upon him sitting on the dais, she could understand why. He sat tall and straight, not slumped or indifferent to those who stood quaking before him. His eyes remained focused on the person presenting his grievance, causing most to look away, unable to meet the intensity of his stark blue eyes. Even the dark red of his clothing caused intimidation since tongues wagged about it being the color of spilled blood. And of course there was his face, so sinfully handsome that the women whispered he could be no other progeny than that of Lucifer himself.

Faith sighed quietly, her eyes and thoughts remaining on her husband. She stood just inside the large doors of the great hall having returned from a walk with Rook. A chill wind and gathering clouds had forced them to shorten their usual lengthy walk, as did Faith's tired and protesting limbs.

Truth be told, she could not fully blame her husband for her tiredness. It was her own unrelenting desire to pursue the dark lord and make him hers. He treated her well and was generous in all he gave her, except he had yet to tell her he loved her.

And those words she intended to hear spill from his lips.

Her hand covered her mouth, hiding one of the many yawns

that had been attacking her since early morning and she looked
down to see Rook agree with his own wide yawn. Her glance
returned to settle on her husband and he motioned for her to
join him. She was about to do so when a commotion at the door
had her moving out of the way.

A messenger, dirty and haggard from a long ride, rushed in,
demanding to see the dark lord.

Faith watched her husband's blue eyes narrow and his jaw
tighten and she smiled when Colin and Borg rose to full, intimidating height on either side of Eric. The three were a sight to
behold and the demanding messenger suddenly turned timid
and fell to his knees before the dais.

Faith heard him clearly, his strong voice intentionally filling
the hall with his news.

"Lord and Lady Donnegan will arrive within the week. They
have graciously sent their priest, Father Peter, ahead to offer his
blessings on this keep and all within. He will arrive within a
day's time."

Eric simply nodded as if the news were unimportant and ordered one of the servants to see to the messenger's care.

Faith made her way toward the dais, not the least bit concerned with her father and stepmother's impending arrival. She
was confident that her husband had no intentions of returning
her to them, though she wondered why he had not informed
them of his decision. She would ask him—of late she found
herself asking him many questions most husbands probably
would find objectionable or refuse to answer. Not Eric—he satisfied her curiosity either with a demonstration or a thorough
explanation.

She was smiling to herself and was caught off guard as the
messenger stepped in her path. Rook immediately alerted the
man to his guarding presence with a low, ominous growl that
had the man taking a hasty step back.

"Your stepmother has a message for you," he said in a low
tone that was meant for her ears alone.

She regarded him with cautious eyes.

"She instructs that you follow her edict and take penance
and communion with the priest. She says do not disobey her or
you will be sorry." As he said this, he cast an eye to Rook.

He moved away from her before she had a chance even to
consider a response. How dare her stepmother threaten her in

her own home and with words she knew full well would affect her. She began to tremble as she approached the dais. She grew angry at herself for being frightened and grew more angry at stepmother's audacity for threatening her in her home where she had finally felt safe and secure.

Her legs suddenly felt too heavy to move, or perhaps it was because she trembled so that she found it difficult to take another step. Her head felt much too light and she was much too dizzy, as though concentration was impossible. She heard Rook whimper, as if in the distance. Why did he whimper? She would let nothing happen to him, nor would Eric. He would protect them both—of that she had no doubt.

She looked at her husband who seemed to be rising out of his seat and taking flight across the dais as she softly called out his name.

Faith never hit the ground; Eric caught her safely in his arms as she fell into a dead faint. Colin went after the messenger, grabbing the stunned man by the back of his tunic as he attempted to take flight. Borg joined Eric after instructing one of the servants to fetch Bridget.

Rook licked Faith's pale face and continued to whimper in concern for his master.

Eric grew so alarmed he shouted at Borg, "Do something."

He was saved from responding by Bridget's frantic shouts for everyone to move out of her way.

In minutes Bridget had the situation in hand. A chilled wet cloth was applied several times to Faith's pale face while whispers were spreading like wildfire that the lady of the keep was with child.

Eric, Borg and Bridget heard them and Eric sent Bridget a questioning look.

"I do not know if she is with child, my lord," Bridget said quietly.

"Good possibility, though," Borg said with a grin and Eric shot him a warning look that did little good. "You play, you pay."

"Nay," Bridget said testy, "'tis my lady who will pay when she lingers in the torturous pains of childbirth."

This time Eric paled and Bridget felt contrite.

"My lady is strong, my lord. I am sure she will find the pain bearable."

Faith began to moan softly.

"She comes around," Eric said relieved.

"I think you should carry her to your chambers. I can better tend her there."

Eric scooped her up into his arms and stood with the ease of a man carrying a light bundle, though he held her with a precariousness and concern that brought many a tear to the women in the hall.

Colin came to his side after having posted three men to guard the messenger.

"Find out what words he spoke to her," Eric instructed sternly and Colin simply nodded, understanding he was not to fail. Eric motioned for Borg to join Colin, though the large man was already on his way with a look of determination that Eric was certain would cause the messenger to answer every question that was asked of him.

Bridget hurried in front of Eric, scurrying up the steps, Rook speeding past her, to reach the room before her. She had the blanket pulled back from the bed and the pillows plumped. Eric deposited his wife down gently, leaving enough room for him to sit beside her. Rook sat on the opposite side, his head resting on the bed and his big eyes fixed on his master.

"What happened?" Faith asked, finally coming fully awake.

"You fainted, m'lady," Bridget said.

"I never faint," Faith said and looked to her husband, who did not wait to ask the question that was heavy on his mind.

"Are you with child?"

She thought a moment and while there was a distinct possibility she was, she could not yet be sure. She answered honestly. "'Tis too soon for me to know."

He stared at her with troubled eyes and she turned to Bridget. "Please brew some chamomile leaves for me."

The young woman understood that the lord and lady wished to be alone. "I will also fix you a light fare."

"Thank you, Bridget," Faith said with an appreciative smile.

When the door clicked shut Eric spoke. "You frightened me."

She pressed her fingers to his lips. "The devil frightened?"

He kissed her warm fingers and took them in his hand. "A husband frightened."

"There are two of you, then?" she teased.

"Aye, there is and it is the husband who is concerned about you and the devil who keeps you from harm."

"I think the devil visits me at other times as well," she said with a laugh.

Eric found himself smiling and feeling completely relieved that she was her usual bold and beautiful self. "He sneaks in on occasion, but right now your husband worries."

"I am fine," she assured him.

"Then why did you faint?" he asked.

Faith's first recall was that of her husband taking flight over the dais. "You flew," she said, startled by her image of him in the air.

He nodded. "That I did. Rook was whimpering loudly and I realized he was sending a warning, smart dog," he said and patted the animal's head. "I realized you were about to swoon and took the most direct path to you."

"Over the dais?"

"In one leap and I caught you," he answered proudly.

"I knew you would never fail to protect me."

"I will always protect you," he confirmed.

She suddenly needed his arms around her. "Hold me," she pleaded softly.

He laid down beside her and drew her into his embrace. She snuggled contentedly against him. Rook, understanding her safe, walked over by the hearth and plopped down to take a much-needed nap.

Neither spoke, though both thought on the incident. Faith recalled the messenger's words to her while Eric wondered what those words were and both wondered what had caused her to faint. Was it the messenger's words or was she with child? Or was there more to her sudden swoon than she would admit to her husband?

Eric left his slumbering wife in the care of Bridget with a command to Rook to guard his master well. The sleeping dog had immediately come to attention and when Eric finished giving him instructions he had walked over to the bed and sat directly beside it, where Faith lay.

"Make sure Rook gets a big bone tonight," he said to Bridget before he left the room and headed to his solar.

Colin and Borg were waiting, both men feasting on a well-stacked platter of food and several flasks of wine. The delicious aroma assaulted Eric as soon as he walked through the door, and caused his stomach to growl.

"Do we toast?" Colin asked with his goblet raised high.

Eric understood what he asked. Bridget had informed him that the keep was buzzing with the news that Lady Faith was with child. He himself was disappointed in her answer, though he would not admit it to Faith or anyone else. Though he did smile, telling himself he would have to try harder.

"She is not sure," he said quickly when the two men were about to cheer, assuming his smile was a positive response.

"Spend more time with her," Borg urged.

"He is right," Colin agreed. "The winter fast draws near. Warm yourself with her."

Eric reached for the wine flask and filled a goblet. "I have done little else."

The three men laughed.

"What did the messenger tell you?" Eric asked, grabbing a hunk of cheese and a piece of bread off the platter before taking his seat by the hearth.

Colin refilled his goblet, Borg reached for a thick slice of stewed meat and slapped it on a piece of dark bread and then both men took seats opposite Eric.

"As soon as he took one look at Borg he talked incessantly," Colin said.

"Repeating the same words over and over," Borg added before biting into his food.

"Which was?" Eric asked Colin since Borg's mouth was full.

Colin rubbed at his neck. "He spoke of Lady Terra and her insistence that he deliver a personal message to Lady Faith. And that the message was for her ears alone."

"What is it she said?" Eric asked, curious. He did not like the fact that a message was sent to his wife without him being first told of it. He was the lord of this keep and no message was delivered without him hearing it first. Lady Terra well knew that. And besides, he wanted nothing said to his wife that would hurt or disturb her.

Colin spoke. "He was told to tell Lady Faith that she was to seek penance and communion from the priest and she was not to disobey this order from her stepmother or she would be sorry."

Eric sprang forward in his chair and both men drew back.

"She dared to threaten my wife in her own home?"

Both men simply nodded their heads.

"Does she think me a fool?"

Borg answered that one. "I think she foolishly thinks that your wife will not confide in the devil."

Eric remained silent. Faith had not told him of the threat, but then she had fallen asleep before they could talk further. But would she tell him? The idea that she might not tell him disturbed him. He wanted her full and complete trust. He did not want her fearing to ask or tell him anything. It was imperative to him that she trust him. Trust was the very issue that almost caused him to lose her and he would not have the issue come between them again.

"She has not spoken to you of this threat?" Borg asked.

"Nay, she has not, but then I was concerned for her health and gave no thought of a threat. Not here in my keep. Never in my keep," he said angrily.

"What will you do?" Colin asked.

The dreaded cold, soulless eyes Eric wore into battle were aimed at his two friends and they shivered. "I will welcome Lord and Lady Donnegan into my home and I will teach them *never* to threaten my wife again."

"Does Faith know you never requested her return to her father?" Borg asked, shaking the chill off his large body.

"Nay, she knows only that I sent a message."

"Then she must have assumed you intended to return her," Borg said.

"Possibly."

Borg continued. "Then she still may think you have intentions of returning her and perhaps fears confiding in you."

"Nonsense," Eric said, standing to refill his wine goblet.

Colin nodded. "I agree with Borg. Perhaps she does not feel as secure here as you think."

"You two need to talk," Borg urged.

Eric returned to his seat with a full goblet. "Like you and Bridget."

Borg laughed. "Bridget talks. I listen."

"How do you get her to stop?" Eric asked.

Borg grinned. "I take her to bed."

"Which reminds me," Colin said, standing. "I have an appointment with a young woman."

"I am working on that, wife," Eric warned with a raise of his goblet.

"A waste of time, my friend. There are too many women waiting for me to pleasure them."

Borg laughed. "Then it will be your luck to be stuck with a woman who does not favor your favors."

Eric laughed, along with Borg.

"Funny," Colin said, "but there isn't a woman around that I cannot charm. And with that said, I go to charm a woman."

When the brothers were alone Borg offered wise advice. "Talk with her, Eric. Discover what it is she hides. We want no surprises when Lord and Lady Donnegan arrive, and Faith has every right to feel safe in her own home."

Eric reached out and gave his brother a firm pat on the shoulder. "I can always count on you to speak the truth to me."

"I can speak nothing less."

"Then you understand why I want you to tell Colin to post extra guards around the castle and the keep itself."

Borg nodded. "Colin already has."

Eric grinned. "Another one I can always count on."

"Now that you realize this, go talk with your wife."

"And what of you and Bridget?" he asked, standing and placing his empty goblet on the table.

"What of us?"

"You wish to tell me you plan to marry her."

Borg's expression grew serious. "She is no servant to me and I will not ask your permission."

Eric shook his head and smiled. "Did you really think I expected it of you?"

Borg grew contrite and rubbed his chin. "Nay, and I am sorry. It is just that I am—"

"Protective of her, as I am of Faith," Eric finished. "And I wish you much happiness, a long life and many children with her. I will find another to see to Faith's care. You inform Bridget that she is no longer a servant and is free to pursue her own choices."

This time Borg shook his head and smiled. "She will have a

fit if I tell her she will no longer care for Faith. Besides, Faith does not treat her like a servant. She treats her like a friend."

"Then you remain here with us?" Eric asked hopefully.

"For now," Borg assured him. "I may take her north to meet our family."

"But you will return?"

"I do not think Bridget could leave Ireland permanently. The land and its people are forever joined and she would not be happy anywhere but on Irish soil."

Eric agreed with a nod. "It is a strange feeling, hard to explain to others who do not possess Irish blood. It is as if the land is an intricate part of you and when you leave you ache to return as it aches for you to return. I suppose it is like a mother who yearns in desperation for her children, not content until all are safely home."

"Are all safely home, Eric?"

Eric thought a moment. "I am not sure, but I will find out soon enough."

Twenty-six

Eric took a quick stroll around the castle grounds before returning to his chambers. He wanted to ascertain for himself that his orders were being carried out as directed and that the castle was now more heavily guarded and stood at full alert.

While the keep's safety was always uppermost in his mind, the safety of his wife was his main concern. He would never allow any harm to come to her and he would never allow her to be threatened in her own home. He wanted her always to feel safe at Shanekill Keep no matter where she walked or who she spoke with. He intended that she feel confident that no harm would befall her.

Secure with the guarded precautions in place, Eric returned to the keep. He walked with haste, wanting to see how his wife fared. He did not like the idea that she was threatened under his own roof and he intended that her father and stepmother taste the devil's wrath for their grievous mistake. But for now he wanted nothing more than some time alone with his wife.

His entrance to his chambers was abrupt and caused Bridget to jump from her seat, her stitching spilling from her lap to the floor. A quick survey of the room alerted him to his wife's absence.

"Where is she?"

"She felt the need to pray, my lord."

Eric searched the room once again and Bridget answered his silent query. "Rook went with her."

Eric immediately turned to leave, instructing Bridget that she would no longer be needed tonight. He had hoped Faith trusted him enough to speak with him about her fears regarding the message and spending the evening alone with her would afford him the perfect opportunity to broach the subject.

He entered the tiny chapel in the keep quietly, not wanting to disturb her prayer time, and was taken back by the solitude of the small room. The two chairs draped in fine tapestry and intended for use by the lord and lady of the keep sat empty. She was not there.

For a brief moment he grew alarmed, then recalled Borg telling him of Faith praying on the west baricon. He instantly made his way up the steps to the baricon that presented the most stunning view of the impressive castle grounds below, the winter-ready fields and the abundant meadows that spread out for miles. However, the view would be obscured with dusk almost upon them so why would she go there now to pray?

Her back faced him as he stepped out on the baricon and an alert Rook announced his arrival with a happy bark. Faith simply turned around to greet him, not at all surprised by his appearance.

"Rook heard you coming up the steps and alerted me long before your appearance."

He walked up to her, but addressed Rook. "Two bones for a job well done."

Rook seemed to understand his words. His tail wagged gratefully and he cast an anxious eye to the steps.

"I will protect your master now. Go get your reward."

Rook wasted not a minute; he was gone in a flash, leaving the lord and lady alone.

Eric wrapped strong arms around her shivering body. "You are chilled."

She rested her head on his shoulder. "Nay, the brisk night air feels good and your embrace warms me."

He held her close. "Bridget told me you went to pray."

"I felt the need," was her only explanation.

They looked out as dusk covered the land, racing shadows across the fields and meadows. Night brought with it a peaceful calm that Eric favored. It was a time to relax and savor the day, share food and drink with friends and a warm and welcoming bed with a woman. Only now he did not have to search for a willing woman—he had one. He had Faith, who was not only willing, but was his wife, and he suddenly felt an overwhelming gratitude that she belonged to him.

He raised her chin and moved his lips downward. "I am glad you are my wife," he said and kissed her.

The kiss surprised her and her first response was hesitancy. He drew back and cast a cautious glance at her.

"I am sorry," she said and rubbed her cheek to his. "I have much on my mind."

"What troubles you?"

She answered without hesitation. "My stepmother."

"Tell me," he urged, wanting to hear the words from her.

"I cannot understand why she hates me so. I was so very young when she married my father and I can still remember her first words, actually warning me to 'behave or else.' I did the best I could to obey her but somehow it was never enough. She always found fault with me and after a while I simply stopped trying to please her."

"Do you fear her?" he asked.

"I did when I was young," she admitted. "Her hand often left its harsh mark upon my face. But after the attack I found a strength I never knew I had and while I made certain not to antagonize her, I did not feel as fearful toward her. It was Rook's safety I constantly feared for. She always warned it would be him who would suffer if I did not obey her."

A low growl in his chest alerted her to his annoyance. "She will not hurt Rook—that I promise you."

She smiled with such relief that it stabbed at his heart. "Your promise fills me with joy."

"You need not worry while she and your father are here. This is your home and you are safe." He caught a hint of doubt in her eyes. "You are safe here with me," he repeated and it sounded like a decree by a powerful lord.

"Safe with the devil," she whispered. "A strange guardian to watch over me."

"A fearless guardian," he corrected.

"You do not ever fear?" she asked.

It was his turn for honesty. "It is a foolish man who does not fear and it is a wise man who confronts his fears."

"Have you confronted all your fears?"

"I have confronted and conquered many, but I expect there will be more."

"Facing your fears is difficult," she said.

"For some impossible."

"How did you confront and conquer so successfully?"

"Tenacity," he answered with a smile.

She laughed softly. "You are tenacious."

He claimed a quick, sharp kiss. "That I am, but then so are you."

"I am not as brave as you," she argued.

"No," he agreed.

She looked disappointed at his response and her eyes widened as he continued, "You are much braver."

"Me?" she asked, stepping away from him and pointing at herself.

"Aye, you," he said, pointing back at her.

"Why do you say that?"

"You fought for your life against great odds and you not only won, you thrived and grew in strength and courage. You are a great warrior and I am proud to have you as my wife."

His sincere words touched her heart and she melted into his arms, her lips reaching out for his. Their kiss immediately turned frantic, as if they had been denied each other too long.

There was an urgency about them, their hands hungering to touch and their bodies hungering to join.

Eric was the one to tear them apart, his strong grasp firm on her arms as he held her away from him. "I want you with a fierceness that I find hard to deny, but it is your health that concerns me."

"I am fine and I want you," she insisted, attempting to break free of his grip and finding it impossible. His potent strength was simply too much to fight against.

"What if you faint again?"

She sighed dramatically. "I will faint from the want of you if you do not release me and see to your husbandly duties."

He laughed. "You are a bold one, wife." He reached out to swing her up into his arms but she backed away. He eyed her sternly. "You play games with me?"

"Nay," she said sweetly with a shake of head and then a

glance to the night sky. "I was thinking what it would be like to make love under the stars."

He looked over his surroundings and then up at the night sky which was just beginning to twinkle with stars.

"Too difficult of a task?" she challenged.

He had grown hard from their fervent kisses, but he now swelled with an ache that had him throbbing. "You tempt the gods, wife."

She smiled and teased him more. "Your Viking blood races."

"Vikings ravish," he said with the one ounce of control that remained. "Is that what you want? To be ravished here on the baricon?"

"Are you up to it?" she asked with another smile that sealed her fate.

He rushed at her with such speed and agility that she yelped with fright. And she was stunned to find herself plastered up against the stone wall of the keep. His mouth and hands took charge and even with her clothes on he managed to slip beneath and touch and tempt her in places that were soon swelling and moistening with need. Her whimpers turned to moans and then to soft pleas.

She was grateful for his fast entrance, grateful still for his hard, unrelenting thrusts and even more grateful for the feel of him so potent and powerful inside her. His orders were sharp and concise and she followed them without question. She wrapped her legs tightly around him, her arms went around his neck and she tilted her head back to stare at the stars so brilliant in the night sky as he took her, soaring to unimaginable heights of pleasure.

Her eyes caught and held a falling star and she burst in a stunning climax, both her and the star dropping to the earth together in a final explosion.

He throbbed violently inside her, his climax so intense that his seed filled her to overflowing. If she was not with child, she surely would be after this. He rested his forehead against the stone wall and kept his firm hold on her even though his legs felt near to collapsing. He did not want to release her; he wanted to remain nested in her, feeling her muscles quicken around him and feeling his own intense pleasure blend with hers.

He loved this time with her, this moment when he felt totally at one with her.

Love.

He could no longer deny it to himself. He loved her and would do anything for her, even give his life.

Besotted.

"Aye that I am," he murmured.

"What say you?" she asked, her breathing still labored.

"I say we seek nourishment and then our bed."

She kissed his cheek. "Can we make use of the chair first?"

He laughed and then kissed her soundly. "With the way you tempt and tease me, you will forever be with child."

"Nay," she said softly. "I know of a potion that prevents a man's seed from taking root."

He immediately moved away from her, though his arms held her waist firmly. "Have you made use of this potion?"

She looked stricken that he should ask. "Nay, I would never stop your seed from taking root unless we first discussed it."

He rested his forehead against hers. "A foolish question I asked, forgive me."

She cupped his face in her delicate hands.

He shuddered at the cool feel of her skin on his warm flesh.

"I am anxious to feel your babe grow inside me."

He smiled and brushed a kiss to her lips. "I am anxious to see him root there."

She grinned. "Then we best keep trying."

He smiled and silently thanked the heavens for sending her to him. He then scooped her up into his arms and carried her into the keep and down to his chambers.

A low growl from Rook near dawn and his own alert senses warned him of an impending visit, and he reached for the dagger he kept hidden nearby.

A soft rap on the door was followed by its slow opening and then a soft, urgent summons came from Colin. "Trouble."

Eric eased away from a slumbering Faith, though he did not expect to wake her. They had engaged in several delightful and feverish bouts of lovemaking and she had slipped into a heavy sleep, exhausted. She would not wake until morning. He was accustomed to sleeping lightly regardless of the circumstances, so quick to hear and respond to noises in the night.

He was dressed and out the door with a quiet order to an alert Rook as he passed where he lay in front of the hearth to watch over Faith.

Colin gave him the news as they entered the great hall where Borg waited by the doors. "A servant woman has been murdered."

Eric stopped abruptly. "Where was she found?"

Colin seemed reluctant to answer.

"The stable?" Eric asked.

Colin nodded. "A guard found her body a short time ago and summoned me."

"You better take a look," Borg said and the three men made their way to the stables as dawn crested on the horizon.

Two guards stood outside the stable door and one remained inside beside the body. A chilled air filled with familiar scents was tainted with an odor he had not smelled for some time. It was the stench of death. It had filled his nostrils for too many years. He had walked the battlefields after each battle, gathering his wounded and his dead. He would not allow any of his men to be left behind with the hundreds or sometimes thousands of rotting corpses that no one would claim. He made certain every one of his men was accounted for and looked after. But that stench was hard to be rid of—it penetrated the nostrils and lingered for days. The smell of blood and human waste and worst of all fear was so heavy in the air.

Colin pulled back the brown wool blanket that covered the lifeless body. Borg and Eric simply stared down at the young woman. She looked to be at least two score, of ample build, plain brown hair and dark eyes and she had been viciously and repeatedly slashed about her body with a knife.

Eric went down on bended knee to take a closer look. Borg joined him.

"This wound is similar to Faith's," Eric said, staring at the thick cut that ran down the girl's face, along her neck and over her breast.

Borg cast a curious eye over all the wounds. "I would say that particular wound was inflicted after the attack. It is too precise to have been made during a struggle and she looked to have struggled."

Eric agreed, taking note of the wounds on her hands and arms and the condition of the stable itself. Someone had grabbed frantically for anything that could be used as a weapon only to find herself being slashed repeatedly until no strength remained.

"Who is she?" Eric asked, standing. "She does not look familiar."

"That is another problem," Colin explained. "The guards do not recognize her. We are going to have to wait a few hours until all are up and about to begin questioning people."

Borg stood. "I will put extra guards on the keep."

Eric looked to the two men he would trust with his life. "I want Faith guarded at all times."

"We can take turns," Colin offered, covering the body.

Borg agreed. "One of us will always be near her, and then there is Rook."

The three men smiled knowingly.

"I never thought I would be glad that big, ugly animal was around, but I know he will let no harm come to Faith," Eric said and then his expression grew serious. "I want to know how this happened. How someone was able to invade the safety of this keep and do harm. Everyone is to be questioned. Start with the guards—see what they know. By noonday I want a full accounting of everyone's whereabouts last night."

Colin and Borg nodded.

Eric looked with blazing blue eyes from one man to the other. "This murderer will be found and punished."

Neither man spoke a word. They both knew full well the devil would have his way and soon, or all would taste his wrath.

"You best tell Faith of this before someone else does," Borg said.

"I was thinking the same myself," Eric agreed. "I have no doubt this will alarm her and I do not want her to worry needlessly."

"Worry and gossip will only fuel the fears," Colin warned.

"That is why this will be seen to immediately," Eric ordered. "Colin, see to finding out her identity, and Borg, see to the questioning of the guards first. Enlist Stuart's help and any others you feel are trustworthy. I go to speak with my wife. We will talk at noonday in the great hall."

The men acknowledged his orders with a nod and immediately set to work as Eric took leave of the stables.

The great hall was stirring when he entered, the servants

scurrying about in preparation of the morning meal. He made his way up the steps to his chambers to find his wife still sound asleep, cuddled deep beneath the blankets, on her stomach with the pillows scattered around her and none beneath her head.

Rook lifted his head, acknowledged Eric's entrance with a low grumble and returned to his slumber.

Eric slipped out of his clothes and beneath the blankets to join his wife. She was warm to his touch, her skin silky and smooth. He pushed her hair aside and gently kissed the back of her neck, his hand trailing down her back, over her slim waist to her round backside and finally making his way between her snug legs.

He nibbled along her pale shoulders, pressing his body close against hers as his fingers slowly and gently penetrated her warm, moist nest.

She stirred then, and so did he.

"Wake up, wife," he whispered in her ear. "I have something for you."

She mumbled and moved her body suggestively against his.

"Wake up," he said again, teasing her with aggressive nips along her neck and stroking her with fingers that had her responding in familiar fashion.

She grumbled and before she could turn around he yanked the blankets off her, pulled her to the edge of the bed with a sinful smile and wink at her startled expression, grabbed her legs, swung them over his waist and entered her most rapidly.

She gasped, sighed and gasped again at his surprisingly intrusive entrance and his teasing manner. It did not take long for her to respond to his demands and took even surprisingly less time for her to climax with a startling cry.

His laugh was full of satisfaction and it took only a few more decisive thrusts for him to join her in climax, though he did not cry out, he simply growled low and viciously as he collapsed over her.

"And a good morning to you," she said after regaining her breath.

"Aye, that it is," he said and then thought of the news he had to tell her.

He slipped off her and pulled her to him, wrapping her in his strong arms, holding her tightly to him, protecting her from harm.

"I like the way you wake me," she said on a yawn.

He kissed her forehead. "We must start our day often like this."

He did not want to tell her how his day had begun; he would deliver that disturbing news soon enough. Right now, at this moment, he wanted her to feel safe and secure in his arms.

His good intentions came to an abrupt halt when Bridget burst into the room, announcing, "My lady, a servant has been slashed to death."

Twenty-seven

Faith thought her world was crumbling around her. The more she learned of the murder, the more terrified she grew. Eric had immediately ordered a contrite Bridget from his chamber and then he proceeded to inform her of the details. He had not spared her—he told her everything, for which she was grateful. If she had learned of this news from others she would have questioned the validity of their remarks, but hearing it from her husband, she knew it to be the truth.

She had dressed in a deep red wool shift and tunic and was standing before the fire, but still she felt chilled to the bone and she could not prevent her limbs from shaking. It was as if her nightmares had become reality. She had dreamed often, almost nightly following the attack, that it had happened again and again and again. It took her own strength and courage to chase away the frightful dreams, but now it was not a dream. Someone had been murdered and left with a scar similar to hers.

Had her attacker returned?

Faith's hand rested on Rook's head and Eric had noticed that since he had informed her of the murder neither she nor Rook had left each other's sides.

"No harm will come to you," Eric assured her.

She nodded, though he felt her doubt and her feeling of insecurity haunted and angered him.

A knock at the door startled her and Rook immediately

jumped in front of her, taking a guarded stance and emanating a low growl.

Eric walked to the door and opened it, admitting Borg and Colin.

They talked quietly at the door and Faith took a seat by the fire, Rook spreading himself out across her feet. She pet his shiny dark coat, her eyes steady on the flickering flames. She had grown frightened at the news of the murder and even more frightened when she learned the details. Was her attacker near? Did he intend her harm? What was it he wanted from her?

She had lived with the fear of his return following her attack. She had spent too many sleepless nights wondering, waiting, watching for him. Those nights had slipped by until little by little they had all but faded from her memory. But she had never truly confronted the fear that had caused them and now she was fearful once again.

Would she hide or would she finally face her fear?

Borg and Colin approached with Eric, and she stood.

"We will take turns guarding you," Eric said. "You are to go nowhere without one of us by your side."

Faith started shaking her head with his first words. "Nay," she said with the insistence of a tenacious woman.

"Nay?" Eric said, annoyed that she should disregard his command and his concern for her safety.

"I will not be a prisoner in my own home."

Borg and Colin smiled at her courage and Eric had to admit he was proud of her defiant stance. But still there remained the fact that she could be in danger, and he was not about to take a chance with his wife's life.

"You are not a prisoner," he reassured her. "But until this matter can be resolved to my satisfaction you will have the company of one of us no matter where you go."

"I have Rook," she said, in objection.

Rook barked and snarled to confirm his presence.

"Of which I am pleased," Eric said with a pat to the dog's head. "But it is a warrior I want beside you and it is a warrior who will be there."

She attempted to protest but he raised his hand. "I will hear no more. Borg, Colin, or I will haunt your every move and if you attempt to disobey my edict you will find yourself sequestered in this room until I decree otherwise."

She realized it was hopeless to argue with him. It was best to obey and best to face her demons head-on even if one happened to be her husband. "As you wish, my lord."

Bridget suddenly appeared in the doorway hesitant to enter. "Pardon, my lord and my lady."

Eric bid her entrance with the wave of his hand and then looked to Borg. "Tell her not to fear me."

Borg laughed. "After the way you thundered at her this morning, that is not possible."

Eric shook his head in disgust and looked to Bridget. "You will fear me no more and you are no longer my wife's servant."

That brought startled gasps from both women.

Borg just laughed harder.

Eric growled low, which caused Rook to do the same.

"She is to marry Borg—she is no longer a servant," Eric informed all, hoping that was explanation enough.

Faith threw her arms around Bridget. "Why did you not tell me this?"

Tears filled Bridget's wide eyes and she kept her glance on Faith. "I did not think it real."

"What?" Borg boomed, his deep voice carrying throughout the room.

Colin and Eric looked on with smiles, enjoying this moment.

"I am a servant, you are not," Bridget said, turning to face Borg.

"What matters that? I love you."

"Truly?" she asked hesitantly.

"Truly," he told her and sealed his vow with a heartfelt kiss.

"I will secure another servant for you," Eric said to Faith.

"I do not need one," she said.

"I will continue to see to her care," Bridget insisted.

"You are no longer a servant," Borg added.

Bridget was adamant. "I wish to care for my lady."

"Nay," Borg ordered firmly.

"Impossible," Eric said.

Faith smiled and walked over to Bridget and with a wink said, "We will be friends."

"Aye, my lady, that we will," Bridget said.

The three men looked skeptically at the two smiling women. Bridget grinned back but spoke to Faith. "I think the morn-

ing fare is ready. Let us see what they have to warm our in-
nards."

"A good idea," Faith answered, and together they walked toward the door, Rook following at the mention of food. They
paused and Faith glanced back. "Which one of you will be my
shadow?"

Colin hurried over to join them. "I have the honor," he said
and held out an arm to each woman, which they readily accepted then strolled out the door with him.

"I am going to find that charmer a wife who will see to it he
charms no one else but her ever again," Eric insisted.

"I will help you," Borg added with a determined glint in his
eyes.

The only talk at the morning meal was that of the murder. The
young woman was yet to be identified. Many people had gone
to look, most just out of curiosity, but none knew her. And
stranger still, no one had complained or spoke of a woman gone
missing in the keep or the surrounding castle grounds. Everyone appeared to be accounted for, which made for more gossip.

Who was she and where had she come from?

While Eric spoke with Colin and Borg on the matter, Faith
and Bridget were holding their own discussion.

"Where have they placed the body?" Faith asked quietly.

"It remains in the stables for now, my lady."

Faith wanted to correct her and offer simply to call her by
name as Borg did with Eric, but she knew that would take time,
so she made no mind of it. "I think it would be wise for me to
view it."

"Whatever for?" Bridget asked.

Faith shook her head. "I do not know. I only know I refuse
to be frightened in my own home and I will not hide my head
and look the other way while more in this keep could be in danger."

"You are a brave soul, my lady."

"Stubborn is more like it," Faith said with a laugh.

"But how with one of them"—Bridget indicated with a nod
Borg, Colin and Eric who were huddled in conversation—"always nearby do we manage it?"

Faith was pleased to see that she included herself in the

scheme. She may be brave but it would be nice to have a fa-
vorable companion beside her as she faced her nightmare.

"Simple," she said, gliding easily out of her seat at the dais.
"We take our leave."

Bridget followed quietly, the two women sneaking out
through the kitchen where Rook joined them, having finished
his meal while the three men remained deep in conversation,
oblivious to their departure.

Faith approached the two guards stationed at the stable
doors as if she had all the right in the world to be there. Bridget
trailed beside her, with healing basket in hand.

The two guards looked oddly at her approach.

She smiled sweetly, rubbed her hands together and then
tucked them beneath her red wool cloak. "Feels more like a
winter chill than autumn."

Both men nodded in agreement.

"I have come to tend the body," she said and wisely waited
for their approval.

The younger guard seemed to understand and stepped aside.
The other guard remained where he stood, still skeptical.

"She is going to fix her up some before they bury her," the
younger guard said.

It proved to be a reasonable explanation and the man
stepped aside.

"If there is anything you need, my lady . . . ," the younger
guard offered.

"Thank you," Faith said, "but I think I have everything."

Faith and Bridget trembled as the door closed behind them
and they stood close beside each other, holding shivering
hands. The place was stone silent, the horses made no sounds,
no birds could be heard chirping in the rafters and there was no
scurrying of cats after the mice that frequented the stable. It was
as if the living creatures were paying their respects to the dead
with their silence. The two women did the same—the only
noise was that of their soft chattering teeth as they walked over
to where the covered body lay not far from the stable entrance.

They stood silent and unmoving, gathering their courage.
Then slowly, with hands still shaking, Bridget placed the basket on the ground away from the body. Together they approached the shroud-covered corpse and together they drew
back the corner of the blanket.

They gasped when their wide-eyed glare fell upon the deceased woman and the blanket slipped from their hands as they took startled steps back, Bridget whispering, "Sweet mother of God—it is Nora."

"How?" was the only word Faith could say, and she repeated it several times.

"I do not understand," Bridget said, tears streaming down her cheeks.

"How could she have gotten here?" Faith finally asked but really expected no answer.

"What are you up to, wife?" an angry voice replied.

Faith and Bridget stumbled as they hurried to turn and face the devil. Borg stood beside him, shaking his head while looking directly at Bridget.

Faith ignored her husband's temper and with a trembling voice said, "Her name is Nora and she was a servant at Donnegan Keep."

"Are you certain?" Eric asked, rushing to her side. Borg joined him and both men used their sizable bodies to block the mutilated body from view.

Bridget nodded, wiping at her tears. " 'Tis true, my lord, it is Nora."

"How, Eric?" Faith asked, as if he would know the answer. After all, did not the devil know everything? "How did she get here?"

Eric answered, as she suspected he would. There was not anything at the keep that went on without his knowledge. Faith amended that, peeking between the two men's broad shoulders and catching sight of Nora, though she doubted it would be long before her husband had his answers.

"I have just been informed that your father and stepmother's arrival is imminent. Their wagons now crest the rise."

"Why would Nora arrive ahead of them?" Bridget asked.

Borg explained. "One of the guards told us that Father Peter arrived late last night shortly before the young woman and had informed them that a young woman would be arriving to speak with him. It was dark so the guard could not tell us much about the woman except that she was of ample weight."

"Nora," Bridget confirmed sadly.

Bridget was the only one present who did not notice that Faith paled considerably.

Eric was instantly beside her, his hand firm on her arm. "Come, we will talk," he said and with a nod to Borg he directed Faith quickly out of the stables.

He walked with her toward her healing cottage, the crisp cold air returning color to her pale complexion. She kept something from him and he did not like the fact that she harbored secrets or that she did not feel secure enough with him to share them.

"Why did you want to see the body?" he asked, though his first thought was to shout and scream and demand that she never frighten him again by disappearing. He had been terrified when he looked over where she had been sitting at the dais to find her gone. His terror intensified when she could not be located in the keep and he grew completely outraged when he had learned she had gone to the stables.

He was grateful the older of the guards had decided he should be informed of Lady Faith's presence in the stable. With the knowledge of her safety, he was flooded with relief and now he simply wanted answers.

She responded honestly. "I wanted to confront my fear." Admitting her weakness brought tears to her eyes and she hastily entered her healing cottage, setting to work lighting the logs in the hearth and lighting the numerous candles.

Eric followed her in, but remained silent, allowing her to go about her tasks, knowing she needed this time to regain her emotions and face him with courage. He would have much preferred to reach out and take her in his arms, protecting her, tucking her away from her fears, but that would not do. She wanted to confront the fear that had haunted her and he would help her, not hinder her.

He finally asked as she lighted the last candle, "Did you face your fear?"

She shook her head and a teardrop fell from her cheek.

He could keep his distance no longer—he was upon her in a flash and had her wrapped in his arms in seconds, squeezing her to him. Her quiet tears turned to whimpers and then to sobs and her anguished cries tore at his heart.

He gathered her up in his arms and walked to the bed, sitting down with her on his lap. He held her like a child in need and let her cry.

"I feel a fool," she said between sobs.

"You are no fool," he assured her. "You have every right to fear."

"I thought it was done, over—" her sobs interfered from her continuing.

"For you, it is. No one will harm you—that I promise."

She knew his word was like a decree and he would keep her safe—but how could he if she did not speak the whole truth to him? Before her decision could be made, a soft knock sounded at the door and Colin peeked his head in after Eric bid him enter.

"Lord and Lady Donnegan arrive shortly."

"Where is Rook?" she asked Colin nervously.

The dog heard his name and stuck his head around the door. She called him to her and she slid from Eric's lap to grab hold of the large animal and hug him tightly.

Eric nodded to Colin and he discreetly took his leave.

Faith stood, her hand resting on Rook's big head. "I must get ready to receive my father and stepmother."

"I will walk with you back to the keep," he said, wanting to pursue more deeply her fear that lay hidden away and concealed and which he was certain she had shared with no one. There was something about that night she never spoke of—not to a living soul—and it had caused her fear to grow.

But no longer—she would tell him and confront her demon in front of the devil himself.

Faith had freshened her face with a hasty splash of water to wipe away the remnants of her tears and then she arranged her flaming red hair to conceal her scar—or as her stepmother had often called it, her shame.

It was strange that since Eric learned of the scar she had found herself not bothering with hiding it. More often than not her husband would push her hair aside and nibble most deliciously along her neck, over the scar. He seemed not at all offended or troubled by it and she felt relieved he accepted the blatant remnant so easily.

She and Rook descended the steps and entered the great hall while the commotion of her parents' arrival sounded outside. She hurried to the dais where her husband looked to be lounging in his chair and where Colin and Borg sat at either end of the long table just as uninterested but extremely alert.

"Come, we must greet them," she said anxiously to her husband and held her hand out to him.

He rose out of his chair, his towering height, powerful size and those blazing blue eyes intimidating even her. She was about to draw back when he reached over the dais, grabbed her under her arms and lifted her with the ease of a small grain sack over the table, depositing her in the chair next to his.

"You will stay seated for their arrival," he ordered in a voice she was wise enough to obey.

This would infuriate her stepmother and not please her father. That thought brought a smile to her solemn face.

"Rook, go stay by Colin," Eric ordered firmly and the dog obeyed without question, taking up a proud stance beside him.

Lady Terra and Lord William burst through the double doors with a gush of wind, startling both of them and disrupting not only their grand entrance but their appearance. By the time they reached the dais, their hair was disheveled and their clothing was covered with a fine film of dust.

"A fine welcome you offer," Lady Terra said in a scolding tone and sent a look of disgust at Faith.

Eric's hand rested over his wife's where it lay trembling on the armrest. He gently gave her delicate fingers a soft, reassuring squeeze.

Lady Terra unwisely continued to berate her stepdaughter. "I knew you incapable of proper manners." She took a breath and more unwisely attacked the Irish devil. "He at least has an excuse being part barbarian, but you—"

Faith was out of her chair in a flash, surprising everyone in the room and stunning her husband with her words.

"Do not dare malign my husband with your vile tongue. You are in my home now and will show respect for my husband and all here or you will not be welcome."

The silence hung so heavy in the air that it seemed that all held their breath in anticipation.

Lady Terra stood with her mouth agape and her eyes rounded in stunned disbelief.

To add to the already uncomfortable situation, Faith flung her hair back away from her shoulders and neck, exposing her scar to full view.

Her stepmother gasped and her shocked glance went first to her husband and then to Lord Eric.

Eric rose slowly out of his seat, standing to his full height. His shoulders were drawn back, his chest expanded and the sides of his dark hair were plaited. He was at that moment a mighty warrior, a leader among men and a lord to dark souls.

All in the room took one or two steps back even if they stood a good distance away from him. Faith herself felt compelled to move away, but fought the impulse, placing her hand securely in his.

He held her hand firmly. "We have several matters to discuss, Lord William, before I decide if I will allow you to stay at Shanekill Keep."

Lord William looked irate but handled his enraged emotions more wisely than his wife. "I am sure we can settle your concerns in no time and enjoy a friendly visit."

"We shall see," Eric said.

"In the meantime, perhaps my wife and I could retire to a chamber where we may refresh ourselves after this long and tiring journey."

Faith almost moved to do as her father bid, but her husband's firm grip kept her rooted to where she stood beside him.

"First we talk," Eric commanded. "Lady Terra will remain here in the great hall until we are finished."

Lord William looked ready to burst with anger. It was Lady Terra who remained calm this time. "I will visit with my stepdaughter."

Eric immediately corrected her. "Until you offer my wife an apology for the threat your messenger delivered to her in her own home, you are forbidden to speak with her."

"You-you-you . . ." Lady Terra found speech difficult, she was so incensed by his edict.

Colin and Borg laughed and several other laughs and giggles could be heard circulating the room.

"This is an outrage," Lord William protested.

"I agree—and one that you will pay for dearly," Eric warned, and the laughs instantly ceased.

His remark immediately quieted the complaining man.

"Rook," Eric said and the dog hurried to his side. "See to your master." He then sent a silent command to Colin to join the two. He leaned down, brushed a gentle kiss over his wife's lips and whispered, "Keep yourself busy and out of trouble until the evening meal. Your parents will either be gone or repentant when you return."

She smiled and brazenly kissed him soundly in front of all and finished in a strong voice, "As you say, my lord."

He watched her walk past her stepmother without a glance or word and out the front door with Colin beside her and Rook at her heels. He felt safe knowing she was in good hands. He turned his attention back to his visitors.

"Make yourself comfortable, Lady Terra. Food and drink will be provided for you. Lord William, you will join me and Borg," he said, pointing to his brother who stood to his impressive height.

The rotund little man paled considerably and reluctantly preceded the two trailing men out of the hall.

Twenty-eight

Colin followed Faith as she toured the castle grounds, visiting those who suffered from ailments and stopping to chat with those who called out a greeting to her. They shared the current gossip, mostly speaking of the poor girl who was murdered and how the Irish devil, bless his soul, would make certain the culprit was caught and punished.

Colin did not prevent her from stopping at the Donnegan wagons to see if any needed tending, but he did make certain to remain by her side, as did Rook. None made mention of Nora's death, but then the news that the identity of the girl had been established had not been circulated. Eric thought it wise to keep that bit of information secret for the moment.

They were near upon the portcullis when Faith asked Colin, "Can we go to the meadow near the back of the castle wall?"

"What is it you want in the meadow?" he asked.

"A breath of fresh air from confinement and more heather."

"Is the heather necessary?"

She sighed and shook her head. "I could probably make do with the batch I have, but collecting extra would not hurt and it would sweeten the rooms in the keep."

Rook agreed with a bark, though she was well aware that a berry patch sat close by and the last of the berries were falling from the bushes. It would be Rook's final treat before winter set in.

Colin found it difficult to deny her simple request, but he took no chances—he ordered one of the guards to fetch Stuart. "We will not go out alone," was his only explanation.

While she waited she sought to borrow an empty basket from a woman in a nearby cottage. The older woman gave it to her only too gladly, and was pleased to be asked to tend Lady Faith's healing basket while she was off gathering plants.

Faith breathed deeply of the fresh, sharp air as they made their way to the meadow. Rook ran ahead and Stuart trailed behind them, his sword in hand and his attention alert.

She loved this time of the year when the land prepared for winter. The fields so ripe from birthing, their last harvest smelled sharp and pungent. The rolling hills wore their purplish gray coats for the crisp weather yet to come and she was certain the lakes sparkled with a little more silver and the brooks babbled just a little more quietly. She was beautiful, this land. No matter the time of year, she was a sight to behold and Faith never tired of viewing her splendor.

"Are you Ireland's son?" Faith asked Colin.

His grin was wide, his bow low. "None other, my lady."

She smiled with joy. "And where is it you call home?"

His grin quickly faded. "My home is wherever Lord Eric is."

That he did not wish to discuss his origins was obvious, but Faith was curious. "Before Lord, Eric, where was home?"

"Eric mentioned your persistence."

She noticed the familiar use he made of her husband's name but did not mention it. "South? North?"

"North," he confirmed.

She said naught, aware of the many struggles and losses that persisted in this land of beauty, birth and sorrow. "How did you meet Eric?"

"That is a story a lady should not hear," he said with a laugh that had her thinking the tale was more salacious than dangerous.

"You tempt my curiosity and yet fail to appease it—that is not fair."

"What is not fair, my dear Lady Faith, is what I would suffer if Eric learned I told you the tale."

"I would not tell," she offered.

"He would find out anyway."

"Aye, that he would," she agreed and yelled to Rook not to wander off. "How does he know everything that goes on? I hear the keep gossip and many whisper of his *powers*."

"The only power Eric possesses is the ability to listen and hear more clearly than others, even when more than one person speaks. Therefore, he hears and knows much."

"He knows, then, you want a wife?"

"His threats are but teases."

Faith shook her head. "But I think a wife is what you want."

"Trust me, Lady Faith, I would not make a good husband."

"I think otherwise."

"You think as all women do."

"Do you not wish to love?" she asked, stopping not far from where the heather grew profusely.

Colin turned serious eyes on her. "Aye, I ache to love, but I charm instead. I am not capable of loving, and that is all I will say on the matter."

Faith knew better than to pursue the subject but thought to discuss the matter with her husband and see if a good woman could be found for Colin. He was a handsome man, kind of charming but scarred—not physically like her, but inside—and she wondered just how deeply the wound went.

Rook ate berries and Stuart and Colin helped her collect heather. It was a joyful trio and dog that returned to the safety of the castle grounds. After collecting her healing basket and promising to return the borrowed basket even though the woman insisted she keep it, Colin and Faith, along with a tired and full Rook made their way back to the keep.

They were not far from the stone and wood edifice that countless men continued to work on all through the day when Faith bluntly asked, "How do you think Eric will explain that he no longer wishes to return me to my father as he wrote in his letter?"

Relaxed and caught off guard from his enjoyable trek, Colin responded without thinking: "Eric demanded your father's presence but made no mention that you were to be returned to him." He halted abruptly after the remark escaped his mouth and turned a suspicious glare on her.

"Thank you," she said and gave his cheek a light kiss. "You confirmed my own suspicions." She ran ahead, her step light and her smile bright.

Colin chased after her and caught up with her before she entered the keep. "I think it would be best for me if you did not mention where you learned that bit of information."

"I will not tell him," she said, then added, "He will find out anyway."

"Then I am done for," he said dramatically and dropped his head.

She laughed. "You cannot fool me, Colin. I know my husband would never inflict harm on you."

Colin raised his head and she was surprised to see his expression serious. For a moment she thought she caught a peek of his wound that had scarred him so badly, but he quickly concealed it from her.

"Nay, that he would never do. Lord Eric is a good man no matter what they call him and I am happy and pleased that he has found an angel to heal his soul."

He pushed the thick wooden door open before she could respond and they silently entered the great hall.

The hearth in Eric's solar blazed with its usual intensity, keeping the large room at a comfortable temperature and the occupants warm. Unfortunately, Lord William found the room not at all to his liking. It was much too hot—why else would he be sweating so profusely?

He dabbed repeatedly at his damp brow with his square lace cloth and also patted along his equally damp neck. He felt the moisture building beneath his arms and crawling over his body and he wanted nothing more than to have done with this business and be on his way.

Eric watched the short, pudgy man's nervous actions. His own fear had him sweating like a man too long in the summer sun and his constant use of his lace cloth would have it drenched in no time. Eric was pleased by his unsettled attitude; it meant he was frightened and a frightened man was always foolish. But then Lord William was a foolish man no matter what the circumstances.

Lord William gladly accepted the tankard of ale Borg offered him but Eric declined it, too anxious to ask questions and even more anxious to hear the answers.

The three men sat in the chairs in front of the hearth,

William taking the one that was the furthest distance away and keeping his square lace cloth in hand.

Eric wasted no time with unnecessary talk. "Why did you lie to me?"

"About what?" William asked, his voice trembling.

"About what?" Eric repeated irately. "Does this mean you lied to me more than once?"

Borg kept his smile well concealed and enjoyed watching the cat and mouse game Eric played with the man.

"I-I nay, nay I—"

"What is it you lied to me about?" Eric demanded sharply.

"Fai-Faith," he stammered, attempting to answer,

Borg prayed the man was wise enough to say naught against Lady Faith.

"Faith needs protection," he finally got out and paused to wipe his brow yet again.

Borg was relieved, though it was short-lived.

William unwisely continued, "From herself."

"What say you?" Eric said much too calmly and leaned forward in his chair.

William immediately realized the foolishness of his words and hurried to rectify them. "She is stubborn and persistent instead of docile and obedient as a good woman or wife should be. She speaks without thinking—"

"A family trait, I see," Eric finished for him.

"I have done well by the girl," William insisted, feeling courageous with each gulp of ale he took. "After all, who would take a soiled woman as a wife?"

"The devil?" Eric asked casually.

The man paled and wiped his brow. "Y-you insulted her virtue."

"So you demanded I compensate for the insult."

"Y-yes, of course. What kind of father would I be if I did not protect my daughter?"

"Yes, what kind of father?" Eric asked slowly.

William once again gathered his courage. "You are wed, your vows consummated, you cannot return her to me."

"Did I ask that you take her back?"

William shook his head. "Nay, but I thought—"

"Thought what?"

He shook his head again, though followed it with no response.

"You thought little of your daughter and even less of me."

"I did what was best," William said, his hands trembling.

"Best for you," Eric confirmed.

"Best for all," William insisted. "You sullied her with your sinful words and she condemned herself with her shameful actions. She deserves the devil for a husband."

"And she has got him, which you would do well to remember," Eric warned and stood, his large shadow looming over the small man like a beast rising from the depths of hell.

"Why did you summon me here?" William asked, wishing to end his torment and be on his way.

"I want to know of her attack."

William appeared shocked. "Why?"

"Think before you speak," Eric warned.

William did not heed his caution. "She acted foolishly and suffered the consequences."

Borg thought now the perfect time to interrupt; Eric looked about to kill the man. "Lord Eric, perhaps it would be best to allow Lord William time to rest and refresh himself before evening's repast. Tomorrow will be time enough to talk again."

Lord William stood, nodding his head repeatedly. "A much appreciated suggestion, my good man. Lady Terra and I are exhausted after our strenuous journey."

Borg smiled graciously and waved his hand toward the door. "Come, let me show you to the guest chambers."

The giant and the short man were almost out the door when Eric's sharp voice stopped them. "Lord William."

The trembling man stood behind Borg and turned to venture a peek past the big man's wide shoulder.

"We speak tomorrow," Eric said. "There is much you have yet to answer for."

Lord William gave him a brief nod, turned and hurried out of the room. Borg simply turned a smiling face on Eric before closing the door behind him.

Faith was not certain when her guards changed. One minute Colin had been beside her and the next moment she looked, Borg was there. She shook her head in confusion and went about her task, attempting to disregard her new and large shadow.

Rook must have sensed the problem, or perhaps he was attuned to her own sense of fear, for he did not leave her side for more than a brief moment and his alert eyes followed her every move.

She was busy seeing if all was well in the kitchen, a place Rook was more than happy to linger in. Mary had not been feeling well, though most of her sickness cleared by midday and the remainder of the day she was her old self. Faith was relieved to see that today she looked healthy and full of energy.

Faith sniffed the air, the delicious aroma causing hunger groans to attack her belly much too loudly.

Mary shook her head. "Your belly needs filling, my lady. You do not eat enough." With that she sliced a thick piece of brown bread from a loaf she had recently taken fresh and hot from the stone oven. She covered it with a generous spread of butter, then drizzled honey over it.

Borg and Rook's mouths were watering as she handed it to Faith.

Faith thanked her and asked if she required any more help. Mary laughed, shook her head and shooed the three out of the kitchen. By the time they returned to the great hall, Borg and Rook were sharing Faith's slice of bread.

They would have been caught off guard if it had not been for Rook who scurried in front of her and with the chunk of bread protruding from the side of his mouth, growled and snarled at someone who was about to emerge from a darkened corner.

Borg immediately joined Rook, his dagger drawn.

"I will speak to my stepdaughter," Lady Terra demanded as if she were lady of the keep.

"Only if Lady Faith so desires," Borg informed her.

"I will—"

Borg did not allow her to finish. "Do as you are told."

Lady Terra grew red with anger. "How dare you—"

This time Faith interrupted her. "What is it you want?"

Borg stepped aside, though remained beside her.

"I want to talk to you," Lady Terra said sternly.

Faith nodded to Borg and he and Rook stepped a discreet distance away, giving the two women privacy yet keeping them in sight.

Lady Terra was quick to attack with her tongue. "I hear that your shame follows you."

"Whatever do you speak of?"

"I was told that Nora was viciously attacked as you once were but she had the decency to die."

Faith stared at her with horrified eyes. "You think it was decent of her to die?"

"She was a good girl and knew better than to bring shame to her family. At least in her death she retained her honor."

"Do you not even care she is dead?" Faith asked incredulously.

"I care that you did not respect your family enough to have done the same."

A look of sheer disgust crossed Faith's face. "You are not only cold and callous, you are foolish and crazy."

"You think me foolish and crazy?" she all but laughed at Faith. "You who is married to a man of no importance and who cares naught for you. He will be on you until he fills your belly with his child and then he will find his pleasure elsewhere. You are nothing more than chattel to him. And he is nothing more than a barbarian who bought his title, land and wife with the blood of Irishmen."

Faith advanced on her stepmother, her voice clear and strong. "You know nothing of kindness, goodness and truth. It is you who care naught for anyone or anything but yourself. You may think me shameful, but I think your selfish ignorance disgraces the name of every Irish man, woman and child who died fighting for this land."

Fury raged over Lady Terra's reddened face and her hand arced wide as she swung toward Faith.

Rook charged for the attacking woman, pouncing on her with a fierce snarl and causing her to stumble and fall on her backside. The large dog stood, his sharp teeth bared, growling over her until Faith summoned him to her side.

"I should have killed that dog when he was a pup," Lady Terra said, stumbling as she attempted to stand on trembling legs.

"Do not ever threaten my dog, Lady Terra, or you will be sorry," Faith ordered and turned on her heels, Rook beside her, Borg following and Lady Terra staring at the departing trio in disbelief.

•   •   •

Faith walked the castle grounds with Rook. Dusk had long since fallen and night was full upon the land. The air was crisp and fresh, the stars were bright in the dark sky and raised voices, laughter and song could be heard from the great hall.

Borg sat nearby, watching her and waiting. She was expected in the hall, should have been there by now; yet she could not bring herself to enter the same room as her father and stepmother. But she was lady of the keep and expected to act accordingly, which meant joining her husband and guests at the dais.

"Finally," she heard Borg say and turned to see her husband approach.

He looked so handsome and intimidating. He wore all black tonight; not a trace of red could be seen. He blended with the darkness as only the dark lord could.

He spoke quietly with Borg. The large man nodded his head and then walked off.

"What keeps you out here, wife?" he asked as he approached her.

She wanted to run to him, throw her arms around his neck, beg him to love her as much as she loved him and beg him not to make her go inside.

"Rook needed a walk." The feeble excuse sounded poor to her ears and her trembling voice did not help her lie.

He raised her chin with his hand. "I respect the truth, as do you. Why do you not speak it now?"

She sighed and reached up to take his hands in hers. "I do not want to go into the hall, Eric."

To her amazement he answered, "Neither do I."

"You don't?" she asked, fearing she had only heard what she wished to hear.

"Nay," he assured her.

She felt hopeful. "Where do you wish to go?"

He leaned down and stole a brief kiss. "I know where we go."

"Where?" she asked, still hopeful.

He kissed her again, then whispered, "Follow me."

Twenty-nine

Faith hurried alongside her husband, taking two steps for every one of his. She was surprised when they came upon her healing cottage and she saw two men standing guard by the closed door.

Eric greeted the men with a nod and a command. "No one passes through this door." Their quick nods told him they understood, and he opened the door.

Rook entered before them and when Faith entered she gasped. The room was lit with a preponderance of candles. The table was prepared with a small feast; the finest of linens were used; and the two chairs were draped in a rich, thick tapestry for the lord and lady's comfort. Extra pillows had been added to the bed and a soft, white wool blanket was drawn back in anticipation. A fire burned brightly in the hearth, keeping the room comfortably warm.

Rook settled himself contentedly with the large bone that had been purposely placed on the rushes he usually napped on.

Faith looked with grateful eyes on her husband.

"He deserves the treat for a duty well done."

"And the rest?" she asked with a wave of her hand around the room.

He walked over to her. "You deserve this."

"Why?"

"I command it," he teased and took her in his arms.

"Do you want me?"

He nibbled at her neck. "I always want you."

"Are you sure?" she asked and teased his lips with her own nibbles.

"Shall I prove it?" He stepped back and stripped to his waist. The firelight made his body appear golden—more like a god than a devil—and his naked flesh glistened as if touched by the morning dew.

"Come to me," he ordered softly, and she did.

He brought her up against him and kissed her with an urgency that made her understand they would soon be in bed. But this time she wanted their joining to be different. This time she wanted to know how he felt toward her and she knew where she would start.

"Have you always wanted me, Eric?" she asked between kisses.

"Always," he assured her and struggled to remove her soft green tunic.

She assisted him, though grasped his hands when he took hold of her shift. "You want me here, Eric?"

He smiled and slipped his hands out of hers. "Here and now."

Her shift came off in a flash and his mouth descended on her breast. Her nipple disappeared into his wet mouth and he suckled on her like a man in need.

"You don't want me gone, you want me here?" she repeated.

His response was to attack her other nipple in the same fashion.

She held firm to his muscled arms as she asked, "Then you will not be returning me to my father?"

Her words stopped his pleasure and he raised hot blue eyes at her. "What nonsense do you speak?"

"The letter you sent my father when we first arrived here. Did you not advise him that I would be returned to him?"

He smiled much too wickedly. "You know I did not; Colin told you so. What is this about?"

"Why did you not return me? Why do you wish me to stay?"

Eric brushed a soft kiss over her lips. "Easy answers, wife."

"Then tell me, husband."

Eric had waited for this moment, not sure when or how to tell her of his feelings, but now it seemed so natural, so right, so perfect. And he did not wish to wait any longer to hear the meaningful words spill from his lips.

His blue eyes softened, his voice grew gentle and he pulled her closer as he spoke. "I never intended on returning you and I wish you to stay here with me and be my wife because I love you. You captured my heart when first we met and my suggestive words caused you to fall on your backside. You won my admiration and respect when I watched you deliver that babe on our wedding night, and I discovered my deep, unrelenting love for you after our wedding when we spoke while riding my horse and you slept in my arms. I knew then and there that I would spend the rest of my life loving you."

Tears stung her eyes but she ignored them and kissed him. "You truly love me."

"I truly love you."

She kissed him again and whispered, "I love you."

He returned her kiss more feverishly. "You alarmed me when first you spoke those words." He paused and resumed their kiss, only to pause again. "I dared not believe my own emotions and I dared not hope that you could return that love." He kissed her full and hard before pausing again. "And then I wished—no, longed—to hear you say those words again."

She obliged him. "I love you."

"Truly?" he asked with a soft laugh as he nibbled at her neck.

"Truly," she giggled when he struck a sensitive spot.

He hoisted her up into his powerful arms and carried her to the bed. "We need no clothes, wife." And in seconds they both had each other stripped naked.

Eric came down on her, covering her with the length of him. "You trust me, Faith?" he asked, his body already moving slow and steady over hers.

"Aye, I trust you, my dark lord," she said, her body responding in kind to his familiar rhythm.

He tempted her lips with kisses that left her full yet aching. "Then this night you will surrender completely to me."

"I always surrender to you," she said softly, running her fingers through his hair to grasp hold of his head and draw his mouth down to hers. "Tonight we both surrender completely."

Their kiss started a wave of pleasure that built in intensity with every touch, every move, every word. There was not a place their hands and mouths did not explore on each other. There was not a word that was spoken that did not speak of their love. There was not a moment shared that each did not fully surrender to the other. They made love as only two people who deeply love each other could, unselfishly and willingly. And together they shared a climax that took them beyond the stars and back.

They lay wrapped in each other's arms, their bodies replete, and their heated flesh glistened and scented with the aftermath of potent lovemaking.

"I love the devil," she giggled after her breath calmed and she ran her hand lovingly over his chest.

He sighed, feeling more satisfied than he could ever remember. "True enough, but the devil possesses something he never did before."

"What is that?" she asked, curious.

"Faith."

She looked up at him with joyous eyes. "And that Faith is yours forever."

"What a lucky devil I am," he said with a laugh and a grateful heart.

She snuggled against him, resting her head on his damp chest. "We are both lucky."

Eric would not argue with that. He had not known true joy, pleasure and contentment until he met her. And while he was certain she felt the same way, there was one dark cloud hanging over them and he wanted it gone and out of their lives forever.

"When two people love, they trust," he said.

She raised her head, her glance curious. "This we have already agreed upon."

"Then trust me, Faith."

"I do," she insisted.

He shook his head. "Nay, if you trusted me you would tell me the truth about the attack."

Her body grew taut against him. "I told you of the attack."

"You told me what you wanted me to hear. What is it you are reluctant to tell me?"

Her reluctance suddenly dissipated, wrapped in the protection of her husband's love and strength, and this time she finally surrendered her fear to him.

"It was so dark that night and when I think on it, I know it was no darker than any other night and yet . . ." She sighed. "It was the darkest of nights for me."

Eric gave her a reassuring squeeze.

"The man grabbed me from behind and I struggled. It was when he knocked me to the ground and fell on me that I realized he wore the brown, coarse wool, hooded robe of a cleric and my eyes caught the heavy cross that hung down from around his neck. It was that cross that kept my attention as he spoke. He told me that the devil resides in all women and that it was his duty to purge their souls of evil. That was when he began to cut me." She stopped, unable to go on.

Eric spoke calmly and firmly, yet beneath he raged with fury at the terrifying ordeal she had lived through. "No one will ever hurt you again. I give you my word on it."

"I do not worry, my lord, I know you will always protect me."

"With my life, if necessary."

She would never want him to surrender his life for her, but she made no mention of it. He was a warrior—a man of pride and honor—and she respected his way.

Eric sought further confirmation of his suspicions. "This is why you fear men of the cloth?"

"Aye," she admitted with a nod.

"I suspected as much."

She looked at him with surprise. "Does nothing escape your attention?"

"Nothing," he confirmed seriously. "I grew suspicious when I realized you avoided the chapel. Then I recalled you suddenly took ill the day a traveling priest visited. But the single thing that disturbed me most was what Bridget had told me."

"Which was?"

"She told me of your words that night when you cried out for God to save you from the devil. You were speaking of the priest in the room."

Tears sprang from her eyes and she fought them. "I thought he had come back to finish purging me of the evil. I was so frightened. I knew that if I named the priest I would be condemned and persecuted. And I could not say for sure that the cleric who attacked me was the one who served the keep."

"So you kept the horrifying knowledge to yourself."

"I had no choice. It would have done me little good to accuse a man of the cloth. No one would have believed me, they would have thought me crazy or worse. My only recourse was to remain silent and keep my distance from the cleric."

"No other attacks followed yours?"

"None," she confirmed. "Tongues wagged, as is common, and soon there was talk that I had met"—she halted for a moment and turned sorrowful eyes on him—"my lover and that he had attacked me in a fit of rage."

"And since no other such attack followed, the gossip was accepted as fact."

She nodded. "It took time to recover from the damage done and at first I thought the task impossible, especially when I realized no one cared that I recover. My own tenacious will made me fight."

He lifted her to lie across him. "I like your tenacity." He sealed his declaration with a sound kiss.

She gently laid a finger to his lips as if requesting he remain silent as she spoke. "After the attack I wondered why I wanted to live. Death would have been easier for all concerned, especially for me. After I healed, my stepsisters would turn their heads from me and people would whisper as I passed by and each time I would wonder why I fought so hard to remain alive." Tears filled her eyes. "Now I know why. I was meant to love you."

His large hands, so strong and swift when in battle, reached up gently to capture her face and bring her lips to his in a soft kiss. "I am sorry for the pain and sorrow you suffered, but I am so very glad that you fought for your life. You have made life worth living for me. I had thought I had achieved all I had fought hard to gain and when I met you and realized how very much I loved you, I realized what I had achieved was nothing compared to loving you."

He wiped at the tears that started to spill from her eyes and kissed her with a gentle intensity that sent their hands exploring, their bodies responding and passions soaring.

They remained in the healing cottage all night, talking, feasting and loving. Toward dawn Faith heard the guards outside change for the second time. Her husband slept silently, his arm and leg draped over her, and she felt safe and content.

She had hoped and often prayed the dark lord would love

her as much as she loved him, but then he insisted he loved her more. And when she made to protest, he warned her that it was not wise to argue with the devil.

Devil.

He certainly was no devil. He was a kind, good and caring man and if she dared tell him so he would probably laugh, as would his men. But then none knew him as intimately as she did—there is where she discovered his true nature. She would keep her secret and let them all think him the Irish devil, but she knew the truth and that was all that mattered.

She snuggled against the warmth of his hard body and his arm tightened around her and she drifted into a peaceful slumber.

Colin greeted them in the great hall early that morning. The keep was just beginning to stir and few were about and Faith realized that Colin had news to tell her husband.

"I will take Faith to our bedchamber," he said to Colin. "Meet me in my solar."

"Go with Colin," she insisted of her husband. "Rook will be with me."

Eric looked to Colin and though no response was heard or gesture exchanged that Faith could make note of, Eric turned and took her arm. "I will see you to our chamber."

"Is something wrong?" she asked as they entered the bedchamber.

"I am about to find out," he said, running a quick, cautious eye around the large room. "You are to stay here until Borg comes for you."

She nodded.

"Rook," he said, his voice firm. The dog immediately gave him his full attention. "Watch your master."

With that final command given he gave Faith a kiss, a smile and a gentle pat on her backside and headed out the door.

Eric made a brief stop at Borg's chambers, instructing him to guard Faith and telling him he would be in his solar with Colin. He then proceeded to the solar, wondering what news Colin had for him. He understood from the concerned look in his friend's eyes that it would be better for Faith not to be alone. And Eric had no intention of taking any chances with his wife's life.

Last night had been like a dream and he still had to remind

himself that it was all real, that he had a beautiful, courageous wife who loved him. He had never expected such happiness from his marriage. Marriage had always been simply a minor part of a larger plan. And love had never been part of his plan; but then he had thought love fleeting, an emotion that was impossible to find and possess. That had all changed with Faith. He found and possessed a deep love with her and she was now a major part of his life and his plan. Together they would forge a future and spawn a family that would carry his name on for generations and generations, establishing roots deep in Irish soil.

He entered his solar alert and feeling good.

Colin grinned. "A night of lovemaking does wonders for the disposition."

Eric laughed. "That it does, especially when it is shared with a woman you love."

Colin gave him a hardy slap on the back. "The devil finally sees the truth of it."

"The devil can be stubborn at times."

"At least he is no fool and admits the truth when he sees it."

"With the help of friends," Eric said, and Colin nodded with a smile.

Colin followed Eric to the chairs in front of the hearth, and as they sat he said, "I have news."

"I thought as much."

"It seems that the priest who arrived the evening of the murder left the castle grounds before dawn that morning. When I questioned several servants in the Donnegan party I was informed that their priest had stayed at a nearby village to hear confessions and give the sacrament. He only arrived this morning. His name is Father Peter and when I spoke with him he insisted that he had not stepped foot on Shanekill soil until this very day."

"Do you think he lies?"

Colin shrugged. "It is possible."

"I respect your opinion, Colin. Tell me what you think."

"I think the priest tells the truth, but I also think that the murderer remains within the confines of the castle walls."

"Any ideas of who the person could be?"

"Someone with the Donnegan party," he answered. "Faith is

too well liked and respected here for anyone to be foolish enough to do her harm."

"I agree," Eric said, rubbing his chin in thought.

"You have your own ideas?"

"Does it not strike you odd that Faith's family seems so indifferent to her? They care naught for her. If her fool of a father had a brain he would have realized many years ago that she could have been an asset to him—yet she was treated as if she were worthless, chattel he simply wanted to dispose of."

"The man is a pompous idiot and his wife cruel-hearted and it does my heart good to know the devil rescued her from such a pitiful fate."

"I think it was fate that rescued the both of us," Eric said. "And I will not question fate, though I will thank her. She gave me a special gift I will cherish for the rest of my life."

"Besotted," Colin said with a laugh.

"Completely," Eric agreed.

"Does Borg now guard her?"

"Rook does for the moment; Borg will be there presently."

"Perhaps we should talk with Faith of this. She may provide an insight we have overlooked."

"A good suggestion," Eric agreed, "but first tell me more of this priest, his garb, his manner and if he wears a heavy cross around his neck."

Colin looked at him oddly.

Eric leaned forward in his chair and in a whisper, as if he wished no one to hear his words, he related the story of Faith's attack to Colin.

Thirty

Bridget joined Faith shortly after Eric left and she knew all too well Borg would soon follow. She thought to protest all this unnecessary attention, but realized it would do little good. Her husband intended to have his way and once the dark lord made a decree, his word became law.

Faith did insist that Bridget no longer needed to serve her but Bridget had other ideas: "I feel the need to be with you, my lady."

Faith sensed the young woman needed to talk and sat quietly while Bridget combed her hair, after having already helped her change into a soft green shift and tunic.

"The night I tended you, I always felt there was more that I should have done for you."

"You did all that you could, all that you were permitted to do," Faith assured her.

Bridget shook her head. "I feel I should have done more."

Faith turned around on the bench and took Bridget's hands in hers. "Nonsense. If it were not for you I would have died. You helped save my life that night and I have been forever grateful. And I am even more grateful that we can be friends now."

"Friends with a lowly servant?" came the sharp disapproval from the open door.

Both women turned to see Lady Terra entering the room.

"What nonsense do you speak?" the woman demanded of Faith.

Faith stood, her stance full of self-confidence and her tone firm. "This is my home and I do as I wish here. And you were not invited to enter my chamber."

"How dare you speak to me with such disrespect."

"How dare you disrespect me in my own home."

"A home you have no idea how to run properly. Why, you did not even have the decency or manners to join your guests last night."

"Manners and decency had nothing to do with my absence from the hall," Faith said. "My husband and I simply chose not to share a meal with you and Lord William."

The woman grew incensed. "How dare you insult me."

Faith walked right up to her. "This is my home, I dare anything I choose. Now you will leave my chambers and await my presence in the hall. I will speak with you there, but only if you keep a civil tongue."

Lady Terra grew red with indignation and, as was her way, she made ready to raise her hand. Rook made his presence known with a bark and a snarl and the woman immediately changed her intention and fled the room.

Bridget clapped her hands and cried out with joy. "You are most brave, my lady."

Faith turned a pale face to Bridget. "Not that brave. My legs are trembling, my hands shaking and I feel light-headed."

"You should sit," Bridget said and moved to help her. She was not fast enough, but Borg was. He ran into the room and caught Faith before she hit the floor in a dead faint.

Eric entered the room, followed by Colin, to see Borg placing his unconscious wife on the bed. He hurried to her side.

"What happened?" he demanded, sitting down beside her and taking her limp hand in his.

"I saw Lady Terra leave here in a snit and I hurried to see what it was about," Borg explained. "Faith was dropping to the floor when I entered the room and I made it to her just in time."

Eric looked to Bridget who had placed a moist cloth on Faith's forehead.

"Lady Faith and Lady Terra had words," she said, and with a smile, added, "And Lady Faith ordered her from her chambers."

The three men grinned.

"A true warrior she is," Borg praised.

"Brave and courageous," Colin said.

Eric finished with, "And she is mine."

"The devil always gets the choice ones," Colin grumbled.

"Lucky he is," Borg said.

"And grateful he should be," Bridget said, startling all three.

She trembled when the dark lord cast his intense blue eyes on her. "You are right, Bridget, and I am very grateful Faith is mine. Now tell me why she fainted?"

Faith began to stir and Bridget rinsed the cloth once again and returned it to her forehead. "I suppose the confrontation with Lady Terra upset her."

It was not the answer he wanted to hear. "She has been feeling well otherwise?"

Borg's hearty laughter interrupted her answer. "How can she not be with child? You never leave the poor girl alone."

Colin continued the teasing. "You rut after her like a stallion after a mare in heat."

Bridge giggled.

Faith heard the conversation, and thinking herself in a dream, remarked, "Aye, that he does—and he's built like a fine stallion, too."

Bridget turned bright red and the three men roared. Colin and Borg slapped Eric on the back.

"Not a better compliment could be given," Borg said.

"And so Faith is not embarrassed when she wakes we will take our leave," Colin said.

"A wise choice," Borg agreed and reached for Bridget's hand. She looked to Eric.

"I will see to her care," he assured her and turned to Colin. "Inform Lady Terra that Lady Faith is delayed and will speak to her later."

"My pleasure," he answered with a charming smile, a dramatic bow and a knowing wink before he exited the room.

"That man could charm a witch," Borg said.

"He will have his chance then with Lady Terra," Bridget confirmed and shivered. "That one is pure evil."

Eric and Borg exchanged concerned glances.

"Oh, my," Faith said softly, her eyes fluttering their way open.

Borg nodded to Eric and with Bridget's hand in his they hurried out of the room, closing the door behind them.

Faith sighed and gathered her jumbled thoughts as her eyes drifted fully open. "I cannot believe I fainted again, Bridget."

"A growing habit."

"Eric," she said, surprised when her eyesight turned alert.

"Is there something you wish to tell me?" he asked, his blue eyes full of concern and his voice gentle though anxious.

She wondered if his hand rested intentionally on her stomach or if his own thoughts brought it there. She did not wish to disappoint him and yet she still could not confirm if she was with child. There was an excellent chance she was and in one more week or two she would be certain, but she could not admit to carrying a child now and then possibly disappoint him. Besides, she was feeling simply wonderful. She ate without her stomach protesting, did not tear for no reason and felt wonderfully hungry in the morning. She displayed no signs of being with child, though she was aware that some women were prone to fainting spells when they carried.

She decided honesty was her best answer. She placed her hand over his. "I will be certain in a week or two."

He would have preferred a more definite answer and while he told himself to be patient and wait, he already grew anxious about her health. "You feel well?"

"Never better," she admitted and pushed herself up to sit. "Actually I am suddenly quite famished."

Again his disappointment showed. "Your stomach does not protest?"

"Only lack of sustenance."

He stood. "I will see that food is brought to you."

She slipped off the bed, her smile bright. "I think I prefer to visit with Mary in the kitchen—this way there will be more for the choosing."

"That hungry are we?"

She nodded and headed for the door.

"Your stepmother waits in the hall."

That stopped her and she turned. "I had forgotten about her."

He walked over to her. "Bridget explained what happened."

"I could not tolerate her another moment."

"You need not, this is your home," he said, pushing her fiery red hair away from her face. She had stopped concealing her scar weeks ago and that pleased him. But what pleased him more was the fact that she felt no shame when naked in front of him. He simply regarded the long, thin scar as a badge of honor won by a warrior who had been victorious in battle.

His hand drifted to the back of her neck and he pulled her to him as he leaned down to share a kiss. The mutually loving exchange brought sighs of satisfaction and whispers of promises each would fulfill for the other before the day was done.

A loud grumble from Faith's stomach caused them both to smile.

"Come, I will make certain your belly is filled."

She giggled as they left the room. "I think you have already done that, my lord."

He stopped and captured her chin in his large hand. "I would be proud for you to carry my child."

She broke free of his gentle hold and raised herself on tiptoes to deposit a fast kiss on his lips. "And I would be the happiest woman in the world to have your babe."

"Now that we have agreed on that and you have made it known that I possess the size and potency of a stallion, we will—"

She gasped and grabbed his arm as they proceeded down the stairs. "It was not a dream? I really spoke those words to you?"

He smiled. "Not only to me." He then proceeded to give her a full accounting of her remark. It was a red-faced Lady Faith who entered the kitchen.

"I do not think we should be doing this," Bridget said as they walked toward the Donnegan wagons near the castle gate, Colin following not far behind them.

Faith held tightly to her healing basket, afraid her trembling hands would betray her nervousness. She had eaten a hardy meal with Eric and with duties of the keep calling him he had turned her over to Colin's care. He thought her to be busy with tending the ill today, but she had other thoughts. "I need another look at Nora's body."

"Colin will not allow it," Bridget whispered. "I heard Lord Eric instruct him to keep a careful eye on you."

"I know, I heard the same instructions myself, but . . ." she said, her voice falling low. "I do not think Colin will enter a cottage where a woman close to her birthing time is being examined."

"But how will you sneak past him?"

"Colin cannot be in two places at once and Rebecca has two doors to her cottage. We enter through the front door and I will exit out the one that opens onto her garden. It will take me only a few moments to reach the empty cottage where Nora's body waits for burial tomorrow. A quick peek and I will be back."

"I am going with you," Bridget insisted.

Faith protested with a shake of her head. "You cannot. You must remain at Rebecca's cottage in case Colin calls for me."

"And what if you faint again?"

"I will revive on my own soon enough."

Bridget looked at her with concerned eyes. "It is dangerous for you to go off on your own."

Faith smiled. "I will not be on my own. Rook will come with me."

The large animal followed beside her, his attention steady on his surroundings and on her.

"You will not be gone long?"

"Nay, I will have my look and be on my way." She would not be deterred from her intentions. She felt she had missed something when last she had looked upon the scarred body, and she wished another look.

They both stopped talking when they came upon the cottage; Colin moved to follow them in.

Faith blocked his path with a raised hand. "I think it is best if you remain outside."

Colin smiled. "Lord Eric has instructed I not leave your side."

She returned a smile as charming as his. "Then you will stand beside me while I examine Rebecca, who is large with child?"

Colin's smile faded. "I will wait right outside this door."

"A wise choice," Faith said and disappeared inside, shutting the door behind her.

Faith explained her plan to Rebecca and the young girl eagerly agreed, feeling privileged that Lady Faith would place such trust and confidence in her. Faith switched hooded cloaks with Bridget and she quietly slipped out the other door with Rook at her side.

She moved swiftly, avoiding open areas and keeping her hood pulled down to conceal her identity. She was glad for the fine mist that began to drizzle, causing many to seek shelter and others to speed their outdoor tasks before a heavy rainfall began.

No guards were assigned to the cottage. Nora was now Lady Terra's responsibility and she had ordered that the young servant be prepared for burial and requested a plot of earth from Lord Eric. Faith was relieved to learn that Nora was to be buried on sacred ground—that of the soil behind the castle chapel.

Rook followed Faith inside the small cottage. It was dark and damp and a dense chill filled the room. A single candle glowed beside the girl's cold, stiff body. Her dress of brown coarse wool and white tunic looked familiar and Faith realized the clothes belonged to Bridget; they were her best garments when at Donnegan Keep. They were no longer necessary to her. Eric saw to it that the servants of the keep were finely outfitted and Bridget with her stitching skill created handsome garments for herself.

Faith approached the corpse slowly. Nora had been washed, her torn skin stitched and her hair washed and plaited. Her eyes held a stitch in each one, the living fearing to look into the eyes of the dead, frightened death would try to steal their souls and return. She looked asleep—as if in peace—and Faith was glad that she had been tended by caring hands.

Rook positioned himself by the door, protesting with whines and whimpers in steady intervals. He evidently did not care to be there, but then neither did she.

She ordered him quiet with a promise that they would leave soon.

Hasty steps took her to the head of the table where Nora lay in repose. She moved the candle closer to her face to study the scar that had been stitched. She remembered the wide gash and even now, with numerous stitches holding it closed, one could see how jagged and deep it had been. The scar followed down her neck in a haphazard path. Seeing the wound again for herself made Faith realize that the person who had inflicted it did so in a rage of unbridled anger.

Faith's attacker had not been angry but rather on a mission against evil. His cut was precise and intentional, as if he understood or at least believed exactly where evil resided in a body. But the person who had attacked Nora simply had slashed out at her with the sole attempt of killing her. The thought that someone would kill so maliciously frightened her, for surely such a person was possessed of insanity.

She shivered and Rook whined.

"I agree, boy—let us be off."

Colin pushed away from the cottage wall he was leaning against as Eric approached. He had positioned himself under the eave of the cottage roof to avoid the fine mist that fell and which would surely dampen his clothes. Dark clouds had moved rapidly toward them from the east, causing the wind to pick up and the rain to start, making Eric's arrival timely. He would want Faith returned to the keep before the rain turned heavy.

"Lady Faith is inside," Colin informed Eric as he drew near.

Eric joined him under the eave. "Will she soon finish?"

Colin shrugged. "She has not been in there that long."

Colin's eye caught a fair maiden walking a short distance from them. She was wrapped in a soft green wool cloak, her pretty face a lovely sight to behold.

Eric grinned and shook his head. "You will learn to curb that wandering eye when I find you a wife."

Colin dramatically clasped his hands over his heart. "If I cannot have a wife as brave, strong and loving as Lady Faith, I fear I cannot marry at all."

"I doubt another like my wife exists but I promise I will do my best to find one similar in nature and quality," Eric insisted just as dramatically.

Both men grew silent as their eyes watched the intentional swaying hips of another maiden that passed by. Her generous smile settled on Colin.

Colin was about to call out to her when Eric stilled his response with a firm hand to his arm and a finger to his own lips for silence. Colin obeyed, remaining silent along with his friend, and listening—though for what he was not sure.

After several moments Colin understood what it was Eric had heard.

"Two voices," Eric whispered to Colin, and he nodded his agreement. "And neither one belongs to my wife."

Both men stood and approached the closed door.

Faith meandered her way around the cottages so as not to be noticed. In her haste and with Rook close on her heels and the rain beginning to fall in earnest she hurried her steps, causing Rook to grow anxious from her nervous pace and race up against her.

Caught off balance from the weight of the large dog being thrown against her, Faith found herself tumbling to the wet ground facefirst. She sputtered and spit dirt from her mouth and staggered to her feet with difficulty, her garments wet and muddy and weighing her small frame down.

She cast Rook a reproachful glance and with no time to waste she hurried her steps once again though with her weighted garments her steps were not as quick.

Faith entered the back door of Rebecca's cottage with a sigh of relief, her face marred with mud and her garments soaked.

Bridget and Rebecca sat at the lone table near the hearth and cast stunned eyes upon the frightful creature that stepped through the door. After a moment of shock was replaced by recognition, the two women stood at the same time the front door was thrown open and Eric and Colin marched in.

Eric cast shocked eyes at the woman in the doorway, shook his head along with Colin and set his eyes upon her once again.

"Faith?" He seemed to ask the question of himself and then he growled that low rumbly growl that portended his anger.

Faith did not respond; she wisely chose silence.

Bridget and Rebecca dropped back down in their chairs.

Colin smiled and kept control of his desire to laugh out loud.

Rook sneaked past Faith and over to Colin's side.

"Smart dog," Colin whispered to him.

Faith decided at that moment to explain. "Eric—"

She never got past his name; he was on her in a flash, grabbing her, hoisting her over his shoulder and marching out the door without a word to anyone.

Thirty-one

Faith kept her hood pulled down over her head as Eric marched boldly across the castle grounds, through the keep and up the stairs. She heard whispers, giggles and laughter and while she hoped all who saw the outrageous incident would simply think the dark lord was about to folly with a servant, she could not easily convince herself. All at Shanekill Castle knew the Irish devil loved his lady and the only woman he would hoist over his shoulder and carry to his bedchamber would be his wife, Lady Faith.

Gossip was probably already spreading, the women admiring Lord Eric's romantic actions and the men boasting of his potency. The topic would entertain the wagging tongues for days.

Eric bellowed for a bath to be brought immediately to his chambers as they crossed the great hall and mounted the stairs. Faith heard the servants scurry at his command and she also heard their giggles and whispers.

His booted foot kicked open his bedchamber door and he walked to the middle of the room where he deposited her much more gently than she had anticipated.

He stared at her briefly and then rubbing his chin and jaw he began to circle her slowly. Faith remained as she was, though a chill seeped into her bones from her damp clothes. Still she thought it wise not to move.

He stopped circling and asked, "Do I want to know where you have been?"

She thought to respond but he supplied the answer himself.

He began circling her again. "Nay, I would grow angry if I learned you disobeyed my orders and had gone off alone."

He stopped and glared at her, his blue eyes bright with tempered rage.

She remained still, though her teeth were near to chattering.

He continued walking around her. "And if I learned that my wife decided to take it upon herself and sneak off to—" He stopped abruptly both in talk and movement and glared at her for several minutes before he sought another answer. "Did you go to see Nora again?"

She opened her mouth to reply and once again he responded to his own query.

"But of course you did. You knew that I would forbid you access to her disturbing corpse so you set out to see it without permission."

She was about to nod a reply when several servants carried the large wooden tub into the room and placed it in front of the fiery hearth. More servants followed, filling the extra-large tub with buckets and buckets of steaming water.

Faith wanted to cry at the thought of the warm water seeping into her bones and chasing her deep chill away. Instead she shivered.

With a softly muttered oath her husband was upon her. "If you grow ill because of your rash actions I will thrash you." He then proceeded to strip the sopping wet cloak off her and when he felt her cold skin and realized the depth of her chill he released several more oaths and shouted an order for the servants to hurry.

Bridget entered the room just as the last of the buckets were being emptied into the tub, after which Faith sighed with relief.

Borg followed just behind, with Rook beside him.

"Out," Eric ordered, to everyone's surprise.

Bridget attempted to protest, but a warning look from Borg and a firm hand to her arm stopped her. The servants hurried out, followed by Borg who shoved Bridget out in front of him with Rook trailing behind, his tail between his legs and his ears drooping.

Eric said nothing; he stripped himself to his waist in an instant and then he proceeded to strip her. His hands worked fast and steady and as the warm air in the room hit her skin she shivered and her teeth chattered.

"I should thrash you now," he said, though his voice held more concern than anger.

"I-I—"

"Not now," he ordered and scooped her naked body into his arms. He carried her to the tub and gently lowered her into the steaming water.

She sighed loudly from the exquisite pleasure of the hot water seeping into her bones and chasing away the awful chill that had consumed her. She slipped down under the water until it covered her shoulders and again she sighed.

"Thank you, my lord," she said, looking to her husband who kneeled beside the tub.

"You are a sight," he said in an attempt to scold.

Faith dumped several handfuls of water over her face to rid herself of the mud.

Eric reached for a cloth on a nearby bench, dipped it in the tub and wiped away the streaks of dirt that remained on her face. "Why? Answer me that?"

With his tone more neutral and his blue eyes tempered, Faith discussed her adventure. "I felt I was missing something when I first looked upon Nora and I could not rest until I took another look."

"And what did you find?"

"Rage," she said with a shiver.

He looked at her, confused but also curious.

"The scar was jagged."

"Aye, it is," he agreed before Faith dunked her head to soak and cleanse her thick hair.

He helped her to squeeze the wetness from the heavy strands.

"My scar is thin and almost a perfect line. My attacker made his intentions clear with the path his weapon took. I knew if I did not fight back he would dig deeper and deeper along where his knife had already traveled until he released the evil he insisted resided within me. My attacker possessed madness. Nora's attacker possesses rage."

Eric thought on the wisdom of his wife's words. She was

right. Each attack was different and therefore caused by two different people, though made to resemble the other.

Eric nodded slowly. "The person who killed Nora had to have been aware of your attack."

It was her turn to nod. "Precisely."

"Hurry and finish," he ordered, "before the water cools and returns your chill."

She did as he directed and when she was done he stood holding a large towel to wrap her in, and he did just that. He carried her to the bed and rubbed his hands over the towel so it would seep the wetness from her skin.

"Promise me you will not act foolishly again."

With her arms tucked snugly beneath the towel she was at his mercy—and his heated blue eyes confirmed it was intentional. But she did not fear the devil; she loved him and she knew he loved her so she answered honestly, "I cannot."

His jaw tightened, his nostrils flared and he shook his head. "How did I know that would be your answer."

"Because I speak the truth," she said with a tender smile.

He smiled as well. "Another answer I was aware of."

"You know me well, my lord."

He skimmed her lips with his. "Not well enough, or I would know how to control that stubborn will of yours."

"I am not stubborn; I am determined."

He laughed. "You play with words, but that does not change your tenacious nature." His smiling face grew serious. "I love you too much to lose you; please do as I ask."

How could she deny him? He did not demand or command. He simply expressed his true feelings and fear to her and it would be most unkind to deny him.

"As you wish, my lord," she answered sincerely.

"Thank you, dear wife," he said and captured her mouth in a kiss that had her wrapped body wiggling to get free.

"Eric," she protested with a cry when his hand moved beneath the towel and tormented her most feverishly.

"A fit punishment," he said with a laugh and continued to tease her into a feverish frenzy. It was not long before his own body felt the same passionate frenzy and they were soon naked and wrapped solidly around each other.

She helped him slip into her. She loved the feel of him in her hand—hard and thick and silky smooth, and she took her time, her fingers stroking in a fashion that ignited his pleasure and her own.

"Enough," he said harshly. "I will be inside you when I spill myself."

Her legs spread slowly in invitation and he accepted, entering her with swift precision and setting a fast and furious pace they both maintained until they burst one after the other in a final breath-stealing, body-shuddering climax.

Faith fell asleep within mere minutes of Eric slipping off her. She had had little sleep the previous night and with this morning's unexpected adventure exhaustion finally caught up with her.

Eric tucked the blanket around her. She lay on her stomach, her head nearly buried beneath a pillow and her breathing close to a light snore. He moved off the bed gently so as not to disturb her and dressed all the while, keeping his eyes on her.

He did not know what he would do if she were not in his life. He had grown so accustomed to her presence that he did not think he could function without her by his side. He would have once thought that notion ridiculous. Any woman can warm a man's bed, as warriors often bragged, but as his father tried to explain to him, only one woman can touch a man's heart. He had not understood those words until now. Faith touched his heart. He felt lonely when she was not near and he ached all too often for her touch. He had fallen deeply in love with a woman who possessed the strength, courage and *faith* to love the Irish devil.

And he had no intentions of seeing any harm come to her.

After he was fully dressed he walked to the door and opened it, finding Rook spread across the doorway, as he knew he would be. He leaned down and gave the large dog a rub behind his ear. "Good boy, now go get Borg and Bridget."

Rook woofed softly, as if understanding his master slept, and hurried off.

Borg arrived shortly, along with Bridget. With a quick request for Bridget to watch over Faith and for Borg to post a guard at the bedchamber door, he hurried off.

Colin was entering the hall at the same anxious speed as Eric. "The cleric from Donnegan Keep has arrived."

"Good; we will talk with him now," Eric said, and the two men headed for the front doors that Colin had just entered.

"Lord Eric!" came a shrill call.

Eric and Colin both winced at Lady Terra's high-pitched voice.

Eric turned. "Another time, Lady Terra—I have business to see to."

Her dark eyes widened and she marched straight toward the two men. "You have the audacity to summon my husband here and then the ignorance to ignore him. If you do not tell us of the reason for your summons we will take our leave today."

Colin took a step back, aware that Eric's temper was about to erupt.

And it did.

"You will take your leave when I order you to," Eric said sharply, walking forward to meet the woman who stopped in her brisk approach and took several steps back as he continued to advance on her. "You will do as I direct. You will speak with a respectful and civil tongue to my wife. And you will learn why I summoned you when I am ready to tell you. Until then you will obey my every command or suffer the consequences."

Lady Terra turned pale, trembled and remained silent.

Eric insisted on a response. "Do you understand me?"

She nodded slowly.

"Then I expect no more problems from you or your husband."

He turned to leave, stopped and approached her once again. The fearful woman looked near to fainting.

"You will not trouble my wife with any of your petty matters. She will speak to you when and if she wishes."

Lady Terra nodded most vigorously this time.

Colin followed Eric out of the keep but stole a backward glance to see Lady Terra hit the floor in a dead faint.

Eric and Colin walked toward the chapel on the castle grounds. It was a simple structure, made of wood and covered by a thatched roof. The outside had recently been completed; rows of benches had been added inside and an altar of wood graced with fine embroidered coverings had been installed. A beautiful cross that had been hand carved by one of the castle carpenters hung on the wall behind the simple altar and the women kept the small room lit with a wealth of candles.

The only missing item was a permanent priest. Eric supposed that was why so many were anxious to seek Father Peter out to hear their confessions and receive the sacrament. Which would explain why a line formed outside the chapel door.

"The priest announced that he would say a special mass tomorrow morning and hear confessions until dark," Colin explained.

"There is a confession I wish to hear," Eric said, and not caring who he disturbed in his pursuit of a madman marched straight into the chapel, people moving out of his path without hesitation, though with respect. The priest would save their souls, but the devil would protect their lives.

Father Peter rose from the bench where he sat, as did Mary, whose confession he had heard.

Eric made his apologies to Mary for the interruption. She bobbed her head respectfully, explained she was finished and hurried out of the chapel. Colin closed the door after Mary departed and stood in front of it.

"I am most pleased to see that the lord of this keep wishes to confess his sins," the priest said solemnly.

He was a small, reed-thin man, and he possessed large sorrowful eyes that were more filled with despair than hope. His brown hair was so thin you could see his scalp and his brown coarse wool robe hung loosely on his frail frame. He did not appear to be strong enough to fight anyone, but then Eric had learned that looks could deceive.

Eric smiled pleasantly. "Father Peter, there is not enough time to hear the devil's confession."

The little man was startled by his admission. "My son, do not speak such blasphemy. The devil resides in us all and must be vanquished with confession and prayer."

"Do you ever favor cutting the devil out of anyone?" Eric asked seriously, and his question was taken just as seriously by the priest.

"If evil goes deep and takes root it is sometimes necessary to purge the soul."

Eric did not like his answer. "And have you purged a soul?"

"Nay, I have not found it necessary; confession and prayer work miracles."

"What say you of Lady Faith?" he asked bluntly.

Father Peter shook his head and sat down on the bench. "A sweet young woman, and so very courageous."

Eric sat down beside him. "You did not think her evil?"

The little man rubbed at his sad, tired eyes. "Nay, she always had a smile for everyone and a kind word. That was why it was so difficult to believe she was possessed by evil."

It was Eric's turn to appear startled. "Who told you this?"

"A young servant girl at Donnegan Keep."

"Do you know her name?"

"Aye, I do, and she is here now."

"Who is she?" Eric asked anxiously.

The priest freely gave her name. "Her name is Nora."

Eric shot a quick glance to Colin and he approached.

"Nora?" Eric repeated to make certain he had heard the name correctly.

The priest nodded. "A fine young woman who carries her duties out most diligently."

Colin joined the questioning. "This Nora, is she the one who arrived with you at the keep the other night?"

The priest looked as if confused. "Only I have arrived."

Colin corrected him. "The guards informed us you arrived two nights ago just before a young woman and departed alone at daybreak."

The priest shook his head. "As I told you once before, it was not me. I stayed at a small village a day's journey away to pray with an ill peasant family. The Donnegan party traveled on without me."

"When did Nora inform you of the evil in Lady Faith?" Eric asked.

"The night of the attack," the priest answered. "She hurried into the chapel and pleaded with me to come with her; that Lady Faith had fornicated with the devil and had met an evil end."

Eric looked about to strangle the frail priest and Colin asked the next question. "And what did you do?"

"I immediately hurried to the poor woman's side. She looked to be possessed, screaming out that the devil was there with her."

Eric snapped at the ignorant man. "She was slowly bleeding to death, you fool."

"She surrendered herself to the devil and suffered the consequences."

Eric reached out and grabbed the cleric by his coarse robe.

"She fought a raging lunatic and survived, and for that she was persecuted."

Colin laid his hand over Eric's and Eric reluctantly released the trembling man.

"You will think on this matter, Father Peter, and tell me anything else you recall about that night, no matter how unimportant you think it is," Eric ordered sternly.

The man nodded. "As you wish, my son."

"I will speak with you in the morning."

"After mass," the priest added.

"One thing, Father," Eric said.

"You wish confession?" the frail man asked hopefully.

Colin grinned. "You are tempting fate, Father."

"All souls are worth saving, my son," Father Peter informed them both.

"Not all, Father," Eric disagreed. "I order you to keep your distance from my wife."

Father Peter appeared startled by his edict. "Why? I assumed she would wish confession."

Eric laid a heavy hand on the priest's thin back. "What absolution can you offer a woman who surrendered to the devil?"

Thirty-two

Faith came awake with a start, grabbing the blanket to cover her bare breasts. She instantly searched the room in a hasty glance and caught notice of Bridget peeking out the door.

"What is it?" she asked anxiously, sensing something was amiss.

Bridget closed the door and hurried over to her. "Lord Eric and Lord William are in a shouting match."

"Over what?"

"You," Bridget said with a grin.

Faith jumped out of bed and rushed to the chest, throwing it open and reaching for her dark blue shift. "I must get dressed. I wish to hear what they say. Does anyone guard the door?"

Bridget hurried to help her, her own curiosity peaked. "Nay, Borg and Colin are in the hall—neither wanted to miss this confrontation. Borg ordered Rook to stay by your side."

The big dog sat by the door, whining. He was just as anxious as they to investigate the shouts.

With fiery red curls falling wildly around her face and Bridget pushing Faith's soft green tunic up on her shoulder, the curious pair made their way to the steps. They hugged the granite wall as they slowly descended the curving staircase and listened to the shouts that echoed through the great hall and up the steps.

Not wanting their presence known, they kept against the

wall and out of sight, listening to the raised voices, one deep and self-assured, the other trembling and full of doubt.

"I need not answer to you; the matter does not concern you," Lord William insisted with a quivering voice.

The thick wooden table groaned when Eric slammed his fist down hard upon it. "Faith is my wife and anything to do with her concerns me."

"The attack took place years ago and matters not."

This time the table cracked when his fist met it with a hefty blow. "What matters is you failed to protect your daughter and then you failed to give her proper care after the attack. Such selfishness is unpardonable."

"I was doing what was best for her," Lord William said, his quivering voice sounding shrill as he raised it.

"And you think leaving your daughter to die is best for her?"

Colin and Borg moved closer to Eric, afraid he would reach out and snap the rotund little man's throat since he looked so furious, though their hands itched to inflict similar damage.

"Her reputation was soiled. What good was she to me? She would bring no substantial marriage contract and she would forever be branded with her shame."

Eric growled low and deep and he clinched his hands at his sides, his knuckles turning white. "So you left her bleeding and in the care of a lone servant."

"At least in death she would have retained her honor."

"You know nothing of honor," Eric said. "You are a coward and a fool."

"If I am the fool, then why is a shamed woman your wife?" Lord William remarked snidely.

Eric hit the table for the third and last time. It split down the middle and parted, though remained standing. "Are you really so ignorant that you would think I would take a woman for a wife that I did not want?"

"You had no choice," Lord William insisted, sweat beading on his full face.

Colin and Borg laughed, making the trembling man all the more nervous.

Eric shook his head and folded his arms across his wide chest. "A fool you most certainly are if you think I married Faith because of your threat."

Lord William stared at him in disbelief.

"Faith was the only one of your daughters I would choose to marry, and choose to marry her I did. Your threat meant nothing to me. Your other daughters were unacceptable, none suited me nor appealed to me. Faith I wanted from when first I laid eyes upon her and Faith I intended to have. I married her by choice, not by threat."

Lord William remained silent, not knowing how to respond.

Lord Eric continued. "I will have an apology from you to your daughter before you leave this keep."

"Never," Lord William shouted, losing his anger and his senses. "I will not apologize to a *whore*."

Eric was on the stunned man before Colin and Borg could stop him and before they tore him off the screaming man he had delivered two hefty blows that left blood pouring from his nose and mouth.

"You will be gone from this keep by morning tomorrow," he ordered and stormed off, leaving Colin and Borg to deal with the sniveling man.

Eric felt the overwhelming urge to gather his wife in his arms and hold her tightly. He may have lost a mother young, but his stepfather had been a good man and treated him fairly and with much love, as did his stepmother. But Faith's own father cared naught for her and her stepmother was a cruel woman. He would make certain she received the love so long denied her.

He bounded up the steps, his focus on his thoughts, when he was suddenly confronted by a pair of weeping women.

"Borg," he bellowed and swept his crying wife up into his arms.

Borg was at his side in no time.

"See to your woman," Eric ordered and carried his wife up the steps and to their bedchamber.

He placed her on the bed and lay beside her, cradling her in his arms. "I am sorry that you had to hear that."

Tears gushed from her eyes like a fast-flowing river.

"Do not let it upset you, Faith," he urged. "The man is not worth wasting tears on."

"Nay, he is not," she agreed between sobs.

He drew back and looked down at her in surprise. "Then why do you cry?"

"You chose me," she said, her tears still falling. "You chose

me as your wife because you wanted me, not because you were
forced to accept me."

"Of course I did," he said firmly. "The devil does as he
pleases and it pleased me to make you my wife."

She wiped at her tears. "I am pleased to be your wife."

"If you must know the truth," he admitted with a grin, "I did
not plan on leaving Donnegan Keep without you."

She smiled, her tears finally subsiding. "I will be truthful,
too. I found you most attractive when first we met."

"I know," he laughed and received a jab in the ribs. He
laughed again. "I saw the passion in your eyes and I was determined to taste it."

She tugged on his long dark hair and her soft glance ca-
ressed his face. "I love you, Eric."

He kissed her with a tenderness that made her want to weep
again. "I love you, wife, and you will hear me declare that love
until my dying day."

She pressed a finger to his lips. "Nay, do not speak of death.
I could not bear to live without you. We will always be."

"Always, I promise," he whispered and kissed her again and
again and again.

The keep and castle grounds were abuzz the next morning in
preparation for Lord and Lady Donnegan's departure. Colin
was assigned first guard of the day for her, Eric and Borg being
presently occupied with an important matter, though with what
Eric refused to tell Faith.

Faith had not seen her father or stepmother, nor did she wish
to. Eric informed her that they would be departing Shanekill
Keep before the morning meal and she was relieved. They
would finally be gone and probably for good, the thought did
not disturb her.

What did disturb her was that she received an unexpected
message from her stepmother requesting that she speak with
her. She awaited her presence in the chapel.

Her first thought was to decline her request, but giving it a
brief consideration she decided it was best to face her one more
time and be done with it. And besides, she knew that her stepmother chose the chapel as the meeting place in order to intimidate her. And she refused to be intimidated by her or the chapel
any longer.

She also possessed a margin of safety with Colin and Rook at her side, so she informed Colin of the summons and he agreed it would do no harm for her to meet with her stepmother.

The day was lovely. The sky was bright and beautiful and dotted with full white clouds; the air was cool and a soft breeze blew. The castle grounds were busy, with most going about their routine chores. The clang of swords could be heard on the practice field in the distance. It was a marvelous day and Faith was grateful to be alive. Grateful for a husband who loved her and for friends who cared and for a new home where life would finally be good.

Rook chased after a stick that Colin had been throwing to him, which Colin dropped, to the dog's disappointment, when they stopped in front of the chapel.

"Stay out here and play with him; I will be fine," Faith said, feeling guilty that Rook had been denied his playtime for the last few days.

Colin looked hesitant and before he would agree he glanced inside the chapel. Fewer candles than usual burned and a lone figure sat with her head drooped near the alter.

"Hopefully, Lady Terra is praying for forgiveness."

Faith smiled. "Then she has a lot of prayers to recite."

Colin laughed as he retrieved the stick from the ground and gave it a toss. "Call out if you feel the need."

She nodded. "Aye, I will." She entered the chapel with reluctance.

The place was darker than she expected—shadows danced in the dark corners and along the stone walls, though perhaps it was her fears that made her see it that way. The few lit candles along the altar cast a dim light and the heavy silence reached out and welcomed with a somber embrace. She spied the lone figure on a bench up near the altar and hurried forward, wanting this done.

With her thoughts centered on the confrontation about to take place, Faith did not notice or hear another figure quietly close the door behind her and drop the latch across it.

"Lady Terra," she said as she approached. She was taken back when a person in the brown hooded robe of a cleric stood and turned.

"Faith, I am so pleased to learn you wish to take confession," Father Peter said, standing, his pale face looking ghostly in the glow of the candles.

Faith froze when her startled glance fell upon the heavy wooden cross that hung around the priest's neck.

"Come, let us get started," he said, holding out his hand to her. "You must have much to confess."

Faith still could not move.

Father Peter talked softly, urging her not to be afraid. "Come now, Faith, I am an instrument of God here to do his work, you must not be afraid of me. I would never hurt you."

Faith thought she spied a shadow moving up behind Father Peter, but she could not be certain. Did her fear create the apparition? She squinted her eyes against the darkness, attempting to see clearer and suddenly the figure began to take shape. She ignored the priest, who continued to babble about saving souls from evil, and watched as an arm raised up and out of the shadows, a shiny dagger clasped firmly in the thin hand.

Eric paced the floor in front of the dais. "Where is he?"

Borg sat on a bench a few feet from Eric, waiting patiently. "Probably giving as many blessings as he can before he leaves."

"I demanded his presence here and he ignores me."

"Or is occupied."

Eric glared at his brother. "I do not care what occupies the cleric; when I demand, he obeys."

Bridget entered the hall and hesitated, but Borg waved her forward. He slipped his arm around her waist and kissed her cheek. "He is angry because the priest keeps him waiting."

Bridget nodded, still a bit fearful of the dark lord, especially when he displayed his temper.

"Perhaps Bridget can answer some of your questions," Borg suggested.

Bridget looked to Eric. "How may I help you, my lord?"

"Will she never simply call me Eric?" he asked of Borg.

"'Tis the Irish way—ignore it."

"'Tis the Irish who have the manners," Bridget informed them sternly. "And the Vikings who do not know any better."

"She told you," Borg said with a laugh.

Bridget turned bright red. "Oh, Lord Eric, forgive me."

He laughed and waved his hand at her. "Nay, Bridget, I admire those who speak the truth, especially when they take their life in their hands in doing so."

This time Bridget paled.

Borg laughed harder and squeezed her to him. "He but teases you."

Bridget was not taking any chances—she clung to Borg for dear life.

Eric finally asked his questions. "Do you know that Nora fetched Father Peter the night of Faith's attack?"

"Aye, she was instructed to do so."

"By whom?"

"Lady Terra," Bridget answered. "She wanted Faith's sins absolved before she died."

"What were her words?" Eric asked.

"I am not certain, though I do recall Nora saying something about Lady Terra telling her that Lady Faith had met an evil end."

Eric stared at her. "Are you sure?"

"I cannot be positive, though Nora repeated them often enough, reminding me of her part in helping Lady Faith. She boasted to me and other servants that it was because of her that the priest was there and waiting for Lady Faith when she was carried into her room."

At that moment a young servant girl entered the hall with a message from Father Peter for Lord Eric. As soon as Eric learned that the priest was hearing Faith's confession at her request he rushed out of the hall, Borg and Bridget close on his heels.

Faith's scream did not come in time to save the priest. The dagger plunged in and out of his back with lightning speed and the frail man, his eyes wide with fright and a whispered prayer on his lips, fell to the floor.

An unexpected vicious blow to her face sent Faith stumbling backward but she managed to remain on her feet and she cast angry eyes at her stepmother.

Shouts, barks and incessant pounding on the door brought a laugh to Lady Terra. "Fools. They built this place to keep the women and children safe from their enemies. They will never get in."

Faith glared at her, not concerned at the moment for her life or with her escape, but curious for answers. This woman had wanted her dead, and had left her to die. And now she wondered if she had something to do with her attack. She wanted answers; she needed them after all these years.

"Tell me the truth," Faith simply said and waited, her posture that of a proud lady of the keep.

"With pleasure," Lady Terra said, her eyes bright with madness. "No one wanted you. Your mother came from poor stock, the fifth daughter of a near-penniless landowner. But your father wanted that land so he married your mother; to his relief she died in childbirth. Unfortunately you lived."

Faith refused to show any response to her malicious remarks. Her words left her with a heart full of sorrow and much regret for a mother she had never known and for a woman who never had the opportunity to know a love as potent and powerful as the love she shared with Eric. But she loved her mother most dearly, for she had given her the most precious of gifts— the gift of life.

The pounding on the door continued along with the shouts, and Faith was certain she heard Eric calling out to her. She smiled to herself. He would not let her die, nor would Borg or Colin—and of course there was Rook. They would save her.

Lady Terra laughed softly. "No one will save you, just as no one wanted you saved the night of your attack." She looked with disgust on Faith. "William and I were always of the same mind. We thought you nothing more than a piece of worthless property, better left to rot or pawn off on someone. My daughters were the ones we wished to arrange substantial marriage contracts for and you stood in the way."

"Why not have married me to just anyone and have me out of your way?"

Lady Terra shook her head. "You will never make a good mistress of a keep, you are too ignorant of the way of things. If William offered you to just anyone, then he could not expect to do well by my daughters. You needed to be completely out of the way."

"And you arranged it, though it did not go as you hoped."

"You foolishly fought the idiot," she said almost in a shout and stopped, her hand quickly covering her mouth. She took a few deep breaths, lowered her tone and continued. "I told the man I hired to have his way with you and then kill you. Your death would have served us well. Poor William would have been able to mourn his daughter who died saving her honor and soul—but instead you lived and brought us shame."

"I shamed no one," Faith said proudly.

Both women heard the door crack and the pounding continue.

Lady Terra turned wide eyes, but a soft voice on Faith. "This will be done here and now. I had thought it done with when William and I plotted to marry you off to the devil—a fitting arrangement. You were of no more concern to me and I had cleaned up quite nicely myself, doing away with your attacker, though there was one loose end."

"Nora," Faith said in a whisper.

Lady Terra nodded. "Dear, sweet, caring Nora—but not quite bright. She never realized that I had given her specific orders to fetch the priest because you had met an evil end. I had assumed you already dead and had yet to be informed that you still lived. When William told me of your husband's summons, I thought, what an appropriate wedding gift to give you while ridding myself of one last nuisance."

"So you sent her to the keep ahead of everyone and she dutifully obeyed whatever foolish order you gave her and then you followed her."

"Was it a pleasant surprise, dear?"

"You are mad."

The splintering of wood warned that they would soon have company

Lady Terra raised the blood-stained knife. "I am very mad, my dear. When the Irish kings learn of Lord Eric's banishment of Lord William from his land, they too will shun him for fear of losing the Irish devil's favor. That I will not tolerate."

Faith went to take a step back and Lady Terra rushed forward, grabbing her hand. "You will meet the fate you should have met years ago and I will be the sorrowful stepmother who saw it all. I will tell your grieving husband how gallantly you fought your attacker for the second time, but how in the end he inflicted a mortal wound that claimed your life just before he died."

Faith jumped, startled by the screams of help that Lady Terra called out. "Hurry, you must hurry. He is going to kill her."

"My death will not change my husband's feeling toward you," Faith said and yanked her arm, trying to free herself.

"The fool loves you so much that he will be lost in his misery and nothing will matter to him, least of all your father and I."

The next few seconds went by in a blur. Lady Terra raised the blade, the door crashed in, falling to the ground, and her husband stood in the doorway, the height and bulk of him filling the small space and his elongated shadow falling down the aisle across Lady Terra.

"Drop the weapon," he warned and took several steps inside the chapel, Colin and Borg following behind him while Bridget remained outside.

"Stop," Lady Terra screeched, and within the blink of an eye she had the knife held firmly against Faith's throat. "I will kill her."

Eric stopped abruptly, as did Colin and Borg. Rook was the only one who continued on, no one but Faith having noticed him enter in a low crawl on his belly and proceed silently around the benches, headed to where she stood.

"You bitch," she screamed at Faith. "You have ruined everything. You should have died the first time I ordered it."

Eric carefully took a step closer, his heart pounding with fright.

"Stop," she screeched again and pushed the blade against Faith's neck, causing a drop of blood to fall.

Eric immediately remained where he was, fear for his wife's life suspending all movement. "This is not necessary. We can discuss this."

"There is nothing to discuss," Lady Terra yelled. "It is over. I will finally see to it being over."

Eric looked ready to pounce on the demented woman.

"Nay," came the soft whisper from Colin beside him. "She is too far away."

Eric agreed with Colin's caution; Faith was too far away for him to reach her in time. The mad woman would have her throat cut in an instant. For the first time in his life he feared the outcome of a battle. There was always another maneuver to attempt, a plan to try, a possibility—but in this case there seemed to be nothing left but defeat.

Faith looked on him with brave eyes. She did not whimper,

cry or beg for her life. She stood proud and courageous, this woman who loved and trusted him.

He could not fail her, he could not. He vowed to protect her, even with his life.

She smiled at him as if she knew, understood his troubled thoughts and in her silence he thought he heard her plea.

"Do not worry, Eric," she said.

He realized she spoke aloud.

"Shut up," Lady Terra warned.

Faith disregarded her warning and continued. "I love you."

Eric grew frantic. What did she think to do?

Colin and Borg grew concerned as well and without thought moved to take a step.

"No," Faith cautioned. "Do not, she is insane."

"Fools," Lady Terra shouted.

Faith saw that Rook was now close enough to attack and she looked to her husband, and spoke her heart in case this did not turn out as she hoped. "I will always love you, Eric."

Before he could respond, think or act, Faith, in a shrill voice, called out, "Rook!"

The big dog seemed to appear out of nowhere. His large body sailed through the air, his growls sounding like mighty roars as he lunged directly for the two women.

Given an instant to act, Faith grabbed for the dagger at her throat and struggled with the woman, placing Lady Terra in Rook's direct path. With a chilling roar and his teeth bared Rook knocked the startled woman to the ground and with limbs flying frantically it was all Lady Terra could do to keep the angry animal from going for her throat.

Eric rushed to his wife's side, taking her in his arms and holding her as tightly as he could without stealing her breath from her. "I was never so fearful," he whispered against her ear.

She hugged him just as fiercely and with a tearful laugh of relief said, "The devil, fearful?"

"Nay, a husband," he said and kissed her.

Colin and Borg were attempting to get Rook off Lady Terra but his snarls and snaps would not permit them near him.

Faith was about to order Rook off her when Eric spoke up. "Cease, Rook, and you will be well rewarded."

The big dog stopped and turned large eyes on the couple. He

then gave the trembling woman one more snarl and loud bark and moved off her to stand directly beside Faith.

She immediately dropped to her knees and hugged the huge animal, kissing his snout and telling him how much she loved him and how brave he was. Rook responded with several lavish licks.

"Enough," Eric called out. "It is my turn." With that he swung Faith up into his arms, ordered Colin and Borg to see to the crazy woman and ordered Rook to follow him, and then he marched out of the chapel.

Thirty-three

Faith stood by her husband's side and watched a grumbling Lord William and a bandaged and raving Lady Terra helped into a wagon. Dermot MacCathy, king of Cork, had responded immediately to Eric's request for men to be sent to Shanekill Keep to handle this matter at once. The king agreed and sent an escort of fifty men to return Lord William and Lady Terra to Donnegan Keep where he would be waiting to deliver their fate.

The king had already informed Eric that he intended for all Donnegan holdings and properties to be added to Eric's holdings and that he himself would arrange marriages for the Donnegan daughters. He also intended to banish Lord William and Lady Terra from Irish soil.

Faith held firmly to Eric's warm hand as she watched their departure. Rook placed the large bone he held in his mouth down on the ground and released one loud bark, as if announcing his pleasure at their leaving.

"I agree with you," Eric said to the dog and gave him a generous rub behind the ear.

She smiled at the scene, recalling how not so long ago Eric found Rook big and ugly and now he spoke of the animal as if he were the most intelligent, brave and handsome of creatures.

Colin approached with a fat stick. "We never finished our game, boy."

Rook barked and jumped, ready for play.

Colin looked to Faith and with a respectable bow said, "Forgive me, my lady, I should have been more diligent in my duties to protect you."

Faith shook her head. "Nonsense, Colin, I had no doubt I would be rescued."

"Your husband was of the same mind," Borg said, joining the trio with Bridget in hand.

"Aye," Bridget agreed. "Lord Eric was a sight to behold, pounding the door with his mighty fists, commanding the wood to crack and then delivering several forceful kicks to the stubborn door."

"You kicked the door down?" Faith asked with surprise.

Bridget answered. "The three of them did."

Faith looked to each man with wide, grateful eyes. "I am ever so pleased to have two such caring and loving friends and a generous and loving husband."

Colin gave her his usual charming smile, Borg blushed and Eric simply squeezed her hand firmly, though his blazing blue eyes hinted at a more intimate emotion,

"So 'tis there a wedding celebration to prepare for?" Eric asked of Borg.

Faith smiled with joy. "We must have a grand wedding for you both."

Bridget was about to protest when Borg kissed her silent and then answered, "A big wedding celebration that will long be remembered."

"So it shall be," Eric declared. "And you, Colin—"

"Need a wife," Faith and Bridget echoed in unison.

Borg laughed. "Now he is done for, with two women seeing to him wed."

Colin attempted to debate the issue. "I need no—"

"So it shall be," Eric declared once again, and all present knew Colin would be exchanging marriage vows soon enough.

Colin grumbled and Borg clapped him on the back. "Come—we will share an ale or two and you can settle all the wagers you owe me."

"Owe you?" Colin said with a laugh and a shake of his head. "It is you who owe me."

"Nay, you are foolishly mistaken," Borg protested as they

walked off, his arm on Colin's shoulder and his hand locked with Bridget's.

Faith stared after her friends with a mixture of tearfulness and joy. She had never thought she would know such endearing friendships and she felt overwhelmed with gratitude.

"Are you all right?" Eric asked, catching her attention and taking hold of her other hand.

She looked one last time at the departing wagon about to exit the castle grounds and cast another look at her friends, then she turned to her husband and with a nod, answered, "I am fine and I am glad it is finally all at an end."

"Nay, wife, it just begins." He scooped her up in his arms and with a loud laugh that attracted all eyes to them he marched into the keep. They passed by more curious eyes and whispers soon spread and followed them up the staircase to their bed-chamber.

"You feed the wagging tongues once again," she said with a laugh when he dropped her on their bed.

He returned to the open door and ordered Rook, who sat looking curiously at them with the fat bone in his mouth, to the kitchen for another treat. The dog obeyed without question and he shut and locked the latch.

He walked back to the bed, stripping his clothes off in the process and went to work on hers after falling gently down over her.

She giggled as his fingers fumbled with her garments. "It is but midmorning, husband."

"Aye," he agreed, "a fitting time to plant a seed that will root deeply in fertile soil and forever remain a part of Ireland."

Faith cupped his face in her hands. "Your seed has already taken root and is but the beginning of many strong sons and fine daughters yet to come."

His smile was filled with joy and his blue eyes ablaze with love. "I am most pleased with you, wife." Then he kissed her like a man long deprived, like a man who finally had found his way home, home to a loving wife and home to Ireland.